THE FRENCH COMANCHE

THE FRENCH COMANCHE

A Novel

Stanley T. Noyes

SUNSTONE PRESS

SANTA FE

Sunstone books may be purchased for educational, business, or sales promotional use.
For information please write: Special Markets Department, Sunstone Press,
P.O. Box 2321, Santa Fe, New Mexico 87504-2321.

Book and cover design › R. Ahl
Printed on acid-free paper
♾

———————————

Library of Congress Cataloging-in-Publication Data

Names: Noyes, Stanley, author.
Title: The French Comanche : a novel / by Stanley T. Noyes.
Description: Santa Fe : Sunstone Press, [2019]
Identifiers: LCCN 2019006403 | ISBN 9781632932570 (paperback : alk. paper)
Subjects: LCSH: Comanche Indians--Fiction.
Classification: LCC PS3564.O98 F74 2019 | DDC 813/.54--dc23
LC record available at https://lccn.loc.gov/2019006403

———————————

WWW.SUNSTONEPRESS.COM
SUNSTONE PRESS / POST OFFICE BOX 2321 / SANTA FE, NM 87504-2321 /USA
(505) 988-4418 / ORDERS ONLY (800) 243-5644 / FAX (505) 988-1025

 *Characters in this Novel*

The French:

Jean-Pierre: Narrator, Indian Trader, also known as Bluejay and El Gayo.

Antoine Lefort: Fellow trader, also known as the Canadian and "Kills-Far."

Arsène: The French son of Colonel de St. Maurice, named "Amabate" (Comanche for "The One Without A Head"), later re-named "Tosaporua" (Comanche for "White-Bear").

Colonel de St. Maurice: Former governor residing at Natchitoches Post, and owner of the trading company that bears his name.

Hélène-Eulalie: The French cousin of Arsène and niece of Colonel de St. Maurice.

Barré: "Buffalo" in French, an unscrupulous trader.

Tournier: Head trail worker.

Engagées: Trail workers for the trading company.

The Comanches:

Taoinan: Comanche friend, also known as "La Flauta" or "The Flute."

    She-Scolds-Her-Dogs: Older wife of Taoinan.

    First-Frost: Older wife of Taoinan.

    Sehêbi: Taoinan's youngest wife, "Le Saule" in French and "The Willow" in English.

Toyamancare: Comanche war chief, also known as "Big-Mountain," adopted father to Arsène.

Mano de Hierro: A divisional Comanche chieftain, also called "Iron-Hand."

Cunabunit: "He Who Sees Fire," also "Sees-Fire," a Comanche leader.

Paraginanchi: "Deer's-Ears," a Comanche warrior and close life-long friend to Arsène.

Taoinan's three real brothers:

> **Tosapoy:** A war chief,* "White-Road," or Chemin-Blanc. (Tabo-ui, his wife "Rabbit-Knife")

> **Red-Woman:** A civil chief,* or "Ybienca."

> **El Chamaco:** A half-brother.

Pagabipo: Older generation medicine man, "The Arrowmaker," also called "Basin-Paunch."

Tuchubarua: "Bearbeard," Toymancare's brother-in-law and Arsène's father-in-law.

Manos-Amarillas: "Yellow-Hands," a civil chief and medicine man.

Ooa: "Little Screech Owl," Sehêbi's adopted daughter from the Osage raid, later named Louise Margurite by Hélène-Eulalie and Jean-Pierre.

Dead-Hide: "Cuero-Matado," another warrior.

Other Names:

Tzena: Small wolf, or coyote spirit who appears to Arsène

Piamupitz: "Great-Big-Man-Owl," a spirit bird.

Buffalo in English, "Cuhtz" in Comanche, Barré in French.

Comanche group names: "Comanche Orientale," also known as "Kotsoteka," also called "Haitans" (English name). Comanche called themselves "Nuhmuhnuh."

*The war chief plans and executes battles. The civil chief plans the journeys and handles domestic disputes in order to maintain peace.

1   *Summer 1794, El Rio Pecos*

It was, as I remember, anno Domini 1794. Summer. We were riding south by Rio Pecos behind the bronzed, sweating back of our guide, a young warrior on a pinto pony. The river trail was sufficiently wide so that Antoine Lefort and I could ride beside each other, he leading the three packhorses. We conversed as we went, accompanied by the ripple and splash of water. Ordinarily the voyageur was taciturn, but I had persuaded him to relate some of his experiences in the north, when he had been a coureur de bois and lived with the tribes. He liked to reminisce. I learned from his anecdotes and found them enjoyable, especially while passing through badlands, as at present.

"Une fois," he continued, "quand j'étais au Marais des Cygnes. Tu sais òu ça se trouve, n'est-ce pas?"

"Bien sûr."

"Nous avons rencontré une partie de ces peau-rouges qui s'appellent les 'Renards.' Guerriers, qui nous cherchaient. Tout de suite, il y avait une bataille, des flêches volant partout." He described a skirmish with Fox Indians, who had called the Osage warparty "women," explaining how he and his warrior companions had chased the Foxes across the river, after killing three. Then, he told me, the warparty he accompanied scalped and cut off the heads of the fallen and set them, bloody, with staring eyes, draining upon stakes along the riverbank, where they would become carrion, a warning to any other enemy who might seek the Osage villages up the Marais des Cygnes.

"Do they raid down here?"

"Into comanchería, sometimes. More often they harass the Pawnee-Piquées.

"But they're enemies of the Comanches?"

"Yes. And now the Spaniards and French, too."

"And some speak French. You say they call you people, 'the Heavy Eyebrows.'"

"Yes, 'I'n-shta-heh.'"

I laughed.

Imperceptibly the country was changing from bare to lush, with great cotton trees on either side of the river. Soon we passed fields of sunflowers, with wild turkeys feeding upon the seeds. Then before I was fully aware, we had approached and were entering the great Haitan, or Comanche, encampment. A pack of dogs greeted us, little mongrels and great hairy canines indistinguishable from wolves, who howled at us in counterpoint to the barks of the smaller dogs. They began to pester the horses until our guide shouted at them and swung his quirt, when they retreated, although still trotting ahead and on either side of us.

Proceeding past staring women and frightened children on a path between tepees, we soon approached the lodge of someone apparently important. His war horse was staked nearby, his shield suspended upon his lance, facing east so as to absorb the power, as they believe, of the sun's earliest rays. The smaller tepee of what must have been his secondary wives was erected at a brief distance. Several children, apparently his, on glimpsing our advance, scampered inside, while two women stared at us timidly.

Abruptly from within the master's lodge voices grew louder, a man's and a woman's, wrangling. As we neared its entrance a woman plunged out and spun around, followed by its apparent owner. Each seemed in a rage, the woman, a fine tall being, was backing but shouting at a shorter, scarred and stout but powerful-appearing man, who was berating her. So absorbed were they by their quarrel, they appeared not to see us at less than a rod's distance. Still backing, the woman became aware of our proximity first, turning her face our way. Simultaneously the man swooped, seized, and swung a Spanish cookpot, striking the woman upon her forehead with a ringing sound, felling her.

As we passed, she lay before the lodge, surely unconscious. For an instant, the warrior glared at us, then turned and swaggered into his tepee, while the other two women rushed to the fallen one. I swung round in the saddle to look back. The two women had been joined by another. The three were attempting to revive the prone figure to no avail while we remained within sight of them.

I turned to Lefort, riding beside me, with a questioning look. I had witnessed much as a prairie trader but not this.

He shrugged. "La femme est obligée d'obéir."

Of course. Wives had to obey. But nevertheless. We rode on.

2

We were passing between tepees where women squatted or knelt graining buffalo robes with children playing around them, when I saw a familiar face. She—a girl—clapped her hand to her mouth, her eyes big, turned and ran off so swiftly she was immediately out of sight in that forest of tepees. So, thought I, with a surge of elation, Taoinan was here. I was pleased. The girl, whose name was Sehêbi, was my good friend's youngest and favorite wife, the other two, who did almost all the work, being older, probably in their twenties and already beginning to look worn. When I had first met Sehêbi, the band was camped by a stream. I had asked her what her name meant, and she ran to the bank and brought me back a twig from a willow growing there. I understood, therefore, that her name would be "Le Saule" in the French language and "The Willow" in the English. In this instance the child's slim figure made that name appropriate.

As we progressed between lodges, several with the owner's warhorse picketed by them, others with shield and lance before the door, two young women, red disks painted on their cheeks, appeared out of a doorway and stood looking at us and our entourage of barking mongrels and howling wolfdogs. Glancing back, I noticed Lefort turn in his saddle and smile at them. Shyly they returned his smile, blushing around the paint. I drew in César and let the Canadian ride up beside me.

"Antoine," I said. "We'll see some pretty young women here, like those two we just passed. But we have to be very careful—you know?"

"D'accord. With this band. You know the story?"

"Seems to me Taoinan mentioned something. I don't recall. I know it's dangerous."

"Years ago a trader from the north. They made him welcome. Some big man, warchief, lent him his wife. Later she had a child. The kid was deformed, hands like a bird's feet. Face like...you know, a monster. They left it out on the prairie."

"Now I remember. So no lending women to outsiders. Strict rule, right?"

"Right. Don't worry. I'll keep it in my pants."

"Good. Me too," I said diplomatically. "Now our business is to find Arsène, if he's alive, and here, and then—"

Ahead of us, sudden hoofbeats: Taoinan came toward us at a lope riding bareback on a piebald pony, his loose hair flying, scattering our escort of dogs. He was smiling, arms extended, rein loose on the pony's neck. He drew up, flinging himself off his horse, limping toward me. I quickly dismounted and we embraced in the Indian manner.

"I'm astonished to see you here, brother," he cried in Spanish. "What a good surprise! Tell me why you're here." His smile was frank and warm.

"In a little while. It's complicated."

"You must come to my lodge right now. My wives are fixing a meal."

Taking leave of our guide, Lefort and I followed The Flute—for that was the meaning of my friend's name—to his tepee, which was located around the middle of the southern part of the camp. The two older wives were busying themselves around an iron pot on a fire at a little distance from the doorway in a cloud of smoke and a good smell of broiling meat. They looked up and smiled as we approached. But Sehêbi, in an elaborately fringed buckskin dress, stood before them beaming at us.

"Jean-Pierre, how are you?" she cried in French. "Comment ça va?"

I laughed at her remembering the French phrase I'd once taught her. "Magnifique! Magnifico! Now that I'm here."

I should explain here that neither Sehêbi nor Taoinan were typical Comanches—or, as we Americans call them, 'Haitans.' But who in this world is typical, anyhow? I know I'm not—too squeamish, a defect that has hampered me on more than one occasion in following my profession of Indian trader, and which I have always attempted to conceal. In any event Sehêbi was a favorite child. Which means of course that she was spoiled. But she was also bright and at that age pretty. Among the People there were few favorite girls, while every Comanche boy was a favorite child. Sehêbi at fourteen or fifteen years was also a favorite wife. This too made her an exception. But in spite of being spoiled, she was charming, partly I think because with the luck she had had she was less shy than most of the other girls and younger women of the tribe. When I first came to know her, she giggled every time she saw me, so I flirted with her. Then I saw she was taking me seriously, was herself becoming serious, and I abstained. Afterward she would sometimes regard me with a hurt look. Taoinan was my good friend. Indeed he called me, "brother." Reason enough not to toy with his child wife, of whom he was clearly fond.

Taoinan was an unusual man. He would have been unusual among any group of men, including the Europeans and Americans I have known. I had met him on a number of trading expeditions, and we had quickly become friends, then close friends. He had first attracted my attention by his pleasant expression, which was thoughtful with a searching gaze and was coupled with a limp and a deformed foot—the last, like any deformity, a rare sight among the natives. One of my traders who also understood the hand signals employed by these people had told me a story about Taoinan which intrigued me. Briefly it was a matter of his warparty encountering hunters of the Ute tribe near the mountains of Nuevo México with bison they had slain. The two peoples are enemies. The Comanche war party pursued and attacked and had quickly succeeded in killing all but one of the hunters. But this man had fought so valiantly, even when wounded and surrounded, that my friend ordered his companions to desist and promised the enemy his safety if he would surrender his arms and accompany them back to their camp. The hunter, faced with certain death, accepted the offer. At the camp Taoinan took the Ute to his own lodge and had his wives tend to his wounds. For some time he fed, cared for, and protected the enemy warrior and when the man had recovered his strength placed him upon a horse and sent him back to the mountains and his own people—all of this because of the warrior's extraordinary valor. I have to confess to an admiration for such gallantry. As a result I sought out this remarkable Comanche warrior, and we quickly became friends.

Taoinan had a way, on greeting a person, of examining his features and looking directly into his eyes, of seeming to penetrate to his soul, and truly seeing that person distinctly with his faults, weaknesses, and virtues. So it was now with Lefort, an old acquaintance whom the Indians called, "Kills Far" owing to his rifle and marksmanship. Taoinan looked and the Canadian gazed quizzically back, a humorous pucker at the corner of his mouth. The Flute warmly grasped the hand Lefort was extending,

At any rate Taoinan's history was unusual and doubtless responsible at least in part for his being the man he had by a remarkable effort become. He had told me of his past at the start of our becoming close friends—"brothers," he had said. At the time I'd had the impression of being probably the first person he had spoken to about that history. I believe he was free to do so only because I was an outsider, foreign to his band and his people. And that this disclosure was a relief to him, since tears had slid down his cheeks while he was telling me one night, the two of us alone in my tent.

The story went that he had been born with a deformed foot, though otherwise normal. The midwife, directed by his father, and according to custom, carried the infant out on the prairie, laid him down and returned to the camp. Unknown to her, another woman had sought and retrieved the child. With difficulty, she managed to raise him. But when he was old enough to understand, she told him he was a special person. When she had found him that night he had already ceased crying. Around him, plain in the moonlight were the tracks of a big wolf, its paws of course much larger than a dog's, then marks where it had lain beside him. Since the wolf was sacred to the People, she told him he was honored and would someday have great power. This secret he said he had never before told anyone.

This woman, an outcast, had once been surprised under a buffalo robe with her husband's friend. The man had paid for his offense by giving horses in reparation. But following a custom, not invariably enforced, I believe, because it lessens the value of the woman, the husband had cut off his wife's nose and ejected her from his lodge. The result of this mutilation, as I have observed on several occasions, is to render the most attractive woman hideous. This poor creature lived in a tepee at the edge of camp and depended for many years upon the charity of a few who pitied her, dropping game by her doorway. In good times she and the boy ate. In hard times, particularly in winter, they often went hungry.

Still they were not allowed to starve, owing mainly to the woman's former lover, who was the most steadfast in supplying food to them, in spite of having his own wife and daughters to feed. He had even given the woman an old horse and the boy, later, a mustang colt he had captured and planned to eat, immediately before the band had discovered a herd of bison. But by the age of fourteen Taoinan had become an excellent horseman and a capable hunter in spite of his lameness. After that his adoptive mother and he rarely lacked for meat. Afoot he hobbled in a distressing fashion but mounted he rode with such grace he appeared to be inseparable from his pony. The Flute was outstanding among a tribe of extraordinary horsemen, so much so that he caused his deformity to be forgotten most of the time. He early mastered the use of the lance. But he told me he fought best at close quarters. The war club, a short battle ax, later became his favorite weapon, which he wielded with a powerful arm.

As the youth grew, he began to make a reputation for himself as a warrior. Ordinarily calm and mild, he became known for his violence during battle, fighting with a dispassionate ferocity in war parties against the People's enemies, whether Apache, Ute, Pawnee, Osage—or even Kioway, at a time when Comanches and Kioways were still enemies. Rival Comanche warriors had come to respect him, to look up to him for his cool courage and good judgment. In this manner and by becoming an accomplished horsethief he gained horses and prestige as well as, eventually, three wives. By this time his actual parentage had become an open secret among his band. The resemblances to his true mother, father and brothers could not be overlooked. But his blood relatives, even then, refused to recognize him. As for his adoptive mother, he gave her horses. Although she still was shunned, she lived well.

There is more to this story, but that later.

When Lefort and I had seated ourselves in the prescribed places and postures within the lodge, and when we had puffed and I had passed the pipe back to him, Taoinan asked me again in Spanish why we had come the great distance across the prairie from our home at Fort St. Jean Baptiste de Natchitoches to these woods on Rio Pecos.

"Remember when the governor's son was lost? Seven years ago. We never found him."

"I remember. We asked among the People."

"Lately soldiers patrolling this river, looking for Apaches, reported meeting a Comanche youth who spoke French."

"Spoke French?"

"Spanish too, of course."

"Speaks Spanish. There are many who speak a few words, but few." He frowned, a flicker of distaste crossing his features. "Yes. There's such a one in Toyamancare's "Wanderers." We call them, "Those-Who-Go-Far-Alone." They remain mostly up and down this river. But I think he's a born Comanche, maybe one of Toyamancare's sons. I don't know. I've only seen him a couple of times, but I think he looks Comanche. I believe he's one of these extremely ambitious young men—like I used to be," Taoinan laughed.

"Does Toyamancare's band keep apart (aislado) from the People?" asked Lefort.

"Yes. In my band we don't much like them."

"Can you take me to this young man this afternoon?"

"No. He went with a war party. Down river. Looking for Apaches—horses, scalps, women."

"Any idea when they'll be back?"

The Flute smiled at me. "You know I can't tell you that. Maybe today. Maybe in two moons."

I looked at Lefort. "We may be staying here for a while."

"It will be dangerous when we leave."

"And how long will you stay? Do you know that, at least?"

My friend laughed. "No. Here's food. Let's eat. We can talk later."

After we had eaten, venison which Sehêbi served self-consciously, I asked Taoinan what occasion accounted for the assembly of so many bands of the Comanches Orientales, or Kotsotekas.

"We've been discussing war against the Utes and Navajos." His expression had become thoughtful, grave. "I'm against it."

"Why?"

"We've already had our revenge against the Utes. The Navajos rarely come into this country. They live beyond the mountains at a great distance. To go there our men would have to cross the province of Nuevo México, and I'm afraid some of our younger warriors couldn't resist the horses of those people. There would then be trouble with the Spaniards, and possibly even an end to the treaty and trade which have worked well for us." He sighed. "But I'm afraid the council will decide for war. That's our way."

"Why fight the Navajos?" I had heard of those distant people.

Taoinan explained. Early during the previous fall a combined war party of Utes and Navajos had entered the prairie from the province of Nuevo Mexico to raid the Nuhmuhnuh, as the People called themselves. Finding a Comanche encampment whose men were absent hunting buffalo, the war party had attacked it, killing the old people as well as those women and children they had no wish to capture. Afterward they had departed with their prisoners and the horseherd. Some time later a Comanche war party rode across the mountains into Ute country. Taking a Ute camp by surprise, they massacred the inhabitants and returned with what booty and horses they were able to collect.

Satisfied with their vengeance against the Utes, the People then began planning a similar strike against the Navajos. It was at this juncture that the governor in Santa Fe heard of their intention from Comanches visiting the capital. The governor immediately sent messengers to Navajo Captain General Eduardo demanding that he bring all Comanche captives to his palace as soon as possible. His visitors he dispatched to Captain General Mano de Hierro of the Comanches, asking that he and his people defer vengeance and forebear until the Navajo leaders returned their prisoners and otherwise gave the Nuhmuhnuh satisfaction. Mano de Hierro (Chief Iron Hand) had agreed to wait in order to see what the Spanish governor could arrange. Meanwhile groups of the eastern and southern Comanche division had convened at this place, a favorite hunting spot of the Kotsoteka's westernmost band, on the banks of the Pecos River. During this interval the leading men of these Orientales occupied themselves by holding councils, discussing their proposed invasion of Navajo territory, while waiting for a messenger from Santa Fe.

As I recall, the messenger from Tucumcari Mountain did not arrive for several weeks, since it turned out that the Navajos were reluctant to return the Comanche women and children they had seized. Eventually, however, at the governor's insistence they complied. In the meantime life in the great encampment continued in a lazy and harmonious fashion, since game was still to be found in the area and the weather, although hot, was agreeable, with a breeze nearly every afternoon and warm, pleasant evenings. On our second day we had distributed to the chiefs and leading warriors most of the gifts which our pack horses had carried, saving a few presents in anticipation of any emergencies during our return journey. After that we had nothing to do but provide for our daily meals and wait.

It was no messenger but our former traveling companion, Warchief Toyamancare, who arrived in camp at the end of the first week. His name meant "Seated-On-The Sierra." But since he was a heavy man of medium height, I always thought of him as "Big Mountain," and as such will refer to him in my narrative. He had joined us at the Pawnee-Piquée (or Wichitan) villages after passing a month as the accidental but pampered guest of the honorable governor of the Provincia de Tejas. He had then ridden alone from San Antonio de Béjar through comanchería to those villages. Lefort and I had raised our tent at several hundred paces from the lodge of The Flute and that of his two older wives, She-Scolds-Her-Dogs and First-Frost. Taoinan had as usual invited me to stay with him, but from the beginning of our friendship I had politely but repeatedly declined that honor in favor of my own tent. Over time The Flute had learned to humor me.

Here we had erected our shelter at the edge of the woods under a huge cotton tree whose leaves protected us from the sun, scattering shadows on the canvas and on the ground around us. It was a hot afternoon and I was lying sprawled on a buffalo robe before its entrance, half-listening to the drone of nearby voices and half-listening to the rustle of leaves overhead which shattered the sun into yellow arrows darting into my half-shut eyes. Taoinan was sitting cross-legged near me, his eyes closed, as if in a trance. We had talked ourselves out for the time being. Often I caught a whiff of fragrance from Lefort's pipe. He was entertaining Sehêbi, his dark eyes lively, using a mix of Spanish and sometimes French words, as well as gestures, responding to her questions about his adventures long before with the Indians in the north. I had noticed she seemed more nearly adult than the last time I had seen her. She was perhaps even fifteen—or more likely fourteen. She was clearly intrigued by Lefort. Apparently she liked exotic men and was curious about the moeurs, customs, of other peoples—for instance about how we lived in Natchitoches.

She had told me on several occasions that she wished to visit there and see our houses and the river and pirogues and our medicine house, or church, with its ornaments of jewels and silver and gold. Taoinan had informed me she had miscarried that spring, but she seemed as well and energetic as before. She had shot me several haunted and haunting glances which were not those of a little girl. I tried to eject these images from my head, but they remained to disturb me as I lay on my buffalo robe in my tent at night, with Antoine snoring nearby. But now it was so peaceful with the murmer of voices and the rustle of leaves that I began to doze and was beginning once more to explain the gist of Rousseau's Contrat Social to Arsène, whom I seemed to see before me again as a boy of twelve whom I was tutoring, when rapid hoofbeats halted almost on top of us. I sat up.

"Hóla amigos!" Toyamancare was astride his pony, grinning down upon us, bare-chested as usual but without his weapons.

"What?" I exclaimed, pointing, with the Comanche word for horse—"Puc! Su caballo." He was riding, bareback, his pinto, buffalo and war horse. It had been stolen one night during our long journey from the Pawnee-Piquée villages.

"Si," he smiled. "Those Caihuas are pretty good horsethieves. "Me, I'm better."
"Bravo!"

His smile faded. He had noticed Taoinan. For a moment the two warriors regarded each other, as if to speak. There was no hatred in either expression, not even dislike. They simply stared as if separated by an invisible screen they were helpless to breach. Taoinan rose and, casting a look at his favorite wife, hobbled to his black, piebald pony. Grasping its mane, he swung upon its back, turned and rode off. Sehêbi rose quickly to her feet and meekly followed.

Lefort was now standing, shaking hands with Big Mountain.

"Come," I said in Spanish. "Get down and have something to eat." It was mid-afternoon, with heatwaves wiggling on the prairie. But Comanches were always ready to dine. Of course, especially on the warpath, or when buffalo were scarce in their region, they were likely to miss a number of meals in succession. Without hesitation, Toyamancare slid off his pony, handing the rein to the Canadian, who tied the animal in the shade near César. The big brute, all of seventeen hands, switching his tail from the flies, nickered and touched noses with the pinto. He evidently liked the other gelding. During our meal the two horses, though greatly disproportionate in size, stood nose to rump, César hanging his head, the pinto raising his, and flicked flies from each other's faces.

We had plenty of freshly killed turkey, along with fish from the river. But as both were tabu to Comanches, Antoine was contrained to offer cornmeal mush and jerked buffalo meat, of which the band chief ate heartily, accompanying them with cups of cold water from the nearby spring.

"They tell me," I said, when we had finished eating. "There's a young warrior in your band who speaks good Spanish. Right now he's away with a war party. But I wonder if he could be the governor's son I was talking to you about. Because that boy would have spoken Castillian as well as French."

For a moment the Comanche scowled, looking down, evidently embarrassed. "Well, you're my friends now. I'll tell you. I did adopt a French boy. I don't know about 'governor's son.' But he said he was françés."

"How did you get him?"

Toyamancare looked down, hesitated. "Traded for him. Two ponies. With the Tonkawas. For a slave. For my wives."

"I thought they were your enemies."

"Not always."

"Do you know where the Tonkawas got him?"

"No."

"Didn't you hear we were looking for him?"

"I heard, a long time after I got him. We don't see others of the People often."

"Why didn't you bring him in? There was a big reward, many trade goods."

"I wanted to keep him. Right away I saw he was smart and brave. So I adopted him. Now he's a good fighter. He's my son. Amabate. One of my best young men. That's why I didn't tell you when you asked me before. Because I still want to keep him. But you're my friends, and you may take him if he'll go with you."

"You think he won't?"

"I don't know. Maybe he will. He likes our life. But maybe he will."

"What did you call him? Ah-mah-bah-tay? What does that mean?"

"The One Without A Head." His expression did not change.

I reflected for a moment on this and discounted it. Most Indian names seem to have been arbitrarily given. "You have any idea when that war party will come back?"

"No. But before we leave this place."

After that talk, my spirits, instead of rising, sank. If it were true that the warchief had purchased the boy from the Tonkawas, the French youth was probably not Arsène. The Tonkawas lived farther south, close to the gulf coast. It would be unlikely that they had been near La Rivière Rouge during the storm in which I had lost him. Once more guilt weighed like a boulder on my chest. The youth was probably not even French but through confusion and misunderstanding had only seemed to be. He would, I speculated, turn out to be some local mestizo or Criollo who had been stolen at an early age and who spoke only a gibberish so contorted that the Indians mistook it for French. Our trip would be wasted, his father the colonel bitterly disappointed. I remained gloomy for several days.

It was during an afternoon about a week later that The Flute sent for me to come to the council in Iron-Hand's lodge. As I approached the oversize tepee, I recall being uneasy. My command of the language was lamentably imperfect. Furthermore I could not imagine what the gathered chiefs, elders, and leading warriors might want from me, a prairie trader with no official ties to the government of New Spain. Shown to a place beside Taoinan, I seated myself and looked around with some difficulty in the dim light of the silent lodge at the circle of expressionless faces, each warrior poised in ceremonial dignity. The pipe was passed around to me, starting from an old man I at once took to be Mano de Hierro, the divisional chieftain, who wore a silver medal suspended from a scarlet ribbon hung around his neck. From previous experience, I suspected it bore the image of the Spanish king and had been presented in Santa Fe. The chieftain, or Paraibo, had a deeply lined face, with an intent gaze and an intelligent, benign expression. I puffed. Taoinan took the pipe from me. Others in the circle passed it back to the head chief. Iron-Hand turned to a young man—a boy, really—who was seated beside him and spoke quietly to him for a minute. Fortunately for me, as I discovered later, this lad had studied for three years at the viceroy's seat of government in Mexico, and now the chief employed him on all official occasions as his interpreter.

"Welcome," said the boy in flawless Castillian. "Your friend The Flute has told us you are like a son to the People's old friend, formerly governor at Natchitoches, Colonel de St. Maurice. He says, moreover, that you do not make foolish judgments, that you have a clear heart."

"I thank my friend, Taoinan. I hear your words. It's true I respect and admire Colonel de St. Maurice. And, yes, it is also true he is like a father to me, as he has been a father to the People. Now, to make my heart glad, tell me what I can do for the chiefs and members of this council, and I'll try to do it."

The boy interpreted my response, loudly, in the Comanche tongue to the head chief and the circle of men. He spoke clearly. From the words I was able to comprehend, I surmised that he had translated me accurately. I detected looks of approval from some of the warriors. Again Iron-Hand spoke to the boy, who once more addressed me:

"As you know, we have been waiting to hear from the governor in Santa Fe. It has been a long time, and no messenger has come. He is a good man, the governor, but we are beginning to think that our Navajo enemies are laughing at us. They are perhaps talking one way to the governor but doing nothing. They are not bringing our horses or our children and women to Santa Fe, or the messenger would have come to tell us so."

The interpreter apparently repeated these remarks in Comanche, and there was a growl of agreement from some around the circle. "Now there are those among us who wish to cease waiting and to send out a big war party right away. There are others who believe we should wait longer, until we hear from the governor. We have asked you to come here this afternoon to help us decide what we should do. You know the colonel well if he is like your father. What do you believe he would advise us to do?"

"You ask my opinion," I said, after some moments of reflection. "I am not the colonel, but I'll try to answer as I believe the colonel would. First, I'm sure he would advise you to continue to be patient." I spoke slowly, and the boy translated my words to the council at each pause. I could see that, among the younger men especially, "patience" was not what they wished to hear. "I think also he would recommend that you immediately dispatch a messenger to Santa Fe from here or from your post at Tucumcari Mountain. This messenger should be a man of importance who would speak to the governor himself. He would find out whether the Navajos have begun bringing in your people. If they have not done so, he would tell the governor that your warriors are weary of waiting. He would convey your offer—" I looked at Iron-Hand. "At the next round moon to send a party of your best warriors to the capital to go with the Spanish soldiers and militia and the governor himself if he wishes, or one of his captains, to punish the Navajos for breaking their treaty with him and for earlier attacking one of the People's camps." I waited for the interpreter to finish and beyond into a moment of silence, in order to let my meaning sink in. I read, it seemed to me, some signs of satisfaction in the faces around the circle, especially in the old divisional chief's expression. "Of course," I continued. "If in the meantime the Navajos begin to comply, it would be understood that the governor would inform you at once, and that he would enforce his previous terms with their leaders to give you satisfaction for your losses in their raid against your antelope band. In that case it would not be necessary to send the war party. Your people and horses would be peaceably returned to their relatives and owners." I paused a long moment to allow the boy to catch up. "Although I'm only a friend of Colonel de St. Maurice and a trader for his company, I believe I have told you what he would advise you to do." I looked around slowly at each face in the circle. "That is all I have to say to you now."

Chief Iron-Hand spoke rapidly to the interpreter, regarding me the while with a look of approval.

"Jean-Pierre tuvo razon," said the boy, continuing in Castillian. "You have a clear heart. Like our friend the colonel, you have spoken sensibly, good words, and we thank you for them."

After that there was much discussion in Comanche, apparently for and against my advice. At first I tried to follow it, but several warriors harangued at great length and their oratory was so fast and impassioned that I was able to pick out a word only now and then. I was able to guess, though, that these men were opposed to my suggestion and desired immediate action against their enemy. Among these the most passionately vociferous was the band and war chief, Big Mountain. I listened attentively to him, trying to grasp the gist of his meaning, while inwardly congratulating myself that he had called me friend, since his expression was as fierce as that of any man in the the lodge, and he was a person I would not wish to have as an enemy. One word, "Teconiuap," or "valiant," I recognized, as he struck his chest several times, and I received the impression that he believed the Navajos would consider him and all Comanche warriors women if those gathered in the tepee delayed seeking vengeance one more day. Another warrior responded, evidently arguing the opposite view, though more calmly, and the discussion went on and on until I wished there were some way I could creep under the raised flaps of the lodge unobserved. But this was of course impossible.

Out of boredom I studied faces in the circle. Soon with a start I recognized the man who had felled his woman with the iron pot. Like Big Mountain, he was of the war faction. His face was memorable, appearing to be composed of dark chiseled rock, if that were possible, with eyes set close together, wide nose with flared nostrils, heavy lips curled downward in an expression of disdain. Like Big Mountain he appeared to be a warchief, a fighting-man conscious of his authority and not to be crossed. For an instant our eyes met. I looked away, hoping to avoid any involvement with such an individual.

In the end it was Iron-Hand who decided. For a long time, perhaps another half-hour, he meditated, while the lodge remained politely silent. But midway through the divisional leader's reflections a commotion erupted outside, and the camp from that moment became anything but still, with the sound of excited voices, running feet, a mixture of unintelligible shouts and, shortly, fast hoofbeats. I of course became increasingly curious, wondering whether a messenger might have arrived from Santa Fé. But of the faces around the circle, including that of Big-Mountain, not one revealed any emotion other than that of patient submission to ceremonial protocol. Finally about the time I was beginning to fear a cramp in my right calf, Iron-Hand pronounced in favor of waiting longer to retaliate—indeed in favor of my plan in most of its details. The council concluded as formally as it had begun.

Outside I found Lefort seated in the tepee's shade waiting for me. He rose as I came out.

"Your war party," he said. "Ils arrivent."

"No! Good God." For a moment I lost my voice. "What happened?"

"They found Apaches. Took scalps, horses, even a prisoner."

"Wounded? Dead?"

"Three wounded, they say. Nobody killed. There'll be a big celebration, dancing."

We were walking quickly toward our tent while I was trying to think, adjust to the realization that very soon I'd either be seeing Arsène again, after sending him into the blizzard seven years before—or else would find that our trip had been futile. Women, boys, girls were running by us toward the south end of camp, where our tent was. Occasionally a horseman would lope by. I continued to question Antoine. It evolved that the warchief had sent in messengers from several miles out, while he and his warriors painted in preparation for their victorious entrance. The warchief had apparently wished to wait for the following morning, a customary time for a successful arrival. But hunting had been so poor that the group was entirely out of food, even the jerked meat and mesquite meal which had been their emergency rations, so that his warriors had persuaded him to return without delay. I hurried into the tent to seize a bridle and saddle to throw upon César, when an outburst of warwhoops, shouts, drumming erupted, along with the sound of women singing. I dropped the tack and ran outside, knowing the party had reached the encampment, and that I was about either—once more—to face Arsène, or to suffer a grievous disappointment.

At first I could not see the war party for the welcoming crowd, both on foot and on horseback. But then the singing women parted. A column of warriors, painted and wearing their war apparel, rode toward camp. In the lead rode a man with a powerful, though plump physique riding a red roan pony splattered with white spots. Under his horned headdress, the warrior's face, however, was cruelly scarred, a fact visible even under the paint, pitted from what had to have been smallpox. He rode sitting straight, holding his shield and a lance from which dangled a scalp. In his free hand he held a cord by which he was leading a man, apparently Apache, about his own age—perhaps mid-thirties—who was thin but appeared strong. The captive, whose skin was so dark as to appear charred, was covered with wounds, dried blood and dirt, his hair tangled and wild. Yet wounded and hungry and exhausted as he must have been, he staggered proudly behind the horse, wearing only breech cloth and moccasins, noose around his neck, wrists bound at his back.

Next I was scrutinizing the half-dozen warriors who rode in a cluster behind, each of whom appeared also to have strands of black hair hanging from the blade-end of his lance. All of them, painted and horned or feathered, appeared typical Comanche fighting men, of whom I had seen many in my seven years as an Indian trader. I then stared at the dozen or so warriors riding at intervals behind this group, trying my best to detect the familiar features of the governor's son, but as the party approached closer and closer, I failed to recognize any hint of that face. Last of all came two youths driving a small herd of what were apparently captured horses.

"Le voilà." Lefort nudged me. "There he is."

"Where, where?" My heart flopped over. As I looked at the scalp-bearers passing now directly before us, I fixed on one younger than the rest, proud and painted like the remainder, a single feather tied in his own black scalp lock, indistinguishable almost from the others, utterly Comanche. And yet...there was something. The youth's gaze flicked across Lefort, then, startled, returned. Then met mine. The fierce, haughty expression vanished, and the mouth dropped open.

"Lefort!" Arsène cried out. "Jean-Pierre! Jean-Pierre!" Instantly he slid from his pony, and we embraced, he still holding his horse, shield and lance in his free hand. "Mon dieu que je suis content de vous revoir!"

"Mon petit Arsène," I said, embracing that sweaty, hard back, and laughed. "No longer petit, though. My God, no." The tears were sliding down my cheeks. I shook them off, stood back and looked at him, laughing: a long pink scar, like a worm, crossed his chest.

"Ah, Lefort, mon vieux," he seized the Canadian's outstretched hand, "Comment ça va? Como estas, amigo?"

"Bien," laughed Lefort, "Muy bien."

The last members of the war party were passing, all looking down at us, with curious, puzzled expressions.

"My father—he's well?" Arsène's expression was anxious, even guilty.

"He misses you. I'll tell you all that. Go on with the others. Greet your friends. There's our tent, over there. When you can, come back. Antoine killed a deer. We've got venison."

"Your tent...over there. But, my God, that's not—that's César! You rode César here? César!"

He, too, began to laugh, and while he laughed the tears were slipping down his face, over the warpaint, and flipping off his chin. As he began turning to mount his pony, I slapped him on the shoulder and gripped it for an instant. The motion brought me near his fist holding the weapon, and there was a whiff of carrion. It was the scalp, with long black hair, dangling from his lance. He turned, sprang upon his pony, kicked it, and charged after his companions at a gallop.

3

We sat before the tent, Antoine Lefort and I, waiting. A warm breeze blew from the prairie, rustling the leaves overhead, scrambling their shadows around and over us. A redtailed hawk flew over, high, and vanished over the boscage. Had the hubbub of celebration from the encampment diminished? Perhaps a little, I think. The Canadian sat cross-legged, musing, smoking his pipe. Sitting with my back against the tree, I too was reflecting upon the war party's arrival and upon Arsène, this new Arsène. I realized that in spite of his affectionate greeting, he was a different being than the boy I had tutored long ago. Would he be willing to return to a civilized life? In my mind I kept seeing his warpainted face the instant before he had recognized me—that hard, proud, challenging look. He had been headstrong as a boy. I feared that in the end Arsène would do only as he wished, regardless of the promise I had made to his father.

"What do you think—" I began to ask Lefort, who was poking our tiny cooking fire with a stick. Then we saw him.

Arsène was riding toward us on a different pony than earlier, a brown-and-white pinto. Following him were two other horsemen—or as I soon realized two other horses ridden by young women, two of them mounted upon a gray and the other upon a scruffy white. The girls were smiling broadly, giggling to each other. Each had red disks, like setting suns, painted upon her plump cheeks. When he was almost upon us, Arsène whirled his horse to face the girls, as if noticing them for the first time. Speaking sternly to them in Comanche, he waved them away. After a moment, with laughing words among themselves, a fluttering of eyelashes and with final giggles, the girls swung their ponies around and trotted back toward the nearest tepees.

Arsène slid from his pony and tethered it to a sapling. Stepping deeper into the shadows to where César was tied, he rubbed the big sorrel's neck, slapped him on the chest, and came out to us smiling, He squatted before the fire. For a moment the three of us were silent, as if each had simultaneously realized once more, with a shock, what an extraordinary reunion this was. Again I examined Arsène closely, while he submitted to my gaze with a proud expression. Yes, I could see traces of the old Arsène under the new: the large dark eyes, with long lashes which had given him, as a child, a faintly feminine look, were the same. He had inherited his father's aquiline beak and bony features, but all had set, hardened. He was a man, the softness of the child gone, a little taller than medium height, not particularly muscular, but hard and more lean than thin, tanned as dark as any of the Nuhmuhnuh, with his black hair worn loose and as long as that of any other young warrior. He was dressed like the others in moccasins, with buckskin leggings to the thigh, and breechclout, a horseman's garb—and then that great scar across his chest.

"At last we've found you!" I said in French. "We've wondered for years whether you were alive or dead—though your father always believed you were alive. You simply disappeared. We looked and inquired everywhere, even up among the Osages."

"I'm happy too, Jean-Pierre. Happy to see you." At the mention of the colonel, his expression sobered. "How is he, my father?"

"As remarkable as ever. He'll be overjoyed." I did not mention his palpitations, the doctor's alarming diagnosis, saving that for a final argument, in the event that the youth refused to return with us. And in the event that the old man died before our return? We would face that, if necessary, at the time.

The sky to the west above the woods had turned an intense blue-pink. The breeze, fainter now, rustled the leaves. Yes, the camp had quieted prior to the festivities planned for later. Lefort had risen and was roasting steaks of venison on willow sticks over the coals of the fire.

"A bit different from that last time, seven years ago, no?" asked the Canadian.

Arsène grimaced. "I was a little fool. I should have died."

"You forgive me for sending you into the storm? The blizzard made me crazy." I didn't care anymore whether Lefort heard the great secret I'd hoarded for so many years.

"Of course. I was a fool. I shouldn't have bothered you when you were trying to pitch that tent, and everything was blowing away. Then I was furious. An infant. I went out after the horse, and immediately I was lost. Immediately. Then I got scared. I was wandering around in the snow, bawling. I couldn't see anything. I was sure I was going to die. I don't know how long I wandered. Not very long, I suppose. And then these horsemen. I nearly ran into them. One of them—it was Big Mountain—slipped off his pony. He wiped the snow off my face, peered at me. Then he grabbed me under the arms and slung me up behind his saddle. He mounted and we started off. Couldn't see anything. I didn't know who they were—just Indians. But I hung on to his waist, still crying but glad to go, anywhere, hugging him. He saved my life."

So, I thought: the warchief really wants him. "He says you're his son."

"Yes. Now I have two fathers."

"And you just took a scalp. That must please your Comanche father."

"Yes. He gave me horses. Our leader—Cunabunit—gave me three horses, too."

"That name. I forget. What does it mean?"

"Cunabunit? 'He-Who-Saw-Fire.'"

"And he's had smallpox."

"Yes. He married into another band. His wife and many others died. Years ago. Then he came back."

"I see. Well, Arsène, for a white man your age you've had a full life already. How did you get that scar?"

"Jean-Pierre, I am no tabebo." Again the cold, haughty expression. "I'm Nuhmuhnuh—Comanche."

"All right, all right. And the scar?"

Arsène drew himself straight and smiled. "In Castillian and French it is not comme il faut to boast. But in Comanche we may boast of our true deeds. I'll tell it to you simply. It happened very fast. We were on the warpath, a small group of us, looking for a Lipan camp. Lipan Apaches, like those we just fought. A bad people. We hate them."

"Worse than the Utes and Navajos?"

"Yes. Much worse."

"Worse than the Pawnees? The Osages?"

"The Pawnees, I don't know. We never see them down here. Or Osages either. But the Lipans are not worse than the Osages. Both are very bad people."

"Go on. What happened?"

"We didn't know, but a Lipan war party was tracking us. One of our scouts saw them. We stopped behind a hill. We were talking about what we were going to do. Then they rode over the hill. We began fighting at once. Our leader—again it was Sees-Fire. He blew his war whistle, and we attacked. There were more of them, but we were ready. They galloped toward us. Arrows flying everywhere. My friend. We were the youngest. He was eighteen. I was seventeen. He got an arrow through the arm, right away." He squeezed his upper arm. "I rode with the others, at a run. I was very excited—the horses too. I'd never fought that close before. As we came together, my horse was leaping around, and spinning, so we bumped into one of the Lipan warriors from the side and behind. He was a strong man, but we were too close for him to use his bow or lance. He pulled his knife and got me here." Arsène ran a finger over his scar. "At the same time my pony stumbled, an arrow in him, and started to go down, falling against the Apache horse. I'd dropped my lance and got my own knife out, and with my shield I was fending off that man's knife. With my shield hand I grabbed his hair and, as my horse went down I pulled him with me, and he fell on top. But I'd twisted in the air, with my shield between us, so I had one chance. I shoved my knife into his throat. Right here." He placed a finger on the soft spot a little below the Adam's apple. "Even then he kept on fighting, trying to kill me. He was so strong! But then he stopped, dead. That day my Puha—my power—was stronger than his."

"Toi, t' as eu de la chance," said Lefort. "Here, take this and eat." He passed a stick holding a steak. "You were lucky that day, mon gars."

"You must have been bleeding badly," I said, wincing as I looked again at the scar.

"Yes. I was covered with blood, his and mine."

"And you fainted?" offered Lefort, his eyes amused. As a boy Arsène had once fainted at the sight of his own blood.

Our proud young warrior regarded him for a long moment. Was he blushing?

"Yes."

"And then?"

"When Sees-Fire came back. They were losing the fight, so the Lipans ran. Our men chased them for a while, but our ponies were already tired. When Sees-Fire came back, he told me afterward he found me sitting by my dead horse and that Apache, still bleeding. I had that warrior's hair in one hand and my knife in the other, but I was too weak to raise my knife. He jumped off his horse and scalped him for me."

"How did they stop the bleeding?"

"Cactus. We skin the stalk and press the inside against the wound. It stops it."

"But it didn't infect? It healed all right?"

"Oh yes. Pulp. You chew the stalk and mix the juice with your spit. When you have plenty, you spit it into the wound. It heals well. Look, didn't it? Sees-Fire did that for me. He's a great leader. I'd go with him anywhere."

"And you, yourself, were a great warrior when you returned?"

Arsène smiled. "Not a great warrior. But everyone was happy, especially my father, Big-Mountain. He gave me horses, and I kept the Apache's. It's a good warhorse, better than the one that was killed. That one was crazy."

From somewhere in the camp drumming had begun.

"And the girls," smiled Lefort. "They all wanted to marry you—or at least crawl into your lodge at night, no?"

Arsène laughed. "Maybe. But I have no time for girls now. I don't want to feed a wife. And children. I'm too young. Maybe later. Now I want more horses."

"Speaking of girls," I said. Arsène turned. A girl was approaching with an older woman—that is, a heavy woman in her early twenties, one who looked thirty. The girl was Sehêbi, with She-Scolds-Her-Dogs, Taoinan's first wife. Dressed for the dancing, both wore new moccasins and handsome buckskin dresses.

"Will you eat with us?" I asked.

"We've just eaten," said She-Scolds-Her-Dogs, speaking slowly so I would understand, and seating herself by Arsène. Sehêbi sat down beside her. Arsène, after the first glance, paid no attention to either. "Your brother," she continued, addressing me, and speaking very clearly and slowly, as if to a little child, "has gone away, with your father, Big Mountain." She looked at Arsène. "Along with five others, to see the governor in Santa Fe. Iron-Hand asked them to go and speak for him. Your brother asked me to tell you that while he is away, you can ask me for anything you need."

"My brother is kind." I was disappointed. I saw The Flute so rarely.

"You're dancing tonight, of course?" Sehêbi asked Arsène. The drumming was louder now.

"Yes. I have to go." He rose. "Jean-Pierre, will you come?"

"No. I've seen scalp dances. That Apache—after the dance what will you do with him?"

"We'll give him to the old women."

"I see." I knew what he meant. "And after that?"

"There will be no 'after that.' Antoine, are you coming?"

"I'll be there," said Lefort. For an instant his eyes rested upon Sehêbi, and she smiled, a little embarrassed smile, and looked quickly at the other woman.

I was aware of a pang of jealousy. For a moment I studied the girl, her lively brown eyes, unpainted oval face, narrow, straight nose, thin lips. Her hair was parted in the center and hung loose, dangling below her shoulders. But these features revealed an eager, joyous, and adventurous spirit contained in that child's body. "Well, anyway," I said at last to Arsène. "Congratulations on your war party's success—and the scalp. You'll be a warchief yourself before you know it."

"Thank you, Jean-Pierre. I'll come again tomorrow. But not early. We'll dance all night."

When Arsène and the women had gone, Lefort and I exchanged a look.

"You know what he meant," I said, "about the Apache. 'Give him to the women.' You know what that means."

With a faint smile, Lefort shrugged. "All these savages are the same. The Comanches are a good people, better than most. The Pawnee Piquées are worse, much worse. The Apaches—the Lipans, like that unfortunate—are the worst of all. I've seen everything. Up north…believe me, even whites. Once, I tried—Most traders ignored it. Useless. And risky. Sacré enfant, it doesn't bother me any more. Don't let it bother you, Jean-Pierre. There's nothing you can do. Don't think about it. In any event, I'm going to the dance."

"Good. Enjoy yourself."

He stood, put on his hat, knocked out his pipe, refilled it, and lighted it with a twig from the fire. "Alors, see you later. Good night."

"Yes. Antoine—remember, the women. Be careful. There'll be plenty there. Probably good looking girls, some opportunities. But remember."

Leaving, he turned back with a smile. "Don't worry. I'll keep it in my pants."

I sat for a long while in the dusk before the embers of the fire, smoking my own pipe. I was troubled about the captive, surmising what would happen to him. Of course he or his people would do the same or worse to a captive Comanche. Lefort had been right, though. There was nothing I could do to prevent it. With difficulty I forced the Apache out of my mind. Then Arsène. Already it seemed clear to me that he was determined to remain with the Indians. With pained amusement I recalled the colonel having once casually remarked that he conceived the frontier to be the boundary between Civilization and Savagery. Now his only remaining child, whom he loved dearly, had crossed that line and was, it seemed, likely to remain upon its distant side.

4

The drumming from the center of the camp had grown louder and faster. From time to time there were warwhoops and shouts, high-pitched singing of women sounding a little like prairie wolves. I pictured Arsène dancing with other warriors, waving their lances and scalps, around the bound Lipan. I shook my head. It was a warm, fine night, with stars, but I was beginning to slap mosquitoes on my neck and hands. Rising, I went past the red coals of the fire into the tent. By feel, I located the pack containing the flask of Armagnac the colonel had given me on my departure, and of which Lefort and I had partaken sparingly on several occasions during our journey to this place. In the dark tent I raised the flask, after sniffing it, to the colonel and his son, took two small swallows, corked it, and put it away. I lighted a candle, placed it by my buffalo robe and dropped the flap. It was cooler outside but with the candlelight the mosquitoes would be worse there, and I wanted to read for a while, knowing I could not sleep in my present state of mind, especially with the drumming and commotion from the dancing ground. Stripping completely, I lay down on my robe on the other side of the tent from Lefort's and, resting comfortably on an elbow, took up my battered copy of Voltaire's *Essais sur les Moeurs*, opened it at the bookmark, and began reading.

After a time I began to doze, then fell asleep on the book. I had a series of troubled dreams, including a nightmare, part of which I still recall. I was in the colonel's house, and I entered his office, seeking him. But seated at his desk was a black, shaggy figure, like a shadow, but darker. From it wafted a powerful smell of carrion. That was all, but I cried out for help. Suddenly I was in my mistress's shanty, and although she was not there, I could hear her calling me, "Jean-Pierre, Jean-Pierre." I replied in return, "Oui, Michelle, me voici." But the voice became a mosquito's mixed with Sehêbi's softly and persistently saying, "Jean-Pierre, Jean-Pierre." Slapping my ear, I opened my eyes to find Sehêbi standing at my feet, repeating my name. She was wrapped in a black-and-red trade blanket, hugged around her as if she were cold, although it was hot in the tent. Her ankles and feet were bare. Naked, I half-way sat up, dumbfounded to see her there. She became silent, continuing to regard me with a look that was at once timid and beseeching. The candle had burned low, but the din from the dancing ground was as loud as ever. Lefort's bed was empty. She had closed the tent-flap behind her.

"What?" I stammered in bewilderment.

In response she opened her arms and dropped the blanket, standing there as naked as

I was, a slim, sturdy figure of a girl, already more woman than child. I stared at her face with a questioning look, speechless. "Jean-Pierre," she said once more, then, crouching, came to me, kneeling on the robe, pressing her face to my chest, lowering her body upon mine and sliding up so that her cheek pressed mine. Although I was stricken with terror, I embraced her, almost as a reflex. The skin of her back proved to be so smooth—une peau douce— that what reason, what resistance I had, vanished. I drew her so close we began sweating together, while two or three mosquitoes whined around us and glutted themselves on our blood.

I am not a saint. I never have been. Much of my life I have been a frontier Indian trader, and I fear have almost always behaved like one. In the struggles between my mother, the Massachusetts bluestocking, a moral woman who educated me so rigorously, and my father the French artillery captain, the soldier has usually won. On this occasion my mind and body became the battleground for two emotions: guilty terror and intense desire, the terror because it is nearly impossible to conceal any action in an Indian camp. The more furtive the act, the more quickly discovered and gossiped about. Everyone, I told myself, while caressing the girl and responding to her caresses, everyone would know about this in the morning. Furthermore this child was the favorite wife of my good friend, Taoinan, who would probably kill me when he learned what I had done. I told myself it would be a heinous betrayal of a friend to enter her, but lust easily won that little struggle. So she rolled to her belly and we copulated. But the first instance, as I recall, was not entirely satisfactory. She was slippery inside but because of her age her organ was slightly too short for mon membre. Furthermore we were both so eager we could not at first coordinate our rhythms, resulting in a jerky slapping together. But the second time was good, I being so intensely stimulated I seemed to go on indefinitely, until she gave a muffled shriek, and I soon afterward a groan, and it was over. But then, shortly, as we lay there, finally disengaged, the cold terror began to seep back into the marrow of my bones, even as I saw and slapped a mosquito on her firm little buttock, leaving a spot of blood. Thinking clearly about the reality of my situation, I lost even the dregs of desire and mon membre shriveled further.

"Antoine could come back any minute," I said, using a mix of French, Spanish, and Comanche.

"No," said Sehêbi, as she nuzzled and clung. "He's with..." And she gave a girl's name which I forget. "I saw them at the dance. They went into the dark together."

Good, I thought. Fool. Then the two of us will die.

"He asked me first." She pressed her nose to mine, her eyes big, regarding me indignantly. "But I said, 'no, of course not.'"

So. Le salaud. "I thought you liked him. You've been looking at him all the time. You were flirting with him, weren't you?"

"That was to make you notice me. You weren't noticing me any more."

"Taoinan's my good friend." Again a pang of guilt...and fear. "We've betrayed him. What will he do when he finds out? Kill me? Cut off your nose?"

"No—"

"Do you love him?"

"Yes. He's...like a father. An uncle."

"Chut," I hissed into her ear, raising my head, gripping her shoulder at what I thought were footsteps outside the tent. For a moment, rigid, I stopped breathing. All was silent except for the sputtering of the candle, about to burn out. "You'd better go. Right now. I heard sounds outside."

"No, I want to stay." With her arms gripped around my neck, she pressed her cheek against mine so fiercely it hurt. She remained in that position for minutes, while I held her gently, stroking her back, listening. The candle flame flickered once more and ceased. The tent was dark. I could feel her breathing, her back heaving. My cheek and neck were wet.

Again I thought I heard sounds outside. I seized her arms. After a moment of naked wrestling I broke her grip around my neck. "Please, you must go," I panted. "There's someone outside."

She tore away, stood, a barely visible silhouette, seized and wrapped her blanket around her, turned and raised the tent flap, silently left.

For a long time I lay thinking as my anxiety froze to a lump of ice in my chest. I'd been an idiot, I told myself. For a few moments of pleasure. Fou. Loco. Poisá. Crazy. Yet what could I have done? Told her to get out? While she stood naked before me with that timid and beseeching look? No, I couldn't have done that. After a while I called Antoine's name, wondering if he had been outside and heard us. But there was no response. Finally after an hour or so of painful thought, I slept.

 5

The sun rose that morning, as on any other. I woke from its light through the canvas. At first the night's events seemed unreal, as if I had dreamed them. But I knew I had not. Now I had to face the day and the Indian camp. Fortunately Taoinan was away. But he would be back. Lefort's robe was empty. He had not returned, unless... I rose and went outside into the bright morning. Antoine was lying curled under the big cotton tree, not far from the horses, wrapped in saddle blankets. On my return from the bosque, I stood looking down at him as he slept, shining with dew, angelic. My stomach felt as if I'd been drinking all night. Evidently he had heard us and out of delicacy had slept outdoors. No, I was not quite in a position to reproach him for his amorous behavior.

I never learned with certainty whether he had heard us in the tent or not, although I have always suspected he had. When I had built a fire for our breakfast, I turned and found him sitting up rubbing his face.

"Bonjour. How was the dance?"

"Good," he said, stretching. "Good dancers. Arsène too."

"Really? Just like the other warriors?"

"Yes. No difference."

"And the Apache?"

Lefort shrugged, and yawned. "Poor devil."

That was all he said, and I let the subject drop. "So you decided to sleep outside."

"A hot night," he said, as he rose. "Cooler out here."

"Mosquitoes weren't bad?"

"They were bad," he said, heading toward the woods, then turning, not quite meeting my eyes. "But the breeze—it was cool."

Later, restless, I saddled César, seized my musket, and went for a ride, first through the encampment. I expected a difference in the way people would look at me. I expected everybody to know about Sehêbi and me. But nobody—women scraping their staked out hides, little boys playing with their bows, a warrior leading a bay gelding—paid any particular attention to me as I rode by. If they stared, and many did, it was at César—a giant at seventeen hands—not at me. I forced myself to make a detour in order to ride past The Flute's and his wives' tepees. I was in a state of suspense in approaching them, fearing that if Sehêbi were outside she would by her expression or greeting reveal our relationship, making it obvious to everyone around—if it were not a common topic of gossip already. But I was irresistibly drawn to the place. As I drew near, I saw both with relief and disappointment that Sehêbi was not in sight. Instead First-Frost and She-Scolds-Her-Dogs were piling firewood before their husband's lodge. We exchanged greetings as I passed. First-Frost smiled, with a friendly look. But I saw from She-Scolds-Her-Dogs' expression, something in her eyes, that she knew. It was a neutral look, not unfriendly, actually indifferent, but the knowledge was there. I don't know how I knew, but I did. I rode away unsettled, my petty sum of equanimity spent. This had been inevitable. I had known it would happen. But I was once more badly disturbed.

I left the camp, making a long circle around it, and rode north, the way we had come. For many English—or American—miles I rode a dim path at the edge of the dense woods which followed the river. Reaching the northern limit of the great boscage, I kicked César and gave him a loose rein. With a force that threw me back in the saddle, he leapt forward and stretched out his legs. We were immediately galloping at great speed, yet I continued kicking him, urging him to further efforts, bent over him, tears in my eyes from the wind. Relishing both speed and risk from the burrows on either side, I didn't care what might happen to me. At last, after urging him to run several more miles until he began to be winded and his gait to slacken, I gradually drew in his head, finally managing to stop him. César, frothing and breathing hoarsely, turned and retraced our route under a lighter rein, trotting slowly and sedately as I sat him relaxed with a slightly easier mind.

But it was not long before a deeper uneasiness set in. Its cause was a trifling detail I noticed on our return. When we reached the edge of the camp, I directed my horse to the shortest route toward my tent on the southern perimeter. As we approached the first cluster of tepees, I observed one of them set apart, farther east and north than the others. From its smokehole trailed a thread of smoke, drifting and vanishing in the morning breeze. This I found curious. Already the day was warm, beginning to be hot. Women who were cooking at other lodges were cooking outdoors owing to the weather. Nor was smoke issuing from any other tepee in view. Surely, I reasoned, any female who had built a fire in her lodge in the very early morning chill would have let it burn out or have extinguished it by now. The high sun in hazy blue indicated that mid-day was near. So why the smoke rising from that single, isolated tepee? Why fire? Abruptly an ugly thought, an unpleasant explanation, occurred to me. I turned away from the isolated tepee, leaving it behind me as rapidly as I could.

On my return, Arsène was seated cross-legged before the tent, eating with gusto and talking with Lefort. He had washed the warpaint from his face and evidently shaved. His tanned features and long, loose black hair with feather rendered him indistinguishable from any young Comanche male.

"Bonjour."

"Bonjour," he replied, with a hint of a smile. "I've come to borrow César, if you'll permit. I'd like to race him. I have a friend who thinks he's got the fastest horse on the prairie. I'll bet him five ponies your horse can beat his."

"He's not my horse," I said, sliding to the ground. "He's your father's. Take him. I've just run him. He may be tired."

"Let him rest. The races aren't till this afternoon. I'll come get him."

"Good." I led the horse into the shade, pulled his saddle and bridle, led him farther to the spring, watered him and tethered him under trees where there was mottled sunlight on the dry grass. Arsène was still sitting cross-legged before the door of the tent, now smoking a pipe with a red bowl. I recognized the fragrance of Lefort's tobacco. Mid-day was hot. Both men were shining with sweat.

"Maybe your father will give him to you, if you ask," said Lefort, raising his hat from his face. He was stretched in the shade of our great cotton tree, the rumpled, stained hat once more over his face. He waved at a fly.

Arsène seemed to reflect, slowly puffing his pipe. "It's true," he said at last, with a grimace of pain. "He still can't ride, can he?"

"No," I said. "You're talking about César? I think he would—especially if you were to stay in Natchitoches."

Arséne continued to smoke in silence, ignoring the latter part of my statement. The silence lengthened. Compared to the previous night, the great encampment was quiet, the moment peaceful. I drank tepid water from my flask. I was too warm, but I didn't remove my buckskins, left open at the chest. The bugs bothered me. Some of the flies bit.

"Tell him the news," Lefort said finally, raising his hat.

"What news? Not about the Navajos?"

"Yes," said Arsène. "My father and your brother are on their way back. They met the governor's messengers on the road beyond Tucumcari Mountain."

"They did? They're not going to Santa Fé?" Again, warm as the day was, a shiver hesitated, slid through my spine and ribs.

"No, they're on their way here now. Sees-Fire came ahead. He has a fast horse. To tell Mano de Hierro."

"The Navajos?"

"They've given horses, returned all our people. They're in Santa Fé now."

"Good. So there'll be no war."

"No. There'll be no war." Puffing gravely, Arsène appeared, I thought, disappointed.

"Then camp will break up soon."

"Probably soon as my father and Taoinan and the others get back."

Late that afternoon when the shadows were long and a warm wind off the prairie was fluttering cottonwood leaves and our tent, Arsène came for César. Lefort and I helped him mount, as there was no stump nearby. He rode off bareback, with a tight rein. The big horse was prancing and throwing his head, but Arsène rode him in a relaxed manner, appearing at ease. We followed him between lodges until reaching the eastern edge of the camp, where the level prairie stretched to the horizon and little groups of spectators on foot and on horseback waited, with even a few women and girls among them. The young women were talking and laughing. Among them I recognized the big one felled by her presumed husband. She was mounted on a pretty black mare. Noticing my scrutiny, she acknowledged it with an amused, friendly smile, a look which made me immediately like her.

The course was a level strip of about half an English mile. The earth had evidently been tamped by previous races dating from the establishment of the encampment, for the track was dirt between the dry grass and clumps of a cactus the Spaniards call "cholla."

Some of the ponies standing near its beginning, most with riders, had clearly raced before our arrival, as indicated by their sweat-darkened coats. A murmur drifted through the gatherings of racers and spectators as César's size in contrast to the ponies present became apparent. Doubtless all had heard of a huge horse ridden by the visiting trader, but most had apparently not seen him owing to our secluded campsite and the excitement created by the reunion of various bands, some of whom had been separated for long periods, as well as by the return of the victorious war party. Yet the warrior whose dress and demeanor identified him as the other competitor, Paraginanchi, or Ears-of-a-Sorrel-Deer, appeared, after a look at the big brute, to remain unimpressed and confident. A handsome youth, whom I will for the sake of brevity call, "Deer's-Ears," he sat his mount bareback, like Arsène wearing only breechcloth and moccasins. Also like Arsène, he was soothing his horse by stroking his neck and quietly talking to him. The horse, a sleek bay gelding with long mane and tail, had plainly been raced during the afternoon and, except for a little stamping and sidling, appeared to be composed.

César, in contrast, was obviously agitated, switching his tail, tossing his head, dancing in place. To add to the confusion other horsemen had carelessly gathered around the starting line. As Arsène restrained his excited mount, César began backing, rearing a little, swinging his rump from side to side. In doing so the big gelding collided with the rump of a pony ridden by another racer, a short, robust man with scarred features. The blow struck the smaller pinto with such force that it nearly went down, throwing its rider off balance and almost to the ground. This individual, whom I again recognized as the person who had felled the friendly woman, responded with rage, spitting a furious phrase at Arsène, drawing back his quirt as if to swing it up at the youth. Arsène, still struggling to control his horse, appeared to appologize, but the other man, instantly in a fury, continued berating him, seemingly with insults, simultaneously maneuvering his pony so as to be in a position to strike the governor's son with his quirt. Unable to reach him on the agitated taller horse, he swung the quirt at the horse, striking César on the flank, causing him to bolt forward and to rear so high that I feared that Arsène would slide off. Yet he stuck. Now angry himself, he apparently cursed in Comanche at his assailant, raising his own quirt in a threatening position as he turned his horse and came back to the other man. For a long moment the two glared at each other, the older man with rage and seeming astonishment that any young Comanche would dare defy him, each with raised quirt.

At this the camp-crier, young, loud, plump and pompous, kicked his pony almost between the two horses. "You race next," he told Arsène. "Hurry, come on."

Slowly the older warrior allowed his quirt hand to sag. With a long, threatening look at Arsène, he turned his pony and rode away into the crowd of nearby mounted men.

At a shout from the camp crier, the two horses started nearly simultaneously. César lunged forward fast for a big horse, but the gelding, being lighter and quicker, swiftly drew ahead for about the first twelve rods, evoking shouts of encouragement from spectators. By that time the sorrel had attained his full speed. Steadily he pulled ahead of the bay. Both men were swinging their quirts, bent over their horses' necks, with Arsène soon looking back at the other man. When the two animals passed the judges at the end of the course, César was obviously a length ahead at least, although it was difficult to tell how far from where Lefort and I were standing. The bay came to a halt a little beyond the men on horseback. But the big sorrel scarcely slowed, continuing at a run, despite what appeared to be extreme efforts by his rapidly diminishing rider, as the two grew smaller across the plain. Spectators, greatly amused, laughed uproariously.

"Diable!" exclaimed Lefort. "He's off for Natchitoches!"

Then Arsène was running his mount in circles, which gradually grew smaller, until the big horse slowed and stopped. They returned at a trot, coming directly to where we stood.

"We won. Why didn't you tell me he did that?" Arsène appeared embarrassed.

"He's never done it with me. But I've never raced him. Who was that who whipped César?"

"Voilà, un sale type," murmured Antoine, looking into the mounted crowd.

"I would have killed him," said Arsène, flushed and shaking, stroking the sweating sorrel.

"He looks dangerous. Who is he?"

"One of your brother's—The Flute's—real brothers. Tosapoy—White-Road. Warchief, like my father. They say Taoinan doesn't like him."

"I wonder why," I said. "Let's go."

"I'll meet you back there. I've got to get the ponies I won."

But just before we left, there was another distraction involving once again White-Road and the friendly woman, who I learned was indeed his wife, and named, "Tábo-ui," or "Rabbit-Knife." I noticed she bore, beside a red-and-purple knot on her forehead, a bruise on her left cheek. The incident began by White-Road, after winning his race, dropping his quirt while he spoke with the loser. His gesture to his wife caught my eye as we were leaving, and I paused. She rode at a lope from the group of women. As she approached her husband, she leaned from the black pony, supported only by a heel and, as I knew, an invisible horsehair loop braided into its mane, and swooped up the quirt, handing it butt first to the warchief. It was a display of horsemanship as expert as that of any young warrior I had seen in the past. Tosapoy received his quirt with scarcely a glance at her. With an open, pleased expression, she spun the black mare and loped back to her women friends. But as she rode, I intercepted a quick look directed at Arsène who, also visibly impressed, was watching her. It suddenly opened new possibilities and left me wondering.

Returning, Antoine and I walked in silence, each isolated by his thoughts. Abruptly, to my surprise, I found we were taking the long route and passing before Taoinan's lodge. This time Sehêbi was outside tossing meat scraps to dogs before the tepee, stooped and talking to them as she did so.

"Bonjour," I said, smiling, using one of a number of French words and phrases I had once taught her. "Comment ça va?"

"Bien. Merci." Straightening, she regarded us coolly, too politely, without the slightest sign of familiarity. "Et vous-même, Monsieur?"

"Très bien," I stammered, so disconcerted by her proper—indeed prim—demeanor that I waved and kept on walking instead of pausing to talk. Lefort and I continued on. If I had feared she might reveal through an expression or her behavior what I took to be our new relationship, whether I liked that relationship or not, I had misjudged her completely, so much so I was embarrassed, even faintly humiliated, by her self-possession. Adding to my discomfort was Lefort's silence as we walked on through the camp. Never had I known him to pass an attractive female without offering some comment, frequently ribald. But in this instance he had remained silent.

Arsène returned César soon after we reached our camp. With him was Deer's-Ears, the cheerful young brave against whom he had raced, still riding his bay gelding. Apologizing for his need to hurry, Arsène, who was riding his war-and-buffalo horse and leading the big sorrel, handed me César's reins, promising he would come back and eat with us, but saying he had to accompany the other warrior to where the horseherd was grazing out on the prairie. He had to learn to recognize the ponies he'd won.

Although game had grown scarce in the nearby woods, frightened away by the many hunters from the encampment, Lefort had that morning killed, skinned, and butchered a small bear in the nearly impenetrable undergrowth near the river. The best cuts he roasted that evening over our little fire, saving delicacies, two succulent paws, for the colonel's son. Arsène, late in arriving and hungry, began eating immediately. Lefort and I, having already dined, sat in the dark by our sinking fire, smoking our pipes against mosquitoes and watching him savor his meal.

"That warchief today, White-Road," said Antoine. "Watch your back, mon gars."

"No," said Arsène, chewing the meat from a bone. "We aren't like that. He was insulting me, besides whipping César, so I insulted him. You have to. Otherwise they call you a woman. But someday, in battle, he may save my life."

"He's got a mean look," I said.

"Oh, he likes to make everybody afraid. My father's not. Neither am I."

"I'd watch my back."

"No. There're three of them, brothers. They're probably all right. Though, I don't know much about them. They aren't in my band. They're in The Flute's."

Antoine shook his head. "En tout cas, attention."

Arsène ate in silence for a time. Finishing his meal, he lighted his pipe. The three of us puffed until the fire burned to ashes and red coals. At last he rose to depart.

"By the way," I asked. "That Apache—still alive?"

He stood, a dim figure in the twilight. "I don't know. Bonsoir," he said at last, turned and walked away into the dark.

Again the night was warm. That evening I brought my robe out of the tent and slept—eventually—under the stars, oblivious of the frequent whine and sting of mosquitoes.

The following morning I rose at first light and, queasy, without eating, saddled César, seized my musket and rode off, leaving Antoine snoring nearby. Making a circle around the encampment, I once again rode north, following the bosque and Rio Pecos. I badly needed to sort out my thoughts. Evidently at least two others beside Sehêbi and me knew of our coupling, She-Scolds-Her-Dogs and Antoine Lefort. Taoinan had been due to arrive yesterday. In any event I would have to face him soon. His first wife would certainly report what had occurred during his absence. I could, of course, flee. But that was impossible. All I could do was to wait guiltily and see what would happen.

These reflections had eased my mind a little. It was still that gray light before sunrise, as I recall, when I had completed my circuit of the camp and was about to take the woods-and-river-path. The camp was scarcely stirring, with no one yet visible from where I rode. Then I realized I was passing near the isolated tepee I had noticed before. While trotting by, I stared: the same wisp of smoke was curling upward in the morning air. In spite of myself, I sniffed, smelled nothing but the good scent of cedar smoke. As before, the place was silent. The details of whatever was occurring within remained a mystery. Giving my horse his head, I allowed him to ease from a trot into a lope. We left that locale without looking back.

Once again I rode up the river path, loping north beyond the beginning of the boscage and continuing for several hours. The river now ran through desert country, a broken brown and gray, with hills and arroyos and mesas, yucca and cholla near, mountains far. A north wind blew, cooling a cloudy morning so that it was almost chill. I was becoming hungry, my mind eased a little, and blessedly empty now, when I saw coming over a rise ahead a small party of horsemen following the river directly toward me. Drawing in my horse, I hesitated, wondering whether they might be Apaches and whether I might have to test my mount's speed in a race for my life. The approaching horsemen also drew up, pausing momentarily, as they scrutinized me from the distance between us. Then one of them whooped a Comanche whoop and waved his lance. Simultaneously they started for me at a gallop. Still uneasy, I sat my horse, facing them. But I soon realized that the warrior in the lead was Big-Mountain who, I learned later, had recognized César silhouetted against the skyline. As they drew closer and I waved my musket, I saw that the man riding beside him was my "brother," Taoinan—The Flute. As they approached, Big-Mountain whooped and bellowed, "Hóla, amigo!"

In return I dropped the musket and signaled with my arms and hands, "Good day" and "friends." Quickly dismounting, I held my horse with difficulty, as he was tugging the reins, rearing, backing, switching his rump, excited by the other horses bearing down upon us. Reaching me, the two lead riders flung themselves from their ponies. We embraced—Big-Mountain, who was a little in advance, then Taoinan. I was astonished to see them together. They seemed to have become not only friends but behaved like old friends. There followed much rapid talk in a mélange of languages and signs while I was still being jerked about by my plunging horse. They talked as if they had been gone from camp a month instead of a few days. Shortly we calmed César by placing Toyamancare's pinto beside him, and immediately the atmosphere became more tranquil. Since the sun was by this hour overhead, the former emissarries decided to pause and eat. I of course had left that morning without food, but the two Comanches shared their meal with me. They told me that on the trail north of Tucumcari Mountain, and before meeting the governor's messengers, they had encountered a party of traders, Españoles, from the capital. By bartering some peltry they had thought to bring, they had acquired several loaves of hard bread, sugar, prunes, and dried apples. It was a tempting meal they offered, and all of the party ate heartily, supplementing their diet of pemmican with these delicacies.

But sitting cross-legged beside The Flute, I found my mouth to be so dry and my stomach so unsettled I could scarcely chew, swallow, or indeed desire food at all. As they ate, Big-Mountain was describing to Taoinan the many days he had recently spent as guest of the governor at San Antonio de Béxar, where he had eaten well and been treated almost as that official's son. And how he had ridden alone from Béxar to the Pawnee-Piquée villages, where he had by chance fallen in with us. Finally he noticed my abstinence.

"What's the matter with you, Bluejay?" he asked finally in Spanish, using my nickname, based upon a blue vest I'd once affected. "You don't eat. Are you sick?"

"A little. Antoine killed a bear. We ate some last night." I patted my stomach. "Maybe it didn't agree."

"Bear meat's good."

"Well, brother," asked The Flute, with a smile. "Have you enjoyed yourself with us this time? We'll be leaving the river now, you know."

"Yes. It's been a good stay. We found the colonel's son. Too bad you had to leave. I'd hoped to see more of you. We've hardly smoked together."

"I had to go. It was good. As you see, we've become friends." He looked at Big-Mountain, who grunted, chewing jerked meat with his bread. "And, my brother," he continued, smiling at me. "I'm curious to know—did Sehêbi come to your bed?"

I choked on a piece of dry bread and coughed until tears came to my eyes. But I nodded. I nodded. What else? I was stunned, dumbfounded. And this before Toyamancare, who now watched me with interest. "Yes," I managed to croak. "Yes, she did."

Both Taoinan and Toyamancare seemed amused, although the latter, that lover of good horses, appeared after a moment to become more interested in watching César than in the subject discussed.

"Was she? I knew she liked you. Was it good?"

"Yes," I said, recovering to some extent and nearly overwhelmed by a sense of relief. "Yes, it was good."

The Flute continued to regard me with humor in his eye and the same gentle, amused smile. "I see you were surprised. You know, my brother, that our customs aren't the same—those of your people, the tabebo, and ours. Now you know this one and when I come to visit you someday, and you are married, you'll lend me your wife." Though he was amused, I saw that he was serious and found nothing unusual in what he said. Apparently it was part of our relationship that I had not known about.

"Of course." I was actually blushing.

Both men laughed at my embarassment. Taoinan continued to smile warmly in the most friendly manner, as if my sleeping with that child, his favorite wife, had brought us closer. At this, regaining my appetite, I began again to try the food he and Big-Mountain had offered and was soon eating voraciously, ready to weep with gratitude and joy and relief.

After eating, satiated and content, the entire party jogged along for the most part in silence, I next to the leaders, The Flute and Big-Mountain. The revelation concerning Sehêbi's visit to my tent had been such a shock I had not begun to absorb it. All I felt was relief. But nearly as astonishing was the friendship between the two men riding beside me. I tried to remember the history of that relationship. The Flute had told me the whole story years before. As well as I could remember the two had belonged as youths to the same band, a large band that had since split in two. The split had come about, as I recalled, partly because there had existed already two factions within it: that of Big-Mountain's father, his family, relatives, and friends and that of The Flute's blood father and his relatives and friends. Toyamancare's father, Sonocat, or Many-Peppers, was war chief while Taoinan's real father, Isaquebera, or Long Wolf, was civil chief. Although there had apparently been increasing tension between the factions, the incident which set off the band's separation was the death of a horse owned by Hichapat, The-Crafty-One, Taoinan's true grandfather.

The Flute had told me it happened this way: the band had been camped in the north, next to the mountains of Nuevo Mexico before riding over the pass to the villa of Fernando de Taos to attend the annual trade fair there. During the night a small party of Utes were stealing horses from the herd when they were discovered and fled with the dozen or so they had managed to gather. They were pursued by a group of youths who seized the first fast ponies they could rope. These Comanche youths overtook the thieves. In the ensuing skirmish, the Comanches killed two of the Utes and recovered the stolen horses, while the remaining thieves escaped to the mountains. One of the youths who had killed a Ute was Big-Mountain's older brother. This young warrior was so elated at taking his first scalp that he raced back before the others. But the pony, though swift, was already exhausted by the chase and, within a mile of the camp, collapsed, dead. Unluckily this was the favorite horse of The-Crafty-One, The Flute's grandfather. Even so the youth dog-trotted with his weapons, shield, and scalp the remaining distance to camp and his father's lodge to announce his triumph over the Ute enemy. Many-Peppers and the remainder of the family exhulted at the news, especially the boy's mother, Temumuquit, or Hummingbird, who went at once to inform The-Crafty-One of her son's triumph and of the death of the old man's horse.

With the proud mother went her youngest daughter, a child of seven or eight years. They found the old man within his lodge. Hummingbird first boasted of her son's exploit before telling him of his horse's death and her husband's intention of repaying him for the loss. Now according to The Flute, The-Crafty-One had been a noted warrior and an able medicine man, but in his old age had become bitter and malevolent, living alone, envious of younger men and rumored to be practicing evil medicine, sorcery against the young warriors most admired by the band's young women. On this occasion it happened that the sole thing he loved—more than his son, Long-Wolf, or his grandsons—had been that particular horse, which had won many races and bets for him. Consequently he became enraged when told of the manner of its death.

Hummingbird, who was also hot-tempered, and who had been growing increasingly angry at his lack of enthusiasm for her son's feat, became in turn enraged. Unwisely she taunted the old man, contrasting him with her handsome and virile son, drawing herself up and daring him to strike her, if he were that crazy, in revenge for the death of a mere horse, which was nothing compared to the heroic deed of a young warrior at the start of a great career! Goaded too far, The-Crafty-One seized his war club and hurled it at the woman. Its flint blade struck her head with such violence that it knocked her to the earth, where she lay. Watching in horror, and finding her mother dead, the child ran shrieking from the lodge to that of her father, where the family was still celebrating, and told them the terrible news.

Instead of seeking refuge at a lodge of his son or grandsons, the old man put on his buffalo-horned headdress and seated himself outside the door of his tepee, where he beat his drum, singing his death song over and over, until Many-Peppers and young Big-Mountain and the other three sons came. Many-Peppers entered the lodge and looked down at his favorite wife lying with her skull crushed, exited and drew his knife. The-Crafty-One continued to sing and pound his drum. While the boys held the unresisting old man's arms, Many-Peppers slit his throat and pushed him, gushing blood, to the ground. They then lifted the dead woman and carried her back to Many-Pepper's lodge.

Taoinan told me that many men would not have risked reprisals by killing the old man over the death of a woman, but that Many-Peppers had truly loved this wife to the extent that no reparation, of no matter how many horses, would make up for her loss to him. Furthermore it appears to me, looking back on those years, that feuds were not the usual Comanche way of settling disputes between families. In fact, I don't recall any.

The news spread like grassfire in the wind. Apparently Long-Wolf's first thought as civil chief on learning of the circumstances of his father's death was to send the camp crier around to announce the immediate meeting of a council of the band's principal men, including Many-Peppers. Although self-important and, like his sons, inclined to put on airs, Isaquebera, or Long-Wolf, was a shrewd politician. He saw the imminent danger of an eruption of violence which would leave the band's best warriors dead. His solution, offered during the council, was to advise dividing the band along the line of the two families and their friends and followers. This suggestion was considered by all to be the only way of resolving the crisis. As a result Many-Peppers, with his relatives and friends, broke camp that day and, after burying the woman, set out, their dogs and ponies dragging travois westward. Long-Wolf and his people, after burying The-Crafty-One, departed the following morning, traveling east. Ever since, until the great divisional meeting on Rio Pecos, the two bands, according to The Flute, had been successful in avoiding each other, one of them remaining to the east, the other always far to the west.

Until the time of the separation Taoinan and Toyamancare had been casual friends, but Big-Mountain had accompanied his father and family to the Pecos River region, while The Flute had remained with his mother and Long-Wolf's faction, which included not only his blood relatives but the warrior whose affair with his mother had caused her calamity. He had not even known the grandfather Many-Peppers had killed, except by the old man's evil reputation. He had no affection for a father and brothers who persisted in their haughty refusal to recognize his relationship to them. Yet finding himself treated by all like a distant relative of the leading family, albeit with an obscure connection, he had simply remained with his accustomed circle of acquaintances, which happened to be that of his actual parents and brothers.

But that was before he had begun achieving a reputation, in spite of his crippled foot, as a promising young warrior and before he had begun acquiring horses, far more horses in fact than his brothers had been able to steal. Now all had changed. Many-Peppers and Long-Wolf were dead, as well as many other members of their generation, including The Flute's foster mother.

During their trip toward Santa Fé, The Flute and Big-Mountain had begun discussing the old days when they had belonged to the same band. They talked of people they had known and of what had happened to them. During this time they had become increasingly friendly, until finally Taoinan had said that he knew of no reason why the two bands might not join together again and become a single branch of the Kotsoteka Comanche division. Toyamancare had agreed, adding that he would of course need the approval of his warriors, especially of Manos-Amarillas, or Yellow-Hands, civil chief and one of the few remaining leaders of his father's generation. As a result the two men had decided to invite a council of the warriors from both bands in order to discuss this possible resolution to the old conflict. They were discussing this plan while riding back to camp.

"Well," I said, responding to a question by Big-Mountain. "With more men your band would be safer."

"True," said The Flute. "Of course, I don't know your country well," he said to Big-Mountain. "Only now this part along the river and mountains."

"It will be good," Toyamancare said. "There's plenty of everything for more people than we'll be. In fall we can come here to hunt, and winter camp in one of the big canyons."

"I'll ask my people right away," said Taoinan and relapsed into silence.

The landscape had changed from bare, hilly river country to green forest on our western side. We had been riding along these dense woods for some time and now began approaching the encampment, with smoke visible in the near distance, its scent in the air. A wind had risen and cleared the clouds, leaving the sky blue, with a hot sun. We were all sweating. I was looking forward to dismounting at our destination, drinking cold water from the spring, sprawling in the shade of our cotton tree. At the sight of camp the leading riders, my companions, broke into a trot, then a lope, and the entire party trotted and loped behind us. As we drew near the first tepees, I glanced at the lodge isolated at their edge: a thread of smoke like a strand of gray hair fluttered from its smokehole and disintegrated. As I looked, a figure came stooping out of its doorway, the first sign I had seen of any human presence there or in its vicinity. This person stopped, shading his eyes, gazing at us, as we loped into camp. I only saw him for an instant by looking back, but the figure was familiar. Yes, I thought, riding by barking dogs, between tepees and women and children, it could only have been Arsène.

Two days later we broke camp. Soon after sunrise the women began dismantling tepees, packing cooking utensils, hitching horses to travois, while boys and older girls herded other ponies into camp, and men saddled those they intended to ride. So what had shortly before been a great encampment of lodges, with lounging men, running children, scampering dogs, and busy women had become a barren area of worn grass, dried brush arbors, smoking firepits, discarded bones, other trash, as well as the excrement of dogs, horses, and humans. It was time to move on. Mano-de-Hierro, with his own band and one other, had already departed northward toward Santa Fé, where he would meet with the Spanish governor and reclaim the Comanche captives released by the Navajos, as well as the horses and goods the enemy had offered in reparation for their raid.

Lefort and I were delayed in leaving, since boys had brought us our pack horses late, there having been some confusion as to who owned them. We had already disassembled the tent and packed all of our belongings, saddled César and Antoine's horse. In a moment we had saddled the three pack horses, their pack saddles nearly empty, and were riding out of the dreary expanse where the camp had stood. We hurried into the early sun to catch the now combined band of The Flute, Big-Mountain, and their people. As we passed the trampled circle where The Flute's lodge had stood, I slowed momentarily to gaze at it without thinking, still a little dazed and puzzled by what had happened to me. Lefort, leading the packhorses, rode up beside me, looking also at the vestiges of my friend's and his wives' camp.

Leaving, I turned for a last look and saw with a start vultures gliding the sky over the northern edge, where the isolated lodge had stood. In my hurry to depart, I'd forgotten. Halting César, I stared. In the distance there seemed to be—though I could not be sure—a black object like a sack on the ground. Around this a group of dogs appeared to be quarreling, tearing at it.

"The unfortunate one," said Antoine.

"No doubt. Let's catch up."

We rode at a lope all the way to the dust and horseherd and last travois of the combined bands. At its head rode Toyamancare and Taoinan. Just behind the latter warrior rode Sehêbi, bearing his shield and lance. Sitting stiffly in the saddle, she acknowledged me as I passed with a formal glance, a look very much suggesting, I thought, scorn. After greeting the two leaders, I dropped some distance behind Sehêbi, to where Arsène was riding alone. We shook hands like good Frenchmen.

"Well, little brother," I said. "You lied to me."

"What?" For an instant he looked like an astonished little boy.

"You told me you didn't know whether that Lipan was alive or dead. Day before yesterday I saw you coming out of the lodge where they had him. So you knew, didn't you?"

For a moment he hung his head. "I only went in to look—just for a minute. I wanted to see."

"And—what did you see?"

"He was a brave man." He swallowed. "I hope if I...If ever..."

"If you're ever captured and tortured? Is that it? Arsène, my little brother, my good friend, I won't tell your father, but..." I stopped, fearing I might be prescient.

"I don't care if you do. I'm not staying with him anyway."

"Arsène, mon vieux, you've become...a savage."

Again, that haughty, fierce look burning into my eyes. His knuckles turned white on his lance. Then he smiled, faintly, defiantly. "But not noble, no?"

"No. Not noble."

6   *Autumn 1794, El Llano Estacado*

Our caravan required eleven days to return to the source of la Rivière Rouge, or—as the Spaniards call it—Rio Colorado de Natchitoches. Meanwhile all of us became irritable, with a vague but widespread sense of impending disaster. The first day the weather continued scorching, windy, though it was the time of the autumnal equinox. That night we camped, after a short march, upon a tributary of Rio Pecos where there was sufficient water for animals and travelers alike. But some of the leading men of what had been the band including The Flute were worried and came to see him during the evening.

He and I were smoking alone in his lodge, which She-Scolds-Her-Dogs and First-Frost had insisted upon raising, though many of us slept under the planets. Ironically these visitors were the true half-brothers who continued the fiction that they were unrelated to him. It was also ironic that while Taoinan had regularly resisted accepting any position of power in his former band its leading warriors had begun coming more and more frequently to consult with him. And now, evidently for the first time, his own brothers came, White-Road, warchief of the former band, and he with whom Arsène had quarreled, also Ybienca, or Red-Woman, eldest of the three and the band's civil chief, as well as El Chamaco, The Boy, youngest and camp crier, half-brother to the other two by a different mother.

After the three had entered the tepee and seated themselves properly, and after Taoinan had lit and passed a pipe, Red-Woman, a tall, bony man with a dignified demeanor and look of importance, explained their concern. Manos-Amarillas, he complained, and Big-Mountain were leading the band out on what the Spaniards called the Llano Estacado, an immense high prairie under a vast sky, with few trails or landmarks. As far as they knew, it contained no dependable sources of water. Now this was no frivolous complaint. It had also occured to me that Toyamancare's insistence on taking a short cut to reach la Rivière Rouge might be a mistake. But while I really didn't know Yellow-Hands, the old man had a good reputation as former warrior, medicine man and experienced civil chief. Furthermore I trusted Big-Mountain.

"For example, the horseherd," complained Red-Woman. "They need plenty of water. A few mud holes won't do. Our own saddle horses would drink them up. Anyway, it hasn't rained for a moon. We can't even count on buffalo ponds—they're as much shit as water anyway."

"True," said Taoinan. He reflected. "Of course, the storms cover small spaces sometimes, under just a few clouds. They leave pools."

"And the children and women," said El Chamaco" His frequently sly and mischievous expression had altered to one of anxiety. "We can go without water for a while. But the women with babies..."

"Of course," said Taoinan. "You're right. But this is Toyamancare's country. He knows it. I believe there's little risk."

"Big Mountain told me he'd never come this way before—not exactly this road. He knows the country, that's all. He knows we'll strike the Rio Colorado sometime. That's not enough," said Red-Woman. "Meanwhile we could lose the horseherd, all die."

There was silence in the lodge.

White-Road fixed his unacknowledged brother with his cold stare.

"There's Yellow-Hands," Taoinan said. "He's smart. He knows the whole prairie. He's been traveling around our country all his life. He's not going to lead us out here to die. Remember, he was a great warrior, in your father's time, led war parties everywhere. I trust him."

"He's an old man," Red-Woman said. "Old men forget. The look of the country changes. They get confused and pretend they're not, blame it on bad medicine." He turned to me. "What does the Bluejay think?"

"I trust Toyamancare," I said, hoping I was right.

White-Road snorted.

"Good," said Red-Woman, after reflection. "Maybe. Maybe you are right. We'll follow tomorrow. But if we start to dry-camp, we'll come back to this stream with our relatives and horses and follow it up to Rio Pecos, and ride back to the Red the way we came, where we're sure of plenty of water."

"We'll wait near the crossing," White-Road said. "For a while."

"If you never come back," said El Chamaco, with a little smile. "We'll tell the People what happened to you." Taking leave of us formally, the three brothers rose and moved stiffly from the tepee, Red-Woman first, White-Road second, and El Chamaco behind them.

"One thing is sure," Taoinan remarked at last, wrapping his ceremonial pipe. "A band should have only one head warchief, one peace chief. If they should choose to go, maybe it would be best for us all."

"I think that's what they want," I said.

From its beginning our trip became increasingly dreamlike. In the mornings everyone rose and broke camp early. The days were windy and hot. Whenever possible, Antoine and I took the precaution of loading our packhorses with water, even at the scarce ponds left by rain. Like the Indians we used buffalo-paunch bags in which to transport this precious liquid. Even so I recall hoping intensely by one memorable afternoon's end, when the sun had turned red and was sinking toward the plain behind us, that our straggling caravan would arrive at some agreeable stream with a luxurious plenty of water for horses, dogs, and ourselves. Instead reaching at sundown a pallid playa whose cracked and curling rectangles indicated long absence of moisture, we were notified by El Chamaco, the crier, that this was the spot where we were to camp for the night. Leaving Lefort with the horses, I loped to the head of the column, where Big-Mountain, appearing discomfitted, was already defending himself against the complaints and accusations of Red-Woman, White-Road and other men of their large family. Beside him, rigid in his saddle, was Arsène, sickly yellow under his tan, staring with his fiercest expression at the accusers of Toyamancare, his lance gripped in his fist. On Big-Mountain's other side, and also facing the brothers, was a little figure who could be no one but Manos-Amarillas. He was vainly trying to make himself heard in the din.

"Basta!" shouted Big-Mountain in Spanish. "Show respect. Let the chief speak!"

In the abrupt silence, everyone looked at the old man on his bony horse, a white nag. Like the other men he wore breechclout, hip-length leggings, and moccasins. Under a fanciful headdress of eagle feathers extendng upward and encircling his head with its tangled gray hair, the dark skin of his thin, withered body resembled ancient oiled leather. But still he bore his shield and bowcase, with bow and arrows, slung on his back, and still he commanded awe simply by appearing, with his glittering dark eyes, to be vitally alive. Slowly he raised the arm bearing his shield, pointing to the darkening sky overhead.

"Tomorrow when the sun is there, we'll reach a creek—and after that, later, another. So don't be scared. No water tonight. We went too slow today. But plenty tomorrow—my promise."

"Scared?" scoffed White-Road. "We're afraid of nothing and no one. But nobody can live without water. Neither can the horses."

"Tomorrow we'll reach water early," repeated the old man, calmly meeting the collective gaze of the clamorers.

"Good," said Red-Woman, after several moments. "We believe you." Turning their ponies, he and his entourage rode back to rejoin their families.

The band broke camp early the next morning. As the sun climbed, we sensed that the wind on this day would be even stronger and hotter than it had been the day before, hotter and dryer. Indeed the horseherd had become so thirsty by midday when we reached the promised stream that the boys, with girls and men now helping, could scarcely hold the ponies back. The constant wind also had the effect of making all of us, human beings and animals, weary and nervous, so that when Red-Woman rode to us where we were watering our horses at the stark, shallow creek sliced into the prairie, and when he told us that he and his brothers, and all their relatives, had decided to camp at the stream, I was half-inclined to agree to join them. Lefort and I exchanged a glance, and I could see that Antoine was also of half a mind to remain in this place for the rest of that day and the night that would follow.

"No, I'll go on with my father," replied Arsène, who had been riding with us, and who was watering his mount next to ours.

After that, Lefort and I felt compelled to protest that it was only about noon, and that Yellow-Hands had said there was another stream lying ahead which we would reach early enough to camp beside. We also would push on, after eating, and hoped we might all be going together, as one band. But this time the three brothers and their relatives and friends were determined to halt. Soon we could see their women unharnessing horses, unloading travois, kicking dogs out of the way and beginning to erect tepees. Toyamancare argued for the rest of us continuing on, leaving them to catch up the following day if they wished. But the old chief, Manos-Amarillas, prounounced against this decision, saying it would simply lead to another split and leave us weakened in the event of a later encounter with an enemy.

For the remainder of the afternoon the weather continued to be so windy, dry, and hot that all of us who were not working or guarding the horseherd remained under shelter, Antoine and I in our tent by the stream, with Lefort's mule and César staked nearby, the packhorses with the herd. Early that evening Arsène, who had been spending most of his time gambling with other young warriors, visited us with the news that his father, Toyamancare, and the old chief, Manos-Amarillas, had met that afternoon with Red-Woman and White-Road. All had agreed that it was not possible to continue longer with two civil, or peace, chiefs leading a single band. Together they had decided that soon they would call a council in which those attending would choose one headman.

Finally the wind subsided to a breeze and remained subdued for a time. Pink clouds streaked with charcoal were massing when I stepped out of our tent next morning. Then our journey became rapidly more peculiar. As Lefort and I were eating our breakfast of corn mush and jerked venison, Sehêbi appeared and informed me that my brother wanted to see me right away, that he had something important to tell me.

"You know what it's about?" I asked, rising.

"No." She wouldn't meet my eyes. Her expression was sour.

We went in uncomfortable silence to Taoinan's lodge, where she left me to join his other wives at their tepee a little distance away. The Flute was seated hunched before the charred remains of a buffalo chip fire under a vast, coloring sky.

"How are you, brother?" he said. "I've been sitting here all night."

"I'm well," I said, seating myself near him. "And you, brother?"

"Listen," he said, straightening a little and regarding me intently. "Last evening when I was sitting out here, after the wind stopped, Red-Woman and White-Road came. I invited them to sit by my fire, but they stood. They only stayed a little. They told me that in spite of the talk earlier with Toyamancare and Manos-Amarillas, they'd now decided they would follow this creek down from the Llano out onto the greater prairie, where they know all the rivers and streams. They said they didn't trust Yellow-Hands' directions because he was an old man and perhaps funny in the head. They didn't want to risk becoming lost here without water. They would meet us later at the crossing of Rio Colorado if we wished, but they'd absolutely definitely decided to follow Running Water Creek down to the prairie. I think Red-Woman and White-Road are afraid the council will go against them and will choose Yellow-Hands and Big-Mountain as civil chief and head warchief. Then they, themselves, would be less important than when the band was split. What do you think?"

"I don't know. You're probably right."

"I think so. Here Toyamancare and I have made friends after all these years and brought the old band together, and now our brothers are trying to break it into two parts again."

"I see." I started at "our brothers" but concealed the faint shock I'd felt. "Yes. You're probably right."

"I sat here a long time before my fire. She-Scolds-her-Dogs came and threw more chips on the fire and went to her lodge to sleep, but still I sat here worrying about the band breaking apart again. After a while I fell asleep." Raising his head, he stared at me intently. "Listen to me now, brother. I woke up because I heard someone talking to me. Right across from me on the other side of the fire a wolf was sitting on its haunches looking at me—not the big wolf, piaisa, but the little wolf, tzena, the medicine wolf. The firelight seemed to come right out of her eyes—it was a female with pups somewhere, because her teats were big—and she was talking to me. I mean, her mouth didn't move, but I could hear her words in my head, speaking to me in Comanche, just as clearly as I heard you just now. You understand?"

"I hear you."

"She said that tomorrow morning—now, that is—El Chamaco would come and tell me that soon Red-Woman, White-Road, and all their people would be leaving to follow Running Water Creek down through its canyon out to the big prairie."

"Yes?"

"But that I must tell them there's danger in that direction, that they must not go that way, not south. She said that I must warn everybody to take the old chief's road—Yellow-Hands' road—ahead toward this new sun and a little north. There she said we'll find buffalo and, later, the Rio Colorado de Natchitoches. What do you think about that?"

"Wonderful." A little baffled and flustered, I could think of nothing else to say in response to his interrogating, penetrating gaze.

"Then I thanked Tzena. But I had to ask her, 'You're not fooling me? Making a joke?' 'Not this time, brother,' she said. Then she got up and, still watching me with those red eyes, turned and trotted into the dark. Her full teats were swaying—you know how they do." He looked at me with great, open eyes as if he were not quite seeing me but seeing past me, still seeing firelight and that being he called 'tzena.' "Now, what do you think about that, brother?"

"I think you'd better tell the council."

I tend in religious matters to be tolerant, in favor of natural religion, not superstitious, but in this instance I had a shiver stored in my spine that would not quite develop, like a sneeze hesitating. It remained a while. Taoinan was my good friend and never lied, and his story had strangely moved me. Furthermore one thing I never mentioned to him, then or afterward, was that if Tzena, whom the Criollos know as "coyote," had called him brother, and he and I were "brothers," then Tzena might be my "sister" too. Unsuperstitious as I am, the thought still gives me an odd feeling.

"Yes, that's what I think. But Bluejay this morning I had bad thoughts."

"You did? So does everybody."

"Yes. Our brothers have caused me so much misery, in one way or another, all my life. And now they're about to chop the band apart again. I thought—what if I didn't tell them? Just let them go south? And if they should die on the road to the great prairie, then there would be no more trouble. Of course I'd never do that. But I hate to have had thoughts."

"Maybe Tzena sent them."

"Yes, I thought about that. But I doubt it. I think they came from my heart."

Of course on the way to see Toyamancare and Manos-Amarillas, The Flute did indeed encounter El Chamaco coming to see him. He sent him off to tell nobody to leave camp and to call all the older warriors together and to announce that he, Taoinan, had heard words directly from the medicine wolf's mouth and had something important to tell them. Now the Comanches have great respect for the big wolf and for the little medicine wolf as well, not even eating dogs, as some peoples do. So the crier's announcement brought all the leading warriors hurrying to meet together in Yellow-Hands' lodge.

When I returned to the tent I found that Antoine had saddled our horses. Boys had brought the packhorses as a courtesy, and he had already loosely cinched the pack saddles and loaded two of them with buffalo-paunches filled with water from the creek. He had lashed these in with the cooking utensils and other gear. I helped him strike the tent and load it upon the third horse. After that we sat and smoked our pipes at the ashes of our cooking fire. These Indian councils can last a long time. All we could do was wait. While we smoked, I told Lefort of Taoinan's vision. He nodded, shrugged, and puffed smoke. He had been watching the sky.

"Looks like a storm building."

The great clouds piling to the east had lost their color and taken on more gray.

"We'll be heading into it either way, north or south."

"North. They won't go against that kind of warning. I don't know what's taking them so long."

"Unless they think she may be playing a prank on them."

"Well, that's possible," said Lefort, again looking at the sky. "That's probably it. They don't know what to think."

After a while, I rose and sauntered back to where Taoinan's lodge had stood, and where his three wives were busy packing a travois harnessed to a black horse. As I arrived, I saw several older men hurrying from the council, which had evidently just ended.

"Which way?" I called in Comanche.

"Ahead, and north," one of them shouted, pointing slightly northeast.

We had been riding for a little over an hour when we heard the first thunder. The sky to the north and ahead, eastward, had darkened. The huge piled clouds before us were now blue-black. I looked at Antoine riding beside me leading the packhorses. He half-smiled, with a grimace. We were riding in front of the train along with Taoinan, Toyamancare, the old chief and, a little to our left, Red-Woman and White-Road. While other women rode to the rear, Rabbit-knife trailed her husband, bearing his shield and lance, her expression betraying her impatience with this honorific duty and perhaps a desire to be free to ride where she wished. The thunder boomed again, louder.

"Thunderbird," murmured The Flute, from beside me. I knew he referred to the immense bird the People believe in, Tomouehtecua, a bird with firey wings whose squawk is thunder and whose eyes, opening and closing, flash lightning. Yes, lightning. I looked again at Lefort. This time he grinned. I smiled and shook my head. Earlier when he had been looking at the sky, we had I'm sure been thinking of the same thing: lightning. It is not pleasant to find oneself on vast flat terrain like the Llano with no cover during a thunderstorm. As he had predicted, we were riding directly into it. Despite myself and my faith in reason most of the time, I could not help thinking of Taoinan's vision or dream—and Tzena, the prankster. I wished he had seen Piaisa, the big wolf instead.

"Relámpagos," mused Big-Mountain from my left. "We're going to get it."

"Well, we won't have to worry about water, I don't think," I said. "Maybe we should stop and wait a little."

"Maybe we should," he said.

But we continued on into the flashing blue-black which draped onto the prairie before us. Now the real wind started. Before there had been a little anticipatory breeze, and we had moved in a kind of vacuum before the storm. But now the northwind rushed upon the caravan, blowing and flapping the ponies' manes and everything that was loose, rushing so loudly and powerfully that the horses had to force themselves into it to progress. From the clouds, now an intense purple, to the earth, jagged streaks of lightning were striking nearer, directly before us, lighting the praire intermittently with a dismal pallor, while thunder crashed and boomed. At this moment Red-Woman and White-Road, who had been shouting back and forth, rode over to us. They appeared upset.

"We've taken the wrong road," Red-Woman yelled. "We should have gone south."

"Medicine wolf has tricked us," shouted White-Road..

"No," shouted Manos-Amarillas. "This is the right road. You'll see. But now we must stop and wait." Each of us in the foremost group was, I believe, glad not to have made the suggestion himself. Yet it was acceptable for an old peace chief to have made it, and we were relieved he had done so. All of us were immediately ready to comply. We halted, sending back word we would pause for a time and wait for the storm to slacken. Even so the wind still drove at us from the north and east. The thunder grew louder, crackling and exploding as if from directly overhead, although the approaching lightning, with its line of rain, was still at some distance before us, its flashes jagged in the purple sky.

Yet to stop and sit motionless on our horses was also frustrating. It was our helplessness which made the situation unnerving. There was no cover in that level landscape, nothing much we could do. The Comanches too showed a respect for the lightning and appeared distinctly uneasy as we watched the storm drive toward our frail-looking caravan and the horseherd behind it. At this moment Arsène rode up with a half-dozen other young warriors, all wanting to know why we had stopped. In response the old chief, Manos-Amarillas raised a withered arm and pointed to the sky before us, which at that moment was illuminated by a great flash followed by a shattering crash!

"Why, that's only lightning," shouted Arsène, throwing out his chest. "Brave men don't fear lightning." There was a silence.

"Assez—ne crânes pas," I yelled into his ear. "Pas de bêtises!"

Chief Yellow-Hands giggled. "You are very young," he shouted in his high voice. To the rest of us he cried, "Look, this young warrior wants to fight Thunderbird—he, he, he, he."

Realizing he had made a gaffe, Arsène looked for an instant mortified, while the older men around him managed weak smiles. His fierce expression returned. Turning to the other young men, he waved his lance forward, and called to them, "Come on." Kicking his pony, lashing it once with his quirt, he galloped forward into the storm. Several of his young companions made as if to follow him, but drew in their ponies, looking at each other doubtfully. Still, I was impressed by how much they appeared to admire him.

"Stay here," commanded Toyamancare, his eyes still on the receding figure of his adopted son. "He's being a fool—un tonto."

We watched as Arsène, at the distance of a long arrow shot, sat his pony back on its heels. Then, facing the storm, he raised his shield and his lance toward the great bruise of sky and shook that lance toward the clouds, as lightning plunged to the earth an English mile or so before him, and thunder exploded above. Bravado it was, but also somehow strangely stirring, moving. But then there was a near strike which illuminated the prairie around us, and a vibrant bang from the heavens. He and his horse went down. I thought he had been hit and was about to ride forward when he rose and retrieved his lance. Staggering to his pony, he grabbed its rein and began to tug. The pony got to its knees and remained in that position, as if stunned. We watched as he lashed its rump with his quirt. The pony rose and stood. Lance in his hand, Arsène mounted. Again he raised his shield and lance to the sky. Again he was shouting. This time the wind shifted a little eastward, and we could hear the words clearly through the roar of the storm:

"Ne tzaré Nuhmuhnuh!" he shouted over and over again. "I am Comanche. And I'm not afraid!" Again and again. And then: "Je suis Comanche. Je n'ai pas peur!" Again and again. And: "Yo soy Comanche! No tengo miedo!" Turning and lashing his horse, he rode back at a gallop, drawing up before us and, sitting disheveled on his trembling pony, regarded us defiantly. Overwhelmed as we were by the bizarre spectacle we had just witnessed, no one said anything, simply gazed at the horseman before us as if he had been a ghost.

"Truly," cackled old chief Yellow-Hands at last, in a sudden quiet, as the wind shifted more directly toward the south. "This young man is not afraid."

In spite of that compliment by a respected chief, there was discussion among the People for some time, even in other bands, as to whether the young warrior's act had been brave or poisá, crazy. But even if he were a little crazy, people finally concluded, he was a brave man and probably destined to become a great leader. Actually though, a fit of madness was not the exact explanation. When I asked Arsène that evening why he had done what he had, he replied simply, "It was stupid—I was scared too, but I just got angry."

Although the thunder continued nearly as loudly as ever, the storm with its lightning was shifting south. For a short time we sat under hail and a pelting rain, but that squall soon blew away. Manos-Amarillas, who seemed naturally to have assumed the position of civil chief in spite of Red-Woman and his disgruntled brothers, ordered the band forward again. We had proceeded only a short distance when the old chief rode a little forward of those of us in the vanguard and pointed southward.

"Caramba!" shouted Toyamancare. To the south the storm had redoubled in violence, with cloud-to-earth flashes every few seconds, so that the entire plain in that direction was illuminated from moment to moment. We could even make out the far distant line of Running Water Creek at the center of the coruscations. Then as we watched, that area where the flashes were most frequent burst into flame, fire which was instantly spread by the wind, until the entire prairie in that quarter blazed in one explosive conflagration. "Look," he cried to White-Road. "There's where you would have been if you'd followed the creek. And you say Tzena tricked us?"

Neither Red-Woman, nor White-Road, nor El Chamaco, sitting sodden and bedraggled on their drenched ponies, staring glumly southward, had a response. They appeared to be pretending not to hear Big-Mountain. As they gazed off, I surprised an expression on Rabbit-Knife's wet, shining face as she regarded Arsène with, it seemed, mingled awe and delight. The entire column had halted again to watch the lightning and fire. We remained, fascinated by the spectacle, until the cloudburst following the fireworks extinguished most of the tract of flames, then continued our journey to the northeast, with old chief Yellow-Hands, now our undisputed guide, leading the way.

7

We camped that night along a creek the Spaniards call Tierra Blanca owing to the pale soil on either side. Early in the day we had struck this creek which Manos-Amarillas said we would follow until we arrived again at that vast canyon the Indians call "Hard Wood" and the Spaniards "Palo Duro," and into which the said Blanca Creek runs, there to join the beginning of la Rivière Rouge at its source. For the remainder of that day and for the next we followed an ancient trace worn along either bank by the buffalo and wild horses that frequent this tableland.

Around sunset of the first day, when Arsène joined us for our meal, Antoine took the occasion to chide him. I recall this because it was a rare event and proved how unfortunately astute the Canadian's observations could be. In advance Antoine had told me he thought Tabo-Ui was in love with Arsène, and he suspected they might be having an affair, which would be very dangerous. I didn't believe him. Arsène, when he arrived was out of breath and disheveled.

"I've been breaking a colt." He settled cross-legged before our cookfire.

"I saw you," said Antoine. "Whose?"

"Rabbit-Knife's. She says she can't handle him. But I think he's all right now." He laughed. "He nearly reared over with me one time. Took me by surprise."

"You mustn't do that. It's dangerous."

"What? She asked me to. I'm not afraid of any horse."

"No, it's not the horse. She's White-Road's wife. Listen to me, mon vieux, people are starting to talk. Warriors get suspicious, jealous. You should know that. That warchief's bad medicine. Stay away from her."

"But I'm not doing what you think. She's older than me. It's just that she asked me."

"I know. But it's dangerous. Those brothers. Bad. I've seen it happen. Stay away. Promise me."

Arsène began to protest, but under Lefort's long, level gaze, he finally shrugged. "All right, as you wish. She means nothing to me. Except, she's nice. I like her."

Otherwise that day passed without incident. But on the second night our Comanche traveling companions held their overdue council to choose a peace, or civil chief. The principal task of this chief, or paraibo, is to maintain unity among the various families, along with their relatives and friends, who compose the band, at times a formidable endeavor. The peace chief has the additional responsibility of selecting a site for the winter camp, and of determining during spring, summer, and fall when the band will move and to what spot, a place where there must be sufficient water, grass, firewood and, when possible, buffalo or other game, such as elk or deer. There were of course only two contenders for this important yet informal post. But since each had his fervent supporters the choice was a delicate matter which, if not managed correctly, might well destroy the cohesion of the group, even rend the band. I was thankful not to be involved. At the same time I was curious as to the council's possible outcome. I heard the details later from Arsène who, with two other young warriors, had been invited to attend.

Supporters of both Red-Woman and Manos-Amarillas had been vehement. But finally the decision had narrowed to a single question: who was the braver man? Red-Woman told of how he had as a young man led a war party against a camp of Lipan Apaches and had fought, killed and scalped the chieftain of the band in a dawn attack which had gained the Comanches scalps, horses, booty, and two young women long since married to members of his former band.

Taoinan, chosen to conduct the council, requested that Manos-Amarillas recount his bravest deed. The old man asked whether anybody remembered how many years before when he had been young he had charged alone in advance of a big vengeance party of Pawnee-Piquées he was accompanying into a raiding party of Osages? Fighting alone, he had killed one of them before his companions had reached him. With him leading them, the Wichitan warriors had killed and scalped many Osages.

Taoinan asked Ybienca if he could tell them of any deed he had performed that was braver than this one.

"No, I cannot," Red-Woman had replied at last. Clearly angry, he had controlled himself. White-Road, too, had apparently been angry but had contented himself with staring coldly at Taoinan, Toyamancare and even at Arsène.

Afterward the council chose Yellow-Hands as the braver man to be the peace chief. With no further discussion the leading men of the band had agreed that from the present council forward White-Road and Big-Mountain would be the band's two principal warchiefs and that El Chamaco would continue as camp crier. Taoinan, or The Flute, had formally declared the council concluded.

We broke camp early the next morning. Our departure was marked by excitement because Red-Woman, disappointed but still an important man, had announced through his youngest brother that he had dreamt a big dream predicting that during this day we would encounter wild horses. Tzena had promised it in his dream. Antoine and I put small faith in dreams but were hoping for a meal of horse steak. He, leading the packhorses, rode near an unmarried girl, while her mother remained close by on a pony dragging a travois followed by a wolfish dog. Much of the day I rode by The Flute, who was in a silent mood, so that we spoke little. Around mid-afternoon Arsène left the group of young warriors who usually accompanied him, to join us. He was mounted on his war and buffalo horse, Cuuna, or "Fire," the sleek, frost-faced pinto, with only a pad for a saddle, a reata coiled in his hand.

"Going to add to your herd?"

"Maybe. I've got seven ponies already."

I smiled. "Rousseau, you know, disapproved of private property."

"Voltaire called him a fox without a tail, who didn't want other foxes to have tails."

"You remember that?"

"Of course. Only it's not important to me any more."

"Seven horses already," said Taoinan. "Soon you'll be able to marry. Make many sons."

Arsène laughed nervously. "I'm not ready to marry."

"Fame first?" said The Flute.

"Perhaps."

"You could steal some big man's wife. Run off with her. That would help your reputation."

Arsène studied my friend with a strange look.

Taoinan grunted, relapsing into silence, eyes restlessly sweeping the limitless Llano like the breeze, as we followed what seemed to be an endless trickling stream with its pale, worn banks under a hot sun with a few white clouds building at the horizon before us. I had been surprised at his addressing the colonel's son, whom he usually ignored. Arsène, aware of the older man's coolness toward him, soon left us to return to his young companions.

"Why don't you like him?" I asked The Flute finally.

"He's crazy. That with the lightning. Also the black pony that killed Beaver Child. His sons wanted to kill it. But Amabate gave them two good ponies for it. And it's tried to kill him. Crazy."

"I didn't know that."

We rode in silence again.

"All the time he has to show how brave he is," Taoinan said finally, facing me. "Maybe because he's tabebo, whiteman." He reflected a moment. "But the young men do follow him. Maybe I don't like him because he's too much like I was then, young. I'm different now."

Taoinan was wrapped in his pensive, taciturn mood, so that after a while I loped to the front of the column and took a place beside Toyamancare, who was riding beside Manos-Amarillas. The three of us rode directly behind the foremost horsemen, who were, for the time being, Red-Woman and White-Road, with Rabbit-knife still riding at his back with his shield and lance. The afternoon was still warm, with only a breeze instead of the usual wind. By then the sun had lowered toward the horizon at our backs and was projecting and stretching the shadows of our horses and ourselves on the ground before us. Abruptly White-Road trotted ahead, peering at the ground, and slid off of his pony to examine the earth. "Cóbe," he shouted back—"wild horse." On reaching him, we found that he had discovered recent tracks of mustangs, probably stamped in mud the day of the storm. Red-Woman did not attempt to conceal his delight at this first confirmation of his big dream.

"You see," he cried to Yellow-Hands. "We've seen no buffalo. But here are the tracks of wild horses. We'll meet some soon along this creek."

"Maybe," said the old chief. "But there will be buffalo too—many."

"When," laughed Red-Woman, already gleeful, triumphant. "In five days? In another moon?"

"No. Sooner."

The first sign of the horses was a cluster of little humps far ahead on our side of the stream and off a hundred yards to the south. They had dark tops, somewhat pointed which seemed sometimes to shift in a puzzling manner. In the distance it seemed as if heat waves were causing an illusion of movement which was so odd that those of us in the vanguard paused to stare, straining to identify these curious objects.

White-Road, swinging his quirt at his pony's rump, left us at a gallop with Rabbit-Knife behind him. Shortly, as we watched, they drew up. The dark objects which had moved proved now to be turkey vultures which flapped upward, soaring in slow circles into the warm afternoon sky. With them rose a flock of crows, flapping higher faster. The humps below them we found, following White-Road, were—or had been—horses, now with distended bellies and legs sticking straight outward to the side or into the air. The llano sun had baked them and there was a choking stench of carrion. At Red-Woman's expression, I felt almost sorry for him at this outcome of his big dream. Behind White-Road, Rabbit-knife wrinkled her nose at the atrocious stink. For a moment we sat our horses in silence near the warchief and his shaman brother.

"Your horses," said Yellow-Hands. "Lightning. The night of the storm."

"There were many," said White-Road. "Look at the tracks. The rest are far away now."

"Tzena," said Red-Woman. "Her trick. Or else—Ugly-Game's youngest boy killed a skunk. That spoiled my medicine."

"Maybe," said Yellow-Hands. "It's all right. We'll find buffalo soon."

We did not. By the time the sun teetered on the brink of the western horizon, directing its slant beams from behind us across the llano, the civil chief declared it was time to camp. He couldn't understand it. However we would find a herd tomorrow. Red-Woman, White-Road, and El Chamaco, riding together behind the old man, Big-Mountain, and me grumbled loudly about this failure of The Flute's vision and Yellow-Hands' prophesy. Still Red-Woman had the grace to restrain himself this time, after the disappointing outcome of his important dream.

Later when Antoine and I had eaten our meal of corn mush and jerked meat, he glanced at the sky, which had been clouding since sunset, and suggested we raise our tent because it was going to rain. We did. Lofty, bulbous clouds had been forming in the distance before us, concealing the stars, and there was a fresh wind. By the time we had stretched out on our robes, rain was pattering upon the canvas, which the wind was swelling and sucking this way and that. During the night we heard distant thunder, but there were no flashes, only moderate wind and intermittent rain.

8

On the ninth day of our journey upon the Llano, a terrible event occurred. My misfortune was to witness it. Worst of all, my former pupil, Arsène-Christophe-Alexandre de St. Maurice, known among the People as Amabate, or The One Without A Head, perpetrated the horror, although unintentionally. Manos-Amarillas had directed through the camp crier that we repose for a day at our present location, since we were settled by the little stream and everyone was fatigued and discouraged, notably Red-Woman, his brothers, and their faction following the disappointing outcome of that medicine man's dream, the only reminder of which were a few crows pecking about our lodges, looking for scraps.

The morning shone bright and windy. The women in camp worked at a leisurely pace and gossiped, cooking or bearing water from the stream or dried buffalo dung for their fires, while most of the men lay or gathered near their lodges and sat smoking and chatting. Some few, however, ventured into the praire on their ponies with the faint hope of surprising antelopes or even one of the large rabbits found there. White-Road was one of these restless souls. I saw him pass early before our tent, wearing a sour expression, and with not a glance at Lefort or me.

"Monsieur Chagrin," remarked Antoine, looking after him. "Le mécontent."

At little later, after we had eaten, Arsène appeared on foot. He rejected our offer of a meal but asked if he might borrow César. I assented of course. I could sympathize with the wish of a youth to ride through camp and attract the attention of girls and young women by his unusual mount. The big gelding was picketed beside our tent. Lefort made Arsène a stirrup with his hands, and the young gallant grabbed a fistful of mane, swung up, and rode off bareback at a prance with only a bridle for control.

I gave it little thought and went to see Taoinan, who was camped near Manos-Amarillas's lodge, evidently by the old chief's request. There had been a commotion during the night. I had learned early in the morning that the old arrowmaker had seen something and had at first, believing it to be an enemy, awakened the lodges around his own. But he soon decided he had seen a ghost. I wondered how the old man, blind as he was, could have seen anything, especially in the dark, and put that question to Taoinan when I saw him. My friend said gravely that the old one could see shapes. He could also "see" things that those with normal sight could not. He told me the arrowmaker had awakened to find in his tepee a pale, shaggy being. At first he had thought it a man but had later decided it was more like a big crow formed of fog. It had spoken to him in a language he did not understand.

Then faded away. Later he had realized the voice was familiar—was, in fact, that of the long dead Crafty-One, evil medicine man whom he had known well, and who had been Red-Woman's, El Chamaco's, White-Road's—and, yes, The Flute's grandfather.

The arrowmaker, whose name was Pagabipo, or Basin-Paunch, had sought out Manos-Amarillas early that morning. The two old warriors had discussed the apparition and had decided it meant that the arrowmaker would probably die soon, since he and the chief too had outlived their contemporaries. The-Crafty-One, while alive, had always enjoyed giving bad news. They reasoned that he had probably come to tell Basin-Paunch of his forthcoming death. Or else it might mean that The-Crafty-One was angry that the band had come together again and was warning that it was in grave danger. Or worst of all it could mean that the blurred bird-shape had resembled a huge owl rather than a crow. In that case it could have been Piamupitz, down from his ice cave in the far north, which would portend the death of an important man. But who was Piamupitz, I wondered?

I had no chance to question Taoinan further. A boy came to the doorway of the lodge and announced that Manos-Amarillas wished to confer with him again. Excusing himself, The Flute left. I departed with him without glimpsing Sehêbi and made my way back toward my tent. My route took me past White-Road's lodge. Earlier I had noticed three of his cowed wives yawning, chattering and laughing as they worked near the smoking coals of a cookfire. They were still seated there, but their attention was directed toward a scene that gave me a start and which I watched with abrupt anxiety. Arsène was standing holding César. Next to him stood Rabbit-Knife, smiling. Arsène was speaking seriously to her. As I approached, he stooped and made a stirrup with his hands. Seizing the big sorrel's mane, Rabbit-knife placed her moccasin in that stirrup and sprang onto the gelding's back, exposing her buttocks as she did so. At once she rode off a short distance, turned and loped back to Arsène, laughing with pleasure and leaning down talking excitedly to him.

Almost at the same moment I noticed the watching wives shrink with frightened expressions. Halting, I saw White-Road approaching upon his pony. His head was down, face sullen, no game on his saddle. As he came near he raised his head and saw Rabbit-Knife flirting, laughing down at Arsène, who stood by her bare thigh listening, looking up at her. The warchief's expression became instantly one of dumbfounded disbelief quickly turning to fury. Lashing his pony, he galloped toward his wife with raised quirt. She looked up hearing hoofbeats, saw him and dug her heels into César's flanks. The big horse leapt forward. For the next several moments White-Road pursued her between tepees, around and around. The pony was quicker at turning, the tall horse faster in a straight line. The effect was, though alarming, comical. Even when the warchief approached the woman, her mount rose so much higher than his that he could not reach her upper body, although he managed to lash her thighs below her buckskin dress.

A warrior emerged from a nearby lodge, looked around, stretching. Observing the pursuit, he laughed, clearly further maddening White-Road. Rabbit-Knife's features now revealed panic. Near her husband's lodge she suddenly drew in César, slowing him, and slid off, running, while the horse galloped away. But Tosapoy closed upon her instantly. With the butt of his quirt, he struck the back of her head. She tripped, fell, rolled, sat up, stunned, her hands out before her defensively. Simultaneously the warchief was off his pony, running. Racing behind her, he dropped the quirt and seized the woman's hair, jerking her head back, drawing his knife, almost in one motion. Sensing the blade, or glimpsing it gleam, she screamed, reaching behind her for his wrists. But Tosapoy ripped the knife up through her throat to her jaw. She ended her shriek in a strangled gargle. He was on top of her next, plunging the blade again and again into her chest and abdomen, even after no further sound issued from that fountain of blood, the nearly severed head, no motion from her bloody corpse.

I had seen men killed. I had myself shot men during my brief time with the Continental Army at our war's end. But I had never witnessed anything like this. I stood frozen, unable to remove my eyes from the sight. Arsène, too, stood like a man bewitched, features so pale I feared he was about to topple. White-Road slowly rose, walking a few threatening paces toward him, his expression wrathful, deadly.

"You will pay. You will pay me for stealing my wife. I want your best horse. I want all your horses."

Arsène, now pale, stared, speechless, at the blood-spattered warchief and his red knife, his expression of fury. But after a moment, White-Road halted, spun around and tore up grass, wiped his knife blade clean, threw down the grass, went to his lodge, stooped and entered. Only then did the first wail break from his other wives, immediately taken up by the arriving women in the crowd converging from all over the camp.

"So what will happen to White-Road?" I asked Taoinan that evening, the two of us alone in his lodge near sunset.

He appeared surprised. "What do you mean?"

Now I was startled. "That was murder. He murdered Rabbit-knife."

"It's too bad. She was a bold-hearted woman. She didn't want to marry him. But her father's dead. Her brother made her marry him. I think he wanted the horses, the bride price. Three ponies he got." He reflected. "Also they called her 'Bee's Tongue,' you know. When she talked. They say she stung when she was mad."

"But what will they do to White-Road?"

"Why, nothing." Again he appeared surprised. "She was his wife."

"Her brother? Her family? Are they all afraid of him?"

He thought for a moment. "Maybe they are. He's a big warchief, with many scalps, many coups. Amabatay will have to pay. But she left her family. She was White-Road's family." Again he reflected. "He couldn't make her obey. So he killed her."

"You mean nothing will happen to him? Nothing at all?"

"Yes, nothing. It was not good what White-Road did. But that's his nature. Nobody likes what he did. Especially the women. They're angry." He smiled sadly, sympathetic to my outrage. "But she was his wife. It was his right. That is our custom. It was his right."

I admit I was shocked. I had never known anything like this to happen in my years as a prairie trader. "One more thing—Could that...ghost bird, white crow, that vision the arrowmaker saw?"

"Yes?"

"Could that have meant Rabbit-knife was about to die?"

Again Taoinan smiled sadly, sympathetic to my ignorance. "No. Piamupitz, if it was he, does not come for a woman."

9

So who or what was Piamupitz? What was the word's meaning? I thought about that before falling asleep. With my limited knowledge of Comanche, I knew that "pia" meant either "mother" or "big." "Mupitz" was the big owl. Great-Big-Owl, or Great-Big-Man-Owl, was probably the meaning of the word. But Piamupitz supposedly lived in a cave far to the north, a cave littered with bones. He ate people. He especially relished the flesh of naughty children, who supposedly disappeared from time to time. All little ones were warned of him when they misbehaved. When he walked, he strode with a big staff and was supremely strong. Each time he broke a staff, some important warrior or chieftain of the People died. I tried to picture what such a strange being would look like. What I imagined was a big man with feathered head and curved beak. His body, too, was covered with feathers, but he had arms and hands with which he carried his staffs. He had wings too, like a wicked angel. Mostly he flew, always at night. But when he walked, he stalked with taloned feet. Of course I could not believe in such a grotesque creature. But knowing what my friends believed helped me to understand them as well as others among the Nuhmuhnuh.

Yet to Antoine, as I recalled, Piamupitz was merely a vaporous figure conjured by superstitious Indians. No, he told Arsène and me early that morning, Tosapoy was the true danger. He was a big warchief concerned with his power and prestige. He believed, wrongly of course, that Arsène had stolen his wife, secretly copulating with her, and humiliating him to the extent that he had murdered her in his rage. That rage extended to the man he believed to be her seducer. Already he had threatened Arsène, informing him that he wanted horses, many horses, including Arsène's favorite, Cuuna. Indeed, Antoine thought it likely that the only circumstance restraining Tosapoy at present was the young warrior's relationship to the band's other principal warchief, and Tosapoy's rival, Toyamancare. Consequently, Antoine told the youth, he should go immediately to his adoptive father and, for his continued safety, explain the situation to him and ask for his protection. This, of course, because Tosapoy was going to seek him out soon and demand horses. If he angered the warchief, Tosapoy might very well again become enraged and attack him. It was as simple as that, Antoine warned. For his safety, he repeated, Arsène must act immediately. Still, as we were even then breaking camp, preparing to leave, Arsène delayed.

Red-Woman's wives and several of Rabbit-knife's female relatives had washed and prepared the corpse, dug a shallow hole in the llano, buried the remains, covered the grave with rocks. But the death resonated throughout the camp, creating a general gloom at first, especially apparent among the women. A little after sunrise we moved out, horses stepping nimbly across wet grass whose drops sparkled in the blinding light, following the traces of travois poles. Our mood was at first not improved by a small flight of crows behind us, disappearing and reappearing, or flying persistently over and around our cavalcade, a melancholy reminder.

Yet it was a fine morning. We made good time, as before following the creek. Again I allowed César to move to the front, taking a place beside Taoinan, who rode next to Toyamancare and a little behind Yellow-Hands, the leader. We rode in silence. As we proceeded, after an hour or two we saw that as the sun rose the bank of clouds too was rising, dispersing its vapor, whitening at its edge the blue air. Soon we could see in the near distance a curious long, level pad of mist directly before us and even whiter than the clouds curling above it.

"Mist," said The Flute. "I wonder?"

"Or fog," I said. "Strange."

"Si, neblina," proclaimed Big-Mountain absently, with his eyes resting, however, on my horse, as they often did.

As we drew quite near, I noted that the creek we had been following for so long poured directly into the white pad and that the fog or mist was itself rising and curling into the air like the clouds above it, so that there was now a ragged gap between land and fog. At the near edge, under the rising mist, the llano was speckled and pale, but farther along there was a curious sheen, which we all at once realized was water, a lake from which mist was ascending in patches. Abruptly the sun broke through the disintegrating clouds and shone directly upon the spectacle before us, rimming the mist and its tentacles with a vague iridescence, the whole a brilliant, sparkling landscape.

"Que hermosura!" exclaimed Taoinan.

"Look!" cried Toyamancare. "Buffalo!" Turning, he yelled back in Comanche: "Cuhtz!"

Before us Yellow-Hands had halted and, still as a statue, was pointing triumphantly toward the landscape before us. The sprinkling of dots along the shores of the lake, still in shreds of mist, we now saw consisted of hundreds of bison scattered and grazing, it appeared, around the perimeter of the entire body of water—by the hundreds, perhaps a thousand or more of them. At Toyamancare's cry Red-Woman and his brothers had trotted up beside us and were peering in the direction in which Manos-Amarillos pointed. It was not easy to make out the beasts for what they were at first because of remaining patches of fog and the distance. But soon, as other warriors galloped to us, joining our group, it became plain to everyone that what lay before us was a great herd of buffalo.

"Tzena didn't trick us," Taoinan laughed joyfully. "Look, as she said they would be, there they are!"

Yellow-Hands turned back to face us from his bony nag. "You have strong medicine," he called to Taoinan. Then, "The Flute has big power."

I looked above, around, behind us. Our funereal escort of crows had vanished. I glanced at White-Road. He appeared almost disappointed, angrier and grimmer than ever. Red-Woman's expression was sour, as if he held something bitter in his mouth and were about to spit it out. I turned in the saddle to find Arsène behind me, with a group of young, mounted warriors. He looked melancholy, pale. "C'est beau, n'est pas?"

"Quelle merveille!"

He was gazing back and forth from the lake and herd to Taoinan with a suddenly rapt expression composed of delight, awe, and something like worshipful admiration. I sensed then he would give much to gain what he thought to be The Flute's kind of <u>Puha</u> and that his awe derived from an awareness that it was not a power which quantities of scalps or coups or ponies could win, nor a gift a man could achieve in battle, no matter how heroic his deeds, all of which made it to him the more baffling, wonderful, and desirable. As for me, I had believed that my "brother" had merely dreamed an interesting dream of a prairie wolf. But now, I shook my head—there were indeed some peculiar coincidences. I wondered what Mr. Isaac Newton would have made of them.

"Tell everybody," Yellow-Hands called to El Chamaco, who, with his brothers, gazed in disbelief at the brilliant, diaphanous scene before us, "today we will camp here."

So we did.

We set out from the Rio Pecos encampment about the middle of September, as I recall. But before that Tosapoy came to Arsène's lodge one morning and, as he had threatened, demanded Cuuna, his favorite horse, as well as nine other horses. Arsène confronted the warchief courteously but boldly, explaining that Cuuna had run away into the prairie, and that he had no idea where the pony might be found. As for the remaining thirteen horses, Tosapoy might choose ten, the maximum permitted by custom. The warchief's hand fell to his knife as he fixed Arsène with a stare of disbelief.

"What have you done with him?"

"Two nights ago he broke his lead. You remember? There were wild horses that went by. I think he may have joined them."

Even standing in the sunlight, he could see his horse under the moon after he had slapped him on the rump and told him to *go*. Cuuna had trotted off around twenty paces, halted, and Arsène had shouted and, sweeping up some pebbles, had tossed them. The pony had trotted away some fifty paces and again stopped, turned, and looked back at him, until it finally whirled and trotted away. As he walked back to camp Arsène could see in his mind the big-roweled Spanish spur that Tosapoy switched from heel to heel of his moccasins, attaching it with buckskin thongs, as well as the blood and scars on the sides of his ponies. Now it had made it easier to face Tosapoy and lie to him, which he had managed calmly to do. He could see that the warchief did not believe him, but was incapable of imagining that any man would drive his favorite horse into the wild in order to protect it from his cruelty.

In the end Tosapoy had to be content with the ten ponies he chose from Arsène's small herd. Nor did Arsène have to ask his Comanche father for protection, or have to fight his father's rival, since in spite of Tosapoy's menacing behavior, his implied threats, Arsène finally realized that by a profound unspoken law Comanches did not kill Comanches, and that it would bring no honor to the warchief to kill a youth of the band but, to the contrary, it would probably cause him to lose prestige and to be ostracized.

Later the three of us—Arsène, Antoine and I—left our Comanche companions at Buffalo Lake for their autumnal hunt and pressed ahead in order to profit from the fair weather of the season. So we must have arrived at the Pawnee-Piquée villages around the end of that month or during the early days of October. Our journey was uneventful, its only weather characteristic under mostly sunny skies, the shifting, continual winds. We traveled rapidly, only three men on good horses, with the lightly laden packhorses to substitute for them when we wished to switch saddles and rest our own mounts. We paused for two days at the Pawnee-Piquée (Wichitan) villages and then pressed on.

We were about an hour beyond the villages, riding in silence, the three of us abreast, the three packhorses behind, when we began to see before us the western Grande Forêt, that great woodland stretching north and south to each horizon.

Soon we began to smell smoke. We were on guard at once, concerned about a possible encounter with an Osage war party, since it would not have been unusual to find one in this region. But after gaining and passing through the woods we at first saw nothing but the movement of wind in the grass. We were about to venture out of the shadows when the wind brought distant whoops and shouts. Moments later at about twenty rods distance we saw several buffaloes running before three mounted figures. A puff of smoke. We heard a shot. One of the bison fell. Another shot, and another beast went down. At this the horsemen drew up their ponies, gathering where the second animal had fallen. Clearly all three of them were bare-skinned.

"Indians," I observed.

"But what nation?" demanded Arsène, peering. "Not Osages."

Antoine had begun to laugh. "No. Not Indians. Look at the horses. Hunters from the post. Canadians—my comrades." Riding out from the trees, he fired his rifle into the air, gave a shrill whistle, and waved. Visibly startled but clearly recognizing the signal, one of the tiny figures fired his weapon into the air. All three waved their muskets and arms.

At that Arsène and I left the forest and followed Lefort onto the praire toward the hunters, Canadian voyageurs who, like Antoine, wore during fine weather only a loin cloth, hat and moccasins, and who like him and Arsène were tanned by the sun to a color resembling that of the skin of certain Indians. The hunters rode up and welcomed Lefort, and indeed the three of us, inviting us immediately to share a meal of freshly killed, broiled bison. Since it was then about mid-day, we willingly accepted. These expert woodsmen gave us a jovial reception. In particular they appeared happy to see Antoine and chattered with him so rapidly and in a French that was almost a patois that I had difficulty in following some of the conversation. Toward me they behaved more formally and, after Lefort had explained our situation, they kept directing curious glances toward the governor's son, who looked even more like a Comanche warrior in comparison with these nearly naked but hairy and bearded men.

"My father is well?" that son asked.

When the hunters had assured Arsène that, as far as they knew, the colonel was in his usual health, the youth lapsed into preoccupied silence, his attention focused upon the making of the fire and the preparation of the meal. The Canadians told us they had been away from the post for several weeks, hunting deer and bison, salting meat and collecting hides for sale to Delorme & de St. Maurice, who would later sell them in the interior. One of their number, a Louis Totin, had remained with the meat and bales of hides, in order to protect them from wolves and bears, at their nearby camp in La Grande Forêt. This left the three we had seen from the woods, Jean Hugue, André Rondin, and Jacques Ledoux as our hosts around the tiny blaze where the tongues and ribs of the freshly killed bison were sputtering, dripping, and blackening on skinning knives.

I was relieved to learn that the colonel was alive and to outward appearances well. Since we had not eaten fresh meat for some time, I ate heartily of the tough portions offered, in fact until I was sated. Then, drowsy, I lay back with saddlebags under my head, my hat over my face. Arsène, withdrawn into himself, continued to chew meat from his knife, while Antoine continued his animated conversation with his comrades. Soothed by their voices and the drifting pipesmoke, I dozed at intervals, at other times half-listening to the hunters' now leisurely exchanges with Lefort. Most of the talk was of hunting, of women, and the activities of their distant friends up on the Arkansas. In particular they exchanged remarks about a trader named "Barré," whom one man called "méchant" and another "très mauvais," and whose license out of St. Louis had lately been revoked. Still they laughed at his habit of marrying into each of the several tribes with whom he traded and leaving children in each.

I gave little attention to the gossip but listened more carefully when Hugue related news of the post: a new lieutenant governor, a Captain Gaston Le Noir, had arrived to take charge of the district. He was liked neither by his soldiers nor by the people of the village, who found him self-important, petty, and mean. Also a trader named Petout had attacked an Indian woman on the road. After she had refused him her sexual favors, he had apparently become enraged and had beaten her and her younger child to death. Her twelve-year-old son had run away to tell his people. The Tawakonis, who lived on Los Brazos de Dios River, were in a fury but their chief, an old friend of the colonel's, had persuaded them to refrain from revenge until after appealing to the authorities at the post. This they had done and the new lieutenant governor, after conferring with Colonel de St. Maurice, had sent a corporal of the militia with several men to find the fugitive Petout and return him to the post, where he would be tried and justice fulfilled. The crime had occurred before the hunters' departure, so that they remained ignorant of the affair's outcome.

None of this information was remarkable, but the Canadian's final piece of news, slight as it was, interested me greatly: a Frenchwoman, said to be the colonel's niece, had arrived in Natchitoches from Nouvelle-Orléans and was now living with him. The story was that she had escaped from Paris, that capital of Civilization where, as was well known, the populace had revolted, murdering the king and was now engaged in cleaving the necks of the noblesse. I had heard of course about the terrible revolution taking place in France. But the news that a relative of the colonel had escaped, traveled to La Louisiane, and was now living with Monsieur de St. Maurice—that news made me open my eyes and sit up. The fact that the relative was a woman made the news even more interesting.

"Then this lady must be my cousin," Arsène said abruptly, wiping his knife with grass before sheathing it. The four hunters stared at the youth, their suddenly widened eyes red from the sun, or perhaps from aguardiente the previous evening, hair shaggy, beards greasy, hands and arms and bodies stained with the fat and blood of the beasts they had butchered and skinned—stared together at the tatooed and painted Indian seated by the smouldering fire cross-legged, as nearly naked as they were, who claimed relationship with Monsieur de St. Maurice, the former Lieutenant Governor and his Parisian niece, who—it had been rumored—had ties to what had only recently been the French court. It was not that they doubted he was the colonel's son. They knew he was. Lefort had said so. Yet for that moment they thought it impossible. Then as quickly they recovered their cheerful nonchalance, continuing casually to converse with each other and Antoine, as if they had neither seen nor heard anything remarkable.

We soon left the hunters and continued to ride eastward that afternoon across the prairie, progressing in silence while the windy grass hurtled toward us in repeated waves, beige to silver, then again beige. Soon we forded La Rivière Rouge at the spot where we had crossed on our outward journey. The great charred cotton tree stump at our old campsite remained. Since the sun was still high, with fair skies, we continued to press eastward across that beautiful open prairie, whose grass rose in places to our horses' bellies and brushed our stirrups. We now rode easier in our minds, less on guard. We had passed the zone where we might have expected an encounter with a war party of Osages, who rarely penetrated beyond the western swathe of La Grande Forêt. Consequently we rode on until nearly sunset, when we camped by a stream of clear water.

The remainder of our trip, as I recall it now, passed without unusual incident. We were all impatient by this time to arrive. Unencumbered by laden packhorses, we pushed eastward and southward day after day, progressing from the open tallgrass prairie to a savanna with scattered small oaks, entering from there a pine forest which persisted more or less until we had reached our destination. On the way we passed the usual springs, ponds, creeks, and bayous, the latter sometimes inhabited by alligators. We surprised the usual deer, and an occasional bear, but after leaving the tallgrass prairie, we saw no further buffaloes, wild horses, or even prairie chickens. Sky, water, and pine forest day after day.

Again we forded the Rivière de l'Ours by the Coushatta village, but early in gray light and quietly, so as not to be detained by the formalities of greetings. From there we continued to hasten toward the post, arriving in about seven days. I calculate, to the best of my recollection, that we made the journey from the Wichitan villages to Natchitoches in a little under a month, to arrive at about mid-October, so that we accomplished our entire trip, after leaving our Comanche friends at Buffalo Lake, in only a little above six weeks.

The day of our arrival we paused at an ancient saline (presently a commercial enterprise called the "Salt Works.") It lies some twenty English miles north of the post on the principal road leading southward to it. There the three of us ate briefly and prepared ourselves for our return to Civilization, doing our best to make ourselves presentable to those who had awaited us for so long. With a razor and metal mirror I shaved, save for my mustache and short beard, after heating a little water over a small fire, while Antoine washed and trimed his hair and beard.

Arsène also scraped off his shadowy stubble, a practice he followed nearly every day, as he was self-conscious about the facial bristle that distinguished him from other Comanche youths, and which would always identify him, no matter how respected a Comanche he became, as a tabebo, a whiteman. From the side of my eye, I occasionally glimpsed him washing himself, arranging his hair, and rearranging its eagle feather. Next I noticed what I had feared he would do. He was squatting and, with the aid of his trade mirror, he was carefully painting his face with blue, red, and yellow stripes. I almost remonstrated, but I kept silent, knowing I was powerless to control his behavior. I would leave that effort to the colonel. From his rawhide wardrobe case he selected a necklace of elk's teeth, hanging it around his neck over his bare chest and tattoo. Finally he drew on fringed buckskin leggings and new moccasins.

Fully dressed, he seated himself on a stump, first looking for pitch, making a brushing motion. He remained with his hands on his knees staring blankly ahead. Darting glances, I saw to my surprise that he appeared nervous, apprehensive. Suddenly it came to me that he was anxious not only about the coming reunion with his true father, but probably also guiltily dreading the moment he would have to tell the old man he had chosen another people than his father's people—as well as another father.

Moments later, refreshed and prepared, we mounted our horses and proceeded together toward the post. Although we trotted and sometimes loped the horses, it was for me a long twenty miles, so great was my anticipation of our triumphant return and the approaching reunion of Arsène with his father, which Lefort and I might take credit for. Surely Antoine and most of all Arsène must have felt some of the same excitement, an eagerness which was transmitted to the horses, whose heads had risen, with ears pricked forward, straining against the reins.

As we drew near the fort on the main road, the breeze suddenly brought a stench, an odor of carrion.

"Something dead," remarked Antoine, looking at the underbrush on either side.

The odor grew stronger as we proceeded. There came a commotion of crows cawing, squawking shrilly, as their shadows passed above us. We saw that the source of the smell was a shaggy object mounted upon a pike some fifty yards from the fort. All at once I knew what it must be—and yes it was: a man's head, eyeless, with some features remaining, and it had not been there for many days. Its teeth seemed clenched in a grin. Even at our distance we could hear the flies and wasps around it. Immediately Lefort and Arsène left the road to trot over to look, while I waited upon César. As I have mentioned before, I am squeamish about some things. While waiting, I noticed Madamoiselle Bijou strolling down the road toward me. She saw me at the same instant, recognizing horse and man. Her shriek disturbed the quiet noon. I feared she would faint.

"Monsieur Jean-Pierre!" she cried. "Mon dieu! C'est lui? Vous l'avez trouvé?"

"Oui," I cried. "Dites le lui. Nous arrivons tout de suite."

Madamoiselle was a tall, lean woman. I had never seen her move in any manner other than with controlled dignity. But now she whirled and ran like a deer up the road toward the colonel's house, astonishing me by her swiftness.

I continued to wait uneasily, my back to the post, watching the nearby bluegreen river ripple cleanly rather than the steel pike with its macabre burden.

"Petout," said Lefort riding up. "I knew him, un fumier. It's well—justice to the Indians."

Arsène said nothing, though his blue, wrinkled nose registered his revulsion.

We proceeded along the road the short distance to the house. César, who had long since recognized our route, and who had begun to prance and sidle under me like his old, wilder self, probably represented in his excitement the concealed feelings of of us all. As we turned the corner of the lane, we could see the house dominating the hillock, with its great trees and corral. At that moment from the corral my mare, evidently spying our horses, emitted a piercing whinny. César, now agitated, stretched his head in a response that was more a vibrant shriek than a whinny, continuing, as we progressed, to make deeper, softer sounds.

At the big brute's neigh, the door flung open and Madamoiselle Bijou appeared on the veranda, holding the door for the colonel, who emerged quickly, leaning upon his two canes, his head craned eagerly forward, looking around him. Behind him came a blonde woman in a gray-blue dress. We were only fifty yards now from the porch, approaching under their gaze, Antoine behind with the packhorses, Arsène by my side on his pinto, lance in one hand, shield on his left arm, its red and white feathers drooping in the moist air. I now was able to see the colonel's old tabby tomcat seated majestically by the tip of his right cane and to observe that the pale blonde standing beside him and watching us intently appeared poised and intelligent, attractive enough to merit a stare.

"Bonjour," I cried. "Le voila, enfin, Monsieur le colonel, votre fils égaré!" With that I swung down off César, handing the reins to Antoine.

"Voyez, Monsieur le colonel. Je les ai ramené, tous les deux, sains et saufs, comme je vous l'avais promis!" shouted Antoine.

"Jean-Pierre," the colonel cried out. "Lefort! Non. Est-ce possible? Arsène?"

Arsène had slid from his pony, which stood as trained, its single rein on the earth. Beside me, lance still in his hand, he faced his true father, hesitating. Taking his bare arm, I urged him forward. Together we mounted the steps. Halfway, he halted, awkwardly leaning his lance, with its dangling scalp, against a railing and continued, moving stiffly, proudly, that stern expression fixed upon his pale, painted features. The woman beside the old man stared, clearly fascinated, smiling, appalled. Standing straight, he moved forward to his father, halting like a soldier at attention before him.

"C'est vraiment vous, mon fils?" asked the colonel quietly, peering into his son's face. "Oui, c'est vous." Letting his canes fall, the old man reached and took the youth's shoulders in his hands, and gently he drew his son toward him. For an instant, Arsène stared proudly, resisted, then abruptly his head fell forward onto the colonel's chest and tears began slipping down his cheeks as he pressed to the old man. As we stared, Colonel Alexandre-Philippe de St. Maurice, standing unsteadily, held his son to his chest with a serene expression and the suggestion of a smile.

We had hardly recovered from our journey when, about a week later, Taoinan's party arrived. They had been close behind us and striving to overtake us ever since leaving the Pawnee-Piquée villages, where they had learned of our recent stop there. Traveling rapidly with a Wichitan guide and spare ponies, they had nearly succeeded in doing so. For Taoinan I believe it was merely warm-hearted curiosity. He had decided to see, after our long friendship, where and how his "brother" lived. He was curious about our way of life, so different from his own, and had decided on impulse to follow us soon after our departure from Buffalo Lake. For Toyamancare it was a habitual restlessness, as well as a desire to be with his friend, Taoinan.

I suspect that Big-Mountain knew that by coming to Natchitoches Post with the others he might be more nearly sure that Arsène, his "son," returned with him to the People and the prairie. As for Sehêbi, she had apparently begged Taoinan to accompany him, while his other two wives remained with the band, jerked the meat and grained the hides of the bison he had slain. She too had wished to see the town, our buildings, how we lived. Did she also wish to see me?

Meanwhile for those first few days we recuperated from our journey. I scribbled notes about the trip, read and slept a good deal. Moreover I was relieved with respect to the colonel's health. Strangely enough with his son's return his alarming palpitations ceased. But there had been some changes during my absence. My bedroom, for example, which was the best in the house after the colonel's, had been assigned to his niece, Madame Hélène-Eulalie Marguerite de Fleury. Madamoiselle Bijou had moved all of my clothing and possessions to a smaller room that Monsieur de St. Maurice had used while he was lieutenant governor to accommodate visiting functionaries and officers of the Spanish crown. Arsène, of course, had the use of his old room, which Monsieur had kept for seven years precisely as his son had left it. But the new Arsène, the Comanche warrior, refused during the first days of his return to sleep indoors and instead set up his tiny camp by the corrals.

Another change I soon learned had taken place in the household heirarchy. Now Madame Hélène-Eulalie instead of the colonel gave orders to Mlle. Bijou. For Madamoiselle it was evidently a shock. She was a high-spirited woman accustomed to ruling the household, responsible only to the colonel, who allowed her in most matters to have her way. But now she was constrained to follow the directions of the newly arrived niece. I saw that she found this hard to bear. I wondered even whether she would tolerate the new régime indefinitely without rebellion.

Not that the niece issued her instructions in a peremptory fashion. To the contrary, Madame Hélène-Eulalie had a gentle though penetrating voice and offered her orders mostly as suggestions. Yet it was clear that they were intended to be obeyed, and the housekeeper doubtless found this galling, particularly I sensed because they came from another woman, a newcomer. As for the niece, it was plain from her easy manner that she was accustomed to managing servants, if not black slaves.

I was curious about this blond woman with the frequently raised eyebrows, as she was curious, I believe, about her young cousin and even about me. At first she gave an impression of delicacy, almost of fragility, with her fine features, her shapely hands with long fingers. Yet her erect bearing was one of pride and strength. Observing her closely, I noticed that her features at rest communicated both hauteur and melancholy. But they were rarely at rest. When she spoke, her eyes sometimes sparkled, and occasionally an irrepressible emotion appeared to bubble up from within, shine from her gray eyes, appear in a frown and stare of indignation—or, more rarely, in a sudden laugh, and for that instant she appeared young and merry, a girl. But the next moment she would lapse into an expression that was sober, dignified, sad. I was puzzled by her, but I did decide she was attractive. Taken separately her features—small mouth, large eyes, nose uptilted at its tip, were not exceptionally pleasing. But when I looked at them together, particularly when she spoke or listened intently, I had to confess they complemented each other in a charming manner. I found even her scent alluring, composed as it apparently was of an eau de Cologne combined with the warm emanation of her skin. Still I warned myself to be careful, since she and I occupied such distant, if not polar, stations in life.

I must admit that I was particularly sensitive to social differences because of my upbringing. Although my mother was an idealist and prided herself upon her advanced views, even belonging to a little group of clergymen and women dedicated to the abolition of Negro slavery, she was never unaware of her own status as a member of one of Boston's prominent families. My father, to the contrary, had been unconcerned about his humble lineage. My mother's attitude toward people in our village had frequently embarrassed me when I was growing up and had made me overly conscious of social rank. She had even disapproved of my playing with other village boys, so that I had spent much of my time on the farm with the horses. I had never thought about social differences with the colonel, but the lady's pedigree was clearly on a level with the stars in contrast to my own. Consequently after taking Madame Hélène-Eulalie's measure, as it were, I heeded my own counsel, banished her from my thoughts, and fixed them and my physical appetite upon the handsome young free mulatto woman whose sexual favors I suspected I was sharing with the captain of the militia, Barthélemi de Court.

Rarely did I have any reason to speak with the colonel's niece, except at the dining table, where we exchanged polite remarks. But one day she caught me idling in the kitchen, dangling a ribbon before the cat while listening to Mlle. Bijou's recital of gossip from the village. Mademoiselle had been teasing me with hints of her knowledge of my liaison with

Michelle Pichet, the pretty mulatto woman. I was chuckling at her insight and at the cat's antics when Madame Hélène-Eulalie entered. She regarded me with a penetrating look. I encountered her a little later in the hallway, and she stopped me, her eyebrows raised, with a look of curiosity and the faintest of smiles.

"You seem, Monsieur, to love life. Is that not so?"

"What?" I was startled.

"Your laughter, a while ago. In the kitchen. You do love life, don't you?"

"I suppose so. I've never thought about it. And you...Madame?"

She shrugged. "I envy you, Monsieur."

After she had turned away and departed down the hall, I became aware that I had begun to pity this melancholy being. With regard to my precious liberty I failed to realize that it's dangerous for a young man to pity an attractive woman.

Soon after our return and before the Comanche group's arrival, one cloudy afternoon Monsieur de St. Maurice called me into his office. He questioned me at length about his son, about our finding him and with regard to his actions and behavior and attitudes since. As delicately as possible I related the facts of our reunion with Arsène at the Rio Pecos encampment and of my observations of him since. But I could not soften the impression that interested him most: my conviction that his son had determined to return after a visit with his father to the Comanches, whom he now considered "his people." The old colonel flinched at nothing, not even the Apache scalp and the account of how his son had received his scar. If he was dismayed by my opinion that the youth had already chosen a savage over a civilized life, a choice which must have seemed to him a betrayal of all he had stood for, he revealed it by no sign that I could detect. For some time after I had finished he mused, gazing out the window by his desk.

"Well, he's a soldier," he said at last.

"He's certainly that." I had detected a tinge of satisfaction in the old man's voice. For another long interval he remained silent, musing out the window. It had begun to drizzle. I wondered how long Arsène would remain camped outdoors by the horses rather than in his comfortable room within the house. Soon came a knock on the door.

"Entrez." The colonel turned.

"Excuse me," said Madame Hélène-Eulalie, looking from one to the other of us, her eyes resting momentarily upon mine. "It's beginning to rain. What about Arsène? Shall I try to call him in?"

"You may try," said the colonel, with a shrug and hint of a smile. "The Indians don't mind the weather."

"He's crazy, that boy," she said, and shut the door.

"By the way. She's asked me to ask you to address her as either 'Madame' or 'Hélène-Eulalie,' not 'Madame Hélène-Eulalie.' That's all right for the servants, but not for you."

"Very well." The 'servants' consisted of Mlle. Bijou and María, a silent Indian slave, probably Apache, who lived in an outbuilding and whom Mlle. ruled with her dictatorial will.

Another long silence while the colonel gazed out the window was broken when his big cat, Diablo, emerged stealthily from beneath a chair and leapt without warning into his lap, causing him to start, with an, "ouf!" Turning back to the window, the dripping gray light, the shining leaves, he began idly running bony fingers over the animal, which responded with an amazingly loud purr that filled the room for another long interval. "I could have him arrested and detained on some pretext," he said at last, still facing the window. "Earlier in my life I would have done that." He turned to face me, still stroking the cat. "It would be useless. He would hate me and soon escape. I would never see him again. This way. No, he is now a man. That is evident. In the end a man makes his own decisions. I shall try to persuade him, but..." He shrugged.

"I too will try."

He smiled. "But you know it will be useless?"

"Yes. But...possibly not."

"Of course. Then we will both try for the 'possibly not.'" He turned to the papers on his escritoire. I rose. The cat jumped from his lap, and I held the door for a moment to allow it to trot out with raised tail before me.

A little to my surprise, Arsène joined us for dinner that evening. After the first emotional meeting with his father, the youth had avoided the house and all of us, eating with Lefort in his cabin near the river. Later he explained to me that immediately to have moved into his father's house would have been too great a shock, and furthermore he was now so accustomed to sleeping in a tepee or in fair weather in an arbor or outdoors that he felt confined and uncomfortable under a roof. The prospect of a bed had dismayed him. Yet as we were seating ourselves—the colonel, his niece, and I—he appeared from the kitchen, dry except for his long black hair dangling around his pallid features and wearing a buckskin warshirt I had not seen, as well as fringed moccasins and buckskin leggings which reached up to his breechclout. After seating himself with aplomb, he told his startled cousin, while smiling, that he had carried his clothes to the kitchen door, where Mlle. Bijou had met him with a towel. So, voilà, here he was. After that he remained quiet during most of the dinner, which nevertheless went pleasantly, as the other three of us engaged in small talk about the company trading post in town and the plantation upriver. I did notice, observing him discreetly, that he managed his fork and knife as if he had never left Civilization. While we were eating a dessert of stewed pears bathed in wine, Monsieur de St. Maurice quietly suggested to him, as rain hammered the roof, that he might find his boyhood room a comfortable place in which to spend the night.

"Yes," said Arsène, looking up, with a doubtful expression, the candlelight shining upon his fine bony features framed by his loose black hair. "Perhaps I shall."

Neither the old man nor his niece was quite able to conceal an expression of pleased surprise.

As for me, I thought that, yes perhaps after all, there might be hope. From then on Arsène usually joined us for dinner, eating eagerly and mostly in silence. Mlle. Bijou, an excellent self-taught cook, appreciated vigorous appetites and appeared to enjoy preparing meals for him. But one evening he nearly reduced her to tears. She had concocted an excellent rognon, complemented by an Armagnac sauce tinged with orange. The kidney was delicious. We set about eating it with enthusiasm, praising her as we tasted. She watched and accepted our remarks at the kitchen door. But her proud expression altered when Arsène pushed away his plate, turned and declared:

"Je ne peux pas manger cette viande."

We regarded him with amazement.

"Pour moi, c'est interdit." He explained with some embarrassment that his 'medicine' forbade his eating the inner organs of animals. In the end Madamoiselle served him eggs, but she was clearly hurt, disappointed, angry, even though the colonel, Madame Hélène-Eulalie, and I tried to soothe her disappointment with compliments.

To further increase tension in the house, I next inadvertently angered Arsène. During the early days of our reunion I had often teased him about those aspects of his new life which I considered ridiculous, such as the dried bat attached to his shield as an amulet. I even suggested that he might establish a new fashion among his people by filing his teeth to points in order to suggest fangs. He shrugged off my pleasantries, appearing nearly as much amused as annoyed. I had, however, never teased him about peculiarities of behavior which Lefort informed me were required by his 'medicine.' Arsène would, for instance, point only with his thumb. He was reluctant to pick objects from the ground when he had dropped them. Even though an icy wind was blowing, he would ride out of his way to pass through or stand in the shade, seeking shadows as if they imparted powers of the night from which he might benefit. These irritated me, coming as they did from my bright former pupil. Consequently after the kidney dinner, I baited him by enumerating some of the restrictions imposed by his 'medicine' and declaring that they seemed to me burdensome and stifling.

"What's happened," I demanded, "to that boundless freedom you'd expected to enjoy upon the prairie?"

This time I offended him. Treating me with his most haughty stare, he turned and stalked away. I have observed since, as I should have previously, that there is nothing about which men are so little rational as in their various faiths. In that respect religion is often a pernicious force. Arsène forgave me. But I never bantered him again about any practice pertaining to his 'medicine,' no matter how peculiar it seemed to me.

One other event before the arrival of the Comanches clings to my memory. I remember that I was reading and reflecting one afternoon in my room. I even recall the passage from Pascal which had engaged my attention—"Le dernier acte est sanglant, quelque belle que soit la comédie en tout le reste: on jette de la terre sur la tête, et en voila pour jamais." Or, rendered crudely in English—"The final act is bloody no matter how beautiful the comedy in the earlier ones: they toss dirt on your head and that's the end of it forever." It's a passage I have returned to many times. On that occasion I began reflecting, upon the Comanche belief expressed by Arsène that the Creator lives beyond the sun. Considered critically I found it no less reasonable than my own beliefs. I recall that it seemed to me then and seems to me now that as creatures living in our precarious state we ought to battle each other less relentlessly and ferociously. Voltaire estimated that man has a life-span of merely about twenty-two years. Therefore why not some lenity for our fellow creatures? Even for our animal brethren? Not that I personally am especially kindly, but I admire nothing more than humane behavior, rare as it is upon this earth, especially upon the frontier.

In any event, I was musing in my room with the door half-open when I began hearing women's raised voices. I rose and walked into the hallway. They seemed to issue from the kitchen. Descending the stairs, I went to the dining room and stood by the open kitchen door. Hélène-Eulalie and Mlle. Bijou were standing face to face shrieking at each other, quarreling it appeared over some matter of household protocol. They did not observe me watching. I was fascinated at the spectacle of this Negro slave confronting a woman who had been for a short period, according to the colonel, dame d'honneur or lady in waiting to a duchess. Mlle did not back down (ne se dégonfla pas), but her emotions suddenly overcame her, and she wept noisily and vehemently. Hélène-Eulalie impulsively it seemed reached to touch her, as if to comfort her, but the black woman twisted away, turning her back, sobbing furiously into her hands. After hesitating a moment, Hélène-Eulalie turned on her heel and walked away out of the kitchen, raising her eyebrows in surprise at me as she passed, her features coldly composed. Yet strangely I imagined her eyes were damp.

After that there was music, loud music, such as I had never heard. There was a pianoforte in the salle de séjour. It had always stood dark and closed in a corner. I had never heard it played. Evidently it had been purchased and brought up the river by barge for the colonel's second wife, mother of Arsène, and Monsieur's adored child bride. It was said that she had played competently and had enjoyed playing until the time of the pestilence and her early death. Since that time there had never been to my knowledge music in the house, although Mlle. Bijou had mentioned to me that during our absence a man from Nouvelle-Orléans had tinkered with the piano unharmoniously an entire afternoon.

But now, evoked by the fingers of the colonel's niece, music filled the rooms like sunlight through a window, though the sky outside was bleak. I who had had at that time little experience with music was enchanted. For a while I stood in the doorway listening, until finally Hélène-Eulalie turned her head and called with mild annoyance, "Please—sit down!" I seized the nearest chair. For the first half-hour or so she played loudly with great energy, with too much vigor I sensed but still expertly—or so it seemed to my untrained ear. But then she began playing with a gentler touch, more delicately, to my delight. My mother had played a little. She had practiced and practiced, but she had always played badly. Aside from fife and drum during the war, her playing was all the music I had known. But this was a different and superior thing—it was exquisite. So I rose when she stopped and was leaving the piano and the room. I stammered, "Madame, that was beautiful."

"Thank you, Monsieur," she said, gazing into my eyes for a moment with a gracious smile. She began to move on, hesitated, and paused. "By the way, Monsieur. Please. Can you tell me what is wrong with my cousin?"

I suppose I looked startled.

"He is so very...triste. And he seems ill."

"About an illness, I can't tell you, Madame. Though he has said he suffers from stomach pains. But as for his melancholy—" I explained about the death of Rabbit-Knife and Arsène's feeling responsible for it. My own indignation made me say more than I had intended, telling how the woman's murder had gone unpunished.

Hélène-Eulalie's eyes opened wide. "How barbaric! Savages!" She reflected a moment. "But at least he has a conscience."

"Very much so."

I wanted to add, 'and why are you, Madame, also so melancholy?' But of course I did not.

She continued into the dining room, and from there once again entered the kitchen, closing the door behind her. I followed to the kitchen door and listened for a few minutes. At first Mlle. Bijou's voice was loud, defensive, but Hélène-Eulalie's was soothing and soft. Soon both women were speaking softly, the niece's voice gentle, Bijou's subdued. Until finally I heard quiet laughter, both women laughing—as if suddenly allies, united for instance against male dominance. I went to my room. There was no more music that day, but from then on there was peace between them.

12

I recall our surprise at the Comanche party's arrival.

"There are some Peaux-Rouges camped down by the river," Mlle Bijou announced, serving breakfast.

"Hein?" said the colonel, spooning sugar into his café au lait, glancing toward sunbeams entering a window.

"Yes, they arrived on their horses early this morning and immediately set up their camp."

"What kind of Indians?" asked Arsène. He wiped his butter knife on the tartine he had just prepared. "Caddos? They set up camp?"

"No. I think they must be prairie Indians."

"Prairie Indians?" Arsène exclaimed, stiffening in his chair.

"Why do you think that?" I asked.

"Scarcely possible," remarked the colonel. "They rarely come here."

"Don't they live in tents?" Mlle asked. "These have set up tents. Now they're cooking at fires before them."

Scraping back his chair, Arsène stood. "Please excuse me," he asked his father. "They must be Comanches. They have to be. They must have followed us here. Now, my dear cousin," he said turning to Hélène-Eulalie. "You will see my people."

"Oh, là! Quelle belle surprise," she said to him—it seemed to me—a little dryly. She was violently opposed to his becoming, as she phrased it, "a painted savage."

Yet she came with us, dawdling along with her usual indifferent and melancholy expression when we left the table and tramped down to the river—all of us except for the colonel, who was unable to walk far without great effort. Mlle Bijou had been correct. Figures were crouched cooking at tiny fires burning before a number of tepees pitched mostly in clearings among the great trees, ponies tethered nearby. As we drew near, I saw a lodge I recognized by the painted ring of snakes encircling it with, above them, a series of what appeared to be half-moons. I also recognized Taoinan's shield, supported by his lance, facing the early sun. The woman at the fire stood, turning to look at us, shading her eyes.

"What a pretty girl," said Hélène-Eulalie.

"Bonjour, Jean-Pierre," shouted Sehêbi. "Comment va?"

"Bien," I called. But not waiting to hear the answer, she ducked and ran into the lodge.

"She speaks French?" exclaimed Hélène.

"Very little," I said. "And a little Spanish."

Arsène was striding away from us toward another tepee half-concealed in the shadows under a massive elm. A stocky, powerfully built man came out of it and swaggered toward him. The two embraced. It was his other "father," Toyamancare, or Big-Mountain. Just then The Flute emerged from his lodge smiling, calling my name. I quickened my steps. He limped quickly toward me. We embraced, he pressing his cheek against mine. Sehêbi stood behind him, clearly excited. This time she appeared glad to see me, seemingly delighted with the novelty of everything around her. Hélène-Eulalie, to my surprise, was suddenly alert, beaming. I introduced her to Taoinan, who shook her hand in the manner of the Spanish soldiers he had encountered, even though she was a woman, and then to Sehêbi. They too shook hands and stood gazing at each other with mutual interest, Sehêbi shyly, Hélène-Eulalie with unconcealed admiration and pleasure.

"How are you, brother?" Taoinan asked in Comanche. "Did you have a good trip?"

"You followed us. Why didn't you tell me you were coming?"

"When we'd killed enough buffalo," he said, "I thought, well, let's go and visit Jean-Pierre before winter. The others decided to come too."

"Hóla, El Gayo!" called Toyamancare, advancing with a ferocious expression which turned to a smile. Like many Indians, he called me "Bluejay," or "El Gayo" owing to a blue vest I had worn when first among them. We embraced and I repeated introductions. He stared at Hélène-Eulalie, paying little attention to her after that first penetrating, curious look. "Que casa grande!" Continuing in Comanche, he asked, "How many women do you keep in your lodge? Will you lend me a couple? My wives are at the camp, and I'm horny after this trip. Is this woman one of them?"

"That's the governor's lodge," I said, adding in Spanish, "The Señora's his neice."

"Bueno. I have a new pony, Gayo. Very fast. I raised him from a colt. You'll see. You won't believe."

"That's true, Jean-Pierre," said Taoinan. "He's been running him on the prairie, so no one could watch. Wait till you see it run."

"Jean-Pierre," interrupted Hélène-Eulalie, smiling. "Please. Invite them to dinner, your friend and Arsène's—the girl too." Turning to Sehêbi, she asked her if she were able to join us for dinner.

Sehêbi looked troubled. Evidently she had understood, knowing the French word, "dîner," and realized an invitation had been extended. "Oui, s'il vous plaît, Señora."

"Good," smiled Hélène-Eulalie. "We'll celebrate their visit."

But as she and I walked back to the house, I had to explain to her, much to her annoyance, that Sehêbi would be unable to attend the dinner. For an Indian woman to have done so on such an important, formal occasion would have been a gross violation of Comanche custom. In the end the lady was compelled to observe the customs of her guests, while complaining, "Cela, ce n'est pas juste."

That evening still stands out in my mind because of its unusual events. The guests arrived an hour early—before sunset, that is, the time at which they had been invited. This meant that Monsieur de St. Maurice, Arsène and I sat and attempted to entertain them throughout the long interval before dinner was announced. Hélène-Eulalie was in the kitchen directing, where she had been most of the day after she and Arsène had decided upon the menu and worked out details of the meal. Fortunately the colonel's plantation grew a superior tobacco, and he had a supply of fine cigars which he rarely smoked but was now able to pass out to our friends. These they puffed at vigorously while remaining mostly silent, except for Big-Mountain. The warchief had of course been entertained for upwards of a month by Texas governor, don Jacinto Fermin de Mendoza, and was now displaying his urbanity to his companions by attempting to converse, through a mixture of Spanish and signs, with M. de St. Maurice. The colonel, back in his element and now smoking with the others, appeared to be enjoying himself despite some long and uncomfortable silences. Meanwhile Taoinan sat uneasily in his chair, puffing and musing, glancing around him at the candles and oil lamps that reflected in mirrors and lighted the drawing room into its dim corners, even flickering and shining like wind in poplar leaves off the dark surfaces of the pianoforte.

Our third guest was the warchief Sees-Fire, Cunabunit. Taoinan would at least respond to my questions, but Sees-Fire sat rigid in his chair, smoking, his eyes those of a man staring out from within a cage, his scarred face, with broad pocked nose, prominent cheekbones and round cheeks tight with alarm, all the while ignoring Arsène's repeated attempts to draw him into conversation. We had finally been reduced to silence, even Toyamancare, who had exhausted the subject of his people's need for firearms to defend against the Huazas, or Osages, who received guns from northern traders. Fortunately the old tomcat stalked in and provided a distraction. Actually he was to save our evening. Big-Mountain, who was familiar with housecats from his stay at San Antonio de Béxar, at once leaned down and, flicking his fingers, called the animal, "minino, minino." But Diablo went to Arsène, whom he evidently remembered from seven years before and favored. He rubbed against and twisted around his ankles.

Taoinan and Sees-Fire appeared to be fascinated by the animal, watching it intently. I realized they had never before seen our common housecat and were only familiar with the wild variety, both the smaller, which the Spaniards call the gato montés and the large and dangerous puma. I explained, using my limited Comanche, as well as a few signs, the universal distribution of the animal throughout the regions of the tabebo, or white man, as well as its usefulness in ridding his houses of mice and other vermin. Our guests understood, exchanging approving remarks among themselves. (I did not explain that this particular cat, an excellent hunter, often fetched his prey indoors for his amusement, frequently losing mice or snakes to such an extent as to keep the house well-stocked.) In any event Diablo provided a diversion, easing the tension a little. The colonel, Arsène and I were still, in a desultory fashion, talking about cats, little and big, when Hélène-Eulalie—to our huge relief—entered and called us to dinner.

The table was splendid, with sparkling crystal and gleaming silver, white tablecloth and napkins, all illuminated by two large candelabra. This splendor I learned later had come with M. de St. Maurice's deceased child wife. I had never seen it used before. It was rarely used afterward, but that evening it made a wonderful, shimmering display that appeared to impress and please our guests. Yet the bottle of wine before the colonel and, even more, wine goblets beside the water glasses placed before those guests caused me immediate alarm. I looked at the colonel, whose eyebrows were also raised at this circumstance, and from him to Arsène. But the youth appeared oblivious to potential disaster, his features fixed in the proud, stern expression he adopted among his companions. Hélène-Eulalie, who looked elegant and beautiful in a décolleté gown the blue of pale water, wore a serene smile, clearly pleased with the dazzling effect she had created on the table and the appreciative response from our guests, who were plainly delighted by its novelty.

They still sat silently with expectant expressions, holding the knives beside their service plates, evidently hungry, long since ready to eat and anticipating a savory meal. They were not disappointed. Mlle. Bijou appeared from the kitchen carrying a great platter of rare roast beef which had been basted, at Arsène's suggestion, with a little brown sugar dissolved in dish gravy, because the People greatly preferred the flesh of the bison, none of which was presently available. And they were partial to sweets. There was also a generous amount of that gravy in the pan—perhaps too much, since our guests were expected to eat, according to their custom, with their fingers. Placing the platter before Hélène-Eulalie, who sat at one end of the table opposite the colonel, Madamoiselle raised the bottle, poured a little into Monsieur's glass and at his nod poured more, moving next around to Hélène-Eulalie, then to The Flute, who sat on her right. Mlle. Bijou, who had been, unlike the colonel's niece, raised on the frontier, poised the bottle over his glass, regarding him with a skeptical, quizzical look. The Flute turned to Arsène, who explained that wine was aguardiente, or poisabá. Immediately the Comanche signaled, "niatz," or "no," refusing the wine, as did our other two guests and Arsène as well.

During an anticipatory silence Mlle Bijou began passing the platter, beginning with Hélène-Eulalie and moving to each guest in turn. Then I helped myself, and Madamoiselle moved to Arsène. The platter, with its burden of red meat and gravy was heavy, so that she rested her forearm upon the table before him. Arsène had just taken up the serving utensils and was considering the choices offered, when the old cat, which had been crouched by his chair, sprang into his lap, landing, as he told me later, on his bare thighs with claws only partially sheathed. The youth started, waving, as if to send the cat flying from his lap. But Diablo had other intentions and had already gathered for a second leap. The human movements threw it off balance, so that when it sprang for the table it came down partly in Arsène's plate but mostly in the platter, splashing gravy in every direction. Ignoring the meat, and apparently aware that his behavior was inappropriate, Diablo continued his momentum forward out of the platter and onto the tablecloth, where he stalked forward a few paces, shaking gravy off first one, then the other hind paw and quivering his tail. He then seated himself almost at the center of the table and began licking a forepaw.

All of this had occurred so quickly that none of us had had time to respond, except for Mlle Bijou, who shrieked, released the platter and reached her long arms for the cat. The rest of us, stunned, looked at Arsène. Gravy slid down his face, making an odd effect when combined with red and yellow paint. It had spattered his buckskin war shirt and his hands. For an instant he stared at the cat, calmly licking itself, with an astonished expression. Then he turned to his Comanche companions, those older men he was trying to impress. Sees-Fire, laying down his dinner knife, was struggling to stifle a smile. Arsène smiled back self-consciously, indeed foolishly.

"He's never done that before," he exclaimed in French.

Big-Mountain exploded in laughter, a second ahead of the rest of us. None could resist, including the youth himself. As Mlle Bijou seized the cat from the table and bore it from the room, scolding the animal as if it were a child in disgrace, all of us joined in laughter. Even the colonel, at the head of the table, smiled along with us. Hélène-Eulalie preserved her composure the longest, then clapped her hand over her mouth and a giggle emerged, soon becoming helpless laughter. By this time the Comanche guests, Taoinan, even Sees-Fire, were rocking in their chairs. Dabbing the gravy from his face with his napkin, Arsène gasped and laughed along with them. I too laughed until tears wet my cheeks.

So it turned out that Diablo had saved our soirée. In French we have an expression, briser la glace, "to break the ice." Diablo effectively broke the ice among us, and for the remainder of the evening every one of us, even Sees-Fire, was completely his or her human self, without constraint and more or less at ease. The cat platter was retired and a fresh one brought in, although with the same meat. Arsène excused himself and returned without gravy on his face or garments, and the dinner proceeded with everyone in good humor and even, from time to time, chuckling again. Monsieur de St. Maurice had spoken to Mlle Bijou and soon after calm had returned around the table she carried from the kitchen a tray supporting, I later learned, a pitcher and glasses of a beverage composed of honey and hot water. While our guests and Arsène enthusiastically drank this mixture, the remaining three of us sipped a vintage Bordeaux that the colonel had provided for this occasion.

Hélène-Eulalie sipped somewhat in excess of her usual glass or two with dinner, so that she became, with flushed cheeks, quite talkative, vivacious, and—I had to admit to myself—pretty and delightful. Taoinan, seated upon her right, evidently thought so too and kept Arsène busy translating information about the pianoforte, which he had noticed in the living room, and the sounds it produced, so that, in the end, Hélène-Eulalie gave an animated lecture on the history, principles and structure of the instrument, which to my surprise that unusual warrior listened to attentively, although I am sure Arsène had difficulty in finding Comanche words capable of an adequate description.

Big-Mountain and Sees-Fire ate heartily, with second and third helpings of the sweetened beef, so that the pace of dinner lagged while the warriors, who clearly regarded eating as a serious affair, regaled mostly in silence. The Flute, meanwhile, was questioning Arsène, from what I could understand of his rapid interrogation, about our hostess, her history, marital status, and reasons for leaving France. Finally he turned to her and asked her in Spanish, which he seemed momentarily to believe she understood, to explain to him the big fight that was taking place in her country, as well as what had happened to her husband. Hélène-Eulalie shot her cousin a quizzical look. With some embarrassment Arsène repeated the questions in French. The lady's alert expression was replaced by a stricken look, from which, however, she quickly recovered.

"Well, there were abuses. Certainly there were abuses. I saw that myself. The frivolity of the court, while the people suffered." She regarded the colonel, as well as Arsène and Taoinan. "You know I grew up in the country. I was not prepared for the court. The people revolted against the king, the noblesse, and the clergy—those to whom they paid tithes and taxes, those who rode on their backs with a whip. You understand?"

Arsène, who had been translating with difficulty, exchanged a few words with Taoinan. "Yes, he sees, more or less."

"At first it was not so bad. Then the most extreme began leading the others. The worst rose to the top, even killing other leaders to get there. The worst were crazy with hatred, or simply crazy. Those of the populace who were poorest and who had suffered most followed them and became crazy too, crazy for revenge, for blood. Then the horror started. They began decapitating people till blood flowed in the gutters. Blood ran down the streets. Really. I swear it. Does he understand?"

Arsène nodded. Chopping off heads was something a warrior could understand. Big-Mountain and Sees-Fire were listening now too.

"You ask about my husband. He was much older than I. I respected him greatly. A decent man. But he was of the noblesse. He saw what was coming, and he put me on a ship, very early, a ship for England. From there, later, I came here. I begged him to come with me, but he considered it cowardly to leave. He stayed and died, denounced by the Vigilance Committee of the quarter because he had property and wealth. The Tribunal wanted it, and they killed him." Hélène-Eulalie's voice had begun to thicken, and she paused, her cheeks again flushed, eyes brilliant.

Taoinan and the other warriors watched her, seemingly fascinated by her passion, if not by her words.

"In England everybody thought only the noblesse went to the guillotine—people all thought that, except for us, the émigrées. We knew. No, finally it was anybody whose property they wanted or whom they suspected of lacking enthusiasm for the revolution."

"Really?" said Arsène. "Not the common people too?"

"Really. Common people. Shopkeepers, peasants from the country, children. Yes, children. Let me tell you. Last year when they suppressed the revolts—revolts against Paris and the revolution—in the provinces, the provincial revolutionary leaders perpetrated unspeakable horrors. Listen to me, my little Indian cousin. In Nantes some maniac ordered—I think it was three hundred—no, five hundred—children, peasant girls and boys driven to a field outside the city and, there, shot down. Those showing signs of life were clubbed to death. Children!" She stopped, unable to continue, a tear sliding from her cheek.

I then did something that shocked me. Touched, without thinking, I reached and gripped her hand. It must have been, as I remember it, intended to give her strength. Of course the wine, too, played its part. I had become emotional. It was une gaffe. I gripped her hand for a moment while she struggled to recover her composure. I noticed the colonel was looking, not with disapproval but surprise. She pulled her hand. I released it and withdrew mine as if I had touched white hot iron, embarrassed, even blushing as I recall. She threw me a startled look, and I was even more embarrassed. But no one at the table was looking at me. They were all watching Hélène-Eulalie dabbing at her cheek and her eyes with her napkin, smiling, raising her chin, looking around calmly.

"Perhaps it would be better," said Monsieur de St. Maurice. "To speak of other things. Jean-Pierre, have you heard about the horse races planned for tomorrow? Arsène tells me that our friends here will race their ponies against the horses of the militia. I'm told I may even place a bet."

"Please. I'm all right now," said Hélène-Eulalie. "Let me finish."

After observing her sharply for a moment, the colonel nodded.

"That was not all," Hélène-Eulalie continued, speaking calmly, although with increasing intensity. "The same madman ordered les noyades, the drownings in the Loire. Adolescent boys and girls, old people, invalids, women with infants—they were herded onto rafts, and the rafts were sunk. We heard several thousand of them were murdered, perhaps more. At Lyons, when the city surrendered, more than a hundred men—no, I think it was two hundred—were tied together in a field and killed with cannon, grapeshot. And at Arras, too, the guillotine."

"In Paris the guillotine, all the while, I suppose?" asked Arsène.

"Yes. With the loi des suspects anybody imagined to possess unpatriotic sentiments could be killed."

"C'est ainsi," remarked the colonel almost inaudibly, and as if to himself, "que se termine le siecle des lumières."

After a moment of discussion with Arsène, Taoinan replied that he had understood, and that he was sorry about all that had happened, and sorry for her that there were such bad people in her country. Placing his hand on his chest, he said that if he and his warriors had been there, they would have tried to help her stop the bad things that were happening.

Quickly Hélène-Eulalie regained her composure and, glancing around the table at empty plates, asked with a gracious smile whether everyone had finished eating and was ready for dessert. Everyone was. Meanwhile Big-Mountain and Sees-Fire had been watching her intently, as if under a hypnotic spell. I doubted that they, or even Taoinan, had understood much of Hélène-Eulalie's explanation. Vocabulary and context were missing. But they had clearly been fascinated by her as an exotic form of life and by the force of the telling. Arsène, who you will recall was a youth of but nineteen years, had of course understood. He had become pensive, his pale cheeks flushed, staring with a bellicose expression at the stained tablecloth before him.

Soon Mlle. Bijou bore in a tray of pastries, a dessert which delighted our guests. While we were enjoying these sweets, Taoinan asked Hélène-Eulalie, through Arsène, whether when we left the table she would play music for us from the great black box in the next room. Surprised and pleased, she replied that she would be happy to.

Later, while all of us men sat comfortably smoking cigars in the flickering light from the candles and lamps and the glow from the red embers of the fire, Hélène-Eulalie obliged us by playing what I now know was a clavier sonata by some Austrian. It lasted no more than fifteen minutes and was so lyrical and charming and so well played that it could have been enjoyed by anybody, even without any special knowledge of music. As before, the performance gave me a great and novel pleasure, also pleasing our guests, especially Taoinan, who half-smiled at the end of the recital. Monsieur de St. Maurice listened, breathing smoke into the air, with his eyes half-closed. The others, listening without expression, had enjoyed it more than they appeared to, as I learned at the evening's end. The only exception, I believe, was Arsène, still reflective, who seemed scarcely to listen and whose mind appeared for the remainder of the evening to be elsewhere, perhaps on the prairie, or on some cobbled, blood-stained square in the Paris he had never seen.

Afterward when, with Arsène, I was bidding goodnight to our friends outside the door under a black, starless sky, Taoinan said to me as an apparent final thought, "Jean-Pierre, you must marry that woman."

"What?" I laughed.

"Yes," said Toyamancare earnestly. "You must marry her, Bluejay. You can have her make music whenever you want."

"And the piano? Out on the prairie? You'll drag it behind your pony?"

"We will come here."

"I don't think she can butcher a cow. Or cook."

"No, you can marry the black woman too. She can cook. Your other wives can do those things. But this one can make music from the big black box."

"All right, all right," I smiled. "I'll think about it." A sudden memory made me pause abruptly. With a little shock I recalled the conversation in which he had told me that "brothers" shared wives, that I would share my wife with him.

"You must, Bluejay," insisted Sees-Fire.

"Yes," said Arsène to Toyamancare, still angry, half-joking: "Jean-Pierre can marry my cousin. Then we'll go to France and fight those bastardos, que no?"

Big-Mountain smiled, clapped his shoulder. "Si, when we have no more Apaches, or Utes, or Tonkawas, or Osages to fight, we'll go over the water and fight those bastardos. Bring your horse tomorrow, the big one too."

The three of them went down the path toward the black river, Taoinan limping ahead, leading the way toward the tiny, flickering fires at their lodges, where I knew Sehêbi would be awake and waiting to hear about our soirée. I wondered what he would tell her. Moreover I wondered whether my suspicion of my "brother's" interest in Hélène-Eulalie during the evening was even slightly plausible. Was it simply crazy? I decided it was. In any event it didn't matter, because there was so little likelihood of my ever marrying the colonel's niece. Still the very thought left me feeling uneasy, with a sense that my life might be growing more complicated.

13

The following day I was obliged to leave the house early and spend the entire day, until late in the evening at the company trading post. I saw no one on my return and fell into bed early.

On my way back to the village the following morning, I was surprised to encounter Hélène-Eulalie out for an early morning walk. I said "bonjour" to her and was about to pass.

"Do you mind company for a way," she asked, falling in beside me.

"Of course not." I told her I would be delighted to have her company. But I felt even less at ease in her presence than usual after my involuntary grasp of her hand the night of her party. I felt a need to explain or apologize, but I was unable to find suitable words. We walked in silence for half of an English mile, until she, herself, broached the subject.

"I must thank you for your kind gesture the other night—taking my hand."

"Oh, I apologize. It just happened. I didn't intend to."

"All the more meaningful. It came from the heart. And I do thank you."

We chatted for a bit about the impromptu horse races the Comanches had held the previous day. Apparently Big-Mountain had raced a new pony, a scruffy runt that turned out to be exceedingly swift. With it he had fooled Le Noir, the new commandant at the post, outstripping his thoroughbred. But more significantly he had challenged a reluctant Arsène, insisting that he race and bet and winning from him the horse the colonel had just given him—César. Arsène, considering himself bullied into accepting the race, was so bitter and resentful toward his Comanche father that he had spoken of not returning with him. Even of leaving the tribe. Of course his real father and his cousin were delighted.

"Oh, if he only would," Hélène-Eulalie signed, shaking her head. "But why did that... Big-Mountain do it? I don't understand."

"I think he's too fond of horses. Like some people with money. He can never have enough."

I left her and continued to the company building in the village in better spirits than when I had set out. On my return at about 11:00 o'clock, I opened the front door to the ripple of the piano. In the drawing room I found Hélène-Eulalie playing, practicing I thought until I saw Sehêbi seated in a chair near the piano bench. Even in the dim light I could see by the child's expression and posture that she was enthralled by the music. Or perhaps it was not the sound alone of the lyrical little piece. Clearly she also admired the pianist, possibly even more than the miracle of the music Hélène-Eulalie was re-creating. I took a chair by the window and listened until the end of the piece.

"Did that please you?" Hélène-Eulalie asked in French, turning from the bench to the girl.

"Oui, beaucoup."

"Sehêbi tells me they're leaving tomorrow."

"When? In the morning?" I asked in Comanche.

"Yes," said Sehêbi.

She looked at me sideways, a little strangely, I thought. We had not really talked since the Comanches' arrival. I sensed she wished to talk with me, although she had not seemed to want to be alone with me previously. "In that case, I'm going to go smoke with Taoinan. Are you going back to your lodge?" I asked the girl.

"Yes." She rose.

Hélène-Eulalie embraced her. "I'll miss you. I'll come out with Jean-Pierre and visit you someday soon. I promise."

The girl blushed and turned her face to conceal tears.

When we had left the house, Sehêbi told me she had not seen the "medicine house," or church. She asked me to show it to her on the way. It was not on the way, so instead of taking the path to the river, we followed a trail up a nearby hill. The little building, constructed of cypress wood, and covered with vines and roses, lay on a knoll near the edge of the community. It was dim and empty when we entered, but someone had lighted candles near the altar, and the building smelled of incense. Candlelight reflected from bronze candelabra, partly illuminating paintings depicting saints as well as a pale image of the crucified Jesus beside the altar, an image subtly emphasizing with painted blood the wounds and the spikes through feet and hands. Sehêbi looked around her with curiosity and awe, murmuring, "Que c'est beau, que c'est beau!" But from the crucified figure she turned away, saying she didn't like to look at such things. I tried explaining in deliberate French and in the simplest terms some of the significance of the altar and crucifix to Christians. But when I turned back to her, I found she was not listening. Instead she was looking at me intently with, once more, tears glistening in her eyes.

"What is it?" I gently took her shoulders in my hands.

Still gazing up at me, she spoke so rapidly in Comanche that I understood nothing, except that she was pleading with me. I asked her to repeat what she had said slowly, and the second time I grasped the gist of what she was saying: she did not want to return with Taoinan and the others. I was shocked.

"I want to stay here with you, Jean-Pierre. And with Hélène. And Madamoiselle Bijou." Her eyes were large, her expression fearful.

"But why? Taoinan's a good man. He's kind to you, isn't he?"

"Yes. He's a good man. Ask him. Tell him I want to marry you and stay here. He's your brother. He'll do what you ask. You can give him horses. You have horses, don't you?"

"I can't do that, Sehêbi. I'm sorry. I can't."

"You won't give horses? It's your baby inside me."

"It's not the horses. You're his wife. I can't ask him to give me his wife. You're his favorite wife."

"Yes. His favorite wife," she moaned. She looked at me despairingly.

"The baby's probably Taoinan's."

"No, I don't think so. I think it's yours."

"Anyway, I can't do it. I'm sorry. I'm sure you can stay here with us. Go back next spring with the expedition. But you'll have to ask Taoinan."

The possibility that she might be pregnant with my child had shaken me, although I suspected her remark to be a bluff. Still I was determined to avoid further involvement in my friend's marriage no matter what she said. Yet she looked so pretty and sad and so appealing standing before me, gazing at me with her distressed and frightened expression, that I drew her to me, stroking the back of her head as she pressed her face into my shoulder. When she looked at me again with tears in her eyes, I was unable to resist kissing her gently on the lips, still stroking her back, trying to comfort her. With that, she flung her arms around my neck. I pulled her hard against me and our kisses instantly became less innocent, as our breathing turned to panting. I don't remember quite what occurred next. I may have flinched back a little, remembering my resolve. Whatever it was, something, perhaps a thought, offended her. She wrenched away and stood, red-faced, breathing hard, staring as if she intended to kill me.

"You won't give horses for me!" she cried in French. "You don't care what happens to me! You piece of shit!" She then lapsed into Comanche, delivering a string of what I knew to be insulting epithets, but which I was unable to understand they came so rapidly and with such fury.

"Wait. I told you—"

But she turned and darted from the church, running back down the path and then toward the river. I ran after her a short way, calling her name, asking her to stop. She fled so strongly and swiftly that I soon gave up. Gradually regaining my breath, I followed her at a walk toward the Comanche camp, wondering at her strange behavior. Clearly it was not Taoinan, so what did she fear? What could she fear? After a time I shrugged, attributing her anxiety to vagaries resulting from her pregnancy.

The Flute was seated in sunlight before his lodge, his face raised, eyes closed. I stood a moment out of respect for his medicine, or whatever it was, until he opened them. He greeted me with a pleased look and called behind him for his pipe. I sat down facing him. Sehêbi emerged from the tepee with the pipe and tobacco, stooping and handing them to him. Her features were composed, eyes averted. I kept seeing her pleading in the church even as she stooped and reentered the lodge. We smoked for a time quietly, passing the pipe back and forth in a leisurely manner. The sun felt good. From trees by the river a horse whinnied. Another answered from one of the nearby lodges where it had been staked. The smoke from the cookfires smelled good. A crow croaked and made a clicking sound in a tree.

"You're leaving tomorrow."

"Yes." He withdrew the pipe. "I've been thinking. Listen, brother. That which Toyamancare did yesterday, with the big horse, that was not good. He's our friend, but it wasn't good."

"But you don't like Amabate."

"Well, I don't dislike him. He's crazy, but a good warrior."

"Maybe he's crazy. I don't think so. But he's brave."

"Yes, he's brave."

"I heard him talking with the colonel. He's very angry, sad. He said he might even leave the Nuhmuhnuh if he could get a commission—be an officer—in the army of Spain. His father was happy, said he might be able to arrange it, but it would take time. That's all I heard."

"That would be too bad." He thought for a time. "He's one of our best young warriors. The young men admire him. You know, he has done some big things. Many would follow him, even now. He'll be a warchief in a few years. It would be bad to lose him."

"I think he was just talking. He doesn't want to leave the People—though, as you know, I'd like him to. This is no life for the colonel's son."

With wrinkled brow, Taoinan smoked for a long moment. "If he doesn't want to live with Big-Mountain, he could ride back with me. He could live with me and my older wives' relatives. I'd have my women make him his own lodge, if there's time before the snow. Otherwise, he could sleep in mine for a while."

"You surprise me, brother. I was sure you didn't like him."

"He's like I was, always wanting to fight."

"What's wrong with that?"

"It's tiresome. There's also a time to rest. To eat. To fuck your wives. Hunt. Make medicine. Race your ponies. Enjoy being here, before we go to the other place. You know that, brother. It's stupid to live just to fight."

I laughed. "And you want him to live with you?"

"We have many enemies. We need good warriors."

That evening I brought Arsène to Taoinan's lodge, after telling him the older man wished to talk with him. I said nothing to the colonel or to Hélène-Eulalie, both cheerful during dinner, she quite animated in fact, since they now believed he might remain and seek a commission with the Spanish military. I felt guilty, but I knew I owed at least this much to my Comanche "brother." In any event he could simply send Sehêbi or some other person to fetch the youth.

Arsène was surprised at the request. He revered The Flute as a successful warrior with many horses, but he had long ago sensed that this respected man neither admired nor liked him, in contrast to most other older men, and he was puzzled, incidentally, as to the reason. When we were about to leave the house, he asked for the third time what Taoinan wanted with him. As before, I told him I didn't know. Hélène-Eulalie had found him what she called, "civilized clothing," in the village. On this evening he was wearing trousers without a shirt, along with moccasins and a single eagle feather drooping in his long hair, so that the effect was partly Comanche, partly what became later known among the Americans as, "squaw man," a white who had married an Indian woman and lived with the tribe.

It was dark when we left the house. Taoinan was seated, as before, by the entrance to his lodge at a tiny fire. He greeted us formally. When we were seated, he passed his pipe first to me and upon its return to Arsène. While the youth watched with mingled deference and curiosity, his bony features alternately in firelight or shadow, The Flute in a short, direct talk invited him not only to travel with him on the return trip but extended an invitation for the younger man to live with him among his wives' relatives and a few followers, to become, in effect, a part of his extended family. This was a serious proposal not to be decided impulsively, and Arsène knew it. His head bowed, he sat for a long while pondering the invitation, apparently thinking hard while Taoinan and I waited in silence.

"I'll live with you," he said finally, looking up. "I'll bring you meat for your wives to cook. Now I ask you—you who have great power—will you give me some of your medicine?"

It was a bold request. But if Taoinan was surprised he failed to show it. After hesitating an instant, he puffed his pipe several times toward the stars, then passed it to Arsène, who puffed toward the night sky.

It seemed to me that my 'brother' was even pleased: for a second I thought I saw a smile hover at his lips, even though the occasion was a solemn one. "I will try. Maybe I can't give you my medicine. Maybe I can. But I'll teach you and try to prepare you so that you can dream and see better. That's all I can do, but I will do that."

"Good," said Arsène, rising, standing respectfully. "I'll leave with you in the morning."

"Wait. Sit down." Taoinan scrutinized his features. "My brother tells me you're not well. You look sick. What's the matter with you?"

Seating himself, Arsène shot me a reproachful glance. "I'm not sick. Just pains here sometimes." Embarrassed, he pressed his abdomen. "It's nothing. My Toyamancare says I need to eat buffalo meat."

"Have you searched your things? Have you found anything that's not yours?"

"No. Why do you ask?" He started slightly. "Antoine has looked through everything I have. He found nothing."

"Why?" I asked, surprised. "Why did he do that?"

Taoinan appeared not to listen, apparently pondering. "Has anyone given you anything?"

"No. Well, nothing but a pad saddle. But that—"

"Who?"

"Oh, some women. Friends of Rabbit-knife. But it's an excellent saddle. There can't be anything—"

Taoinan called out and dispatched a nearby child for the saddle. "You think you killed Rabbit-knife, don't you?" He fixed the youth with a hard look.

Arsène looked stricken. "No, not exactly," he stammered. "Everybody thinks... But I just liked her. She was just...a friend. If it hadn't been for me though...." He abruptly hung his head, hiding his face, controlling himself.

"Hear me, Amabate. My father's son, White-Road, is a great warrior. But he has a bad heart. He's bad with his prisoners. Bad with his ponies. Bad with his wives. He's malo, malo, malo. He could not break Rabbit-knife. Rabbit-knife was a bold-hearted woman. No man could break her. So it had to happen. He had to kill her. It would have happened anyway. Now he wants to kill you. You see? His brother, Red-Woman, the medicine man, must have told him how to do this."

"And El Chamaco?" I asked.

"El Chamaco's pure mischief. Both brothers do what Tosapoy wishes."

When the boy arrived with the saddle, Taoinan gave it to Sehêbi and told her to remove the stuffing. At first she drew out nothing except deer's hair. But then she gave a little cry. We turned to her. She held up a bundle of small black feathers. Approaching her husband, she held them out: the quills were bound with black horsehair and fastened to a tiny skull, perhaps of a bat or squirrel, with what appeared to be a drop of dried blood upon its dome. Taoinan, examining the bundle, sniffing, pronounced the feathers probably to be those of a turkey vulture.

He directed the startled Arsène to take them to the river, throw them in, enter and wash himself all over, get out, shake himself like a wolf and make medicine commanding the evil to depart with the stream and to leave him, Amabate, and all of us forever.

Taoinan dreamt that night a dream so strange that he kept it to himself until the next time we met. Of course, he said, it was only a part of a long and confusing dream, most of which he could not recall. But he had dreamt that on the return trip to comanchería, Arsène had become deathly ill, with a face the color of ashes, vomiting, pressing his belly, and telling of pain there. In the dream Taoinan had been unable to relieve this pain by a song or other medicine. Finally, he told me that Arsène's abdomen had begun to swell while he lay on his back and writhed by the fire. Taoinan said that Arsène had cried out as his belly split open like a melon, spilling an evil smelling and hideous green liquid. Then Ah-mah-bah-tay had thrown back his head, rolled his eyes upward, cried out, and died—at least he had appeared to have stopped breathing and to be dead. Of the dream, Taoinan remembered nothing more, but he had puzzled over what it might signify. Finally, he said, since the very opposite of the dream had actually happened, he took heart in deciding that it revealed what might have occurred if Arsène had not escaped the witching by casting away the little bundle of feathers and washing himself in the river.

What had really happened was that by the time the Comanche party had passed a league beyond La Grande Forêt, Amabate had regained his high spirits. His melancholy and pains had left him, and he had recovered his health, evidence that Taoinan's remedy had worked and that Amabate was free from White-Road's and his brothers' sorcery, or so I believed then. Moreover we heard that Big-Mountain, whom he was continuing to avoid, had attributed his adopted son's recovery to a renewed diet of buffalo meat.

The morning began in gray light and drizzle, as I could tell by the dripping outside my window. Although all of us in the house rose by lamplight, we nearly missed our friends' departure. Indeed we did miss the departure of Big-Mountain and his group, who had without ceremony ridden off earlier—Big-Mountain seated upon César, according to Antoine, who joined us at the front door. Arsène had bid goodby the previous evening to his father—painfully and guiltily according to his cousin's account much later—passing the night in the Comanche camp. I had told him I would be out to see him and The Flute away, but I slept badly and failed to wake as early as I had planned. I was scarcely dressed when Mlle. Bijou rapped on my door to inform me that Arsène and the others were leaving. Cursing my tardiness, I rushed barefoot to the open front door, where I was surprised to find not only the colonel but Hélène-Eulalie and Mlle. Bijou standing with Lefort.

"Vraiment un sale temps," observed the Canadian.

The drizzle had turned to rain. Down the road they went, Taoinan leading, followed by Sehêbi and several warriors. Behind them rode The Flute's wives' relatives, except for Sehêbi's, whose family belonged to the distant Yamparica Comanche division. All were already wet and bedraggled, including the ponies splashing through mud. Last but one were several riders with the packhorses. Despite the rain the men rode barechested, dark skin slick and shiny, hair limp and tangled. The womens' buckskin dresses were dark with rain and clinging to their bodies.

I waved farewell to Taoinan. Straight in his saddle and looking intently toward us, he raised both hands, index fingers pointed toward his pony's ears in the sign for "goodby." I waved to Sehêbi. For an instant she looked, then slumped, hung her head and rode on. Was she weeping? I could not tell. I felt a pang of guilt and regret and an increasing sadness as the procession slogged past below us through gleaming puddles and black mud. Last of all rode Arsène on his pinto. None of the other men was dressed ceremonially, or carrying his arms at the ready. But bare from the waist up and painted, sitting straighter even than The Flute, Arsène bore his shield on his arm and his lance, with its sodden scalp, in his fist. Monsieur de St. Maurice, lifting a hand from a cane, slowly waved to his son. Arsène, now permanently it seemed Amabate, or The One Without A Head, raised his lance in a salute to the old man and to all of us. A moment later they were gone, vanishing around the corner leaving, as it were, a gray vacancy in the downpour.

"Ça y est," said the colonel. "C'est fini. Tant pis." His features were composed, except for the faintest of smiles. Turning, with the help of his canes, and now with Madamoiselle's arm, he entered the house and hobbled down the hall to his office.

"I wonder if he'll ever see his son again," murmured Hélène-Eulalie. Her old melancholy expression had returned. She fixed her gray eyes upon mine.

In response, Lefort shrugged, spat, and cursed under his breath. Head lowered, back bent, he walked away in the rain toward the woods and his cabin.

"Who knows? He may come back for visits."

"Will you take me out there someday—on your next expedition?"

"The prairie's dangerous. Not a good place for a white woman."

"I know. I want to go. Will you take me?" She looked at me intently, steadily into my eyes, then glanced down at my naked feet. Her eyebrows rose, accompanied by a chilly smile. The expression was well-known to me. I had seen the same haughty look cross Arsène's face from time to time ever since he had been my pupil. It always had, and still did, amuse me, his assumption of superiority. But on Hélène-Eulalie's features the identical expression vexed me and in my present mood vexed me extremely. But now her expression cleared, suddenly became cheerful. Evidently she found me comical.

"Yes, perhaps someday," I replied, regarding her irritably. Turning, leaving her to enter and close the door behind me, I walked down the dim hall and—abruptly remembering Diablo's predilection for snakes—placed my bare feet carefully, looking down, proceeding with all the dignity I could manage.

Could I have heard behind me—? Was it possible? A barely audible sound? Could it have been suppressed laughter?

Soon after the Comanches' departure I lost two years of my life. It was scarcely life I endured in New England. It was, rather, two years of the merest existence. The interval began with a letter from my maternal grandfather informing me that my mother had suffered an apoplectic seizure which had left her partially paralyzed. She had, however, retained the power of speech. The old man, whom I scarcely remembered, as our families had taken opposite sides during the Revolution, wrote that my mother wished to see me, believing she might not have long to live. Everything in me revolted at the prospect of leaving Natchitoches Post and the frontier. Yet I loved my mother. I could not deny her request.

Goodbyes are frequently painful. This was so with Colonel de St. Maurice. I had expected that. But I also recall my parting with Hélène-Eulalie. Although it should not have been, it was only a little less difficult. I was at the front door with my bags when she came down the hall and stood before me, regarding me with a little frown of pain.

"You'll return as soon as you can."

"I will."

"My uncle is so very old. And his health is so...uncertain."

We stood looking at each other.

"We'll miss you. Have a safe voyage...and come back as soon as you can...Jean-Pierre."

This was the first time she had uttered my first names. I did something then that startled me, which I had seen Le Noir do, that I had never done before, nor ever since. Bowing, I seized her hand and raised it, brushing it with my lips and my mustache. "Au revoir, Madame," I said, as I turned to open the door, merely glimpsing her amused, distressed expression. Grasping my bags, I left without shutting the door, without looking back, quickly descending the path to the port. But in the pirogue on the river moving with its flow down toward the city and the gulf, I found myself raising my hand occasionally to my face to sniff the faint scent of roses.

I arrived in Boston Harbor only a few weeks before Christmas. After disembarking, I sent a message to my grandparents announcing my arrival. I remember snowflakes drifting among the squawking gulls above the bustle of the wharf as I waited by my bags, wiggling my fingers in my pockets and stamping against a cold I was no longer prepared for. In less than an hour my youngest and favorite uncle appeared with my grandparents' phaeton and coachman to take me to my mother's village and her farm west of the city. We greeted each other with a hug. Elliott was my favorite since he had been, beside my mother, the only Patriot in the Rutherford family. Ironically he too had begun as a Tory, but some of his older Patriot acquaintances had "volunteered" him, a little drunk, resisting and protesting of course, for the Continental Army. After serving some months together with his young friends, fighting and suffering beside them, and after observing the burning and pillaging by Hessians and Lobster Backs, their looting of Patriot and Loyalist homes alike, he had switched sides and, to his family's consternation, had become a Patriot.

Ironically again, it was that very fact which had rescued his parents and brothers from the persecutions of our Patriot mobs, the knowledge that the family had a son and brother with the Continental Army. We talked of that within the carriage, trotting through narrow streets of the city and later on the road to the village. We talked of how he had staggered to the door of my mother's cottage, emaciated and ill, after capture, prison, and prisoner exchange to stay with us and recuperate, and how his recovery and help with the farm had released me to enlist in turn, so that I was able to fight in the south at Cowpens under "Old Wagoner" Morgan and, later, to participate in our victory at Yorktown and Cornwallis's surrender to the French and Continental troops there. But first of course I had questioned him about my mother and grandparents.

"Johnny, I hate to tell you. She's had another seizure, a worse one."

"She didn't die, did she?" I asked quickly.

"No. Maybe it would be better if she had. But then of course she couldn't see you. And that's good. You came in time."

"What do you mean?"

"This last one's left her paralyzed...on one side. And she can't speak."

"Can't speak? Not at all?"

"No. I fear not. But we believe she understands what we say to her."

"Mon Dieu, can't talk. Paralyzed. Who's taking care of her?"

"Alice. She moved in at the beginning. She's been there all along."

Thank God for Aunt Alice, I thought. She was my mother's and Elliott's older sister and as good as she was plain. Immediately I was reassured. Distressing as the news was—like being kicked by a colt in the belly—I knew my mother could receive no better care from anyone than from her sister. As for my grandparents, they were evidently thriving.

"They're so healthy sometimes I think they're immortal." Elliott smiled.

"Are they reconciled yet to independence?"

"Oh, no. Not at all. It was a dreadful mistake. We should still be singing, "God save the King!"

I smiled. I was not looking forward to that reunion. We were now entering the village with its white picket fences, plain church, and neat, simple houses. A knot formed in my gut.

"There's one thing I must tell you, Johnny."

"Yes?" My father, then my mother, had called me Jeannot. The family called me Johnny.

"Before this last seizure, Abigail—your mother—asked Alice, and me too, many times...that if she were somehow not able to ask you herself...we would beg you not to leave her until she died. She was terribly eager to see you. And that dread seemed to be constantly on her mind. That you would come, stay a little while, then go before...."

"I won't," I said, after a moment. "No, no, I'll stay...till it's over."

The visits to my mother's bedside were at first, while distressing, not as painful as I had anticipated. The painful part was to sense her anguish, as she lay trapped in a body unresponsive to her intelligent mind, waiting. She was not suffering physically. She lay in bed, her head upon a pillow, pale and helpless. Her long hair was brown for the last six inches to the tips. But above that it had grown in white, making for a disturbing effect. Only her large brown eyes, with dark half-moons beneath, remained expressive. Upon seeing me at first on my arrival, they appeared positively to glow. When I leaned to kiss her, she gripped my hand, using her good hand, with surprising strength, as if she had been drowning and believed I might hold her up. But of course I could not.

Every day I sat by her bed and held her hand and talked to her, told her about my life on the frontier, told her about Monsieur de St. Maurice, and Hélène-Eulalie and Madamoiselle Bijou, about Arsène and Antoine Lefort. Over the months I told her about the Comanches, my friends, The Flute and Big-Mountain—even about Sehêbi, although without reference to sexuality, always a delicate subject with her, as well as with all the family but my father. Her eyes told me she understood what I said, and she always wanted more. She was particularly interested in Arsène, and I told her everything about him I could think of, while softening the bloodier details. I told her about César and my mare, Manon, and the Comanche ponies and wolfdogs and Diablo, the tomcat. But inevitably and soon I ran out of stories and her eyes would ask me to repeat, and I would repeat endlessly. But finally I would sit in silence, and she would doze. But whenever, after a period of time, I attempted to disengage my hand, her eyes would open, startled, and gaze into mine. Breaking away became more difficult each time. She would not willingly release me. That spirit, so strong and rebellious in her youth had become as frail as her body waiting to die. Then my dear aunt would as gently as possible remove her sister's fingers from my hand, while my mother would gaze into my eyes beseechingly, begging me with hers not to go. But I would go.

Many times I would leave the room for the kitchen, sit and slump in a chair at the table with my head in my hands. Aunt Alice would come in later and occasionally lay her palm gently on my shoulder.

"Poor Johnny."

"Poor mother," I would reply, with a shrug.

In my melancholy and boredom I began to drink. I had drunk only sparingly of spirits at Natchitoches Post, and then mostly wine with my meals. In my exile, as I thought of my visit, I drank more, not to the point of becoming overtly intoxicated but enough so that I frequently woke in the morning with a headache. Still, word passed around, and I received my share of disapproving glances. The people of the village were good, God-fearing folk but also priggish and captious, intolerant of anyone whose behavior differed from their own. That I never attended church and that I often drank a glass at the bar of our little hostelry, even in daylight, shocked them, convincing them I was a soul bound for perdition, if not already lost. One well-intentioned little female who had known my mother slightly stopped me on the street one day to ask about her, then clicking her tongue informed me that she was praying for her and—with a knowing look—for me too. I thanked her politely but walked away cursing under my breath.

Sometimes I moped about the farm, which was under the care of old Samuel, indentured worker and a silent, bitter man. From Scotland, he had once been a farmer, then a pauper. I went principally to the stable, with its musty odor and dusty tack, now housing but a single animal, and mused upon the horses once maintained there, two of which I remembered riding bareback when they were colts. That was of course long ago when I was growing up a country lad. But I soon found the visits increased my melancholy. Languid and listless, I left off.

Besides taking long walks into the countryside, even in windy, frigid weather, I read a great deal in my mother's library, especially the English poets, Milton, Thompson, Grey, Goldsmith, Dryden and Pope. Eager for news and reminders of what I regarded as my home, I scribbled many letters, at first only to Monsieur de St. Maurice. But since I received only a few replies—which though affectionate were scant—I ventured after some months had passed to write to Hélène-Eulalie. The summer slipped away, and I heard nothing. Gloomy and disappointed, I reasoned that Her Grace had thought it beneath her dignity to correspond with a simple frontiersman such as I. But I was a little surprised, as well as delighted, to receive that autumn a thick envelope addressed to me in her handwriting. I paused before opening it, fearing its contents would inform me of that lady's marriage to Lieutenant Governor Gaston Le Noir, a widower and aristocrat of her own class. It did not.

I should mention here, with some embarrassment, that at one time I had been jealous of Le Noir. Even while aware I had no chance with the lady—that she was far above my station in life. Yet I considered him unworthy of her. He treated all he considered beneath him like servants. There was also something about his big dark eyes and little mustache and about his ingratiating manners and playful attentions to Hélene-Eulalie, and about her gaily artificial response, that of a lady of the court, when he addressed her, that had annoyed me extremely. Then even when she hinted she might wish to approach me more familiarly, I had responded in a perversely cool and impersonal manner. But one day entering the door of the colonel's house, I had met Le Noir leaving. His face was pink and he stared at me furiously, muttering, "Toutes les femmes sont des garces—toutes, toutes!" Brushing against me rudely, he charged from the building. I must admit I was pleased. After that I was scarcely jealous of him.

Hélène-Eulalie's first letters to me avoided anything of a personal nature. But they were filled with news, even of my Indian friends, precisely what I had been longing for. Antoine had returned that fall from his trading trip with information concerning the Comanches. She passed it on to me. In the back of my mind there had been, since before my departure, a nagging question concerning Sehêbi and her supposed pregnancy. That is I was hoping it was only "supposed." Furthermore I could not stop myself from wondering how she and Arsène would respond to sleeping, along with Taoinan of course, in the same tepee. Examining my anxiety, I had found myself to be at once concerned and jealous—not so much worried about what Arsène might do but about what Sehêbi might risk, and the inevitable following complications. But from Lefort, through Hélène-Eulalie, I learned that Sehêbi had miscarried and had lost the fetus on her return trip to rejoin the People, perhaps from the long journey on horseback. It was a common enough occurrence among the women of these horse Indians. So she had been pregnant—perhaps with my child? In addition I learned that she evidently did not like Arsène, who—I had more than once noticed—paid little attention to her. Evidently she had asked Taoinan to remove the youth from the lodge as soon as First-Frost and She-Scolds-Her-Dogs had completed sewing hides together for his tepee. As a result he had been able to move into it for winter camp.

But with the coming of spring, Arsène had spent little time in his lodge. By the time the tassels were hanging from the boughs of the cotton trees, by Lefort's account he had ridden south at the head of a party of young men, returning a moon later with a herd of fine horses stolen from Mescalero Apaches. Not only had his coup been celebrated in his own camp but it had evidently been talked of enviously within other bands of the Kotsoteka division of the tribe.

Shortly afterward, as Antoine reported, Arsène had been offered a rare though perilous honor. Three older warriors had invited him to join their society, a society which forbade retreat before the enemy no matter what the odds, unless the leader should order it. These men were called, "Wolves," and were distinguished by the wolfskin "tails" they wore. They had no wives or families and devoted themselves entirely to war, spending much time on the warpath, exacting vengeance for Comanche dead, raiding for horses, or attempting to take enemy scalps. During the intervals when they rested in camp, they were treated with marked respect. They were permitted to be arrogant and were admired by all, but if any member of this society should run from an enemy without a command from his leader, he would be dishonored and despised by everyone. The society had only three members within this band. There had been five, but two had recently been killed in skirmishes with enemies. Evidently, according to Lefort, the three remaining men had decided they needed to recruit outstanding young warriors. They had chosen to invite Arsène.

Impressed by the honor, Arsène had nevertheless requested a few days in which to consider their invitation. They had granted him this, knowing the price that membership exacted. He had smoked and consulted with Taoinan and with Toyamancare, and had even asked for advice from Antoine, who had been in camp, along with his traders, packhorses, and bales of goods. All three men had advised against his joining. Not only would he be in danger of an early death, he would have no real life, with the greater part of his time spent upon the warpath. Furthermore, they had told him that those three "wolves," while indisputably brave, were also crazy, a little like the actual wolves that from time to time would run through a camp bubbling spittle at the jaws and fatally biting any animal or person unlucky enough to be in their paths. But of course, as Hélène-Eulalie wrote, for anyone with Arsène's temperament and ambition, such an offer had been irresistible. In spite of all advice, he had accepted it. Even before the traders' departure from the Comanche village, Lefort had found that the now four "wolves" had vanished from camp. Where they had gone no one knew.

There was not much other news. She wrote that the colonel was generally well, although somewhat forgetful, not surprising for a man of seventy-five years. Antoine on his return had been innvolved in an escapade with a militia corporal's wife and had quickly departed again on a hunting expedition with several of his Canadian friends. She mentioned that she had surrendered to Mlle. Bijou most of the decisions affecting the household, which the black woman was managing with as much willful energy as ever. With some of her free time Hélène-Eulalie was exercising my mare, as I had invited her to do. Reading her letter, I was pleased by her enthusiasm over my Manon, a gentle though spirited animal, which I had neglected for some time. She had taken, she informed me, to riding for several hours every morning when weather permitted and had come greatly to enjoy her outings, for which she expressed gratitude. She ended her letter formally, signing it with her full name, Hélène-Eulalie Marguerite de Fleury.

The letter became precious to me. In my dismal state of mal du pays, I reread it many times. I had to admit to myself that it was also valuable to me because of its source, and I recall sniffing its vague roseate perfume and thinking of its author with new feeling. I remember trying to picture her face, along with that of Sehêbi, in my loneliness. I drew upon the letter's contents not only when seated daily at my mother's bedside but also during the periodic, mostly onerous visits I paid to my grandparents in Boston.

These visits began soon after my arrival and continued at monthly intervals throughout my stay, except during periods of severe weather or during the time I was ill. The invitations usually came a week in advance and were generally for a Sunday dinner after they had returned from church. My aunt Alice would of course remain with my mother, who would reluctantly release me, her eyes clinging until I had passed through the door.

I would borrow the gig and old white gelding and trot into the city, navigate the narrow streets, and clip-clop up the alley to their handsome house, which along with others commanded a view of rooftops, chimneys, treetops, and the harbor with its many ships, boats, docks, drays, and constant activity. I had expected the first visit to be a strain, as it was, but I had found my grandparents to be both amiable and kind. My mother had told me bitterly after the death of my father that the family had disapproved of him even before the war, as they had disapproved of anything French or Roman Catholic. They had evidently believed him to be an adventurer and, although he had been an (enemy) officer in the French and Indian War, not possessing a social status sufficient for marriage to their daughter. This from their perspective was probably true, since my paternal grandfather had been a simple solicitor (that is, a notaire) and my father's mother, though reputedly a handsome woman, a village barber's daughter. I had of course expected my grandparents to make an effort to be gracious but had also expected them to take a critical view of me as the son of "that Frenchman," who had also been a Patriot and a Captain with General Lafayette. But my expectations proved false. They welcomed me like a true grandson and a long-missing and missed member of their family.

"My goodness," exclaimed my grandmother, pressing both my hands while gazing into my eyes and inspecting my features. "You've inherited your father's good looks. He was a handsome man."

"And a fine officer too, we understand," added my grandfather. "Although on the... um...other side. But all that's over, in the past, thank God."

"I see something of Abigail. In the eyes. Don't you?"

"Yes. You resemble your mother too. She was a fine looking girl and bright, so bright. Even as a little girl, you couldn't pull her out of a book. Remember, Sarah? A reader. And thinker. She'd have made a fine lawyer if she'd been a man."

"And how is she today?"

"The same, I'm afraid."

"It's so sad. So sad. Tell her I'll come by this week. Probably Thursday. Tell her, Thursday."

"But please come in and sit down," said my grandfather. "We shall be eating quite soon. Will you join us in a glass of sherry?"

Although my grandparents, Jonathon and Sarah Rutherford, were Protestants of a moderately strict sect, they regarded total abstinence as fanatical and favored an occasional glass of sherry before a meal or a glass of porto afterward. During my first visit conversation both before and during the meal was constrained by the limited number of topics we were able to discuss. We could not very well discuss the late war and American Independence. We could hardly talk about President Washington or members of Congress, both of whom they loathed, nor really about my father or any other Patriot. Although the war was long over, their disappointment, as well as the contumely they had evidently suffered from victorious Patriots, appeared still to sting. On this line Grandfather Jonathan did venture to cite Daniel Shays' 1786 rebellion in his own Massachusetts and the Whiskey Insurrection in Pennsylvania, only the year before. These were ominous evidence that our so-called "United" States were sure to fall apart and fail on account of the unruly populace contained by each, in addition to the distrust and bickering among them. He predicted that all of them would end by imploring the king to take them back.

"You see, Johnny, it's a question of some degree of discipline and subordination. Without these, a people becomes a mob. And you have mob rule. Which is what we have already experienced, and what I very much fear we have still—or will have soon."

"I see." I was determined to be patient and not to permit myself to be provoked.

Apparently sensing my uneasiness, my grandmother changed the subject to relatives and began speaking of family members near and far, including many I had never heard of, not to mention a confusing rollcall of spouses' and childrens' names which I immediately forgot upon hearing. My three uncles, nevertheless, I remembered and hoped to see. She promised she would invite them when I should next come, although my middle uncle, Peter, was residing and farming with his wife and three daughters in the state of New York and almost certainly would not be able to attend. The other two, Elliott, my favorite, and Lemuel, the eldest, would surely appear, since they both lived in the city and were employed, with responsible positions, by a transatlantic shipping firm. By this time the sherry had commenced its work upon Grandfather Jonathan, and he leaned back in his chair, crossed his legs, sighed, and regarded me with a benign expression:

"Tell us, then, about your life in the woods. You live in an outpost, I understand, by a river, with a fort, far from the city of New Orleans, and trade with the savages. Am I right?"

I assured him he was.

"But you're near the river they call, Mississippi?" asked grandmother.

"We are."

"It must be a Godforsaken dangerous place to live. Though I perceive you've kept your hair," said my grandfather with a smile. "Pray tell me, Johnny, don't you find life there a bit primitive? Not much amenity, I should think. Don't you long at times for…some of this?" He flung out his hands to take in the polished furniture, the gilded mirrors, the shelves of books, a painting of an armed brig, her sails full, over the hearth, with its red coals and flickering logs, the big, shiny windows with their view of the harbor.

I smiled. "But we have that, sir."

"What? Did you say you had…this? Out there? In the wild?"

"Come, Johnny," said Grandmother Sarah. "Surely you exaggerate."

"No," I smiled. "We do. And more."

"What?"

"More snakes and mosquitoes." I too was feeling the sherry on an empty stomach. After a moment, my grandmother smiled and grandfather followed suit. "No, let me tell you." With that and the aid of the sherry I began explaining how we lived at Natchitoches Post, about Monsieur de St. Maurice and his home with its library and many rooms, about how he had been an officer in the army of France and had become, after the Treaty of Paris, a Spanish lieutenant colonel, and finally colonel, and had served as Lieutenant Governor of Natchitoches district for the Spanish governor in New Orleans. I described his learning, his command of many languages. I said that all of the Indians of the region trusted and respected him and that he had been able to bring the hostile prairie Indians to friendly terms with the Spaniards of New Spain. I told about his being a nobleman whose niece had been for a short time, before the revolution, a dame d'honneur to a duchess at the French court—all of which, I must confess, impressed me. But I quickly observed that my enthusiasm was not shared. A shadow had crossed my grandfather's face when I had said "army of France," and I realized that to my grandparents those I mentioned were neither British nor even American. They were "foreigners," almost surely immoral, and consequently neither to be trusted nor to be considered as objects worthy of interest. Jonathan and Sarah were not impressed. Still I persisted, and when I told them of Arsène, of his having become a Comanche warrior, their eyes brightened and they straightened in their chairs.

"But you mean to tell me this unfortunate boy, this poor young man," said my grandmother, "after returning to his father…"

"Of whom he was evidently quite fond," interrupted Jonathan.

"Went back with his savage friends intending to become an Indian for the remainder of his life?"

"Yes. I believe that's his intention."

"How dreadful! Poor young man."

"I've heard previously of that happening," mused my grandfather, "among children stolen and raised by Indians on our frontiers. When rescued, they always want to go back to the Indians. Curious, isn't it?"

"Have you ever heard of the opposite?" I asked, intrigued. "Young Indians raised by whites wishing to remain with them?"

"Oh, they always run away," declared my grandmother.

"Never," said my grandfather. "Never heard of it. I confess it has always puzzled me. Do you understand it, Johnny?"

"No," said I, although I did have some half-formed thoughts on this subject. I was spared from attempting to express them by the entrance of a big young white woman in what I took to be a maid's uniform and by her announcement that the meal was served. We rose. My grandmother, a thin, sallow woman wearing her hair in a bun and dressed in a long gold-and-green gown, offered her elbow. I took her arm and escorted her into the dining room, while my grandfather, pink and spindly, his wig slightly askew, tottered energetically behind.

During the meal they continued to question me about Arsène. In the end I obliged them by recounting in detail his life as my pupil, his loss in the blizzard, his rediscovery seven years later at the Comanche encampment upon Rio Pecos. I told them even of his part in the battle with Apaches, of his struggle with an older warrior, his close victory, and of the scalp and war honor he had obtained by it. My grandparents were shocked, but I could not help believing that underneath their remonstrances of horror and disgust they were entertained and titillated. Plainly they were fascinated.

In any event the visit turned out not to be the ordeal I had anticipated. Still when I emerged from their house into weak afternoon light and sea air and took the bridle of the old horse, I felt liberated. The atmosphere had been oppressive. My grandparents, I had found, were good people, although they had to my mind deplorable ideas and beliefs. They had been kind to me (which did not mean, however, that they would have been kind to everyone). They were good people, but their views were at once so narrow and proper and held with such conviction that when I was in their presence I always feared some lapse on my part would give me away and scandalize them. To me the decorous atmosphere of their home was suffocating. It was of no importance to me that they were shocked by Arsène. I did not wish to shock them myself, so that I always felt as if I were an intruder tiptoeing in disguise among them.

In the city I left the old horse and gig at a livery stable while I walked about town accomplishing a few errands. The New England climate being more severe than that of La Louisiane, I purchased a greatcoat of a bulk and weight sufficient to keep me warm despite wind, fog, or snow. To complete the insulation I was seeking, I also bought a round hat with high crown and a brim I could pull down. Both were of a sober and inconspicuous color. Dressed in this manner, I was able to walk the streets by day or night, not only secure from intemperate weather but unrecognizable by any family member or acquaintance who might happen to be driving or strolling in the vicinity. Finally because I knew that many Frenchmen had fled their Revolution for American cities, I sought and found a back street shop belonging to one of my father's compatriots. Along with the volumes of French books, this congenial man sold those devices known as capotes anglaises, or préservatifs, for the protection from diseases like the pox associated with venery. But after having equipped myself in this manner, I found that I had spent nearly all of my money. Indeed I lacked for money. I had needed little on the frontier, but now, what with purchasing a few drinks daily, I found myself constantly out of funds, and Aunt Alice could spare little from my mother's savings. Consequently mildly frustrated I returned to the livery stable, paid, and drove the old horse back to the village.

On subsequent visits to my grandparents, they would always ask me, during the course of our chats and sherry, whether I had heard anything from Natchitoches Post and, especially, whether I had heard anything more concerning Arsène. For months I was obliged to disappoint them. But after receiving the letter from Hélène-Eulalie, I was able to gratify their curiosity somewhat more. Although autumn had come, I remember the weather had turned fine, warm without wind. My grandmother decided to entertain family members in her sheltered garden behind the house, where roses still bloomed. On this occasion two of my uncles and my younger uncle's wife shared my news as we sat around a white table with pink tablecloth and at its center extra glasses and bottles of sherry and burgundy.

Seated at a little distance before a rosebush was my little cousin, Abigail, named for my mother. She was a lovely child of twelve years with my mother's eyes, daughter of my Uncle Elliott and his wife. Although she sat demurely with her feet crossed, playing with an doll which might once have been Aunt Alice's or my mother's, there was the look about her of a wild creature, one who might suddenly startle and slip into the shrubbery.

As best I can recall that day my Uncle Lemuel had been talking about Napoleon Bonaparte and the startling success of his Italian Campaign. Seated in full sunlight, swollen and, like his father, of ruddy complexion, he predicted that while this supposed military genius was able to achieve remarkable victories over Italian and Austrian troops, it would be a different matter when, as was inevitable, he should someday confront a British general in command of a British army. Then the world would see how brilliant he was! Or wasn't. He struck the table with a flat hand, causing glasses to clink, bottles to wobble, sat back and sipped his burgundy.

My Uncle Elliott and I exchanged looks. His wife, Priscilla, smiled an amused smile at me.

"Quite right," said Grandfather Jonathan. "We shall see then." But he was obviously bored with the subject, as was my grandmother. "Tell us, my boy," he continued, turning to me. "Anything new about your former pupil who's become an Indian? Has Sarah told you about him?" he asked the others. "Really an extraordinary story."

"Yes, tell them, Johnny," said my grandmother.

I was compelled to repeat what I had told my grandparents. I found Lemuel, Elliott, and Priscilla as interested as they had been, and as full of questions, which I answered as best I could, able only to speculate of course on Arsène's motives. Then responding to their desire to hear more, I described to them his coup against the Mescaleros, how he had sung and made medicine and dreamed, as he told Lefort, a "big dream" of horses held by Lipan Apaches at a camp south of San Antonio de Béxar. Early last spring, starting from the principal fork of the Rio de Los Brazos de Dios, he had led a party of young men to the west and south of the población, to steal that herd from the Apache enemy.

"But wait, wait," interrupted Lemuel. "Apaches...Brazos de something. San Antonio—I suppose that's some saint. But what does it all mean? Where are these places?"

Neither he nor the others knew anything of the Indians or the geography of the southern prairie or of the Spanish Provincia de Tejas, so that I was compelled to explain. I began by reminding them that in 1762, a year before the end of what they called the French and Indian War, France had transfered the Isle of Orléans and La Louisiane west of the Mississippi to Spain, to prevent the colony from falling to the English through the treaty they foresaw they would of necessity soon make with them. The western boundary of La Louisiane formed the eastern boundary of La Tejas. But actually apart from a few small settlements and the capital at San Antonio de Béxar the grand prairie was what the Spaniards called, 'un despoplado,' an unoccupied area. Nevertheless it was occupied by Indians they named, 'the Nations of the North,' namely the Tonkawas, the several Wichitan peoples, of which the Pawnee-Piquées, or Taovayases, were one, and the nomadic Comanches.

My remarks were followed by baffled looks and a long silence.

"Do you mean to tell me," demanded Grandmother Sarah, "that this young man set out upon a horseback trip of a hundred miles or more simply because of a dream?"

"And that he persuaded other men to follow him?" asked Priscilla. "That's the amazing part to me."

"It's their custom. They believe in dreams."

"Extraordinary," said my grandfather.

"Power of superstition," remarked Lemuel knowingly.

"Well, did he find the horses?" asked Elliott, with a smile.

I had to laugh. "Actually he found horses, but not the ones he dreamed about." I explained how, on the way, south of Béxar near the Rio Bravo del Norte, he and his party had happened upon a camp of Mescaleros with a herd evidently stolen from the haciendas of Coahuila. These Apaches were reeling about, celebrating with a fermented cactus beverage of their own concoction. Having escaped detection, the Comanche party had altered its plan. Creeping into the camp at night, Arsène and several of his companions had cut the tethers of the best horses and led them away. This accomplished, the remainder of the party had swooped through the sleeping camp and its nearby horseherd, stampeding all of the horses and leaving these other Apaches afoot and unable to pursue them. Arsène and his warriors had succeeded in driving the herd back to the People's encampment on the Brazos.

"I suppose your young man was a great hero after this...theft," said Lemuel. "But of course, they were at war."

"Oh yes. There were dances in his honor. But the best part was that he was reconciled with his Comanche 'father.'" I explained the rift between Arsène and Big-Mountain.

"Reconciled, how?" asked my grandfather.

"Well, Big-Mountain was so proud of his adopted son he honored him. As I understand from the letter, he sent a little boy with a beautiful pinto mare and her colt to Arsène's lodge. Arsène, after hesitating, as he told Lefort, evidently went to Big-Mountain's lodge and accepted the gift. According to Lefort, the two ended by embracing. Hélène-Eulalie, the colonel's niece, wrote that Big-Mountain had also insisted that his "son" ride the big horse, César, whenever he wished, as long as the warchief had no plans to ride him himself. So it seems that Arsène forgave his Comanche "father," and the two ended on their old affectionate terms."

"Fascinating," said my grandfather. "Strange customs."

"Yes, isn't it though," said Sarah.

"Was Arsène able to keep all the horses?" Priscilla asked.

"He could have. He gave most of them away to his companions. That's what a good war leader does."

"Well, Johnny," said Elliott. "You have quite a life out there. I almost envy you."

"Extremely risky, I should think," Lemuel said. He was squinting, holding his glass to the light. The sun formed a red blotch on his forehead.

"Fascinating, though," said my grandfather. "Really quite fascinating."

"I should say so," added grandmother Sarah.

"I love hearing about it," said Priscilla. "Tell us more."

"You really should write it all down," added my grandfather.

"Maybe I will someday," I remember saying.

All at once there came through the open door of the living room ragged notes, a melody from the pianoforte. I started as if shot.

"Only Abigail practicing," said Priscilla to me, smiling.

But that was not it, not merely the sudden sound of the piano. The child, whom I had not noticed vanish, was playing, although haltingly and mechanically, one of the familiar scores that Hélène-Eulalie played flawlessly. I was seized by such an abrupt nostalgia that I was compelled for an instant to bow my head over my glass as I nodded, in order to conceal my features.

After dinner, when I had said my good-bys, my grandfather showed me to the door. But as I was about to leave, he placed his hand upon my shoulder.

"Johnny, hate to see you looking dejected. I know it's hard. Here, my boy, take this." He pushed money into my hand. "Buy yourself something, amuse yourself. There now, goodbye—see you soon, love to your mother." I departed in the melancholy mood which had come to seize me with increasing frequency. Talking of what had already come to seem "my former life" had brought the Post and the prairie and my friends at each vividly to mind. My poor mother was clinging to life, neither worse nor better than when I had arrived almost a year before. I could not leave her while she lived. I could only attempt to comfort her, which I had been trying to do daily. The pianoforte with its familiar melody had taken me by surprise. Trapped in melancholy, I felt like an animal struggling in a snare. Angrily I drove the old horse to the livery stable and left him with intructions to the hostler to give him a nosebag of oats.

Meanwhile fog had drifted in on a breeze from the bay. Wearing my greatcoat, with hat pulled down, I made for a pub with which I was familiar. I inspected the contents of my pocket. My grandfather had given me twenty dollars—a generous sum. How could I not be grateful? Yes, I would raise my spirits. After a glass of whiskey neat, I returned to a lighted avenue. Soon I began to encounter pairs of the young and pretty whores who emerged at this hour and walked rapidly arm in arm down the sidewalks seeking customers. Before long I accosted two as we met under a streetlamp. These two, simple, friendly girls, fresh-faced and fashionably clothed, claimed that they were petty dressmakers. I accompanied them to their home. There for a fee of a few dollars I dallied with them for a time. Afterward, a little guiltily and with a smile, I wondered whether the family would have been pleased had they known how I had entertained myself. Indeed entertained and cheered, I strolled back to the stable and drove the old gelding from the city down the dark road to the village.

Thus I spent my days, weeks, and months through an interminable gloomy winter. Mostly I read by the stove, this time in my mother's set of Shakespeare's works, *Hamlet*, of course, and especially the historical plays. Henry IV, I and II, in particular, were able to summon a smile. I found myself in sympathy with Prince Hal. I went for long walks, sat by my mother's bed, holding her hand, or conversed in the kitchen with Aunt Alice. Occasionally I would, upon receipt of an invitation, visit my grandparents or my uncle Elliott and his wife and daughters. Sometimes my grandparents or an uncle would visit my mother. Mostly though upon my periodic visits to Boston, I would drink a few whiskies, wander the streets alone until I encountered a fetching pair of sporting girls, with whom I would beguile myself for a time, then come home. But finally even these pursuits ceased to satisfy me, and I sat or lay idly in my mother's house more and more, until Aunt Alice began to observe me sharply and tell me she was worried about my health.

My mother died that spring, the first of May. Another violent seizure killed her. She died, I am glad to write, suddenly and mercifully. Pray, my children, for a good quick death. At first I felt sorrow mingled with relief. Her lying endlessly, it had seemed, in a helpless state had been so painful to me it had worn me down more than I had realized. After the funeral, strangely, the relief disappeared and I was left with something close to despair for no reason I could tell. I went to Boston nevertheless and bought a ticket on a merchant vessal supposed to depart for New Orleans on a date near the end of July.

But then a catarrh went into my chest, worsening rapidly. I began to cough sputum streaked with blood. My cough was accompanied by sharp chest pains. I told myself it was nothing and shrugged it off. I really did not care. But my aunt, alarmed, was watching me. When I developed a fever, she forced me into bed upstairs, ironically the very bed in which my mother had died. It was the onset of pneumonia. I very nearly succumbed. For days I lay, as it were, upon a fulcrum between life and death. It was Aunt Alice who stayed and nursed me through, as she had nursed my mother.

As I lay there one night in the dark, it occurred to me that I might actually be dying, and though I was afraid, I didn't care. Then at that moment, I heard my father's voice. I felt his hand rest on my shoulder as he said, "Ne te rend pas, mon fils! Tu peut vivre. Fait-toi un grand effort—tu vivras longtemps!" I seemed to reach up for that hand and grasped only air. Doubtless it was all a dream or product of the fever. But I slept restfully for the remainder of the night and well into the following morning. That day my aunt found the fever broken, my health slightly improved. Of course I recovered, though I required weeks to convalesce. To regain my strength took longer. I missed my ship in July. It was not until after Christmas that I was fit to travel.

During the months of my recovery I was languid, procrastinating even on the necessity of buying a new return ticket. There had been a letter from Hélène-Eulalie expressing concern about the cessation of my correspondence. It contained no recent news of my Indian friends, only the fact that Antoine, on his summer trading expedition, had found Arsène and the other "wolves" absent from camp. They had been away for weeks and not even Toyamancare had known where they were. After showing the letter to Aunt Alice, who like other family members was interested in Arsène and the frontier, I let it lie upon the kitchen table and forgot about it, too indifferent to reply. But without my knowledge my aunt replied for me, in English of course, describing the principal events since I had last written, to wit my mother's death and my protracted illness and convalescence. To my surprise, late that fall or early in the winter I received a letter from Hélène-Eulalie, shorter and more personal than any she had written before: together with the local news, she informed me that Monsieur de St. Maurice was more and more distrait, or absent-minded, and there were complications to do with the trading post. But the words that struck me were, "J'ai vraiment besoin de vous ici, Jean-Pierre." That and the faint scent of her perfume. It was not "we" but "I." She needed me there. That, with what I interpreted as a sympathetic, solicitous, and very nearly affectionate tone startled and stirred me profoundly.

It set me to soul-searching. If I was so affected by Hélène Eulalie's letter, why had I not tried to draw closer to her at the Post? Looking back, I seemed to recall her making a few subtle overtures, from which I had fled. In the end I realized it was pride. So conscious of her social status, and of my lack of any, I'd been fearful of her condescending to me. Which she had never done. For that reason I had always kept a distance between us. Because of my pride. Here, at a secure distance, I resolved to change my behavior when I returned.

The following morning, weak as I was, I harnessed the old gelding and drove the gig to Boston and the harbor, where I purchased a ticket upon the first vessel expected to depart for New Orleans. Since not many ships put out of Boston that year for La Louisiane, I was obliged to wait for an indefinite period, while the departure of the Mary Ann was postponed again and again, owing to difficulties concerning her cargo. But from that day at the docks my recovery was swift, my strength returning rapidly. Each day, each week, waiting, found me increasingly impatient and eager to board the Mary Ann for La Louisiane, Nouvelle-Orléans, Natchitoches Post, the frontier, and the veritable life I craved once more.

When I finally did stride up the gangplank, it was with no regrets. I had bid my farewellls. I had legally transferred the farm with the house and its contents to my Aunt Alice. Besides the little baggage I had brought with me from the frontier, I carried back only the pittance that remained of my inheritance, as well as a miniature portrait of my mother and my father's sword, to remind me of that northern seaboard and all I willingly left behind.

It was late May before I arrived at Natchitoches Post, after the ocean voyage and another of about a month upriver from Nouvelle-Orléans. With joy I looked ashore from a large pirogue charged with merchandise for the village. The morning was sunny, warm, with clouds exchanging shadows on the piney hills.

At the landing the first person I saw was a stranger to me, a long-haired and bearded trapper, who evidently intended to make the return trip to Nouvelle Orléans upon our pirogue. I was so intrigued by this person's appearance that I briefly stared. Everything about him suggested boldness, his bearing, his expression, his penetrating gaze as he looked about him out of sharply defined, deeply tanned features. I had the impression of a supremely confident man whose will was habitually exercised upon all those around him. Catching his eye, I quickly looked ashore, while he seemed, I thought, to consider how he might best make use of me. Leaving the boat with my bags, I was pleased to know that he and I were headed in opposite directions, and that I would probably never see him again. Yet the features of this individual, called 'Gustave' by a companion, remained, as it turned out, unpleasantly wedged into my memory.

The grass along the bank was green, insects buzzing, foliage damp and shiny. A fresh smell of moisture. Carrying my bags, I strode up the path toward the colonel's house. Some distance from the diminishing commotion of the port, I paused, breathed and listened. The morning was still except for a few birds, as if the village behind the hill still slept. Not a dog barked. Nothing appeared to have changed, yet the familiar seemed unfamiliar to me in my state of inner excitement, and I felt like some foreigner, a little apprehensive about his reception, first arriving on this river littoral. Monsieur de St. Maurice's sprawling house, with its peaceful veranda and several open windows, appeared deserted.

As I approached I noticed the figures of two women bent over in the potager, or vegetable garden, at the river side of the building. I could hear their quiet voices but could not make out what they were saying. Clearly one of them was Madamoiselle Bijou. And the other? Perhaps a new servant? Or perhaps? But that was not possible. Dropping my bags, I hastened toward them. Madamoiselle saw me first, straightening, with a little shriek:

"Monsieur Jean-Pierre!"

I waved and, with a few bounds, was at the edge of the patch. The second figure turned, rising. Could it be Hélène-Eulalie? Yes. At first I hardly recognized her, wearing, as she was, an old dress a slave might have worn, holding a trowel, her hair tousled, her hands muddy, bare arms smudged.

"Madame, bonjour," I smiled.

"Monsieur...Jean-Pierre, enfin. Soyez le bienvenu." She came to me, composed, smiling, shifted the trowel to her left hand, whisked back her hair from her forehead with her wrist, and extended her right. Noticing the mud, she let it fall, still standing, smiling, immediately before me.

I am not an impulsive man, but I rested my hands on her shoulders and, leaning, kissed her gently, tenderly even, on first one and then the other cheek, a family kiss. She continued to look into my eyes, smiling. I noticed several freckles and droplets of sweat upon her nose. I inhaled the earth, her sweat, and eau de Cologne with that scent of roses. I had a powerful impulse to draw her to me and kiss her fervently upon the lips. But I glanced at Mlle. Bijou watching, smiling too, with tears shining on her cheeks, and I turned away and went to the black woman and took her callused hand, holding it between my own two for some moments, as I looked back at Hélène-Eulalie. Her eyes were shining in her sun-darkened face, which seemed to me more pink than was customary.

"You surprised us. You come just in time. Antoine has been holding the expedition for your arrival. Now we'll leave in a few days, as soon as you're ready."

"We?"

She smiled, eyes sparkling, as if challenged, raising her chin a little. "Yes, of course, 'we.'"

"Well. This is a surprise. So Antoine has an expedition ready to depart?"

"Yes. We were just waiting for you."

"Well. You can't imagine how I've been longing for this."

"To the contrary, I think I can." Her expression became sympathetic.

"Thank you." I turned to Mlle Bijou. "Meanwhile, do we have food in the house? Meals on the boat were poor—and how is Monsieur?"

Monsieur, it seemed, was the same as ever. Unfortunately I had missed Colonel de St. Maurice in Nouvelle-Orléans, not having known of his presence in that city, where he had gone, according to Hélène-Eulalie, to visit his lawyer and his own physician, a man even older than he, and to enjoy a stint of social life with the few old friends, men and women, who remained alive. On entering the house, I paused in the hall to gaze through the open doorway into the colonel's office and library. It was with a pang that I observed the old cat curled in the chair at the escritoire. In the chair, that is, of the man who had become a second father to me and whom I venerated and loved almost as if he were my own. Diablo opened a yellow eye to see who was intruding, then shut it as I continued down the hall.

During the days previous to our departure I thought frequently about the anomalous presence of a white woman upon a prairie expedition. My first impression had been that Hélène-Eulalie knew who she was, that she was complete. Now that she was to join the expedition, I worried. Would she, cette aristocrate, be able to endure the heat and wind, the driving thunder showers with their hail and lightning and no place to shelter? Could she live at times on half-burned, half-raw meat? Would she be able to squat and defecate in the bushes, if there were any, as naturally as a female wolf, or behind a tepee like the Indian women, and clean her noble bottom with grass or leaves if there were any? Could she locate and fetch from her civilized identity an older one that could thrive in the wild? A wild animal self?

We rode away from the post a week later and reached the Pawnee-Piquée villages near the end of June. Throughout the trip our packtrain advanced, day by day, at a deliberate pace, with eleven heavily laden horses, five spares, and five engagés, Canadian friends of Lefort's, in addition to Antoine, Hélène-Eulalie, and me. The journey was pleasant, except for the showers that frequently drenched us within the piney woods during our first days. I led the train, although Antoine had efficiently organized the details before my arrival. While retaining his good-humored outlook, he had aged, with deeper lines sliced into his weathered face, becoming in the process more serious and responsible. Perhaps my absence had been good for him, since he had of necessity taken on more duties for the trading house, for which he was now an indispensable year-round employee. He and Hélène-Eulalie, moreover, seemed to have arrived at an easy relationship in which he no longer stood in quite such awe of her but treated her with the same respect with which she approached him, and without a hint of flirtation.

As for cette dame herself, she managed to astonish me at the moment of our departure. I had expected her to ride sidesaddle upon my mare attired in a simple, stout dress. As I have mentioned, she had been exercising the animal and was accustomed to riding Manon. She of course expected me to ride the mare, but Antoine and I decided it would be more prudent for her to continue with her familiar mount until we reached the villages, or even the Comanche camp, where we would find her a suitable pony among the Indian herds. I chose a big gray gelding from the spare horses. He was easy gaited, strong and calm, and suited me perfectly for the trip, although he would not have been sufficiently swift for the prairie, where, as I have written, one's life may depend upon the speed of his horse.

In any event Hélène-Eulalie astonished me by appearing at the moment of our departure seated astride the mare and dressed in new, fringed buckskin. (This was of course the deerhide called "gamuza" by the Spaniards of the north, gray because smoked for water-resistance.) On her head she wore a soft, plumed red cap of the sort favored by coureurs de bois, from which her blond hair protruded, and around her waist a red-and-blue sash. At my astonished expression Antoine and all of his Canadians began laughing, as did the lady herself. Her little surprise had succeeded and I was as amused as anyone. Her garb, if unconventional, was sensible. We departed in high spirits.

At the Pawnee-Piquée villages we learned that Those-Who-Go-Far-Alone were camped upon a tributary creek about two leagues, or five English miles, west and were expecting us. After the ceremonial greetings and smoke within their largest grass house, the Taovayas chiefs urged us to make camp and trade with them, as we had often done in the past, but we appeased them with a few gifts and a promise to tarry and trade on our return. While taking leave, I asked the head chief whether his village had been troubled by the Osages of late as I was concerned about an encounter with a war party of those formidable men, to whom our little caravan would represent an irresistible prize.

"No, not lately," said the chief with a scowl. "The last time they came, they took horses and killed two women in the fields. They bother us terribly. But I don't think they'll come now. Too many Comanches nearby. You'll have a safe trip from here."

Before our departure Hélène-Eulalie, Antoine, and I rode with one of the leading men to where the horseherd was grazing at some distance beyond the fields of maize, pumpkins, beans, and squash, all of the plants green and undeveloped. Three boys and an older youth were lazily watching the herd of about a hundred head from their sleepy ponies. There was a variety of horses of all ages and sizes but one in particular appealed to the colonel's niece. This animal was a well-built dark, dappled chestnut with long white mane and tail, apparently a gelding or stallion, although from a distance I could not be sure which it was.

"What a beauty that one is!" exclaimed Hélène-Eulalie, asking its price in trade goods.

Antoine translated the question. Our warrior escort smiled. The horse, he informed us, was the prize buffalo and war horse of the head chief. No amount of goods would be sufficient to buy it.

"I didn't think it would be for sale," said Hélène-Eulalie, turning the mare, with a last, lingering look. "Oh well, perhaps in the Comanche herd."

It was late afternoon before we spied in the distance the line of trees which indicated the creek we sought. Near the stream's juncture with the river the summer sky blurred above what we assumed to be the cooking fires of the People. Soon we saw from the crest of a rise the lodges of the band scattered along the glittering creek or pitched among the great shadowy trees. Nearer to view was the horseherd, consisting of well over a thousand head, grazing on the prairie, with the tiny figures of the boys guarding them. Behind in the dispersed village itself, mounted figures, some riding double, trotted back and forth passing what were surely children playing near mothers graining buffalo robes or simply sitting. We heard distant barks, occasional whinnies, shouts, children's cries. Our surmise about the discolored sky proved to be correct: smoke rose from scores of tepees or from fires before them and mingled into a vague and transparent stain above the extended encampment. Beyond the trees along the creek, the praire reached to the horizon, stark, though with the delicate shades of the hour. Halting on the knoll, which offered patches of dry grass for the horses, I dispatched Antoine to the camp with instructions to announce our arrival to Manos-Amarillas.

"If it were only this, merely this moment," said Hélène-Eulalie from beside me, "the trip would be worthwhile." Leaning forward in her saddle, with reins dangling, she gazed at the distant encampment, now in the rich light and long shadows created by a sinking sun. Her buckskins, an even gray at our departure, were now worn and shiny, further darkened by more smoke and by grease. I recalled with a smile how surprised she had been when they had first shrunk a little after a cloudburst. They had then revealed a body slim rather than fragile, so that the engagés and I, and even Lefort, had felt constrained to look away in embarrassment. Elle était élégante. Later she had, like the rest of us, learned to wet and stretch the buckskins back to their original shape. Her red hat, too, had faded and molted its plumes, yet remained dashing.

"You wouldn't rather be in France?" I smiled. "Your father's château?"

She continued to gaze at the scene before us. "That was beautiful too. Growing up."

"And Paris? You don't miss it? You did at first, I think."

"I missed France. My childhood. A place that no longer exists. But Paris, no." She turned to me abruptly, almost angrily. "It was beautiful also, that city drenched in blood. I'll never go back to that...horror."

"There's horror here, too. We haven't seen it. I hope we don't. But it's here."

"I'm sure it is. It can be anywhere. But out here...one feels...liberated."

"Yes?"

"I feel...young again. I love it."

I smiled. "Voltaire says freedom is power. Do you think we have power?"

"Of course we do," she said, glancing back at the packtrain, with its bales of goods and armed engagés.

"I suppose you're right."

"You know, Jean-Pierre, I realize you don't believe it. But we think the same way about many things."

I had either a hundred observations or nothing to say in response. I chose to say nothing. In the camp, little figures were mounting ponies. Some were already loping out toward us. Other figures were stirring among the tepees. For a time we sat in a silence which became increasingly strained, while the engagés chatted and smoked their pipes behind us, and the horses stamped and cropped the yellow grass.

"Antoine was saying how well you've stood the trip. Like an old plainsman. The rain, the wind, dust, bugs..."

"I've loved it. Not the dust or bugs, any more than you. But the rest, yes."

"Well, the colonel can be proud of his niece."

"Thank you. What you're saying is that you—all of you—expected me to be a 'lady of the court'—miserable, finicky, complaining, all of the time making difficulties. A bitch. But I'm not like that. Not at all. You think you know me, Jean-Pierre. You don't know me at all."

I had to admit, with embarrassment, under her steady gray-eyed gaze, that I did not. Then the Indians started forward in a body, galloping out from their camp toward us, and we watched in an uncomfortable silence as they came.

"Look," I said as the horses galloped up the rise with a big sorrel far ahead of the others. "That's old César, with Toyamancare."

"Isn't that Arsène?"

"Yes, it's Arsène."

At our backs a packhorse whinnied. Leading, Toyamancare bellowed, "Hóla, amigos!" as he approached. Behind him other men whooped. Then the warriors, most of them riding bareback and without weapons, were upon us, shaking hands. Arsène, in embracing his cousin, pulled her, laughing, nearly from her saddle. Big-Mountain almost cracked the bones in my hand with his grip. Next Taoinan and I were hugging, our cheeks pressed together in the Indian manner.

"Well, brother, you've come at last. It's been a long time."

"Too long."

I turned to shake the hands of other warriors among the swarm around us, even those of men who were strangers to me. This was for me the joyous reunion I had repeatedly imagined and yearned for during my exile.

We trotted back together, the engagés behind us with the packhorses. Arsène and I had greeted each other with a hug, after which he quickly returned to ride beside his cousin on his frost-faced pinto. While responding to The Flute's questions about our trip, I glanced from time to time at the pair, who were engaged in eager conversation with gestures, apparently exchanging details of their recent lives. Arsène, whose features had been lean before, was now gaunt in face and body, with shadows under his eyes, his nose even more hawklike. What had remained of his boyish appearance was gone. His former fierce expression had abated to one more nearly of hard, unceasing determination. Even so, he was able to smile, as he did when he caught me glancing at him and, as I soon found, able to joke and to laugh. Having lived as a hunting and hunted "wolf" for two years, he had acquired the air of an predatory animal and—at the same time, if this were possible—of a reflective wild animal.

The Flute and Big-Mountain, leading, conducted us through the tepees and between the howling wolfdogs and the confusion of shy children and staring women to the big lodge of Manos-Amarillas. Dismounting, handing up my reins to Antoine, I entered with my Comanche companions. The lighted pipe passed from hand to hand around the circle of leading men, of whom I recognized many. The wrinkled chieftain greeted me with a smile of recognition and a brief ceremonial welcome. He made a speech in his cracked, high voice saying how happy he and his people were to see us, and how happy they would be to trade with us, having accumulated many buffalo robes and other skins. After presenting the old man with several rolls of tobacco, and promising better gifts as soon as we had unpacked the horses and set up our camp, I delivered a similar oration, saying what a great and valiant people the Comanches were and how they were our friends and how we were bringing them good things and how glad we were to see them and to be able to trade with them again. Taoinan's brother by birth, Ybienca, or Red-Woman, also made an elaborate and boring speech which I could scarcely follow, welcoming us, while his two younger brothers, White-Road and El Chamaco, listened impassively.

During this discourse my eyes happened to encounter those of Yellow-Hands.' Although the old man's expression was sober, befitting the ceremonial occasion a flicker in his eyes revealed inner laughter. I had even for an instant an odd sense almost of a clin d'oeil, as if he had winked at me. There were other undercurrents at this council. At another time, I found El Chamaco, whom I had always considered a harmless jester, studying Arsène, as if slyly evaluating him in some manner. Noticing my scrutiny, he quickly looked away, resuming his usual expression of innocent importance. The occurance seemed insignificant but it made me wonder.

At last the old chief formally closed the council. Arsène went off with a wave, and I was free to follow Taoinan to his lodge, making our way on foot past clusters of curious women and girls, alarmed children and suspicious dogs with raised hackles, several of which growled and raised their lips as we drew near. Limping beside me Taoinan shooed them and they backed off.

"Well, brother, how are you? Kills-Far told me you went away and got sick."

"Yes. My mother died. I nearly did too."

"I'm glad you didn't. We'll go to my lodge now and eat. We found a little herd of cows near this place. So we have plenty—fresh meat."

"Good. Does Arsène bring you much?"

"Yes. When he's with us. Brother, I'm glad you came. There's something I've been wanting to ask you for a long time."

"Yes? Certainly."

"No, not now. Later."

Taoinan's lodge, as well as Arsène's and that of his wives, was set up in a grassy plot by the creek near a great shade tree. As we approached, we saw a group of women talking and laughing around Hélène-Eulalie and a figure I took to be Sehêbi. Before the women two little naked boys were toddling after an old white dog, plainly part wolf, which with lowered head and tail and an uneasy look, was slinking from them.

"See. I have two new sons."

"Good. Sehêbi?"

"No. She-Scolds-Her-Dogs and First-Frost. Both."

Shrieks of surprise and laughter broke from the group of women and girls around Sehêbi and Hélène-Eulalie. Sehêbi, I saw, had pushed up the sleeve of the Frenchwoman's buckskin frock and was holding her own brown arm beside the other woman's white forearm. Not glancing at the women, Taoinan stooped to enter his lodge. Sehêbi lowered her arm and quickly looked at me. I smiled at her and at Hélène-Eulalie and ducked into the tepee's dim interior.

Antoine sent one of the engagés, Henri Tournier, with my horse and Hélène-Eulalie's mare to fetch us as the sun was setting through a thin string of bubble-like clouds at the horizon. We rode in the day's waning light along the creek beyond the last lodges to the north. About twenty rods farther we entered our camp, already established by the engagés under the direction of Lefort. The saddle horses and packhorses were hobbled and grazing among the trees along the riverbank. The tents had been pitched on the grass between the stream and several boulders, a natural defensive position which Antoine had caused to be reinforced by bales of goods in a semicircle before the narrow strip of woods which followed the creek on our eastern side, as well as upon the opposite bank. Not that we had any particular reason to fear a surprise attack. To the contrary we were probably now more secure from raiders than at any time, except when within the Pawnee-Piquée village, since we had passed beyond La Grande Forêt onto the prairie. The atmosphere was peaceful, even festive here. Yet traveling as we did with a number of horses and bales of trade goods, we made it a habit always to take precautions against a surprise attack at night, or at dawn, the Indians' favorite time to fall upon an unwary enemy or prey.

Antoine was sitting cross-legged smoking a pipe with several of his friends at a fire in the center of our enclosure. We dismounted, handed our reins to Tournier and went to stand by the fire. We had long since discarded any formality. Each man knew his duties, and each diligently fulfilled them. Those around the fire greeted us casually, and we, in turn, greeted them in the same manner with a, "Bonsoir."

"Tomorrow," I said. "We unpack bales taken from the first four horses. We'll start with presents for the chiefs. Antoine and madame and I will go. You watch the camp. After that, Antoine and I will come back and trade. You others can help with everything, but I want all of you to watch carefully, especially the women, or all sorts of things will walk off. The women are very adept at pilfering. Be polite but don't let them take a thing."

Several men laughed.

"Pardon," said Antoine. "But there's another thing we must do."

"Yes?"

"We must find a horse for madame."

"So you can have your mare back," said Hélène-Eulalie.

"You're right," I said. "I'll talk to Toyamancare. But I'm not in a hurry. I'm not riding much here. Tomorrow we work hard, starting early. Goodnight."

The next morning, after sunrise, Hélène-Eulalie and I, with Antoine also mounted and leading a packhorse, rode back to the old chief's lodge, where perhaps a half-dozen of the band's most influential men were seated in a semi-circle awaiting us. We dismounted. Hélène-Eulalie held the horses and observed while we sat and smoked, each in his turn, with the others. I made a little flattering speech, offering the gifts. Antoine then brought me from the packs articles which I distributed. To Manos-Amarillas I presented a plumed hat trimmed with galloons, as well as a big knife, some vermilion, a roll of tobacco, a little mirror. He appeared to be pleased with the hat, putting it on, taking it off, trying it at different angles while staring into his mirror. I distributed to the other chiefs, elders and leading warriors similar gifts, except for the hat. We had been generous. All seemed to be pleased with their gifts, especially with the knives, which were of good steel. Monsieur de St. Maurice had traditionally been generous, had never tried to cheat the Indians, a reason he was liked and respected by all the tribes with whom we had had commerce over the years.

When the ceremonies had ended, and the warriors had begun dispersing, El Chamaco, the crier, rode off on a white pony, threading between tepees, shouting that we were open for trade, with directions to our camp. I spoke momentarily with Taoinan, inviting him to come and eat with us that evening, then turned to Toyamancare, standing nearby, and inquired if I might meet with him at his lodge later, during the afternoon. He agreed, while regarding me with curiosity.

"I need a fast horse for the colonel's niece."

A sly, avid expression came and vanished. As if recalling that we were friends, he regarded me gravely: "I have no horse for you now. I'll try to think of one."

"Good. I'll see you later."

At our tents a crowd of women, with a few warriors, had already gathered.

We worked constantly for the remainder of the morning and well into the afternoon, Antoine and I concluding the actual barters, while Hélène-Eulalie recorded each transaction in a large book. Her help made the tasks decidedly easier for Lefort and me. Meanwhile the remaining engagés guarded the goods, kept order and carried supplies to us from the bales. We had earlier announced we would not trade for horses on this day, so that we bartered principally for buffalo robes and the hides and skins of deer, elk, and bear, rendering in exchange tomahawks, glass beads, little and big knives, vermilion, tobacco, hawksbells, combs, ells of blue cloth, mirrors, red blankets, and sundry bagatelles, including needles, flints, steels, awls, thread, and so forth. About mid-afternoon I announced to the small group of women who remained, feeling, sniffing and picking over the goods, that we were now closed and would re-open on the following morning. After that we stored the goods, ate our meal, smoked, chatted and relaxed with a true Spanish siesta.

Afterward Hélène-Eulalie, still riding my mare, accompanied me to Toyamancare's lodge, which was pitched near the creek not far from Taoinan's. Arsène, whom I had notified earlier, joined us on the way, riding his pinto. One of Toyamancare's wives saw us coming and scurried into his tepee. Big-Mountain came out as we drew up before the doorway, regarding us soberly. A second wife led up his pony, already saddled. We rode side by side east into the great meadow where the herd grazed. For a moment we sat at the edge of the herd beside a large tree and watched the multitude of animals as they plucked grass or stood lazily, whisking flies, dozing in the afternoon sun. The few mounted boys had no trouble in holding them. Those-Who-Go-Far-Alone had rarely been raided, remote as they usually were. The ponies, long accustomed to each other's company, were inclined to stay together, were even somewhat herdbound.

"I've thought of a horse. He's not pretty, but I know he's fast. I've been watching him. I intended to buy him myself, but you can have him. He'll be a good horse for your woman."

"Is he mean," asked Arsène. "Will he try to kill her?"

"No, he's not mean. He was a wild horse once, as a colt. But he's quiet now. We cut off his balls a long time ago."

"Who does he belong to? And will he sell him?"

"He belongs to 'Cuero-Matado,' Dead-Hide. But Dead-Hide doesn't know how good he is. He doesn't know anything about horses. He rides well, yes. But he just wants fast, pretty horses. He got this horse for his youngest son, and that boy raced him when he was lame. Of course the horse couldn't run fast, and he got worse. So the boy stopped riding him. Dead-Hide got him another horse, a pretty one this time. The boy rides that one always in front of the girls, though it's not fast, and he's forgotten about the other. So has Dead-Hide. I think he'll sell him for a blanket."

"The lameness?"

"That's gone. A long time ago. It was his shoulder. I've watched him playing with other horses. He's quick. He's fast. She'll like him."

"You're sure he doesn't strike? Bite? Throw himself backwards?"

"I'm pretty sure he doesn't. He didn't with the boy."

"Well," I said. "Let's see him."

One of the boys rode into the herd and, after a flurry and whirl of dust among the animals, appeared at a fast trot leading a brown pony by his reata. He drew up before us and the pony swung around, watching our horses.

"Good Lord," exclaimed Hélène-Eulalie. "What happened to him?"

The brown pony, which stood calmly eyeing us, was missing much of its left ear. Along its left jaw and its neck were curved marks where the hair had grown in whiter than the remainder of its coat.

"Toyarohco. Cougar," said Big-Mountain, stepping down off his horse. "When he was little. But he got away." He took the reata from the boy. Moving slowly to the mustang, he ran a hand down its neck, then leaned and blew into its nostril. The pony turned its head and looked at him, showing a little white at the edge of its eye. He pinched the muscle along the left shoulderblade. The pony did not flinch. Briefly he examined its teeth, then ran his hands over its body, even legs, flank and rump. After a little struggle, during which the mustang swung back and forth, he picked up its left front hoof, examined it, let it fall. The animal stood calmly, watching our horses. Toyamancare grunted, signaled to Hélène-Eulalie to dismount. Quickly he transfered the saddle from the mare to the gelding, cinching it loosely. Slipping a tether around the mare's neck, he removed her bridle, slipping the Spanish bit into the pony's mouth, securing the horsehair throat latch. He tugged the cinch tight and gestured to Hélène-Eulalie to come. I took the tether, and she went to him a little tentatively. Handing her the reins, he gestured for her to mount.

"Wait. I'll try him first," Arsène said in French, slipping from his pinto and dropping the reins. Moving quickly to his cousin, he attempted to take the reins of the mustang but she held to them tightly. "Here. Give me the reins. I'll try him for you."

"No."

"Come. Give me the reins. He hasn't been ridden for a long time. He may be wild. He may be crazy. Let me just try him first."

"No. I will try him." A little struggle ensued, with Hélène-Eulalie continuing to cling tightly to the reins. Then they stood staring at each other, Arsène, furious, with his old fierce, proud expression, the woman, standing stiffly, with her most imperious look.

Then something odd took place. Or I should say I think it took place. This curious event occurred so quickly it left me with the dizzying impression that I was seeing things. We were standing by a cotton tree at the edge of the great natural pasture where the horseherd was grazing. As I have written, Arsène believed his medicine drew power from shadows, from shade, so that he would frequently ride below foliage or stand in whatever shade might be available. I had grown accustomed to that. In the present instance he was standing within the edge of the tree's shade.

As he stepped angrily away from the tree, his own shadow seemed to become elastic and stretch from that darkness, bulge, and flow like smoke by his feet. But its form was curious, not at all his shape but a squirming smudge. I saw it for only an instant. But for that moment it resembled splashed ink, a ragged outline changing shapes. The strange idea occurred to me, unaccountably, that it was a shred of his soul struggling. Where I got such a peculiar idea I don't know. I saw the shadow for only seconds and could be sure of nothing at the time, even less afterward. But Arsène, apparently glimpsing my expression, stepped instantly back into the shade, his own expression changing from that of anger to one of anxiety.

"As you wish, Madame," he said at last, bowing, pale. "I hope you ride well, my dear cousin." He released the reins.

Without a word, Hélène-Eulalie led the pony back and forth and in a little circle. While we watched, she mounted from the right, the Indian side, loosened the reins and kicked. The pony pranced forward, gave two or three playful bucks, which she absorbed with the small of her back. It broke into a trot. For several minutes Hélène-Eulalie rode him in circles near us, at the edge of the grazing herd, reining him right and left, turning in either direction. Next without a backward glance, she further loosened the reins, urging him into a lope, and headed him eastward, away from the leveling sun, across the meadow, where at a distance, she began turning him in wider, faster circles, first one way then the other. At the first turn, the mustang nearly left her sitting in the air. But after that she seemed to have become a part of him. Finally, heading him toward the rise we had descended on arrival, she let him run. The three of us, and the boys guarding the herd, exclaimed in surprize at the animal's swiftness.

"Bueno," Toyamancare cried. "Bueno!"

"Fast," exclaimed Arsène. "She can ride too. I didn't know."

"You're right. That's a good pony!" I agreed.

"You see," said Toyamancare, as woman and horse ascended and disappeared over the rise. "He'll make a good horse for her."

Yes. For a mustang drawn out of the herd, he seemed surprisingly mild tempered. Moreover smart and tough. A lucky find, and quite possibly just the right mount for Hélène-Eulalie. As for the aberration of Arsène's shadow, it didn't happen again that trip. I didn't mention it to him, finally wondering whether I had seen what I am still fairly certain I saw.

16

Taoinan and Arsène ate with us that evening. They did not remain long. We were all yawning around the fire, even Hélène-Eulalie, still weary after our trip as well as from the morning's trading. The afternoon barter with Dead-Hide for the one-eared pony had been accomplished, although the warrior had been more nearly aware of his son's horse's value than Toyamancare had estimated. But for a red blanket and a kettle, along with some vermilion, tobacco, and a mirror, the exchange had been consumated. The brown pony was now hobbled and grazing with the other horses in the prairie immediately east of the trees by the creek. Hélène-Eulalie excused herself and went soon to her tent, saying she wished to ride him early in the morning. The Flute left shortly afterward. I walked with him beyond the firelight to a nearby sapling to which he had tethered his buffalo horse.

"You said there was something you'd been wanting to ask me?"

He looked down at me in the near-dark, seemed about to speak, then remained silent for a moment. "Not now, brother. Later. There are plenty of days—before you go." Turning his pony, he rode away into the dark, downstream, leaving me annoyed by his increasingly long silences and a new evasiveness. What did he wish to ask me that he could not declare directly?

I proceeded to my tent and buffalo robe, while Arsène and Antoine continued to smoke and talk by the embers of the fire. The smoke and words mingled with vague thoughts and images as I drifted toward sleep. But part of my mind, stupefied as it was, became aware of those words as Arsène described how once when traveling with his two "wolf" companions up by the Río de Napestle, or Rivière des Ark, he had at night entered a Pawnee camp alone, leaving his companions at the edge. He threw scraps of meat to pacify the dogs. He had crawled into a tepee, where a slice of moon overhead beamed into the smokehole. After boasting of what he would do. To impress the older warriors. Then immediately wishing he had not spoken. He had contemplated a glorious coup: to cut the throat of a warrior and creep away while the man's wife and children slept. He had been very frightened, he said, but believed he could succeed and afterward reach the others and their fast horses. Lefort remarked at how risky a feat that would be. With an embarrassed laugh, Arsène agreed. "But," he continued in a strange tone—"Antoine, I couldn't do it. You know, I could see part of his face, even his throat. It would have been easy. He was an enemy. I heard his wife and children breathing. I was surprised. I hadn't expected that. I couldn't do it."

"What did you do?"

"I grabbed the knife lying by his robe, and crawled out and crept through the village and back to the others."

"And then?"

"I stood tall as I approached them and made a show of wiping the blade with grass. I handed them his knife. They thought I'd made a big coup."

"T'as bien fait, mon gars."

A long silence.

"Yes. That time." He spoke with difficulty. "But once before, when I was first with them. I thought I had to prove myself. You know, I was eager to be one of them. I did something I have on my conscience. I've never told anybody." He lowered his voice.

"Yes?"

"I killed an old woman. I didn't intend to."

"How did that happen?"

"It was early morning. We were on foot scouting a camp of those people we call Pacanabos—Painted Arrows. Crawling next to their horseherd. Suddenly there were three old women squatting before us, digging roots. Their backs were to us. But one of them kept looking up, looking around. If she saw us, it would be dangerous. Our leader signed to kill them. But I knew we didn't have to. We could have crept back the way we came. I tried to protest with signs. But the way he looked at me! I was ashamed."

"So you killed them?"

"I thought of crawling back to my horse. Leaving. But when they got back, they would have told everyone. Called me a woman."

"So you strangled...?"

"Together we sprang forward. I with the other two. We each seized one by the throat. They struggled. Tried to scream. Mine turned her head to look at me. Those eyes! I cut her throat. Well, it was horrible. But I did it. She made very little noise. Bled all over me." He was silent for a time. "Horrible but I did it."

"Parfois," said Antoine, after a long silence. "Il faut tuer."

"She'd been looking around. If she'd raised an alarm, we couldn't have got away in time. But I still have bad dreams."

"You know what they would have done to you."

"Yes. What we would do to them." Silence. "You know, Antoine, I wonder whether I could stand it. I'm afraid I might scream like a baby. I'm not a coward. You know that. I'd be so ashamed...even dying."

"You'll stay with these savages? Why?"

"I've already chosen. I owe my life. It's a good life. It suits me."

"You must never permit an enemy to take you alive."

The subject changed. I was so close to sleep and muddled that the words seemed to have been part of a nightmare. Then suddenly I was shocked completely awake. But finally I drifted off.

It was already warm—un temps lourd—as they say, with a hazy sky, when I left my tent, went into the woods and pissed beneath a tree. I looked into the prairie for the one-eared pony, but it was not among the others. Returning to camp, where the engagés were stretching and yawning and the cook was heating coffee, I went to Hélène-Eulalie's tent and called to her several times, each time more loudly. I drew back the flap and looked inside: her buffalo robe was open and rumpled, her belongings scattered about, but she was not within. I concluded that she had departed on her ride and, since all was quiet and peaceful in our present location, forgot about her for most of the morning.

We opened for trade early that day and worked until the mid-morning heat became oppressive and the Indians left us. Arsène, evidently an excellent hunter, had brought us a supply of jerked buffalo flesh. After eating I saddled my mare and rode in the shade beside the stream into the encampment and to Taoinan's lodge. There in the shelter of one of the great trees lining the banks by the river a cluster of men was watching Toyamancare, Manos-Amarillas, and another whom I later learned was Dead-Hide. The three were seated cross-legged before Toyamancare's lodge, gambling upon a deerskin. Dismounting, I saw that Arsène was one of the spectators. I tied the mare in the shade and joined the onlookers. He turned.

"Where's my cousin?"

I had forgotten about Hélène-Eulalie until Arsène's question reminded me.

"She went for a ride." Evidently satisfied by my reply, he turned back to the game. But as I considered the length of time she had been away from camp, I began feeling uneasy and found myself glancing from time to time past the horseherd toward the eastern and northern horizons. Yet before going to Taoinan's nearby lodge, I watched the game for a moment. The smooth side of a deerskin had been divided into sections by white lines. Each player in turn bounced a pair of short, shaped sticks against a flat rock resting upon the hide. The sections upon which those sticks then fell seemed to determine the number of points to be bestowed upon, or perhaps subtracted from, that player's score. I surmised that the stakes were considerable, possibly including horses, from the concentration shown by each of the three men, each completely absorbed. The game was silent, except for an occasional exclamation. All were sweating in a shade where even camp dogs lay with sagging tongues, panting. From time to time an onlooker would draw in his breath, or one would grunt, or several would smile appreciatively.

Far from comprehending the intricacies of the game, I strolled toward Taoinan's lodge. Behind and west of it on the bank of the creek She-Scolds-Her-Dogs was standing butchering a buck which hung from a bough. Nearby First-Frost was seated tickling the two little naked boys with a switch, causing them to toddle about, giggling and shrieking. Occasionally a horse would whinny from somewhere in the camp and another would respond from the distant herd grazing upon the prairie, or a dog would bark, briefly stimulating others to howl. But then the noise would abate and the camp would relapse into a calm so hushed in late-morning heat that between the children's cries I could hear the creek, while every human being who was able to do so seemed to be relaxing in the shade, half-paralyzed.

Abruptly Sehêbi appeared from behind the lodge with an armload of dry wood and stooped to enter. Sweat shone on her forehead. But noticing me approaching, she laid down the firewood, turned, and came directly to me, addressing me by name and holding out her hand, which I briefly held.

"Ça va?"

"I'm well. And you?"

She replied that she was well, continuing to regard me with curiosity. She had filled out, was slightly wider and heavier, with a fuller figure, no longer a girl but still a pretty young woman with lovely dark eyes. "Where's my friend, your woman?"

I tried to explain that Hélène-Eulalie was not "my woman," that her husband had died and she was presently nobody's woman.

"Oh yes," she said, gazing at me with a frank, open expression. "And will she have your baby, Jean-Pierre?"

"No, I don't think so," I laughed.

"I think she would like to."

"Why do you think that?"

"Oh, I can tell," she said, smiling.

I studied her for a moment. She looked extremely pretty, calm, confident. "And you? Would you like to?"

With a slight frown, she looked at me appraisingly, then smiled again. "Yes, I think that would be nice."

"Taoinan's my good friend."

"I know. He's your brother. Shall I ask him?"

I believe I actually reddened, embarrassed and abruptly flushed with desire.

Smiling, she read my mind. "I'll ask him."

"No, not now."

"I'll ask him soon, before you go."

I remained silent, struggling against a mutinous concupiscence. I wanted her immediately. I wanted to take her hand, lead her downstream and, in the woods, kiss her, remove her dress, lay her down and, without preliminaries, enter her. But that was of course impossible, so I controlled myself and regained my composure, while part of my mind observed my agitation with astonishment, incredulous that the woman whom I really knew so little was able to affect me in this fashion.

She regarded me with, it seemed, amusement. But her gaze shifted to the plain beyond my shoulder. Her expression changed. "Look—isn't that our friend, Hélène?"

I turned. She was right. I recognized the pony, advancing from the north along the fringe of trees at a steady lope. But as Hélène-Eulalie drew near—although I was certain she saw us—she surprised me by riding past, going directly to Arsène, who swung around at her approach. Whatever she next said to her cousin, and which he apparently relayed immediately to the other men, caused turmoil among the group around the gamblers. Some ran off to their lodges, while others stood talking excitedly before they, too, began trotting off in various directions. Even Arsène, leaving his cousin, began running toward his lodge, which was established in a grassy area between the tepees of Toyamancare and Taoinan and their wives. But Sehêbi and I intercepted him. Quickly he explained to us that Hélène-Eulalie while returning from a long ride northward along the creek had been engaged in watering her horse among the trees, when she had seen what she took to be a war party of Indians driving a herd of ponies before them and heading north. Hidden in the shadows, she had watched them ride away, her fingers clutching her pony's nostrils, as I had cautioned her to do when concealed, to prevent him from neighing. But the fact that had excited the Comanche men was her mention of the presence within the herd of a horse she had clearly seen—a dappled dark chestnut with flowing white mane and tail. All the men knew that pony and its owner, head chief among the Pawnee-Piquées, their allies. Their obligation was now to pursue, overtake, and kill the thieves in order to retrieve the herd—which had almost surely been stolen by their mutual enemies, the Osages.

Sehêbi ran to tell Taoinan this news. Changing his mind, Arsène accompanied me as I walked rapidly back toward the tree where I had tethered my mare.

"Will you come with us?"

"Yes, I'll go," I said, to my own surprise. In the past I had made it my policy to avoid involvement in Indian conflicts, but on this day there seemed to be little risk in joining the Comanche pursuit. Besides at that moment, stimulated as I already was, the adventure appealed to me.

"Good. Get your weapons and come back." He ran to where the three gamblers, now deserted, bent over their deerskin, still totally absorbed in their game. "Ahpï, father," he cried, "Can I take César? My horse is with the herd."

"Yes, take him, take him," said Toyamancare, not looking up. "Bring me a scalp. We'll come soon."

At our camp after seizing my powder horn and bullet pouch, I woke Antoine from a nap in the shade. He quickly saddled his horse, seized his rifle and rode with me back to Toyamancare's lodge, where the three gamblers scarcely raised their heads at our arrival. Although the pursuit party had not waited for us, we saw them at a little distance, riding north fast along the trees. Immediately we set out to catch them, riding at a run. Some among the group evidently looked behind, for they slackened their pace, allowing us to overtake them. Once we had joined the war party, we galloped in pairs behind Hélène-Eulalie, whose task of course was to lead us to the spot where she had seen the enemy horsemen. After some twenty minutes she slowed and drew up in a hollow with big trees crowded on either bank of the creek. As I rode to join her and Arsène, she was explaining, pointing to the crest of a small hill east of us.

"Good. We'll find their tracks there," replied Arsène. "Now you go back. You're tired. Your horse is tired."

She stared at him indignantly, clearly not accustomed to taking orders.

But Arsène had already turned to his fellow "wolves." He and his three companions, who had ridden in the forefront resembled other feathered or horned warriors, except for straps like tails hanging from behind them and drooping at the sides of their ponies. Otherwise they were nearly naked, carrying lances, bows, shields, with quivers of arrows slung on their backs. Each had painted his features similarly. Arsène's face was striped black and red, with black predominating. At that moment, while observing him confer with his "pack," I recalled his conversation of the night before—or had it been a dream? But there was little time for reflection, for we set off at once up the hill toward the crest, where the tracks of the stolen herd were visible between shrubs, small cactuses, and clumps of grass. The trail was clear and the "wolves" led us along it, up and down a series of gentle hills, some with vales in between.

From time to time there were brief pauses when the trail became momentarily uncertain, as after clattering for a distance over slabs of rock. At one of these delays, as I scrutinized my companions, I recognized to my amazement, under his warpaint, one of the warriors who had been riding before me as my "brother," The Flute. I was, in fact, incredulous. As a warchief he should have been riding in advance, ahead of the "wolves," who had arrogated the leadership of the party to themselves. I pushed the mare quickly ahead and greeted him, gripping his hand. Although he greeted me in an absent-minded, friendly fashion, he was gloomy, self-absorbed. We started again immediately upon the trail, and I fell back with Antoine. But as we rode along I kept wondering what might have produced the change in my friend, who was beginning to seem no longer the person I had known for so many years.

On a level field before a hill I tried to identify the other members of our party, a process rendered more difficult by the painted faces of the Comanche men. I had already noticed two of Arsène's friends, scarred Sees-Fire and Deer's-Ears, the dandy. But with an effort I recognized among those riding before these two Taoinan's true brothers White-Road and Red-Woman. His third brother, El Chamaco, the camp crier, was not present. This made, besides Arsène and his comrade "wolves," and in addition to Lefort, Taoinan and me, eleven of us in the pursuit party, not including Hélène-Eulalie, who continued to lope the one-eared pony behind us, defying her cousin's order. In the field we spread out, all of us riding abreast at a lope, since the horses could not indefinitely sustain the pace with which we began. We continued side by side with Arsène and his fellow "wolves" riding a little ahead as we ascended the hill. But at the crest the "wolves" drew up so abruptly that the two brothers behind them collided with the rumps of their horses.

In the dell before us, after a gentle descent and at not more then fifteen rods away, a line of some twenty warriors confronted us. By their bald heads and roached hair I took them to be Osages. They regarded us out of black-and-yellowbrown painted faces. Eagle feathers fluttered from their roaches, which dwindled behind to scalplocks. They formed a formidable appearing force, armed with lances and shields, warclubs, bows and arrows, even a few muskets, and mounted upon what I recognized as some of the fleetest of the Pawnee-Piquée ponies.

"Sacré enfant de grace!" exclaimed Antoine to my left.

Stunned, we hesitated several heartbeats. Turning, I waved Hélène-Eulalie back. "Run to camp. Tell them to come!" To come bury us, my mind completed. The situation was clear. Their horses were fresh, having been driven. Ours were not, having been ridden hard. Flight would be fatal. They would run us down and kill us separately, except perhaps for Arsène mounted upon César. We paused, yes, all but Arsène. Hardly halting, he charged alone with a warwhoop. To my right Taoinan blew his eagle-bone war whistle and plunged forward whooping, a mere eyeblink ahead of the remaining "wolves." To my left Antoine slid from his horse and dropped to a knee, aiming his rifle. I let my musket, useless to me at present, slip down beside him and, with the rest, started off after Arsène, the warchief and "wolves."

The Comanches were whooping as the Osages charged with responding whoops to meet us. Arrows flew, humming and buzzing, from both sides. With a heavy pistol in my right hand and reins in the left, I crouched in the saddle, envying the Indians their shields. Muskets aimed by two of the oncoming riders flashed orange and boomed black smoke, with no effect I could observe, except to frighten the horses. But then I heard the report of Lefort's rifle from behind and the foremost Osage, a giant of a man, dropped his warclub, fell backward off his pony, which continued running. As we were about to close, Arsène, with shield held high and bent over his lance, galloped well in advance of Taoinan and the three "wolves," arrows flying around him.

The nearest enemy warriors apparently realized at the last instant that his great brute would not stop. They attempted to wrench their ponies out of his path, but Arsène and his horse smashed through the mass of men and horses, colliding with enemy mounts and flinging two to the ground, while sending their riders flying, creating disorder among the enemy array as we reached them. My mare's impetus carried me into that tangle, where I faced an Osage warrior gripping an upraised warclub. Leveling my pistol at his head, I fired, missing him completely at a distance of less than four feet owing, I believe, to the plunging of his horse and the sidling of my own. Fortunately the violent motions of our mounts had an identical effect on my adversary's aim, causing his warclub to descend harmlessly. My terrified mare lunged forward, carrying me past my first assailant to confront another large man wielding a spiked warclub. I had drawn my left pistol, which I presented to his painted countenance, causing him to duck behind his shield and to restrain momentarily his hand. Overly excited, I failed to wait for a better opportunity. I drew the trigger, again missing but further agitating my mare, which—her way blocked by a backing horse—began to plunge and buck, probably saving me from a fatal blow. Dropping the pistol, I drew my father's sword and thrust it into my adversary's face. But he was so adroit with his shield, I could not approach him, especially while trying to control my horse. His next swing with the warclub, I could only attempt to parry. The club struck my sword with such force it stunned my hand, breaking off the end portion of the blade. I was vainly shoving the broken blade at what I could see of my enemy's painted face when Arsène warwhooped at a distance before me, followed by an Osage warning shout. Luckily at that instant my assailant, too, was struggling with his pony, which was whirling in one spot, greatly hampering his efforts to club me.

Again the warwhoop. Directly before me, to the Osage rear, Arsène was once more bearing down upon the battle. Seeing the big horse advancing at a run, all combatants, both Osage and Comanche, desperately attempted to shift from his path. By good fortune César approached to my left. Again he smashed through the mêlée. Thanks to their riders' frantic maneuvers, no horses were struck directly in Arsène's second assault. César, however, slammed with a glancing blow into my adversary's pony, still in the act of spinning, sending it careening and hurling its rider into the air and to the earth. With only an empty pistol and broken sword remaining for defense, I managed to turn the mare and kick her to my right out of the struggling mass, seeing as I did Arsène impale an Osage through the shoulder. I turned my head as I rode. The victim, torn backward off his horse, seized the lance, pulling it with him to the ground, so that Arsène was compelled to release it as he continued his charge. Behind him, the young Osage appeared to bounce to his feet, tearing out the lance and flinging it. But simultaneously White-Road, leaning from his pony, thrust his lance through the wounded man's neck, which spurted blood onto the youth's grasping hands.

At the edge of the fray, separated from it by two or three rods, Taoinan, seated upon his war and buffalo horse, was wielding his own warclub, engaged with an Osage brave, their clubs knocking together in a violent intermittent rapping. The Osage was the stronger man but Taoinan the quicker and more dexterous. But then, running out of the mass, one of the unhorsed enemy warriors drew his bowstring and aimed at my friend's back, holding an arrow poised for a second as the two combatants twisted and rose and ducked upon their circling mounts. I shouted but my cry was lost in the report of Lefort's rifle. The bowman collapsed to his hands and knees, his weapons bouncing away in the dirt. Reining in, I glanced back at the hill just as the figures of two horsemen, clearly Indians, joined those of Antoine and...yes, surely Hélène-Eulalie, who was waving to invisible beings behind her. Even as I watched, more figures, two with lances, drew up their ponies, joining them, only a few at first, then several more, all apparently observing our skirmish below.

But some of the enemy had also been watching, it seemed. Abruptly, as if at a signal, the Osages broke off the engagement, seizing fallen weapons, nimbly catching and mounting the loose ponies and riding so swiftly up the opposite rise that it seemed, after some moments, they had never been present. Even the warrior Antoine had shot vanished with the others. Only the bodies of the leading warrior, also shot by Lefort, and of the youth White-Road had lanced, and of a Pawnee-Piquée pony, remained upon what had been a battlefield. For an instant I watched Tosapoy slip from his horse and run to scalp his bloody victim.

"Ah:he!" he shouted, as he touched him, claiming his coup.

It was hard to believe. The entire engagement had taken only minutes.

I sat my trembling mare looking up at the hill where, from moment to moment more mounted figures appeared. Antoine seemed to be communicating, by hand signals, with two or three of them. Hélène-Eulalie, still seated upon her horse, was looking—could it be at me? Or perhaps it was at her cousin? Arsène had dismounted to retrieve his lance and was now struggling unsuccessfully to climb back upon his horse, which was equipped, like the other warriors' ponies, with only a pad saddle secured by a surcingle of buckskin or hair. Around him riders were standing, talking excitedly, their exhausted horses blowing, heads hanging. White-Road, at that moment, still dismounted and bloody, with knife in one hand, dripping scalp in the other, confronted him.

"Your horse fought well today, tabebo."

I clearly heard him say it.

Arsène froze and stared at the insult, as the warchief turned his back, moving away to his pony, knife and bloody trophy in his hands.

Arsène continued to stare, then looked at me in amazement. His shadow, I noted, was perfectly normal.

Like my mount, I was shivering. All had happened too quickly for me to have been afraid. At the top of the hill at the sight of the enemy, with the prospect of what had seemed to be certain death, I had forced my fear into a closet of my mind, holding it in abeyance, promising to hear its pronouncements later. That moment had come, and I felt very tired. But Arsène, who had managed finally to climb upon his horse, appeared suddenly at my side, agitated.

"Where's Taoinan? He must have followed them."

I looked about. Out of all of us, only The Flute was missing. "Yes. He must have."

"Quick, let's go. We must catch him."

"Yes. Why?" I asked stupidly.

"Why? He's your friend. And mine. Wake up, Jean-Pierre."

By his fierce look, I thought he was going to slap me. "Yes. Very well. I'll go."

He turned his horse, leaning down toward me and hissed, "He said he would die today."

"What?"

"Yes. He had a dream. Said he was going to die today."

With that he kicked his horse into a run. I followed on the mare, moving nearly as rapidly as he at first, immediately clear-headed and anxious. My first act as I followed at a gallop, though falling quickly behind, was to pour powder from the horn into my remaining pistol. I pinched a ball from my bullet pouch, dropped it into the muzzle, pounded the muzzle against the saddle and sheathed the firearm in a saddle holster. My sword, also sheathed and by my side, was still I believed capable of inflicting a fatal wound. Whatever I lacked in weapons, I told myself, I would simply have to make up for with the help of Providence, or with Antoine's "la chance."

We had not ridden far, over the hill and for a little distance on the prairie, when the trail we had been following split into three sets of tracks. Arsène drew up, leaning down to examine each set of tracks alternately. I caught up and rested the mare for a moment. She was flagging, breathing hard.

"This way, I think." He pointed to the earth below and immediately kicked the big horse along the westernmost trace. I followed, with the weary mare quickly falling behind. But soon I saw Arsène look back at me and point forward with his lance. I pushed the mare to further efforts and gained enough ground so that from the next rise I saw in the near distance a figure I recognized as Taoinan defending himself against two Osage warriors who had evidently slowed and, finding themselves pursued by a single Comanche, turned back to attack him. I could see that my friend already owed his life to his buffalo-and-war pony, which was wheeling and whirling at its master's commands, turning upon its hind legs, to face one, then the other warrior, as Taoinan kept both at bay, defending himself with shield and lance. Arsène, far ahead of me, was racing toward the three figures. He whooped. I was near enough to see one warrior quickly turn his head. In doing so he apparently raised his shield. I failed to see Taoinan's fatal lance thrust, but he evidently slipped the blade under that shield and through his antagonist's abdomen, withdrawing it as quickly. I did see the warrior double, drop his warclub, grip his middle, lose his balance, and topple from his horse to the ground, where he writhed, rolling, struggling to his knees. The other warrior, seeing Arsène approaching rapidly with me behind him, swung his pony about and fled at a run. Instantly Taoinan was off his horse, knife in hand. Jumping, coming down knees first on the back of the fallen man, he seized his scalp lock, jerked his head back, quickly sawed at his throat, and rose over his foe's bloody convulsions. Arsène drew up César some dozen rods before reaching our friend, then slid to the ground. Joining him, I looked at him in surprize.

"If I run him any farther, I'll kill him."

The big brute stood with his head hanging, legs apart, sides heaving, breathing hoarsely, gasping, froth at his mouth. My mare, too, was gasping, breathing heavily. I dismounted, held her by the bridle. Taoinan, now squatting, appeared to be scalping his dead enemy. A moment later, while we waited for the horses to recover, some twenty or thirty horsemen galloped over the rise behind us. As they approached, I saw they were Pawnee-Piquées, with a few Comanches. One of the leading men rode the chestnut gelding with white mane and tail, the one we had seen at the village. From that I deduced that these pursuing warriors had recovered some, if not most, of their stolen horseherd. As they drew up around us, Toyamancare greeted us, while looking sharply at César.

"He'll be all right," said Arsène. "I had to run him a long way. But he'll be all right. I'll walk him back."

Toyamancare grunted, his expression neutral. "Isn't that Taoinan?"

"Yes. He killed that Osage. He was fighting two of them. The other ran off. Maybe you can catch him."

With rapid handsigns Big-Mountain translated. The Pawnee-Piquées and the Comanches with them whooped and went off at a run. Toyamancare rode with them as far as Taoinan, where he dismounted. We led our horses to them. When we came up, Taoinan was attempting to tie the bloody scalp to his pony's war bridle, which consisted merely of a buckskin strand looped around the animal's lower jaw, and a single rein, now hanging to the ground. Toyamancare was talking into his friend's ear, but Taoinan appeared not to be listening. I noticed three arrows stuck in his shield and two more in the dirt. Blood was trickling from beneath his buffalo-horned headdress to his black, painted cheek and from there to the ground. An arrow protruded from either side of the top of the headdress.

Just as we arrived, Toyamancare seemed to lose patience and snatched off his friend's horned hat. Blood streamed over Taoinan's face, but, quickly sweeping it from his eyes, he otherwise ignored it, continuing his attempt to fasten the scalp to the chin strap. Toyamancare broke the arrow over his knee, threw away the pieces, handed the headdress to Arsène. Reaching down, he tore up a bunch of dry grass, shook off the dirt, cut off the roots with his knife, sheathed the knife, spit on the grass, rubbed it together into a bundle. He threw a big arm around Taoinan's neck and, with his free hand, placed the grass poultice against the other man's head wound, pressing firmly with a flat hand. All the while Taoinan, absorbed in his fumbling with a string of hide, the bloody scalp, the bridle, paid no attention and the well-trained war-and-buffalo pony stood calmly, as if this were an ordinary morning in which nothing unusual had happened.

We rode back at a walk to the battlefield. The two Osage bodies and the dead pony had not yet begun to bloat in the mid-day sun. Yet above on the same rise we saw first the one-eared pony, then as we came closer, a figure seated cross-legged below it, holding its reins. Arsène was so disgusted and angry at seeing his cousin sitting alone on the hill that he would not look at her as he passed, continuing at a walk with Toyamancare as well as with Taoinan, who was still silent and again wearing his horned headdress, riding between them. I dropped out to look for my second pistol, but it was gone. Giving up the search, I rode up the hill to where Hélène-Eulalie was now standing by her horse.

"Antoine has your pistol."

"Where is he? Why did he leave you?"

"I asked him to."

"And he did? Left you alone? I asked you to go back. So did Arsène."

She raised her chin, smiling. "And I'm still here, aren't I?"

"It's terribly dangerous. Don't you realize? Those Osages had fast horses. You would not want to have been caught by them."

"Antoine told me that once they found a young Frenchman. Alone and helpless. Somehow they stuck him on a spit." She grimaced. "I don't like to think about that. They roasted him alive."

"Well? And you're still here? Alone?"

"I watched the battle. It was fascinating. You were brave."

"I was? Arsène was brave."

"Arsène was heroic. But you were brave."

I shrugged. I had run out of words. "Are you ready to go back?"

"Of course. I've been waiting for you."

I looked at her quickly, then away.

We rode back side by side, mostly in silence. With her sun-darkened face, her blond hair loose, further bleached by the sun, riding with natural ease, her fine hand on the reins, she looked more attractive and desirable than I had ever seen her. She was so beautiful! My head swarmed with contradictory thoughts. It was as if I were an hourglass and when I looked at her all of the sand was draining out of me. Good God, I thought, I'm afraid I'm beginning to love her. Our silence was not a strained silence. It was as if by unspoken mutual consent, and as if through a mutual understanding, some communication that went beyond words existed between us.

It was early afternoon when we returned to camp, and already there was shade and an intermittent breeze that fluttered leaves. A drumming throbbed from somewhere. At an hour when they often slept, people were talking, calling to each other with excited voices, moving from lodge to lodge despite the heat. A few men and boys were riding their ponies near the camp. There was an air of ferment among the tepees. Sehêbi, pale, with a frightened look, greeted us before Taoinan's lodge.

"He wants to see you."

I dismounted, handed her the reins. "He's all right?"

"I think so. I don't know."

I left the two women talking, partly in French with a few Comanche words, partly by simple signs. Stooping, I entered the dim interior of the lodge. Its sides had been rolled up a little, so that there was some movement of air and sunlight scattered at the edges. Taoinan was seated at the far end under his suspended bow, quiver, and warclub. He regarded me calmly, smoking his pipe.

"Come, brother, smoke with me."

Although there was an open kettle of water before him, lines of dried blood ran down his warpainted face to his chin. The bunch of bloody grass remained stuck to his hair, giving him an odd appearance, as if it were growing from his head. I seated myself before him, and he handed me the pipe. For a time we passed it back and forth, smoking in silence. The drumming continued. I could hear the women's quiet voices outside.

"How are you?" I asked at last.

"I'm well. You know, brother, I was supposed to die today."

"You had a dream. Arsène told me."

"Yes. In this dream there were big crows. I was a crow too, but not very big. We were on the prairie. The chief of these crows was a great fat crow, his feathers sticking out all over." He gestured with the pipe and free hand. "The fat crow said to me—when the foxes come, we will fly. I said I don't think I can fly. Then, he said, you will have to hop. You will have to hop and run. I can't run fast, I said." Taoinan raised his eyes from the ground, looked at me. "Because of my foot, you know. The fat crow said, if you can't run fast, they will catch and kill you. You had better run fast if you can't fly. Then all the crows began to cry out, 'the foxes, the foxes'! The crows flapped and rose off the field into the air. I tried, but I couldn't move my wings. The others' shadows passed over me, going away. I tried to run, but my legs moved very slowly, hardly at all. Even trying as hard as I could, I could barely move them, trying to run." He lapsed into silence, handed me the pipe.

"So they caught you?"

"Yes. One caught my foot in its teeth. They bit me and pulled me down and all jumped on me, biting, and they killed me. I was dead. My spirit saw them eating me."

"Well," I said, after a time. "You dreamed that, but you didn't die."

"No, I didn't die. Kills-Far saved me. I don't understand."

"Antoine may have saved you once, but you and your horse saved you against the two enemies. I saw that. You saved yourself and scalped one of them. I saw."

He puffed thoughtfully. "Yes. That's true."

"Maybe Tzena sent that dream to fool you. She likes to play tricks, you know."

"Yes. Maybe. I don't think so," he said, unconvinced, still troubled. "Well, anyway, there's something I've been wanting to ask you for a long time. I should have asked you yesterday, when I was about to die. But I didn't. I don't know why. I should have."

"Yes?"

His expression altered. He looked beyond me.

I turned.

A shadow stooped in the doorway. It was the crier, leaning in. "There will be a council tonight after sunset. You will be honored. All the important men will be there. Afterward, the scalp dance. Everybody will come. But first, the council."

"I'll be there," said Taoinan.

"Good. I'll see you later—brothers," El Chamaco said, backing out, disappearing.

Taoinan looked stunned. "Did you hear what he called us?"

"Us?"

"You are my brother, aren't you? Yes, he called us brothers. That has never happened before. What does it mean? And this honor. I don't know."

"Look. They're going to honor you. That's good, isn't it? Be happy. You're alive. You were brave. Now, what were you going to ask me? I've been waiting for you to ask. What is it?"

"Later, brother. Now I have to wash, then sleep. I'm very tired. You must be, too. Go back and sleep. I'll see you after the council. Then we'll talk."

"But you'll have to dance."

"Yes. Tonight I'll dance. Then, tomorrow. Tomorrow we'll talk."

"Good," I said, yielding, and rising. "Tomorrow, then."

Outside in the hot sun I found that Hélène-Eulalie had departed. The shrieks of children rose from the creek. I too felt very tired. Sehêbi brought me the mare from the shade, where she had tied her. She regarded me anxiously. "He's all right, don't you think, Jean-Pierre?"

"Yes, he's all right. They're going to honor him at the council tonight."

"They're going to honor him?" Her expression brightened. "Oh, that's good." She looked around, smiled coyly, and stepped closer, lowering her voice. "I haven't asked him yet."

"Don't. Don't ask him."

"No?" she said, looking surprised.

"No." Swinging onto the mare, I gazed down at Sehêbi, then rode away leaving her standing, looking after me. I asked myself why I had said that and felt a mix of embarrassment, disappointment, and chagrin. The words of a writer from the last century unaccountably entered my head: "L'amour est une émotion três incommode," and I smiled again, sourly, to myself.

17

When I reached our camp, I found César tied in the shade. I had already watered the mare at the creek. Wearily dismounting, I tied her by the big horse and stripped her of bridle and saddle. Arsène, who had come for vermilion and hawks' bells, and who had been conversing with Lefort, was just departing. His face was still painted. Although I was tired and irritable, I walked back with him to his horse. I noticed the sweat had dried in whitish waves on the big animal's coat. He untied his mount and took the rein.

"Your cousin said you were heroic today."

"Ah?"

"Well, you were. You probably saved us all."

"Did I?" He regarded me sternly, but his expression gradually gave way to one of wry inner amusement. His mouth was set, while his eyes laughed. His lips twitched. He looked back at our camp, and all around him. "I'll tell you, mon vieux, no one else. César bolted. He's not used to the shots and whoops. Twice—I couldn't stop him, so I let him run." He began to laugh, almost silently, until he was bent over, hanging on my shoulder for support, tears glistening on his black warpaint. "César," he gasped, "was heroic, n'est-ce pas?"

Indignation, which I had been scarcely aware of, now boiled from my mouth, "Anyway, more heroic than cutting an old woman's throat. Or setting out to murder a man in his bed, to show off."

He stiffened and stood straight. His hand dropped from my shoulder to his knife. "So you heard, the other night. I thought you were asleep. So that's what you think—murder?"

"Yes. With the old woman, it was horrible. But to save your skin—I can understand that. But to volunteer to kill a man in his bed. To show off. That was your intention, wasn't it? I think that was atrocious."

"Ah, you do." He stared at me, unblinking, hand on his knife. "Though of course I didn't do it."

"Yes, but it was your intention—to make them admire you." Furious now, disgusted with the bloodthirsty 'wolves,' I met his gaze, while it occurred to me that this was probably how he looked when he killed an enemy. I did not think he would kill me, although he might slash me with his excellent knife.

"Do you remember telling me of the Paoli Massacre?"

"You remember that?"

"The Redcoats bayoneted men in their blankets."

"Yes."

"And under Morgan—you fought under Morgan. Colonel Washington. He was the general's nephew, wasn't he?"

"Yes."

"Hammond's Store. You remember? He and his dragoons surprized the Tories at Hammond's store. At dawn. Am I right?"

"You are."

"They bayoneted men trying to get out of their blankets. The militia did. Many, many men. Isn't that true?"

"But that was a battle. That was war."

"A battle? Jean-Pierre, you are naïf." He calmed. Became my old student again. His hand fell from his knife. "You don't think we Comanches are at war? Always? With all the tribes around us? Everyone wants our horses, our buffalo, comanchería. You don't think a Pawnee warrior would not, if he had the chance, and was brave enough...would not crawl into my lodge and cut my throat? Of course he would. Our war is not the same as your war. But look, the British stabbed men in their beds, didn't they? Your Americans did the same. Was it murder then? Bah, think about it, Jean-Pierre, before you accuse me of planning murder."

I simply stared back at him, dumfounded at his having remembered my old talk of the war, exhausted and slightly confused, not knowing what to say. I expected him to begin quoting Cicero to me next.

"As for the old woman, I make no excuse. I'll never forget that. It's on my conscience. Always will be. Come. Help me up on César."

I made a stirrup for him with my hands. Bracing himself on my back, he sprang lightly up onto the pad that served him as a war saddle. Silently he turned his horse and, without a look back, rode away down the creek.

I was too tired to eat. Noting that Hélène-Eulalie must be in her tent, I placed a finger on my lips at Antoine, gulped several dippers of water, entered my own shelter, dropped upon my buffalo robe and fell asleep. I awoke hours later with sunset light in my doorway. I found Lefort snoring quietly where I had last seen him. Men were stretched out randomly where there had been shade. I saw Hélène-Eulalie's horse among the trees near my mare. Making a quick meal of cold venison and dried pumpkin from a mat of the same we had obtained from the Pawnee-Piquées, I caught and saddled my horse, riding quietly away from camp. I had determined to seek out Arsène, or the "Amabate" he had become. Somehow I could understand his murder of the old woman, horrible as it was. He was young. His life was at risk. He was following the orders of his leader. He felt remorse. With the Pawnee, it was otherwise. Although I was repelled by his original intention, I could now reluctantly see some justice in his argument: he had behaved as an exceptionally daring Comanche warrior might be expected to. I found his plan, based upon his desire to flaunt himself, repugnant. Yet the tribe he had chosen as his own would approve of both, though not of his failure to kill. Most of all I had no wish to lose our friendship, which meant a great deal to me and was surely destined to be strained anyway by the differences in the moeurs, or customs, of what had become our two peoples.

It was the time between sunset and dusk when I stooped into Arsène's arbor constructed of branches near his small lodge. The many gaps between leaves admitted pale light and air. He was seated opposite the doorway, under his weapons, examining his face, now yellow, red, and blue, in a trade mirror. He greeted me and I sat down facing him. He had fastened a single eagle feather in his loose black hair.

"Well, have you eaten?"

I told him I had. We sat in silence for a time, hearing the drums at the dancing ground. "I shouldn't have accused you. I know you're a warrior. In your society...it's probably necessary. But you see...I—"

"I've left the society."

"What? When?"

"This afternoon. After we talked. I went to our leader's lodge and told him. Today I could do that because I'm a hero, thanks to César, and no one can say I resigned out of fear."

"But why? Nothing I said?"

He was silent a while. "No. I've been thinking about it for a long time. It's no life. All the time traveling, hiding, being hunted. Counting coups. Stealing horses." He sat silently for a moment, reflecting. "I have enough horses now to marry."

"So you will?"

"I don't know. Maybe. Sometimes I'll go on war parties." Pausing, he seemed to cheer. "I'm a warchief now."

"Like Big-Mountain? The Flute? White-Road?"

"No, not like them. A little warchief. But it pleases me. Someday I'll be like them."

"What about Taoinan? How did they honor him?"

The number of drummers and the tempo of the drums had increased, accented by occasional distant shouts and whoops. Outside the light had diminished. Still we sat there in the deepening twilight while he told me of the council. Taoinan had been made to sit in the first seat north of the lodge doorway, opposite Manos-Amarillas at the other end. After all had smoked, Yellow-Hands had praised his valor and his value as a medicine man to the People. Red-Woman had then, in a long, complex oration, explained why he had decided that The Flute, medicine man and warrior with great Puha, was actually brother to El Chamaco, White-Road and himself. He passed to Manos-Amarillas a round headdress of eagle feathers that stuck straight upward. This the old chief had dispatched from hand to hand around the circle to Taoinan, who accepted it hesitantly, holding and staring at it for some moments before slipping it upon his head and uttering the proper acceptance. It was a high honor, Arsène said, to be recognized in this fashion by your friends or family. Next Red-Woman, whom Arsène described as ambitious to inherit the head chief's position—as well as anxious to gain followers—praised Arsène's deed of that morning when he had twice charged the enemy, disrupting their ranks and wounding one of them.

Rhetorically he demanded to know why Arsène was not wearing the "wolf tail." Arsène replied that he had resigned from the society. Red-Woman praised his deeds with the "wolves," welcoming him back into the community and proposing that he now be considered a warchief who might someday be as renowned as his own brother, White-Road, who had greatly distinguished himself that day by counting coup and scalping an enemy. The entire council approved this suggestion, and shortly afterward, after the pipe had passed once more, Manos-Amarillas had ceremonially closed the meeting.

"You think Taoinan didn't want that warhat?"

"No. He didn't want it. But he took it."

"Why?"

Arsène shrugged. I could see him only dimly now.

"I mean, why didn't he want it?"

"It's like the "wolves," only you don't travel all the time. No, it's not like the 'wolves.' But you can't leave a fight before anyone else. You have to rescue any man whose horse is killed." For an instant he considered. "If you should ever throw your hat away and run, other men can call you 'older sister.' Anyway the hat shows you're a leader, so all the enemy try to kill you."

"But Taoinan's not afraid."

"Yes, I know. Maybe it's because of a dream he had."

"Well, maybe. Maybe it is that."

"Amabate, Amabate," voices called from outside, with an approaching rhythmic tinkling of hawks-bells. Several heads appeared in the arbor's entrance, dim faces of young warriors. "Are you coming? Everybody's dancing."

"I'm coming, I'm coming," he said, rising. "Jean-Pierre, goodnight."

It was evening, with early stars. I found myself meandering toward Taoinan's nearby lodge, although I knew he was dancing. The drumming was faster, louder now, accompanied by more frequent whoops and shouts. I had firmly decided not to go with Sehêbi. Yet it did seem to me I ought to give her an explanation for that decision. What explanation though? That I was becoming increasingly attached to Hélène-Eulalie? That I was in love with her? But was I really? Coals of a cooking fire glowed red before the lodge. No one was visible. Assuming wives and children had gone to watch the scalp dance, I turned back toward Arsène's tepee, where I had tied the mare. But a figure emerged out of the darkness toward me.

"Bonsoir. I knew you would come."

"I need to talk to you."

"Come," said Sehêbi, taking my hand. Her grip was at once gentle and firm as she led me by starlight down toward the creek.

"Where are we going?" I asked weakly.

She was silent, stepping quietly down the path in her moccasins, her hand cool in mine. I could smell some fragrant herb she had rubbed on her skin and in her hair when she had bathed. At the creek she turned downstream toward the river. As we proceeded—she stepping surely, I stumbling from time to time and clinging to her hand for support—I felt my resolve slipping. I knew I should ask her to stop, talk to her in a reasonable manner. But I remained silent. She halted in a patch of meadow under a giant cotton tree where it was quite dark. Releasing my hand, she confronted me, bringing her face close to mine.

"Donne-moi une bise."

I laughed. It was a phrase I had taught her long before, when I had first known her and had believed I could safely flirt with her. I complied, embracing her, kissing her at first gently, little teasing kisses, then more fervently as my resolve evaporated. Soon we were panting. There in the dark she drew her buckskin dress up over her head and tossed it on the grass while I threw off my clothes. We embraced. She turned, went to her hands and knees, then lay on her belly, face to the side. But I knelt beside her, gently turned her over, to her evident surprise, gently moved her legs apart, moved onto her and entered her. She had it seemed been anticipating this coupling for some time and was greatly aroused, a condition which increased my own ardor to such an remarkable extent that I moved within her for what seemed a long interval, until she threw back her head with a little shriek. I finished seconds later. Then we lay motionless, breathing in unison, once again in silence.

The second time was good, though not as good. Afterward we washed, naked, in the creek. Dressed again, we followed the stream up to where we had come down from Taoinan's lodge. It was dark and quiet at the tepees, while the drumming and other noise from the dancing ground was louder than ever. I kissed her and turned to go.

"I asked him," she said.

I turned back quickly. I had assumed she had. "What did he say?"

"He said, 'yes.'"

I rode back to camp in the dark, making a detour to avoid the dancing ground, where the drumming and commotion were louder than ever. Watering the mare at the creek, I hobbled her, stripped off her saddle and bridle, released her to join the other horses. Antoine was seated before a small fire conversing with two of our older men. They looked up and greeted me as I entered the light.

"Madame went to watch the dancing."

"Not alone?"

"No. With the others."

"And you? You're not going? I'll watch the camp."

"No. I've seen enough of them."

"Ah, well. Good. Bonne nuit."

"Bonne nuit, mon bourgeois," replied Henri Tournier, oldest of the engagés.

Undressing again in the near dark of my tent, I reflected a moment upon Lefort's words. I was pleased that Hélène-Eulalie had felt sufficiently at ease with the men to accompany them to the Indian camp. At first, having never encountered anyone like her, they had been uncomfortable in her presence, indeed awestruck. But throughout our journey she had behaved in such a natural, genial, and unpretentious manner that they had come to forget her lineage and social status and had begun to treat her, although still with respect, almost as one of themselves. I had not expected this, and it pleased me. As for Antoine, I was surprised he was not at the dance pursuing some Indian girl. Sitting by the fire on such an evening was unlike him. But before our departure, Mlle. Bijou had confided to me that he was living with a young Frenchwoman, a new arrival in Natchitoches, and it was rumored they would be married as soon as he had saved sufficient money. Could the bon vivant I had known for so long actually have changed?

A wind arose in the night, with gusts so forceful they shook my tent. The wind was followed by thunderclaps, with frequent flashes of lightning that illuminated my canvas interior, followed by violent rain. But the storm eventually passed, and the wind subsided before dawn.

The morning was fresh, clear, and fragrant, the recent haze dispersed, so that colors of sky, earth, trees, rushing creek shone in a new sun. Even spider webs sparkled like strings of jewelry where they stretched between branches above the long shadows of the trees and the rising vapors. Henri Tournier, the old voyageur who cooked, had already prepared coffee by the time I came out. We were squatting around the fire chatting and sipping the dregs of our coffee when Hélène-Eulalie joined us, holding her cup to be filled by Tournier.

"Well, where were you last night?" she asked me, sitting down cross-legged. "The dancing, the crowd...fascinating."

"Did Arsène dance?"

"Yes. He was marvelous. They all were. Where were you?"

Even Antoine was looking at me with interest. "I've seen so many dances. I went for a ride, on the prairie." Strangely, I felt defensive, guilty. She was not my wife. I owed her nothing, really. Yet I felt awkward, a little embarrassed, guilty.

"In the dark?"

"Starlight. It was a beautiful evening."

"Really," she said. "You know I've never thought of that. I'll have to try it."

We had completed our barter with the Comanches the previous morning. I soon dispatched three of the men to the horseherd with instructions to receive the ponies for which we had traded, with an understanding that we might leave them under the care of the boy herders until our departure. I also instructed these engagés to proceed with the new ponies directly to the northern Pawnee-Piquée—or Witchitan—village, where we would next establish a camp. They were to hold the animals there until our arrival.

During this morning the remaining five of us worked together packing the buffalo robes and other peltry we had accumulated, as well as those trade articles already removed from their bales. Antoine and I afterward looked to the horses, making certain that each, including the spares, was fit for travel. With this accomplished all that remained to be done was, on the following morning, to disassemble the tents, pack our belongings, saddle the horses, and secure all the bales upon the packtrain for an early departure. By mid-day we had completed the preliminary preparations and were once again hungry. As we sat together eating, I announced that, as of the present moment, we might all do as we wished until the sun rose the next morning.

The first thing I did after eating was to lie under a tree and fall asleep. Waking later in the afternoon, I found Lefort and the two engagés lounging under another tree, smoking their pipes and talking. I had slept longer than I had intended. Dazed, I sat up, looking around me.

"Madame said to tell you she was going to visit Sehêbi," said Antoine.

"Good." But on reflection I decided it was not good. I had planned to see Taoinan on this afternoon. Now the prospect of finding myself in the presence of both women simultaneously made me uncomfortable. I was ready to see either of them separately, but to be in the presence of the two together on this particular afternoon was not at all what I desired. Indeed the thought made me feel queasy. If Taoinan wished urgently to speak with me, he might ride to our camp. Otherwise I would stop at his lodge on our way out of the encampment in the morning. I had brought along three worn volumes of Montesquieu's

De l'Esprit des Lois. These from a set of the colonel's like one which Hélène-Eulalie had informed me had constituted the favorite reading of her father. For the remainder of the afternoon, stretched in the shade of that elm, I alternately dozed and read within these sensible and humane inquiries.

Late that afternoon Arsène joined us bearing, tied behind his saddle, a doe he had killed with a musket down by the river earlier in the day. Dismounting and passing the body to old Tournier, he led his pinto into the shade, loosened the cinch and tied him. He flopped down beside Antoine, informing us that Hélène-Eulalie had been playing with Taoinan's little boys and would be with us directly. Taoinan himself, and Toyamancare too, had been in council much of the afternoon. This assemblage of the People was about to move, and there was apparently disagreement as to where the buffalo herds were located at present and where the band should go. Each of the leading chiefs and elders wished to voice his opinion, and many took pride in their oratory, although the final decision would be made by the old peace chief, Manos-Amarillas, at some time during the evening.

Our own evening was festive. The trading had been successful. Except for last minute preparations in the morning, we were ready to depart. We were all at ease in each other's company. The broiled venison had smelled and tasted good. Though it was a mild night, after dinner Tournier and Jean Hugue built up the fire, so that we had to move back but could see each other well in its leaping, ruddy light. From my supplies I had provided a bottle of the colonel's good Armagnac, which quickly enhanced the conversation, rendering it louder and more lively.

"So, you think you may marry," I said to Arsène, who was lounging on the opposite side of the fire. "Will you marry one of those girls who've been crawling into your lodge?" Everyone laughed, including his cousin, who was seated cross-legged beside him.

"Yes. Why not? Maybe I'll marry both of them."

Hélène-Eulalie, after exchanging a look with Arsène, regarded me with a merry expression: "By the way, Jean-Pierre, what did you say you did during the scalp dance last night?"

They were all watching me. I sensed a trap. "I told you. I went for a ride."

"In the dark?" They were all smiling now.

"Of course in the dark. I didn't carry a torch."

"I see," said Hélène-Eulalie, struggling, it seemed, to keep from laughing. "How adventurous! And alone, too. Tell us all about it, and where you went."

I looked around. They were all smiling, even Antoine and the two engagés. So they knew. Probably everyone in camp knew. "Well, Taoinan's my brother. It's their custom." I seem to remember I was blushing.

"Yes. That's what She-Scolds-Her-Dogs told me. He gave his permission. I asked Sehêbi. She said, 'Oh yes, it was good!'"

At that detail Arsène appeared delighted.

"Don't be embarrassed, Jean-Pierre," Hélène-Eulalie said, laughing. "I know about your Mulatto woman too. Michelle Pichet. Mademoiselle Bijou told me. You're like most men."

"Thank you," I said.

"But no," she said. "Don't be offended. I had three older brothers. They're gone now. The youngest was wounded in a duel over another man's wife. The middle one caught the pox from a duchess. They were both charming men. The eldest was always very correct— and terribly boring. So you see?"

At a loss for a reply, I was still blushing.

"Tell me, Jean-Pierre," Arsène said with a laugh. "On your ride in the dark, did you trot part of the time? Or did you mostly gallop?" With that, he again appeared hugely amused.

They were all laughing. I had to join in, as trying as it was for my dignity. In the end, we had a jolly evening. The fine evening, the fire, the alcohol had relaxed all of us. Even Antoine began talking more than usual, in this instance about some of his experiences in the north The conversation turned to the capture of whites, and Antoine spoke of one Barré, a fellow Canadian whom he despised and who was known for having more than once been a guest in an Indian village when a white prisoner was brought in and having encouraged that person's death in order to gain possession of any valuable belongings, such as a pocket watch or gold or silver coins, that the natives had little use for. Lefort went on to say that Barré had long ago invited him to take part in a trading venture up the Missouri River but, knowing the trader's ugly reputation, he had refused, greatly offending the man, who had never forgiven him. "Your father," he remarked to Arsène, "When he was Lieutenant Governor of the district, sent orders to the commandant at Arkansas Post to have him arrested."

"Why?"

"No license. He was selling aguardiente and guns to the Arkansas. But he must have heard and slipped away."

"What happened to him?"

Antoine shrugged. "Who knows? Once he worked for Chouteau. Out of St. Louis. But maybe he's still up on the Rivière des Ark." He paused. "A curious type," he added, staring into the fire, "he thought only of his own advantage."

Arsène, who was still lolling on the other side of the dwindling flames, raised himself higher on an elbow, and looked at me with a faint, mischievous smile, his eyes mirthful.

"What is it?" I asked, puzzled.

"Barré, La Barre," he said. "Remember? The Chevalier de la Barre."

I remembered and was forced to smile at his remembering. Truly it was nothing to smile about, entirely the contrary, as I was compelled to explain to the others. During the Ancien Régime, some thirty years before the Revolution, a youth named the Chevalier de la Barre was arrested for failing to demonstrate sufficient respect for a passing religious procession. He was tried and condemned by a court to have a hand amputated, his tongue torn from his head, and his body burnt. Voltaire had unsuccessfully attempted to have the sentence annulled, but the Parlement in Paris had, on the youth's appeal, merely reduced his punishment to decapitation before burning. When long ago Arsène, then a ten-year-old, and I had discussed this affair, the punishment had seemed to him as well as to me so grotesquely disproportionate to the offense that he had begun to giggle. We had both finally laughed helplessly, while at the same time realizing that the matter was at the furthest remove from the comical.

"That's not amusing," declared Hélène-Eulalie, frowning from Arsène to me. Her mood had darkened. "Your story's horrible—and in poor taste when we're enjoying ourselves."

"Nevertheless," I replied. "Unfortunately it's true."

She rose stiffly, bid us all goodnight and went, momentarily à la manière d'une grande dame, a difficult feat in buckskins, to her tent.

Lefort, gazing at the stars, whistled for a moment tunelessly.

Tournier smiled.

Arsène looked after her, grinned at me, and shrugged, for an instant his former self, my pupil.

The rest of us, soon regaining our good humor, remained for a time longer at the subsiding fire, while Lefort, at our urging, recounted more of his and other voyageurs' adventures in the far north. During a lapse in the conversation I asked him to tell us more about the trapper and trader, Barré, about whom he had aroused my curiosity. Had he no redeeming virtues, this voyageur? And what other mischief had he accomplished to earn himself such ill repute?

Antoine thought for a moment. "Gustave is a big man, very strong, very brave. They say he killed a grizzly—the one the Indians call the white bear—with his knife. The Indians of many tribes admire him. The women too. He has married into several tribes, made children. When he tires of the women, he leaves them. But those people still trade with him."

"There are many men like that," said Arsène, "though not among my people."

"No, not many. Sometimes the Indians kill them. But not Barré. Maybe they fear him a little. He's afraid of nothing. When he's angry, he's dangerous. He's also an excellent shot." Lefort smiled. "Once he challenged me to a match, and I beat him. He hates me for that, I believe."

"Encouraging the Indians to murder is terrible. But could he have feared for his own life?"

"As I told you, he fears nothing. But let me tell you a story. It was much talked about at the time. When he was younger, he went with an Osage warparty to raid the Kadohadacho on La Rivière Rouge above the Post. On their way home along the prairie they encountered a Frenchman hunting with his young son. They cut off the father's head and made the boy carry it during the long trip to their village for their ceremonies. Barré did nothing to stop the murder or help the boy. In fact, he later laughed about it. What do you think of that?"

After this anecdote, our conversation failed, each of us becoming reflective for a time. Our silence was broken by an owl in a nearby tree. Arsène started violently, staring up into the dark.

"That's an owl—mupitz," said Antoine. "Not an Osage."

We all laughed. When we at last stood, yawned, and stretched, Tournier kicked a broken branch onto the fire for the benefit of the engagé on guard duty, causing flames to flare and spray up sparks, a miniature fireworks instantly absorbed by the dark.

It had been on the whole a jolly evening. Still after lying down in my tent, I was conscious of an inner ache. In spite of Hélène-Eulalie's merriment at moments, I had sensed that she was annoyed with me. Because of my lapse with Sehêbi, I could tell that our relationship had been damaged. She perhaps respected me less. Those invisible cords I had felt tugging between us had loosened or parted.

The following morning I stopped with her at Taoinan's serpent-painted lodge on our way out of the Comanche camp. I had already sent Antoine, with Tournier and Hugue, ahead with the packtrain. Sehêbi smiled and took my reins, greeting my companion with evident pleasure:

"Hélène, tu vas bien?" Turning to me, she told me in Comanche that Taoinan was waiting to see me. As I entered the tepee, the two women were leading the horses toward the shade where First-Frost played with the little naked boys. Taoinan was seated under his weapons opposite the doorway. As soon as I sat down, he lighted his ceremonial pipe with a coal from the smoldering fire. He puffed in the four directions and passed it to me.

"So. You're leaving now. I'll ride out with you."

"You've been wanting to ask me something." I said, after I had puffed smoke and returned the pipe.

"Yes. I should have asked you when we were riding to the battle. But I didn't." He puffed for a moment in silence. "I wonder why." He mused, and changed the subject, regarding me gravely: "You know, I had a dream last night. Bad."

"You did?"

"About Amabate."

"What? What about Amabate?"

"I saw him by a fire at night. A shaggy bird, round eyes...yellow beak..." He held his arms wide to indicate great size. "...was holding Amabate's head back, by his scalplock, with a knife under his chin. There was a little moon. I think that creature was Piamupitz, the big owl-man. Those were feathers, I know. I didn't see his staff."

"Yes. And then?"

"I think he began to cut his throat. Then a cloud crossed the moon. I couldn't see any more. That's all I saw. But I'm afraid he'll die soon."

"Well, it was only a dream. But don't tell anyone. Don't tell him."

"I think the tababos don't believe dreams. But we do, certain ones."

"I know. But please don't tell anyone."

He passed the pipe. "I won't. If you wish it. But I think you should warn him."

"Is that what you wanted to ask me?"

"Oh, that. No."

"Well? You can ask me now." I was becoming annoyed, but one cannot become impatient in ceremonial circumstances. I gazed up at the new, feathered headdress suspended with his bow, quiver, and warclub.

"Yes," he said at last, still smoking. "It's about Sehêbi."

I started. "It is?"

"When... If I am killed, will you take her? You will, won't you, brother?"

I stared. "You mean...marry her?"

"Yes, my heart has been troubled about her. My other two wives will be all right. But Sehêbi—I've been worrying. You will take her, won't you?"

I stared at him, my good friend, a torrent of thoughts rushing through my head. There was no alternative. "Yes," I said at last. "Yes, if you're killed, I'll take her. But you're not going to be killed."

"Good. Now, I'm happy."

He passed me the pipe. When I had smoked and passed it back, I knew with a shock that my life had altered, that I had taken a solemn oath which—should circumstances result in my friend's death—bound me from this time forward to assume responsibility for Sehêbi. After this, Taoinan became cheerful, his usual self. But as we emerged from the lodge, I looked at the sun shining in leaves under an intensely blue sky with the ghost of a moon in it, and the world itself seemed to have tilted slightly since I had entered that serpent-ringed tepee.

As we stood there, Taoinan and I, Hélène-Eulalie was sitting in the shade by our tethered horses. Seated near her were Sehêbi, First-Frost, and She-Scolds-Her-Dogs. Hélène-Eulalie was holding one of Taoinan's sons on her lap. When the child saw his father, he cried out and raised his arms, as if asking to be picked up. Quickly rising, Sehêbi stooped and passed the boy to The Flute, whereupon the other toddler began to bawl, holding up his arms in a desire to join his half-brother. In doing so, he flailed his hands back and forth. In one of them he held a soft buckskin ball, a present from Hélène-Eulalie. In his excitement he released the ball, which, flung hard, struck his startled brother on the nose, causing him to howl. Simultaneously the four women began to laugh.

Jumping up, First-Frost swung him into Taoinan's other arm. I have even today, after all the years, a clear picture in my mind of the laughing women and of my friend standing before his lodge holding his two little naked sons, chuckling, stroking, talking to them calmly, affectionately, while their mothers and Hélène-Eulalie continued to laugh, and Sehêbi watched it all with a pleased, wistful smile.

Taoinan, Toyamancare, and Arsène rode beside us for a little distance out of the Comanche camp. After embraces and farewells, we left them on the crest of the rise from which we had first looked down upon that same horseherd and the tepees scattered among the trees of the stream. This time we rode diagonally toward La Rivière Rouge de Natchitoches, loping eastward. As we approached the wooded riverbank, Hélène-Eulalie drew up her one-eared pony and turned to look back. The three horsemen remained motionless upon the hill, no doubt watching us. As we gazed, on that vivid day, where each tree, each twig, each blade of grass stood out sharply under an intensely blue sky, a tiny cloud passed over the rise, casting its shadow upon the three mounted figures. Arsène raised his arm and let it fall. In response, Hélène-Eulalie waved, again and again. I looked at her, and she turned toward me. Tears were shining on her cheeks. We moved on. I glanced back for a final look. They were still there. But as I watched a fourth horseman joined them. Because of the distance and the shadow of the cloud, I could not identify him. But I thought it might be pock-marked Cunabunit, He-Who-Saw-Fire.

18

I remember when Monsieur de St. Maurice first urinated in his breeches. He was fully clothed, no longer in his dressing gown but still recovering from his head injury. It was directly before our noon meal. He and I were in his office discussing problems associated with the death of M. André Duval, longtime manager at the firm of de St. Maurice, when, with the help of his canes, he struggled to his feet. Abruptly a spreading stain appeared on his trousers and dripped from his pantsleg to his shoe. He regarded me with dismay, but quickly regained his composure.

"Oh là," he exclaimed. "Voyez vous, Jean-Pierre, que mon corps m'abandonne!"

Such humiliations were infrequent, however. The colonel, still an intelligent and disciplined man, henceforth kept an eye on the clock on the shelf by the skull within his bookcase. At appropriate intervals he would rise and tread in his halting manner down the hall to his bedroom and to his commode and chamber pot. Even so this first indignity, like his accident, was a token of his seventy-nine years and consequent failing powers. Indeed it was that very commode placed near his great, formerly marital bed which became the source of his injury when he had fallen one night and struck his head against its corner.

Upon our return from the prairie we had found him in that bed, scarcely conscious and reportedly dying. The American Dr. Matthew Snag, who had visited the day of the fall, had examined the unconscious man and had informed the agitated Madamoiselle Bijou that her master's condition was hopeless and that he would succumb within hours. But that good woman had not given in to despair.

"Bah," she had exclaimed afterword to the village apothecary. "Celui-là c'est un charletan! J'en suis sûre. Vous verrez, Monsieur. Il vivra!"

As events evolved, the good woman's suspicion was proven true by an American traveler who had once known Snag as an undertaker in his native Pennsylvania town.

By the third day after the accident, when the colonel had opened his eyes and asked for his deceased child-wife and for Arsène, Madamoiselle had managed to spoonfeed him a little water and some broth. After our return on that day, she and Hélène-Eulalie, by ministering to him continually, managed gradually over a period of weeks to restore the old man to a state of health approaching his previous condition. Eventually he was back in his office daily, along with his cat, reading or working at his escritoire.

Yet on first regaining his senses, Monsieur de St. Maurice had been confused, often confounding past with present, the dead with the living. For example he had awakened with the idea that a certain El Chato, a renegade Apache who had made himself chief of the Comanches' Tonkawa enemies, had captured Arsène and was holding him for ransom or death by torture. Feeble as he was, the colonel had insisted we immediately dispatch a party with trade goods to the Tonkawas to ransom his son. His niece and I had tried to disabuse him of that delusion, since El Chato was long dead, as we both knew, as a result of the colonel's own conspiring, and we ourselves had only recently left Arsène thriving among his Comanche companions. But the colonel would not be persuaded and for the sake of his recovery we humored him by feigning to send Antoine Lefort at the head of a party to ransom his son. The pretense satisfied the old man for a time. But one morning a few weeks later, while Mlle. Bijou was attempting to catch the cat in order to toss him from the chamber, Monsieur de St. Maurice sat up in bed, exclaiming, "Mon dieu, cet Apache est mort depuis longtemps. Donc, c'est pas possible."

Consequently Mlle had to reveal our deception. The old man was pained to realize the extent of his recent confusion. But after the first shock, he sent for Hélène-Eulalie so that she might give him a detailed account of our recent trip and especially the situation and condition of his son. This she did, telling him, for instance, of Arsène's exploit against the Osages while he had been mounted upon César, formerly her uncle's horse.

The colonel appeared visibly amused and cheered when he joined us at the dining table in his dressing gown at our next meal. Hélène-Eulalie had asked me about El Chato (the flat-nosed one), but I then knew very little of the story and had never wished to embarrass Monsieur de St. Maurice by asking him to explain what seemed an uncomplimentary account of his behavior. During our mid-day meal Hélène-Eulalie, who evidently possessed complete faith in her uncle's rectitude, tactfully raised the subject. At first he frowned, looking down upon his plate, then raised his bald head, removed his spectacles and slowly smiled, his brown bony cheeks coloring slightly.

"Perhaps I wouldn't do the same today. But possibly I would. You know, it was my only conspiracy." He appeared embarrassed.

We both looked at him expectantly.

"Well, I'll tell you. I've never talked about this, but... You see, years ago when I was lieutenant governor of this district, English smugglers regularly came to the coast of Tejas. They lay offshore and sent boats up rivers of that province. These smugglers would trade arms to the Indians, who would then use them to fight the Spaniards. The viceroy of New Spain, which of course includes Tejas, had forbidden the sale of arms to all Indians. But the governor at La Nouvelle Orléans, who took orders from La Havane, not from the viceroy in Mexico City, had approved the sale by our licensed traders of firearms to the friendly tribes. The Tonkawas, principal intermediaries in the contraband trade, were not at that time friendly toward Spain. This hostility was attributed to the influence of their leader, known as "El Chato," who was not even a Tonkawa. Although my orders came from La Nouvelle Orléans, as I have said, and we followed a policy different from that of New Spain, I was obliged to assist the governor of Tejas in every way possible. When he wrote asking that I attempt to remove such a detestable enemy from that people, I determined to undertake the task."

"The tribe was at peace with your district?" asked Hélène-Eulalie.

"They found better opportunities in the Province of Tejas. Besides, they feared our Caddoan allies."

"Therefore?"

"I had him killed." The old man went on to describe how he had invited El Chato and three of his most ambitious rivals to the post on the pretext that, should they establish friendly relations, they might engage in trade, possibly even that of firearms. The three men came, unaccompanied, probably because they had no wish to share their presents. The colonel entertained them in his home and made much of El Chato in particular, flattering him and even embracing him as 'brother,' so that the Apache suspected nothing. But he suborned the others. On the return trip one of the rivals, knowing his chief was unable to swim, shoved him from his horse while they were crossing a river. Thus the unfortunate Flat-Nosed one drowned, relieving the province of Tejas of a person considered by its governor to be an especially perfidious enemy. Soon afterward the Tonkawas made peace with the Spaniards."

"But...you were certain he was dead?" Hélène-Eulalie asked.

"I'd promised them each a musket, balls, and powder, as well as additional gifts if they would bring me his head. They did. Unfortunately they had turned from being the dead man's escort and friends to proud assassins boasting of his murder. Before reaching me, they displayed the head to a patrol of our men, and even to poor Madamoiselle, causing her nearly to faint."

There was an uncomfortable silence while we considered this account. But the colonel had not finished.

"Of course the affair and my part in it were whispered throughout the post and the village as well."

"The Tonkawas found out?"

"Never. But Arsène heard...not long after he returned to live with me at the age of ten." He gestured at the door to the kitchen, lowering his voice. "Probably from our own beloved gossip."

"Ah, Arsène," murmured Hélène-Eulalie. "What did he say?"

"Poor boy, he was upset. Very upset."

We continued to regard the old man, who was now pensive, smiling faintly.

"He came to you directly?" asked Hélène-Eulalie.

"He's the only one who has ever reproached me to my face. No, I saw him from my window. He was dueling with a shrub, slashing furiously with my sword. I'd forbidden him to play with the sword, so I hobbled out and confronted him. When he turned to me, I saw he was weeping, his face red and contorted, angry. I asked him first for the sword. He gave it to me, then stood, his head bowed, weeping. Now what can this be about, I thought? I saw how upset he was and went to comfort him. But he stiffened and shoved me away, nearly causing me to fall. Recovering, and baffled by his behavior—because he had always been respectful and well-behaved—I asked him what was wrong. He raised his head and looked, through tears, into my eyes, standing before me as if at attention. 'What you did was treacherous,' he said, still regarding me reproachfully. What? I thought. I asked him what he meant. 'When you had that Apache killed,' he charged. Ah, El Chato, I thought. I had almost forgotten about him."

"Poor Arsène," said Hélène-Eulalie with a sad smile.

"You see, he was disappointed in me."

"Yes," I murmured. "He thought you were perfect." I too had believed him perfect. I was not disillusioned, but I realized with a pang that he was more like the rest of us than I had imagined.

The colonel sighed. "Poor boy. He had discovered that this world, and his father, were not what he believed they ought to be. I took him into my office and sat him down. He wished to be a soldier, I told him. I reminded him of a soldier's obligation to follow the orders of his superiors and to perform his duty. I explained the obligation I'd had at that time to the Spanish crown and to the honorable governor of the adjoining province, who also served that crown. I spoke to him of the distinction between such an act, which he had called 'treacherous,' when it was done for selfish reasons by individuals and when it was done in the interest of the state. I told him that in the latter instance such an action, while not admirable, was often imperative for the good of the kingdom and its people—that is, an act which would be immoral when done by individuals for their own good was not necessarily immoral when done for the good of an entire people."

"That's true," murmured Hélène-Eulalie, with a thoughtful expression.

I looked at her quickly in surprise. This was not my opinion. "Well, did you convince him?"

"I cheered him. I reconciled him to the disinterestedness of my act. I'm not sure I convinced him, but I think he understood my explanation and forgave me." He plucked a handkerchief from his sleeve and blew his nose. "Now, let's talk of other things."

Later, walking in the hallway, I remarked casually to Hélène-Eulalie that I was surprised she would condone acts by the state that would be immoral if practiced by an individual. Instantly she halted, faced me and told me with acerbity that she, herself, was surprised at my naïveté if I believed that kingdoms might be guided by moral principles like those appropriate for individuals. She was annoyed, as her hard stare indicated. "A government that lies and deceives," I said, feeling my own anger rising, "loses the trust of its people and creates a cynical, disaffected populace. And rightly so."

"I'm astonished at you, Jean-Pierre. Such naïveté is childish. You must realize that state affairs transcend individual morality. As my uncle said, the well-being of entire peoples may depend upon the occasional use of duplicity."

"Then you'd also justify torture, when it's for the good of the nation? Say the end justifies the means, you know."

It was then that madame stamped her foot. "Under no circumstances, ever, do I approve of torture for any purpose whatever. Never, never, never. And it's insulting of you to suggest it!"

"Then you're being inconsistent," I began. "Can't you see..."

In the end our tempers overcame our self-control, and we descended into a violent, noisy quarrel. I think there had been an increasing strain between us for some time, something to do with mutual attraction in conflict with our fears and doubts about each other. The issue at hand had provoked its expression. In any event our combined fury on this occasion created a chilly atmosphere between us for some time to come.

So that summer passed. There are periods in a person's life that are so tedious he would sooner forget than remember them. The fall of 1798 through the winter of '98-'99 were such an interval in my life. Monsieur de St. Maurice continued his convalescence and gradual recovery, which was greatly assisted by the devoted care of Mlle. Bijou and his niece. As for cette dame and me, we continued to circle each other cautiously like two wary animals. We were compelled, though, to take the principal responsibility for the affairs of the trading house, owing to the death during our absence of M. André Duval.

This punctilious individual had been employed by the firm of de St. Maurice for nearly his entire adult life. For some forty years he had been keeping the books, supervising the larger sales, and ordering goods as required. While Monsieur de St. Maurice had busied himself sporadically with the business during the earlier years when still an officer in the army of France, Duval had proven such a loyal and dedicated employee that the colonel had begun training him to assume the position of manager. This was, if I remember correctly, in the month of November upon the colonel's employment by the Spanish crown in 1769. Indeed, after buying out his relative, M. Laurent de St. Maurice in the late 1760s, Monsieur de St. Maurice had bestowed upon Duval the title of "M. le Directeur," and had relegated all but the most important decisions to him.

Fortunately for us, Duval had kept clear, precise accounts, although their aggregate implication was a shock. There were debts, enough of them to indicate a severe downward drift in profits. The firm appeared to have been operating with the same volume of trade as during previous decades, yet sales of buffalo robes, other peltry, and horses seemed to have contributed little to the firm's fortunes. Working together, Hélène-Eulalie and I discovered the cause for dwindling profits. We found, to our surprise, that Duval had also been responsible for keeping records of the plantation, which had regularly operated at a deficit, one which had steadily increased. Funds from the trading post had been diverted, doubtless by the colonel's orders, to compensate for its losses over the years. But these had increased to the extent—what with diseased or disappointing crops of indigo, cotton, and tobacco—that the plantation was dragging the firm of de St. Maurice into insolvency. The obvious solution, we agreed, to the firm's faltering profitability was to sever its connection with the plantation—and, indeed, to sell that foundering enterprise before it entirely consumed the old man's assets.

Hélène-Eulalie proposed to her uncle that he take that action. To her surprise, and to mine when she told me later, the colonel was reluctant to discuss his financial difficulties. His response to her suggestion was politely vague. He thanked her, and me through her, for our continuing efforts in the trading house. He said he had been giving thought for some time to the problems she had mentioned and would carefully consider our suggestions, which he appreciated. He would, he added, consult with her when he had more closely approached a decision—especially since any decision he made would necessarily affect her inheritance, as well as Arsène's, and whatever he might leave to me. With that he, in effect, courteously dismissed her, turning back to the papers on his escritoire.

Afterward we let the matter rest for a time, thwarted by the old man's determination to retain control of his affairs. Also the two of us refrained from further discussion of government. Although the colonel had remained a staunch royalist, his niece apparently had not. From remarks she had made I inferred she wished to see a form of government more nearly resembling that of the present United States than a monarchy in France. "Surely something better than the past must come out of all this horror," she once remarked at the table in response to her uncle's regrets for the Ancien Régime. "You mean, 'liberté, égalité, fraternité?'" I joked. Her eyes sparked. "Why not? It's not entirely impossible, you know." Monsieur de St. Maurice, as I recall, had smiled his doubt at what he evidently considered her naïveté. As for me, I admired her spirit and agreed with much of what she said, although I frequently dissembled, concealing my agreement with a neutral expression.

I attributed Hélène-Eulalie's startling convictions, so unusual in a woman of her class, to the influence of her father, whom she had evidently adored and about whom she had told me much. Widowed late in life after the departure of his sons, he had lived for years alone in his château with his daughter and a few servants. As a young man in Paris he had associated briefly with the Libertins Erudits, or freethinkers. He had formally disavowed their ideas before matrimony. After his marriage he had lived quietly on his modest estate in Gascogne, overseeing the management of his vineyards and livestock. Not a particularly sociable being, as his daughter described him, he had nonetheless taken a responsible part in local affairs, as befitted his station. Apparently he had been a loyal husband to a constitutionally anxious and excitable wife, as well as a firm but kind father to his sons. His twin passions had been hunting upon his estate and his books, of which he had owned a large and varied collection. Particularly he had been interested in the new thinking of the Encyclopédistes, such philosophs as Diderot, d'Alembert, Helvétius, Condillac, Turgot, and of course, Voltaire. Liked by his peasants for his mild and fair practices, he was protected by them during the Revolution and had died in his bed of heart failure during his daughter's sojourn in England.

As Hélène-Eulalie had once remarked, she and I agreed on most of the essentials. Why, then, were we so cautious, si retenues, with each other? By the demands of the trading house and of the household we were thrown together constantly. Yet each of us maintained a cool reserve toward the other, especially after our quarrel. She certainly trusted me less after my evening with Sehêbi. But that was not all. She knew of "my" mulatto woman, Michelle. Her knowledge made me uneasy. I hated that fact. After my increasingly rare visits to the woman, I would catch her looking at me next morning in a peculiar manner that made me uncomfortable. There was no accusation in her look. It was not the raised eyebrows, the amused tilt of the lips, that troubled me but the tinge of distress on her features. Why could she not be more cynical, I asked myself, after her days in the French court? Yet I did not really want her to be cynical. It was her unusual idealism, in conjunction with her realism, which touched me deeply—so deeply that I found myself thinking once again of those delicate and wounded features as "lovely." Did this mean that I loved her? And was it simply my cursed pride and her distrust that kept us apart? It was the question that had haunted me for some time and which continued to haunt me.

I could not decide how I felt. I did not wish to love her. I did not wish to marry. I did not wish to lose the freedom I had sought and found upon the frontier. I was suspicious of romantic love. There is little reason in it. There were other, practical barriers. She had brought with her to Natchitoches Post some property, money. I had nearly none beyond my mare and my personal belongings and had come almost to regret my generosity to my aunt Alice. It would be unseemly, humiliating, I thought, for me to marry a woman with some little wealth—or in any event more than I possessed. She would wish to marry in church, an act impossible for me, or so I believed at the time. Then there remained our different stations in life: she, of the noblesse, I a bucolic, a simple frontiersman.

Still there were occasions when I found myself glancing longingly at her when her attention was fixed elsewhere, and my heart would bump and I would have to look away. And there were moments when I caught her regarding me sadly and was able for an instant to read her mind, and I knew she was thinking, "Why are we wasting so much of our lives, when the precious days and weeks and months go by and we might be truly together? And what is wrong with us that we are not?"

Then one evening when the two of us were standing by the staircase prior to mounting to our rooms, and we were both in exceptionally good humors, I confessed to her my promise to Taoinan, preparing to tell her how burdomsome I found it. Perhaps it was an additional glass of claret I'd had at dinner that evening that was talking. It was imbecilic of me. In any event she stared at me with a shocked, then pained expression:

"You marry Sehêbi? Not Sehêbi?"

"Well, he's my 'brother.' What could I say?"

Seeing her distress turning to wrath, I immediately began explaining how on our next expedition to the Comanches I intended to ask Taoinan to release me from my oath, assuring him that in exchange I would, in the unlikely event of his death, take full responsibility for the happiness of his favorite wife as long as I lived. But I saw that words were useless. I had blundered badly.

"Well, Jean-Pierre, congratulations!" she spat. "I'm sure you'll make a brilliant squawman." With that, she turned and rapidly climbed the stairs.

I stood below for a moment, hoping never to see such an expression on her face again. And yet, when I contemplated her fury, I didn't know whether to be badly upset or flattered—or even both at once.

19   *Summer 1799, The Southern Plains*

At the Pawnee-Piquée village one of Toyamancare's sons was waiting. He was a portly stripling of some sixteen years with features resembling his father's. Already a warrior, he sat painted, mounted upon a white pony, and bearing in addition to his bow and quiver a shield and lance. This boy was only one of several well-favored youths fathered by the warchief with different wives—although, strangely, Big-Mountain preferred his adopted son, Arsène, to his own boys. As for his girls, they scarcely counted, except for receiving benevolent pats from time to time, of the sort he might bestow absent-mindedly upon his favorite ponies.

The youth greeted us gravely, informing us he was to guide our trading party to the present location of the band. He was clearly pleased with this trusted mission and sat on his horse so proudly that for a moment he resembled his father, even to the manner in which he puffed out his chest, so that I had to turn my head to conceal a smile. His imitation led me to reflect upon the extent to which some sons imitate their fathers, while others are their opposites. I sensed hidden reserves in Arsène, for instance, which caused me to speculate that as an old man he might considerably resemble the colonel. But then I reflected that as a warchief for a people whose motto was, "the brave die young," there was a question as to whether he would ever reach old age.

We accepted the boy's proposal, of course, and the following morning set out after him, proceeding whenever possible along the northern bank of the Rio Colorado de Natchitoches, or La Rivière Rouge. At the end of several days we reached a fork of that stream and pursued its northern branch, which led us ultimately to a range of peaks whose silhouettes suggested high, irregular rockpiles plastered with earth under a pale blue sky with few clouds. The river or its tributary—I forget which—passed before a cove in which lay the tepees of the Comanche encampment, while their herd of horses, guarded by boys and older girls, grazed by the glittering stream beneath a summer sun.

On that final day of our trip when we were yet at a distance of several leagues, I had sent our guide before us to announce our imminent arrival. An hour or so later a horseman appeared in the distance, loping toward us by the stream.

"Isn't that Arsène?" asked Hélène-Eulalie. "It looks like his horse."

After a moment it became clear that the approaching horseman was indeed Arsène. Mounted upon his frost-faced pinto, he had come with shield and lance, tanned darker than many of his people, wearing only his breechcloth, buckskin leggings, moccasins, and with an eagle feather in his flying black hair. After we had exchanged affectionate greetings and embraces, he rode with his cousin and Lefort and me at the head of our column. He was in high spirits, clearly happy at our reunion. As we bore northwest along the river, he entertained us with his latest news and that of the band. Manos-Amarillas had died the previous winter, he said, and Red-Woman was now acting as civil chief, faute de mieux, though his position was hardly secure. Arsène himself was now married he told us—three sisters, for whom he had had to give many ponies. But better than that, he announced, he was now the father of three sons.

"What, already?" cried Hélène-Eulalie. "Three? Not already!"

"Why not?" He was piqued.

Antoine smiled, but Hélène-Eulalie laughed so hard tears shone in her eyes and she had to grasp the pommel of the saddle to steady herself. "Not possible," she laughed.

"And Taoinan? How is he?" I refrained from asking about Sehêbi.

"Oh, he's a great hero. And his young wife, Sehêbi. You remember Sehêbi," he said to me, with an amused sparkle in his eyes.

"Of course. What about her?"

"She has a little girl."

"Oh, how marvelous!" cried Hélène-Eulalie. "She had a child after all."

"She didn't 'have' it. I gave it to her. I gave it to Taoinan, and he gave it to her."

"You what?"

It was a long story. Arsène explained that only the previous month they had met with two other bands of the Kotsoteka Comanche division in order to determine how to punish the Osage people, some of whose warriors had encountered and surprised an outnumbered war party from one of these bands, a party who were riding north to fight the Pawnees. The Osage warriors had killed all the Comanches and taken their scalps and ponies. The families of the slain men had demanded revenge. A great council of elders and leading men had decided to send a substantial war party comprising warriors from several bands northeast to the Osage country to attack one of their villages. After much discussion, the council had decided upon Taoinan to lead the warriors. It was a great honor.

The Comanche war party had ridden a long way until their scouts had located an Osage village by a river. Taking care in his preparations, Taoinan had directed a dawn attack, when all the people of the village were asleep. Although the Osage warriors had come out of their rectangular lodges and had fought to defend their families, the raid had succeeded: The Comanche men had killed nearly everyone in the village, taking plunder and scalps. No enemy had escaped, except for two young women seized by warriors of other bands, as well as a little girl of about five years, whom Arsène had discovered cowering and weeping in one of the lodges just as he and the others were setting them ablaze. He had snatched her from the flames and ridden away with her seated before him on his pony, intending to give her to his wives to raise, since he could neither tolerate the thought of leaving her to starve nor of cutting her throat. But on the first evening that they had camped Taoinan had asked Arsène to give him the child for his young, childless wife, to make her happy. He had willingly done so, relieved to be no longer responsible for the little girl.

"You didn't kill any children, did you?" asked Hélène-Eulalie quickly. "No, you wouldn't do that. You couldn't, could you? And how many people have you killed?"

Arsène looked away, was silent for a moment. "I fought men only."

"And Taoinan?" I asked, curious.

"No, he led. I was right behind him. Before the attack, he told me, 'You and I will kill only warriors.' Of course their men were surprised and on foot, while we were mounted. They fought bravely, but we killed them all. He took three scalps, I only two."

"You lose anybody?"

"Five wounded. One, not from our band, died. But it was a big victory."

"But the others killed women—children?" insisted Hélène-Eulalie.

"Yes. They would have done it to us. It's our way, my dear cousin."

She shook her head, sighed, looked away across the prairie toward the shadowy beige mountains rising before us.

We halted our caravan and established camp at a bend in the stream at a little distance from the People's lodges. Leaving the engagés and the packtrain in charge of Antoine and Henri Tournier, Hélène-Eulalie and I followed Arsène to the Comanche camp, where we were greeted, as usual, by a howling contingent of wolfish dogs. Within the encampment, Arsène led us between tepees, where children stared and women paused in their work to gaze as we passed. Taoinan's and Toyamancare's lodges were pitched, as in the previous year, by the river in proximity to each other. Both men, according to Arsène, had ridden out to scout the location of a small herd of bison reported to be in the vicinity. Although the People suffered from no lack of food, since hunters daily provided deer and other game from the mountains, some families longed for fresh buffalo meat. The report of a herd nearby was too tempting to ignore.

The plan, according to Arsène, was to locate the herd on this day and to undertake a hunt on the following morning, taking care not to kill a large number of the animals or to frighten the remainder to the extent that they would depart from the adjacent region. If the hunt were properly managed, he added, the herd might linger within a morning's ride. In that case it might provide the band with meat for some time, forestalling the need for a move from this agreeable place for days to come.

At Taoinan's lodge, Hélène-Eulalie was so eager to see Sehêbi that she called her name while dismounting from her one-eared pony. Immediately the young woman emerged through the doorway of the serpent-ringed tepee, squinting, looking about in the sunshine and shadows. She gave a cry of delight as she saw her friend. Talking and signing at once, the two women embraced each other as First-Frost and She-Scolds-Her-Dogs also came out of their lodge and stood beaming, their little boys peering from behind their legs.

Before anything else Hélène-Eulalie wished to see her friend's child. Gesturing that she should wait, Sehêbi ducked into the lodge, reappearing some moments afterward drawing behind her a reluctant little girl wearing a breechcloth. The little survivor hung back, looking up at us with large dark, frightened eyes.

"I call her Ooa," Sehêbi announced proudly.

Ooa, named for the little screech owl, was a shy, frail looking girl with delicate features, thin arms and legs. Even looking down from my saddle, I could see the terror lurking in her eyes. She made me think of a small wild creature that had been plucked from its den and held up in the light. But Sehêbi's pride and delight in the girl were evident. I could see that already the child was beginning to make the cruel shift from her dead Osage mother to this young Comanche woman whom she clearly had begun to trust. When Arsène and I rode off to his lodge, we left Hélène-Eulalie on her knees attempting to coax the little girl to her. But the child continued to hang back and cling, appearing more frightened than ever by the strange buckskin-clad woman with suntanned face, gray eyes, and yellow hair.

The moment we rode up to Arsène's lodge one of his wives ran and seized his horse's rein, while another grasped the reins of my mare. The three sisters were lively, plump girls with broad faces who smiled and laughed frequently. They appeared to me on good terms with each other and eager to please their husband. The elder girl was suckling a round-eyed infant over the top of her buckskin dress as she tended a Spanish trade pot steaming a good smell at the fire before the larger tepee. The other two bustled about, obviously preparing a meal for several people.

The master of all this led the way into the tepid shade of his lodge. He flung himself down facing the doorway, under his weapons, sitting cross-legged, gesturing that I sit opposite him. We smoked a pipe in silence at first, passing it back and forth while my former pupil frequently observed me with an amused expression, as if to say, "Look how far our lives have diverged." It was peaceful in there. For a moment I nearly envied him. Nearly. He seemed contented, proud, pleased with his success as warrior and hunter-provider, pleased with his wives, their babies, his lodge and its contents, and with the many ponies that he knew I knew he owned grazing by the river with the herd. When he spoke, it was to ask about his father, and he appeared relieved, to be reassured about the old man's recovery and present condition. But when I asked him whether—considering the colonel's age—he planned to visit us soon, he said that this was difficult to predict, but possibly after the fall hunt.

"You're happy. You're sure you made the right choice."

"I know I did. I have what I wanted."

"It's a good life for a young man. But perhaps for an old man?"

"There is no good life for an old man. Maybe I'll die in battle. That would be best. Otherwise..."

"Otherwise what?"

"I'll boast with other old men in the Smoke Lodge."

I felt my ire rising. Controlling myself, I fixed him with a direct gaze. "Then all we studied together. All that learning we talked about—mathematics, philosophy, history. Culture from the Greeks onward, the Romans, Christianity, Newton, all that knowledge, all that study, your heritage, was wasted?"

"Not at all," he said, composed, regarding me unflinchingly. "It helped me decide."

"Your family, an ancient one—de la noblcss d'épée. Tu ne vas pas ternir ton blazon?"

He shrugged. "Soldiers. They won that escutcheon by the sword. They wouldn't be ashamed of me. This is a new world. I've chosen to live in this one, not the old."

Despite my efforts, my anger got the better of me. "Then you've a right to be happy. You've become what you wanted to be—that creature Dryden wrote about."

"Ah, dry-den. As you wish," he said, smiling. "At least now you grant me the 'noble.'"

Outside we heard horses and familiar voices. In the dazzle of sunlight before the tepee we found Taoinan and Toyamancare, the former sitting his buffalo horse, the latter mounted upon César and towering over his companion. The ribs of the old horse were visible, perhaps from frequent work and a diet of grass. And here I must pause to report that my command of the Comanche tongue had by this time improved to the extent that I was able to understand and participate in simple unhurried conversations in the language of my trading partners. I had no longer to depend upon broken Spanish and hand gestures.

"Hóla, Amabate," cried Big-Mountain. "Who's your friend? He looks like El Gayo, but uglier. Can it be?"

"It's the trader," said Arsène. "He wants to trade for your women."

"He can have them. Bluejay, how are you?"

"Come. My wives will take your horses. Come eat."

The Flute swung off his pony, hobbled toward me smiling. But I was quicker. We embraced. He pressed his sweating cheek against mine, holding it for a moment. Then we backed away, as the women led the horses to the shade.

"How are you, brother?" he asked. "Did you bring us many good things?"

"Yes. Arsène tells me you're a hero. Your Puha must be strong."

"Yes, it is strong," he said, laughing with pleasure. "Later I'll tell you about our raid. We took many scalps, many things, horses. But the Osages don't have many horses, except for those they steal from us or the Pawnees."

"Look," cried Toyamancare, suddenly turning. "There goes Tuchubarua. He's learning to ride." He regarded an odd figure, a man I had previously noticed in camp. The person, Tuchubarua, or Bearbird, was short and muscular, bow-legged with a big belly and big head. I had noticed him because, although he was ugly, he habitually wore a good-humored, even comical expression. He was clearly eccentric. Presently he looked even odder than usual, seated as he was upon a burro, which he rode bareback, his short legs dangling near the ground, using a single rein and a stick. He appeared not to hear Toyamancare, but as the burro plodded by us, he reached forward and patted its head, crooning in falsetto, "My Piarabo, my little Piarabo."

Taoinan and Arsène smiled. Piarabo was Toyamancare's racing pony, the winner at Natchitoches Post, of whom he was reputed to be inordinately fond.

"Hey, Tuchubarua," bellowed Toyamancare. "Are you still fucking your mares? All your colts look like you."

Bearbird drew up and stepped off the burro, which stood with its head hanging. With a look of great dignity, he walked to Toyamancare and squinted up for a moment at the warchief. He then turned, raised the posterior flap of his breachclout, bowed, and with lips and tongue loudly imitated a fart. At that, he walked with bowlegged dignity to the dozing burro, mounted the animal and, with one triumphant look back, rode away at the same plodding gait.

Bearbird's response had been so unexpected that the four of us laughed, Toyamancare most of all. "My brother-in-law," he said finally, wiping his eyes.

"My father-in-law," said Arsène.

After he had regained control of himself and had nearly crushed my ribs in embracing me, the warchief led Taoinan and me, following our host, into a brush arbor which Arsène's wives had constructed between the tepees. The women served squash and beans and maize recently bought from the Pawnee-Piquées, as well as venison which I found almost impossible to chew. All of us were hungry, especially the two who had been scouting since dawn. We ate mostly in silence, drinking spring water with the meal. Afterward we lay back and smoked, and the two hunters told us about their reconnaissance, as well as the plan for the next morning's hunt. I declined their offer to join in the chase but agreed to bring Hélène-Eulalie as a spectator.

Later when the girls had fetched the horses, and each of us was about to ride off in his own direction, Taoinan asked me whether I had seen Sehêbi and the little girl he had given her. "She's happy now. You must come see her. She talks about you often."

I told him I had. "By the way, I have something to ask you—something important. May I ride with you to your lodge, where we can talk for a little bit?"

"No, brother, not now. I'm too sleepy. I must go back and sleep. Tomorrow, after the hunt. You come eat with us. We'll talk then."

"Next day, you eat with me," demanded Toyamancare, turning as he began to ride off. "Bring your woman and Kills-Far. We'll have fresh buffalo meat."

I rode to where Antoine was to set up our camp. This camp was as usual prepared defensively I saw, packs unloaded, horses and mules picketed, tents pitched. All of the men, including Antoine and Tournier, were stretched out in their tents or in the shade of a few nearby poplars. After looking for Hélène-Eulalie, and finding her still absent, I too lay down in my tent and slept.

20

We rode out together until we approached a windy yellow plain dotted with junipers and a herd of grazing buffaloes. Fortunately the wind was against us. As we rode, Taoinan told me how pleased he was with his two sons who were healthy and growing fast. He would make them little bows this summer. He had already held them upon horses, and they were beginning to learn to ride. In another year or two he would give them their own ponies, and they would be able to ride out and play with other boys. When they had bows later this summer, they would be able to run about and begin hunting birds and rabbits.

"But not bluejays."

He laughed. "No, no bluejays."

"Now they have a sister too."

"Yes," he smiled. "They have a sister now." He laughed. "When I brought the little girl to Sehêbi, you should have seen her. She was so pleased that she cried. Before she was sad all the time. Now she's happy."

"You seem happy too."

"Yes, I'm happy. My Puha has been strong. I have many horses. My wives are content. They don't fight each other. We have plenty to eat now. I've done well in war—I who was less than nothing once, a cripple, am now respected by my father's other sons. These are good times for us."

Hélène-Eulalie and I remained behind, half-hidden by mesquite, on the high ground near the mountains. We watched as the hunters, bearing lances and a few with bows, approached the herd using the mesquite trees at the plain's edge for cover. Already the men and their ponies had diminished in the distance. Above them flew a flock of crows stretching away like smoke. The group of riders was small. Invited by Taoinan, it included Big-Mountain, Sees-Fire, and Arsène, as well as two of his brothers, White-Road and El Chamaco. Except for El Chamaco, The Boy, all appeared to be seasoned horsemen and hunters. But the portly camp crier rode awkwardly, seeming unable to control a white half-wild mustang, which often pranced sideways. They had now approached the herd. Yet the bisons' heads were still lowered as they continued to graze. I had brought along a spyglass which I passed frequently to my companion.

"Your 'brother' looks dashing on his buffalo horse."

"He's in good spirits."

"You haven't spoken to him yet?" She handed me the spyglass. "I don't need this, really."

"No, he keeps putting me off. Maybe this afternoon or tonight." Even without the glass I now could see the bulls at the near edge of the herd raising their shaggy heads and beginning to look about. They were probably snorting. I trained the little telescope upon the group of hunters, moving from one man to another just as the herd began trotting away, then broke into a heavy run. The hunters lashed their ponies and gave them their heads, and the chase began, with the horses gaining quickly upon the herd, most men riding to the left of the running animals. I kept the glass focused upon Taoinan, who had apparently chosen a fat cow and was approaching her rapidly, guiding the pony with his knees, his lance held with both hands, the left or outside hand held at the level of his head, trunk twisted, as he prepared to strike down to the right and forward for the heart. Arsène, also with a lance, was pursuing another cow a little to the left and close behind him. I flicked the telescope a little to the right, focusing for an instant upon Sees-Fire. This warchief was racing to the right of his cow almost opposite Taoinan, holding his bow poised for a low shot forward at his animal's flank, behind the ribs. Close on his right and a little behind suddenly hurtled El Chamaco, whose pony, running away, was bucking. The camp crier was flapping his free arm like a wing, still holding bow and arrow, as he attempted desperately to rein in the mustang with the other. But the pony had pulled its head down, bucking blindly. Even as I watched, the camp crier pitched forward over its ears to its right and the horse, dodging its rider's bulk, collided with the rump and right side of Sees-Fire's pony, throwing the rider backward at the moment he released his arrow, and running on. This imbrolio was so sudden and comical I laughed. But Hélène-Eulalie uttered a little shriek.

"What? What?" I exclaimed, lowering the spyglass.

"Taoinan," she cried out.

"What happened?" But as I watched, Taoinan seemed to be falling from his horse into the path of a bull running a short distance behind him. Instantly Arsène, close at his back, caught up, shifting his lance entirely to his left hand and, leaning, with his right arm, snatched the warchief below his shoulders and drew his body onto the rump of his own horse, veering off to his left, away from the herd and hunters. When he pulled his pony to a halt, he apparently could support the other man no longer. Taoinan slid limply to the ground and, after a few spasmodic movements, lay motionless. With that I kicked the mare forward and set off at a gallop between mesquite trees, with Hélène-Eulalie following.

As we approached the area of the hunt and the dark mounds of fallen bison, I glimpsed White-Road standing beside his seated brother holding the rein of his own pony as well as that of the little half-wild mustang. Farther ahead Arsène, kneeling, held Taoinan's upper body, while Toyamancare was on his knees bending over him. As we arrived, Sees-Fire stood ashen-faced, his hand pressed to his mouth, looking on in apparent disbelief. We slid from our saddles and ran to the fallen man. There was a hole in his chest bleeding profusely. Arsène's arms were bloody, his tanned features a sickly yellow. Toyamancare was leaning down so that his ear touched Taoinan's mouth.

"What happened?" I was kneeling opposite Toyamancare with Hélène-Eulalie beside me.

"How is he?" she asked.

For a few moments no one responded. Taoinan stared at the sky, his head dangling, eyes unfocused, glassy. For several minutes his chest rose and fell wildlly, repeatedly, finally collapsing in a great sigh. There was silence while we all listened for another breath. Time passed. None came.

Arsène squeezed his eyes shut, bowing his head. In his free and bloody hand he held a bloody arrow.

Big-Mountain raised his face, with a stunned, awed look. "Ya está muerto."

"Mon dieu," whispered Hélène-Eulalie. Crossing herself, she turned away, beginning quietly to weep.

I placed a hand on her shoulder. I knew what had happened. It was of course a dreadful accident, the fault of El Chamaco pony. But I had to ask anyway. To respond, Toyamancare nodded toward the arrow which Arsène held, having evidently drawn it from the dead man. Arsène, raising his head, opened wet eyes and passed the missile, still with an appalled expression, to his Comanche father. Toyamancare seized it, examined it closely, turning it in his hands, started, then glanced astonished at Sees-Fire.

"Crows' feathers, I think," he said, smoothing the bloody feathers.

Cunabunit stared with a look of even greater amazement. Apparently struggling to speak, he grasped his throat. His eyes rolled. There was a retching sound but no voice.

"No," said Arsène. "He wouldn't use crows' feathers. Nobody uses crows' feathers."

Toyamancare held out the arrow to him. Arsène looked down, gaped, raised his head, with an astonished expression. The warchief held out the arrow to me.

Accepting it, I peered at the black feathers, tinged red. Arsène, his head bowed over the dead man he supported, had again squeezed shut his eyes, tears dripping, his features fixed in a grimace of pain. Toyamancare glared at the clouds, tears streaking his face, while Hélène-Eulalie wept silently at my side. Sees-Fire, that valiant warchief, looked from one to the other of us, incredulous, aghast, his hand still squeezing his throat as if he were trying to strangle himself. We soon learned that, strangely, he was unable to speak. I glanced again at the arrow I held. As for me, I was too shocked to weep. My good friend, with whom I had been joking not long before, was now a corpse, with eyes fixed and vacant. The explanation, they were telling me, was a bloody arrow fletched with crows' feathers.

Borrowing his brother's pony, El Chamaco galloped away to inform the People of their favorite chieftain's death.

Big-Mountain and Sees-Fire butchered the dead buffaloes, bloody work demanding muscle and sharp knives, while Arsène, a subdued and silent White-Road, and I managed to secure Taoinan's limp body across his horse's back. During this endeavor I studied White-Road, but he ignored Arsène, his face fixed in a grim expression which never varied. Hélène-Eulalie watched and attempted to assist. All this accomplished, we rode back together. Men galloped out upon their ponies and joined us as we approached the encampment. Entering camp, we led a solemn procession, which grew as we proceeded. We had hardly progressed past a dozen tepees when Sehêbi came running. Without a glance at us, she flung her head and arms upon the body, her expression frantic, screaming repeatedly, shrieks which turned to howls and wails as She-Scolds-Her-Dogs and First-Frost, howling and wailing themselves, dragged her away, followed by an appalled Hélène-Eulalie on her pony. We halted before Taoinan's lodge, where we staked the buffalo horse and its burden.

El Chamaco, still mounted upon his brother's pony, approached shouting. As he drew near we could hear he was announcing a council to be held immediately in Red-

Woman's lodge—Red-Woman, that ambitious politician who, since the death of Manos-Amarillas had been acting as the band's peace chief. Now I was certain he would attempt to fill Taoinan's position as head chief. But none of this involved me. I left those gathering and grieving around the corpse of my friend and rode quickly to our camp.

Antoine had already heard the news and expressed his regret as I passed. But I nodded and kept walking. In my tent, I drew the flap, sat down on my buffalo robe and tried to think of what all this meant—especially my promise to Taoinan, Sehêbi's expectations, whatever they might be, my relationship with Hélène-Eulalie, and finally the grief which lay like a tombstone flat upon my chest, a weight that refused to budge.

I sat for a long, long time. The sun on the tent told me it was past midday. Abruptly the flap was flung aside and Arsène stooped and entered. I raised my head from my hands. His face was painted. He was wearing an eagle feather in his hair and was dressed in his ceremonial blue breechcloth, new leggings and moccasins. With his long black hair and dark, bony face he could not have looked more Comanche.

"Come. They're going to bury Taoinan."

"Who is? Where?" I was still not thinking clearly.

"White-Road and El Chamaco have found a place. They'll put him in it. You were his brother. You should be there."

"Of course." I stood. "I must be. Tell me, what's this about crows' feathers?"

"We believe that arrows with crow's feathers will never fly true."

"Do you believe that?"

He didn't answer.

"But how could it have happened? The crows' feathers. Isn't Sees-Fire's father the arrow-maker?"

"The old man can't see. A little boy brought him feathers from a dead bird he found. He said they were raven, but he was wrong. They must have felt all right to the old man, so he used them."

"How do you know the difference?"

"We can tell."

"I suppose they'll kill his horses."

"Some, yes. Maybe not all. His other brothers want them."

"Ah, yes. Of course." Once I had seen a minor warchief buried in a cave. I had never seen the burial of a band chief.

"Before we go, something important." He looked at me intently.

"Yes, what is it?"

"Before he died, he told Toyamancare..."

"Yes?"

"He said, '"Sehêbi to...Gayo.' Did he ever talk to you about her? It's important."

"He did," I said slowly. "Last year. I promised him I'd take her if..."

He looked relieved. "I thought you probably had. Good. Otherwise, they may kill her. Let's go."

"What?" I was stunned.

"You'll see. Taoinan was an important man. They'll say, 'she's only a woman.' The family honors itself by following all the customs. Let's hurry. I'll explain later."

Arsène had already spoken with Hélène-Eulalie, whom we found waiting before her tent, her pony saddled. Riding at a brisk pace, we caught up with the burial party at the base of the mountains, just as they were entering a stark canyon and had begun climbing. Taoinan had been a popular chief, and the group contained more mourners than the usual close friends and kin. We joined at the rear. It was a doleful procession, with the wives weeping and howling and the others wailing. As we slowly ascended a rocky red slope with a few stunted pines and a few clumps of grass, I saw that Red-Woman and White-Road and El Chamaco were leading. Behind them came the corpse entirely wrapped and tied in a sitting position, head bowed, within a red trade blanket and mounted upon the buffalo horse The Flute had been riding. On either side walked a woman holding the body vertical. One of the women was a wife of White-Road, the other the favorite wife of Red-Woman. It was as if the brothers who had rejected him throughout most of his life had now taken possession of him—and his prestige—upon his death.

Behind the body came the three wives. She-Scolds-Her-Dogs and First-Frost, wearing only hide aprons, had hacked off their hair and slashed their faces, arms, legs, and breasts. With faces painted black, they howled and wailed and crooned and moaned as they climbed, already bloody and filthy. Sehêbi, extremely pale, rode between them. She in contrast wore a white buckskin dress and wept silently. As soon as I saw her dressed so differently from the other two wives, I began to feel even more uneasy. As we proceeded to climb the narrowing gorge, I grew increasingly apprehensive. Hélène-Eulalie on seeing her friend attired in this manner turned to me questioningly. I could only shrug and shake my head. Several times I looked at Arsène. But he, with a somber expression, appeared engrossed in thought. I hesitated to violate the solemnity of the moment with questions. Finally not far from the canyon's upper end in vertical rock, a long horizontal crevasse entered from the west, as if the mountain had split there, with a view eastward over river and prairie. Here the procession halted.

White-Road, El Chamaco, and two others stepping carefully on the steep, loose rocks, carried the bundled corpse to the bottom of the fissure. They moved it a little upward upon the west side and seated it, propping it so that the bowed forehead faced east toward where the sun would rise the following morning, and for all mornings forever afterward. Without glancing back, they climbed out. I took a last look at the wrapped and doubled red figure and turned away to gaze out upon the prairie and the distant, shining river. Hélène-Eulalie for a moment clung and leaned against me.

I have written before that I am squeamish. I remember being perturbed by the killing of the horses. The execution, as it were, of the first two ponies, was not so bad, although it was not pleasant watching White-Road cut the throats of young, healthy animals and with El Chamaco shove them so that they fell into that cleft. But with the buffalo horse, it was distressing. He was a clever animal that had been trained—indeed educated—by a patient and affectionate master. He had witnessed the deaths of the previous two ponies. He resisted when El Chamaco led him to the brink of the crevice. The two men managed to control him, but when Tosapoy reached with the knife, he reared and struggled. The warchief swung the knife, partially severing the jugular. The gelding fought the rope and swung his head, flinging blood in every direction and upon those standing nearby, including his two executioners, fought until his knees gave way and he was pushed, still alive and struggling, to fall into the cleft with the others. Sehêbi was also standing nearby a little before Red-Woman and closer to the crevasse. With black paint on either cheek, she was ashen. The dying horse had flung blood upon her buckskin dress, making for a gruesome effect. I thought she appeared about to faint. At my side, Hélène-Eulalie turned to me, horrified.

I was beginning to feel a sense of panic as White-Road, still holding his bloody knife, came back and grasped Sehêbi by the arm. Half-supporting her, he led her toward the crevasse. I swung about and looked for Arsène. He and Toyamancare and Sees-Fire were striding forward and halted behind us. At my look, Arsène nodded slightly.

Red-Woman had begun talking of his brother and the brother of his brothers, Taoinan, about what a great warrior and medicine man he had been, and about how The Flute would now follow the red road that great warriors took, and where his best horses would now be with him, and where his favorite wife, Sehêbi—" He ceased talking and stared, as if abruptly tranced, at the three warriors advancing from behind us upon him and his brothers. Big-Mountain, Sees-Fire, and Arsène halted some thirty paces before them, each with a bow drawn to its fullest extent, arrow in place, aimed at one of the three. White-Road quickly raised the blade of his knife to Sehêbi's throat, and Hélène-Eulalie gave a little cry.

"Cut her, I'll kill you," threatened Arsène. From his tone, there was no doubt that he meant it.

"Hear me, false brothers," bellowed Toyamancare. "You who denied your true brother most of his life. He had another brother, Bluejay, whom he loved better than you. When I talked to you today, you wouldn't believe me. Now I'll tell you a last time—when your brother was dying, he whispered that he wished Bluejay to marry Sehêbi. I heard it. I swear by the sun." He turned to me. "Bluejay, did he not ask you last year to take her if he died?"

I replied that he had, my voice issuing as a croak.

"You hear, false brothers? The woman will go with Bluejay."

Red-Woman, suddenly as pale through his paint as Sehêbi was through hers, appeared stunned, nonplused. After a moment, he gestured to his brother to lower the knife. White-Road did so, grim, splotched with blood, and still supporting blood-spattered Sehêbi by her upper arm. I thought of Rabbit-knife, her end. There was sudden silence. Even the two wives' howling had ceased. At this moment I sensed a darkening mood among the mourners. Several of Red-Woman's friends and relatives were quietly taking bows and quivers from their saddles and were beginning to edge in the brothers' direction. Red-Woman, who was astute, evidently considered the developing crisis and decided to try turning it to his advantage with another oration:

"Do you wish The Flute to enter the other world alone?" he asked dramatically, beginning softly and growing increasingly loud. "To arrive there and find no wife to greet him? No woman to hold his horse or to bring him his food, or to fetch his pipe and tobacco? Is that what you wish?"

"Sehêbi will go with Bluejay," Toyamancare countered loudly, flatly. "That's what Taoinan wished. Let her come to us."

Again there was quiet. The situation had begun to seem an impasse for which there was no solution but violence—which, once started, might I suspected, kill us all. I turned to Hélène-Eulalie, gesturing with my head that she leave. But she looked back at me coolly and remained standing beside me, motionless. Even if death threatened, she would take orders neither from me nor from anyone else, it seemed. I set that fact in my mind and never forgot it again.

The tension continued to grow. Red-Woman looked around at the faces and the number of his supporters in relation to those of ours. Several of Toyamancare's grown sons were present, so that the odds were clearly against Red-Woman's group. I knew he was a shrewd politician and hoped he would know when to retreat. There were also three of the band's best warriors standing with taut bowstrings aiming arrows at him and his brothers.

Finally he looked at White-Road and signaled to him to release Sehêbi. But just as the warchief's hand fell from the girl's arm, there was a shriek and She-Scolds-Her-Dogs ran into the circle and to White-Road, from whom she attempted to snatch the knife, crying out, "I'll go, I'll go. Give me the knife. I'll go to him. I'll go to the other world." Nearly as strong as the warchief, she was attempting in a demented way, with her breasts flapping, to stab herself in the heart with the knife for which the two of them struggled. With this, chaos erupted, everyone except for Arsène and his two companions crying out, exclaiming, shouting at once, rushing toward the struggling man and the half-naked woman, who was covered with dried blood and dirt and resembled a creature glimpsed in a nightmare.

I looked quickly at Hélène-Eulalie. "Help me."

Together we ran toward Sehêbi. But Arsène reached her first. Seizing her wrist, he yanked her away from the struggling pair, nearly jerking her from her feet, dragged her to the two of us, then whirled and aimed his arrow again. We each seized a hand and drew her rapidly the several rods back to the horses, three of which I quickly untied. Boosting her upon the pony she had ridden, we mounted our own and started rapidly down the way we had climbed, I leading and her horse following. Pandemonium continued behind us. After a little distance, I looked back. Riding before Hélène-Eulalie, Sehêbi was clinging to the saddle, pale as her bloody buckskin dress, her dark eyes large and empty. But she was no longer weeping, or wailing, only hanging on.

We had not descended far when we encountered Antoine Lefort riding up to join us. I immediately transferred both women to him, instructing him to conduct them safely, with two of the engagés, to the Pawnee-Piquée villages. He was to set up several tents, leaving Hélène-Eulalie and Sehêbi guarded by his two most trustworthy men. He was then to return and seek me out. He nodded, though with a questioning look, and took the reins of Sehêbi's pony, quickly proceeding down the canyon with the dazed girl behind him. Hélène-Eulalie followed, turning back for an instant on her horse to throw me a distressed look.

I waved and loped back up to the gravesite, flinging myself off my horse and seizing a pistol from a saddle holster. I charged it, spilling powder, as I raced to rejoin Arsène and his companions. I didn't think. I knew they might need me, and that merely the sight of the pistol would cause a delay. The confrontation between the groups of mourners had lapsed into silence. Red-Woman, White-Road and El Chamaco stood as before, frozen in position, facing the two warchiefs and Arsène, who continued each to level an arrow at them. Behind the medicine man his supporters stood uneasily with bows drawn, arrows fitted, but not raised. I was catching my breath behind Arsène when Big-Mountain declared, "I'm going to kill White-Road."

"What? Wait," cried Arsène. "Wait. If you kill him, we'll have to kill them all."

"Kill them all, then. They're evil. They murdered The Flute."

"No. No they didn't."

"Red-Woman's a sorcerer. He put crow's feathers on Sees-Fire's arrows."

"No, no. You heard. That little boy. And the arrowmaker's blind. You know that. Red-Woman's a medicine man. Not a good one but no witch."

"They're evil."

Red-Woman and his companions were pale, regarding us intently, as if they understood that the conversation concerned them.

"Look," Arsène argued breathlessly. "If we kill these men, what will we do about their wives and families? They're Comanches. Yes, and the in-laws too. We'd have to feed all those women and children and old men. I've got plenty to do to feed my own. I don't want to hunt for more."

"I'd forgotten that," admitted Big-Mountain, suddenly with a sober expression.

Sees-Fire sputtered, evidently agreeing with Arsène. The two warchiefs regarded each other for a moment. Simultaneously White-Road dropped his knife and in a supple motion reached back and drew his bow from his case. But in attempting to arm it, he fumbled and dropped the arrow. At that he froze, watching us with an astonished expression, as if he could not believe what he had done. Simultaneously Arsène sent an arrow buzzing over his old enemy's head. "Niatz!" or "no," he cried, instantly fitting a new arrow to his bow. Feeling my own life threatened, I aimed the pistol slowly back and forth toward the warriors of the opposite party. White-Road now stony-faced, remained motionless staring at Arsène. His brothers and their followers stood as if stricken by paralysis.

"You see," exclaimed Big-Mountain. "If we don't kill them now, they'll kill us. Or Red-Woman will witch us. We have to kill them."

"No. They'll leave the band. Hear me, Potaw. You know my piebald colt?"

"Yes. I know that one. The pinto? You don't want him?"

"Look, if we don't do it, you can have him. I'll give him to you. They're ready to go. I can feel it."

Sees-Fire sputtered agreement.

Slowly, thoughtfully, Big-Mountain lowered his bow. Making the sign for peace, he began quietly addressing the brothers and their followers, while Sees-Fire and Arsène remained, as it were, on guard. In the end he quickly persuaded the brothers to leave the band. They were, it appeared, already prepared to depart and go their own way. Both sides orated, an agreement was reached, rendered sacred by passing a pipe. We dispersed all at once and rode down that red canyon in two parties, nearly intermingled.

21   *By the Pawnee-Piquée Village*

We had not eaten fresh meat since leaving the Comanche camp. Meanwhile waiting for Lefort and the others had grown tiresome. Our tents were pitched by La Rivière Rouge de Natchitoches at the base of the northern Pawnee-Piquèe village. With plenty of traded corn and pumpkins to eat, we craved variety. Consequently I had taken my musket and was riding into the nearby hills in search of deer. The governor's neice, bored, had asked to come with me. We were mounting a slope among scattered piñon pine and juniper trees, when Hélène-Eulalie's one-eared pony snorted, halted and looked around, abruptly alert and agitated.

"What do you suppose?" said Hélène-Eulalie, attempting to calm her horse, stroking its neck, while it danced and snorted repeatedly.

"Some predator..." I began, looking around. My mare was also growing increasingly nervous, skittering under me as we climbed. A big puppy, or half-grown dog, on my left was gazing steadily toward a rockpile some two rods ahead and to that side. This dog had followed us from the village, to my annoyance. But my companion had begged and insisted that it be allowed to accompany us. I had given in. As Hélène-Eulalie kicked her pony forward, and I too moved onward, I noticed that the pup's ruff had risen while it sniffed the air. I shifted the barrel of my musket, resting it upon my inner left elbow.

We proceeded. The one-eared pony continued to snort, toss its head, and skitter from side to side, while my usually steady mare had also become difficult to control. I recall that Hélène-Eulalie was reaching forward to stroke her horse's neck in an effort to calm him, when he gave a loud snort, halted stiff-legged, and bucked violently, an act which, catching her unbalanced, sent her flying off his back to her right. She landed on her back and buttocks, from which the momentum thrust her to a seated position. At the same time, springing from behind a boulder, a cougar streaked toward us.

All this I glimpsed while trying to control and remain seated on my rearing mare. The cougar's eyes were fixed upon the dog, which tried to flee, running almost under the hoofs of the one-eared pony. I drew the trigger, missing, I thought. The boom echoed in the narrow canyon. The cat wobbled, giving a little screech, attempting to run before the horse, but the mustang, to my astonishment, screamed and attacked it with both front hoofs, striking the animal a blow that apparently stunned and knocked it from its feet to its side, where it clawed wildly at the horse. Instantly righting itself, it began trying to crawl away. But the mustang struck the cat again with a forehoof, then seized the dazed animal by the neck in its teeth and shook it in the air. I had never seen anything like the fury of the pony's attack, as it continued to shake the cougar, finally slamming it to the earth, landing upon it with both front hoofs, and trampling it again and again, picking it up, shaking it, slamming it down and trampling it once more, leaving it motionless, clearly in its death throes or dead.

But the cougar had, in clawing for the dog, ripped open the side of its belly with a single swipe, nearly disemboweling it. It lay not far from the cat, yelping, shrieking, vainly struggling to rise out of its blood. Throwing my musket clear, yanking a pistol from a saddle holster, I managed to swing down from my mare to the ground, falling to my knees in the dirt, rising and stumbling to Hélène-Eulalie, who was sitting staring at the pup with an expression of horror.

"Are you hurt?"

Speechless, she pointed to the dog.

Running to the pup, I saw that, torn open as it was, the animal had no chance of survival, was probably dying, though still shrieking. I placed the muzzle of the pistol to its head and drew the trigger. I then took it by the tail and dragged it out of the bloody mess to the body of the cougar and dropped it there, where I examined the body of the cat for a moment. It appeared to have been a young one, not fully grown. The ball from my musket had grazed its back, leaving a pink line. Looking around, I spied the one-eared pony racing up an opposite hillside, dodging between piñon trees, boulders and stumps, stirrups flapping, reins flying. My mare stood a short way off, trembling, legs apart, ears forward, eyes fixed upon the dead lion.

Hèléne Eulalie had painfully risen, was dusting her buckskins, her face contorted, silently weeping. As I approached, she regarded me with an anguished expression, hobbling to meet me. Silently I embraced her, drawing her close, stroking her back, feeling the shuddering of her backbone as she now wept loudly, face pressed into my shoulder, clinging to me.

"Are you all right?"

"C'était de ma faute," she cried, glancing up for a moment, then lowering her head, pressing it to me, gripping me painfully, like a drowning swimmer.

At that I lost my reason. "Je vous aime, Madame," I said into her ear, ridiculously, suddenly overwhelmed with pity and the love I'd been suppressing.

She raised her wet face, gazing into my eyes for a moment, gave a distorted smile, and laughed. "Madame? Madame?" Holding to me she continued to laugh. "Et je suppose, Monsieur, que je dois vous aimer aussi?"

At that I too began laughing. We held each other for a long time, my face against her wet face until finally we regained control of ourselves. With my help she painfully mounted my mare. I walked beside her all the way back, leaning against her thigh from time to time in order to press against her. I bore my recharged musket on my left shoulder and scanned the countryside for her one-eared mustang, which she declared she already missed and feared she would never see again. But her admission of love for me was not the only miracle to occur that day.

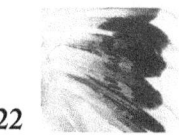

22

I stooped out of the tent to study the sky. It was black and purple. I sniffed moisture in the air, concluded it would shower soon. The wind had risen, fluttering the sides of the tent behind me. We had pitched our two tents on the northern bank of the river within sight of the grass huts. Already we had camped here for five days waiting for Lefort and the others. The fact that they had not yet arrived I took as a good sign: despite the turmoil in the Comanche encampment, they had been able to trade. As I reflected upon this a brilliant flash split the purple followed after a moment by a resounding clap of thunder. I could see from far beyond the village and its fields and horseherd the web of advancing rain. Now another jagged flash and a little afterward rolling thunder. In the intervals between thunder I could hear the river, which was noisier than usual. Evidently it had rained upstream.

"Beautiful, isn't it?" said Hélène-Eulalie from behind me.

I turned. "Do you think the thunder will wake her?"

"I don't think so. I gave her laudanum."

"Again?"

"She's still so agitated. If only Arsène would come with the child."

A gust of wind whipped around us. "We're going to get wet," I said, turning back to the tent. Inside I fastened the flap as wind tore at the canvas and rain pounded and splashed. She sat down on her buffalo robe. I seated myself on mine, facing her. The light was dim, except for intermittent flashes of the storm.

"So, what are we going to do?"

"Must we? Again?" she sighed.

"We still haven't decided anything."

"Do you know what Louis the Fifteenth called Madame de Pompadour?" Her eyes were amused.

"No. I have no idea."

"Madame Putain." She laughed. "That gives one an idea of his court."

"You're worried they're going to think you a whore because we're sharing a tent, Antoine and the others? And back at the post?"

"No, and yes. Of course I don't like the idea of gossip. But it's not that. It's that we haven't decided anything."

"That's what I just said. Here's what I'll do: we'll give Sehêbi and the child Arsène's old room. Or my present room, for that matter. But I won't sleep with her. We'll both be her friends and take care of her and the child, but I won't sleep with her. Then if you insist upon the church, I'll betray my principles, and we'll marry, and—"

"No, we won't marry."

"What? I thought we were going to marry?" I was shocked.

She crawled forward on her hands and knees and, kneeling, took my face in her hands, as the storm flashed and rumbled and tugged at the tent. Her face, smiling slightly, was close to mine. I could see her clearly by the flashes. "No, you must pretend you're married to Sehêbi. I don't like it, but you must. In fact, I hate it. But you promised Taoinan. That's how he understood it. You told me. You mustn't break your promise to your 'brother.' Marriage, their kind of marriage, is what she expects and wants, I'm sure. She'll be very unhappy if you don't. You see? You don't have to marry her in church, but she must believe she's your wife."

"But what about the two of us? We're not going to marry?" I was stunned by her words.

"If I'm going to live sinfully, I'd rather do it unmarried than married. Unlike the ladies at the court. I won't be your legal wife, but I will be your lover. We'll still be lovers, Jean-Pierre. She'll think it perfectly normal, since their men take several wives. Only the people at the post will be shocked, if they find out, and will call it—you know."

"A ménage a trois."

"Precisely. And they'll be right. We'll cause a scandal. But I won't be a Frenchwoman anymore. Or of the noblesse. Why should I pack around that stale wardrobe from Europe? I'll be free. An American woman. I know now I'll never go back. I'll be an American, and you too. We'll live as we wish, won't we, my dear?"

"Thank you for trusting me." I kissed her. "I don't know. But it's going to be complicated. For example, your uncle."

"He'll think you're living with Sehêbi. You're not the first white man to take an Indian woman. She's pretty. You keep your bedroom. She won't like it, but tell her its one of our customs."

"And if you get pregnant?"

"No, that must not happen. That would be too much. You have plenty of those... things?"

"Some. I can get more from Nouvelle-Orléans."

"We can't have a child, but we can share one. Ooa. Isn't that a pretty name? She'll have two mothers and a papa. I've always wanted a child. Poor thing. I love her already."

"Very well. If she gets over her fear of us."

"She will. Did you bring any of those...objects with you?"

"Yes, a few."

Lightning flashed and I saw she was smiling, her face close before me. "And why did you bring them?"

"Just in case of some emergency," I smiled. Actually, I had wondered why myself.

"During a storm," she added.

"Of course."

She rose and stood in the halflight, and next seemed to be undressing with her back to me. I was surprised. "What are you doing?"

"Taking off these filthy buckskins."

She turned and in the next flash was standing naked above me. Rising to my knees, I embraced her legs, rubbing my cheek against her bruised thigh, the side of her blue buttock. She caressed my hair and face as I drew her down to her knees.

"Go get one of those things, will you?"

I went on my knees to the packsaddle containing my articles for the trip, fumbling and feeling within it. I tore off my clothes. As I was doing so there was brilliant lightning and a tremendous crash of thunder that seemed to come from directly overhead. I took one of the little devices and crawled back to her and slid my arm around her waist, feeling the texture of her skin warm against my arm.

"What would happen," she asked, smiling. "If lightning struck our tent?"

"We'd be killed," I laughed. At that moment I hardly cared at all

But there's always an afterward. And afterward we lay on our sides together, our bodies warm against each other, and talked. She admitted she was bothered by the prospect of Antoine and the engagés thinking her a loose woman.

"That's why we should marry."

"No. It would be too late anyway at the post. It's now that bothers me. I know it's silly, but still…"

I pondered for a time. "We could have a Comanche wedding."

"What's that?"

The following day was fresh, damp, sunny. About mid-morning Arsène appeared with Antoine Lefort riding along the riverbank. At first I worried because I could see only two ponies approaching. But as they drew closer, I made out the figure of the child riding before Arsène, with a buckskin doll held before her.

"Here they are."

Hélène-Eulalie came out of our tent, stared, and called to Sehêbi.

Sehêbi ducked out of the other tent, blinked in the sunlight, looking around. She still wore the fringed buckskin dress, with shadows remaining where she had washed away the bloodstains. But she was barefoot, with disheveled hair. She appeared haggard, pale, and dirty, her eyes red from weeping.

"Look," said Hélène-Eulalie. "There's Ooa with Arsène."

She stared, then smiled, gazing with increasing excitement from Hélène-Eulalie to me. It was the first time she had smiled since we had brought her to the Pawnee-Piquée village. When the two horsemen were close, she darted forward to the side of Arsène's pony and held up her arms. Arsène, with his haughty, dignified expression, looked down at her sternly, detached. The child, round-eyed and solemn, seemed for an instant to draw back against him, hesitating. Then she leaned forward and down to the side, holding her arms out, doll in one hand. As the child leaned away from him, Arsène, without changing expression, and as if unknowingly, stroked the crown of her head. Sehêbi seized her, held her, embraced her, pressed her cheek against hers. Swinging round, hugging the little girl, and without another glance at us, she carried her into her tent.

While Arsène spoke with his cousin outside by the horses, Antoine Lefort reported to me within our tent about trade with the Comanches. Despite the dissension in the camp, barter had been moderately successful, with many buffalo robes, other hides and peltry, and a few more horses acquired.

The packtrain, with Tournier and the engagés arrived late that afternoon. The Comanche wedding followed that evening. The day of the wedding began auspiciously. As we were sitting at the fire outside my tent, a boy from the village appeared leading Hélène-Eulalie's one-eared pony by what remained of a rein. The saddle was intact. The mustang had joined the horseherd around dawn, he told us. One of the herders had recognized it as the white woman's horse. So here it was. The 'white woman' jumped to her feet and ran to the pony, encircled its neck with her arms, and pressed her forehead against its cheek. The horse submitted quietly, switching its tail. After a moment I nodded to Antoine. He went to the pony and took the broken rein, waiting. Hélène-Eulalie looked at him in surprise, then smiled and released the animal, which Lefort led away.

Our mock Comanche wedding took place that evening. The little drama occurred after sunset when the sky was still glowing with a few gold clouds and scarlet streaks. We performed it before an audience of engagés and the Pawnee-Piquée chief along with several leading men of the village. There were no women. I had stationed Henri Tournier, the oldest and most dignified engagé, within our tent to give away the bride, acting as her father. To Antoine I had relegated the task of conducting a half-dozen horses to me, the groom, before that tent. But when the time came, I was startled to find that he had arranged a little joke for us. Instead of the modest number of ponies I had asked for, he had recruited boys from the village to help him present the bride with an entire herd. He had appeared at some distance leading a long procession of ponies, all of those we had acquired in trade as well as, I learned later, a large number borrowed from the Pawnee-Piquées. There were horses of either sex and all colors—bays and sorrels, roans red and gray, black, whites, buckskins, chestnuts, along with a multitude of pintos. This irregular line of shifting animals reached back for some twenty dusty rods. With difficulty the mounted boys held the herd together, the village ponies and our new ones jostling, with mares nickering for straggling colts, others snorting, squealing, nipping or kicking at each other, while still others constantly attempted to break out of line. In all, it was a precarious and combustible procession accompanied by flies and giving off a steamy smell of fresh manure. At its head walked Antoine, with a smile, leading Hélène-Eulalie's one-eared mustang. Although annoyed, I could not help chuckling, then giving way to laughter.

None of us had brought extra outerwear, so that when the bride appeared from our tent, she was still in her dirty buckskins. But she had found some yellow wildflowers and twined them in her hair. Looking down as she stepped out, she was at first gracefully composed. But when she looked up and saw the living stream of restive horses before her, her mouth fell open. She looked at me and at Lefort and began to laugh, soon rocking so that she clung to Tournier's arm for support. With an amused, embarrassed smile the old engagé presented her to me.

"Do you really think I'm worth that much?" she cried, laughing, tears in in her eyes.

"More. Much more," I laughed, moved by her beauty as we gazed at each other, accepting her from Tournier. "What else can I give you?"

"Just a ring. A simple little ring."

"You shall have that."

I kissed her lightly and gestured that the horses should go to Tournier as the bride-price. Still smiling, the old man accepted them and signed to the boys to take them away to the horseherd. We then faced our little audience and, embarrassed and not knowing what else to do, I bowed slightly. The grinning engagés applauded vigorously while the Pawnee-Piquée dignitaries looked on with grave expressions. Hélène-Eulalie began to giggle again and hugged me, laughing, her face at mine, and the engagés joined in, laughing too, seeming strangely pleased, as if there had been more significance to our skit than had appeared on the surface. The Indians, unfamiliar with our customs as they were, continued to observe with solemn expressions. Hugging my bride as I laughed, I wondered what they thought of our mysterious behavior.

Antoine, to my surprise, had indeed prepared a feast. Not having any buffalo available, he had ordered one of his men to kill and butcher a two-year-old pony, one of those he had traded for. This animal was now roasting over several fires in our camping area. I was not pleased at the slaughter of a good horse but the smoke from the cooking fires was savory. I said nothing. Antoine appeared pleased at his second surprise.

Twilight came quickly. All of us used our knives and ordinary tin utensils for a meal consisting of corn, squash and horsemeat complemented with cups of water. The meat was tough but good. Our Indian guests ate heartily. I had mostly satisfied my appetite and was strolling with my plate among the three large fires occasionally taking a bite of corn mush when I paused by Arsène and Hélène-Eulalie, who were seated cross-legged side-by-side chatting by the smallest of the fires.

"Well, Madame Fouquet," I said. "How did you like your Comanche wedding?"

"It was lovely," she smiled. "I'll never forget it. The other will be dull in comparison."

"What about Sehêbi?" Arsène asked. "She didn't come. Weren't you going to marry her too, Jean-Pierre? You need at least two wives. Doesn't he?"

"You know perfectly well she's still mourning," said Hélène-Eulalie. "In fact she wouldn't leave her tent."

"I expect to marry her at the post—invite the governor and everybody," I said.

"Oh yes. Of course you will," said Hélène-Eulalie, beginning all at once to sound like a wife.

Arsène smiled.

Leaving the two of them to continue the banter, I wandered to the edge of the firelight. In the dusk I distinguished a figure seated on a large rock. I seated myself on a nearby small boulder. Puzzled, I squinted in the half-light to make out the other man, obviously Comanche, long-haired, bare-chested and dressed in the characteristic horseman's long leggings.

"How are you, brother?" the figure asked.

I started violently. I cannot understand today why I was not even more shocked. I recovered a little. I had always expected the extraordinary from Taoinan but never the miraculous. "I'm well. How are you?" I stammered. I could make him out indistinctly, even a little dark hole in his chest.

"You've taken Sehêbi. Good."

"Yes. She'll come with us. She's in her tent now, mourning."

"It's our custom. Hear me. Someday she may wish to leave you. You must let her go."

"Yes? I will, of course."

"And Amabate. Tell him El Chamaco is witching him."

"The Boy, Not Red-Woman?"

"No. El Chamaco learned. For White-Road."

"What should Amabate do?"

"Nothing."

"Nothing?"

"He must do nothing. Tell him. Otherwise he may die."

"Die? No. I'll tell him. Of course White-Road and his people have left the band."

Taoinan grunted. "Now you have married Woman-Who-Makes-Music. That's good. Those two women will not fight. You will have a new life."

"Yes. She's over there with Amabate. But tell me, brother. Why did you come back? Here among us? Now?"

"Sehèbi."

As he spoke the last word, I had a dizzying, falling sensation and his image grew clear and wavery before my eyes, like a reflection in a river. Laughter exploded from where the engagés sat. Simultaneously a dark, standing figure heaved a log upon the fire, which erupted in flames, sending smoke and sparks into the sky. The man was Arsène. I found I was standing beside him. The rock where Taoinan had been sitting was shining in the firelight. There was no rock where I believed I had been seated. I shook my head. I had not been drinking. Could I have imagined it all? The sparks had no sooner vanished than a comet dragged its tail down the summer night, seemingly from directly overhead, causing cries and a hum from those gathered at the fires.

"Beautiful," I said, as I gazed at the starlit sky.

Arsène remained silent, also staring upward, then left the fire.

We remained for another week at the Pawnee-Piquée villages, trading and preparing for the trip home. We bought ears of corn, melons, squash, and beans, as well as another pony, an old, gentle animal for the child. Meanwhile with the little girl to care for, Sehêbi seemed to have begun recovering from the shock of Taoinan's death and the events following it, washing herself and the child in the river daily as well as taking greater care otherwise of her appearance. Although she continued to grieve quietly, with sorrow persisting in her eyes, her demeanor was more nearly normal. She had gained weight since the previous summer, was pale with dark half-moons below her eyes and looked older than her nineteen years. In spite of this she was an attractive girl—and strangely in a way I could scarcely believe was, I suppose, my wife.

Early one morning at the end of the week we departed for the post. Arsène, with whom I'd had a talk, left at the same time, starting back for the Comanche camp by the mountains. After we had embraced, and he had kissed his cousin on either cheek, he mounted the gelding he had ridden to the village.

"Once again—when will you come to see us?" I asked, swinging up into the mare's saddle. "That's the first thing your father will ask."

"Tell him..." He reflected. "All right. Late October maybe, or November, after the fall hunt. Anyway, I'll come this year."

"Bon, au revoir." I waved and turned the mare and loped to catch up with the packtrain.

"Au revoir, dear cousin and friend," cried Hélène-Eulalie, turning as we rode side by side. "Kiss those babies for me."

Arsène evidently heard her, for he waved once more, a diminishing figure sitting erect upon his pony, again the minor Comanche warchief with a name to come as he rode at a lope westward, upriver.

"You always wonder," Hélène-Eulalie shouted, with a pained expression, as we trotted together toward the packtrain, "when you leave someone out here, whether you'll ever see him again."

I rode to the head of the train to join Lefort. Hélène-Eulalie had drawn up her horse beside Sehêbi's. The old yellow pony on which the child was mounted had trotted between the horses of the two women, who appeared to be trying to converse over the child's head. I looked farther at the column behind me, with its packsaddled horses and armed men, and the spare horses behind with Henri Tournier. It made a long and dusty caravan.

I looked again at the child between the two women and smiled. She regarded me gravely, doll clutched in the saddle before her, round-eyed as before. Like a small owl, I thought, ooa, the screech owl her new mother had named her for, riding solemnly between her two new mothers, one dark and one blonde. If they were both in an extremely peculiar way my "wives," then this little creature, this little Ooa, was also in an odd way my "daughter." I would, I thought, have to begin to know her. I gazed ahead into the prairie before us. Pondering the extraordinary change in my life, I smiled to consider that after all the years of a bachelor's free existence I was now in effect married, and to two women at once—and with a daughter. Even funnier, when I thought about it, was that having a little family all of a sudden constituted a profound change by no means disagreeable to me. I saw it as a new beginning, the beginning of a new life.

23   *The Road to the Post*

I woke to screams. A woman's screams, I thought. Osages, burned like fire in my mind. But here, beyond La Grande Forêt? Confused but awake, heart pounding, I struggled out of my bedroll and seized my musket. I ran, stumbling, to the horseguard, one Totin. The screams ceased. Part of my mind was considering the oddity of no warwhoops. Why not? They must have encountered our tracks on the western side of the forest, followed us here, where they rarely came. From somewhere now a sobbing. Wait— Could it be the child? Maybe it was...

"Qu'est-ce qui se passe?" I panted.

"Je pense que ce n'est rien de grave," said Totin. "C'était la petite qui poussait des cris—un cauchmar, quoi."

I ran, then slowed, panting, to Sehêbi's bedroll, where I could see the two women bent over, comforting the child. Totin's surmise was correct. Ooa, whom we guessed to be five or six-years-old, had screamed awake out of a nightmare. This was not astonishing for a child who had seen her mother murdered and had been snatched from her burning village by one of the Comanche raiders, namely by my former pupil, Arsène-Christophe Alexandre de St. Maurice, who rode away with her past the body of her slain and scalped father and the corpses of other Osage men, some surely also her relatives. Near her now was Hélène-Eulalie wrapped in a blue blanket standing above the child's new, Comanche mother, Sehêbi, who was stroking and comforting "la petite."

This alarm occurred as we were camped for the night on La Rivière Rouge de Natchitoches (also known as El Rio Colorado de Natchitoches) at our familiar ford while returning to the post, Fort St. Jean Baptiste. We had built a fire near the charred hulk of the cotton tree which a storm long ago had apparently deposited on the bank. Here a little east of La Grande Forêt—those two parallel swaths of mostly post oak stretching from northern horizon to southern—I had considered us reasonably secure from any roving Osage war party which might have discovered our tracks. Still I had ordered our customary procedure to be safe, placing bales of hides and other goods acquired in trade in a semi-circle around us away from the riverbank. The evening was fine, with stars. We had raised no tents, laying out our bedrolls. Our saddle horses were hobbled or staked nearby, while Antoine Lefort had chosen several engagés to guard the herd of Indian ponies we had acquired and which were by now accustomed to us and usually content to graze and rest, unless there were a bear or cougar in the vicinity.

After the alarm, Hélène-Eulalie joined me at the remains of our fire. I tossed on a broken branch. It flared. I shook my head, thinking of Ooa and particularly of Arsène, whom we had just left with his people. I tried to dismiss him from my mind. But he was not easily dismissible. It has always proved nearly impossible for me to do so. Often he has confounded me—as for example on the night I overheard his painful confession to Antoine Lefort that when he was a 'wolf' in the Comanche military society of 'wolves,' and was crawling toward a Painted Arrow, or Cheyenne, encampment, he had once been forced to cut the throat of an old woman out digging roots. I would not have believed him capable of that. But he was always able to surprise me.

"This is the place," Hélène-Eulalie reminded me, "where you lost Arsène, isn't it?"

"Yes." I had lost him when he was twelve. This was not a pleasant topic for me. That loss, of course, was merely the first. We lost him to the blizzard. I didn't know it then, but we were to lose him twice more. Once as captive, and finally...yes, finally. The evening was calm and beautiful, with stars, but the place made me uneasy. Too many memories. Too many doubts about the future.

"And Big-Mountain bumped into him in the storm."

"Yes. If Toyamancare hadn't come along..." In my mind I could see the sunny shining windswept empty snow that morning, and throughout each day of our two-day search. Not one track. "Big-Mountain almost surely saved his life."

"And made him his son?"

"Yes."

"And you had to go back and tell my uncle. His only living child. That must have been terrible. Poor Jean-Pierre."

"Sending that news back was, for me...the hardest act of my life."

Hélène-Eulalie soon returned to her bedroll. As for me, roused by the spot and its memories, I was not sleepy and remained, solitary, for a long while under a wisp of a moon before the fading red coals and flicker of the fire. My mind chafed, thinking of Arsène, the boy, and the warchief. Then and now. That night. Memories rushed into my mind. Guilt. One does foolish and cruel things when he is young. A man of my age who says he has no regrets either lies or does not know himself. Or else he was a saint. There are few saints. I was not one of them. When, heading westward, we arrived at this crossing on La Rivière Rouge—also known as 'The Red River'—the wind was already blowing stiffly. Already it was cold. To the north was a blue-black cloud the color of a bruise, such as I had never seen. Advancing. Thunder rumbled, crashing. And from the cloud, lightning, yellow cracks appearing and disappearing. All this coming toward us. Antoine Lefort loped up to me, shouted in my ear: "We must hurry. Tell them to hobble the horses, or we'll lose them." He gestured at the northern sky. "It's going to hit us. We must first unsaddle, secure the horses. Then set up the tents, if possible." I agreed, yelled commands, and the men obeyed, rushing, yanking off pack saddles, slipping hobbles around fetlock joints. By this time the lightning was close and the horses nervous, prancing and leaping, the best they could, now hobbled, with a few of our saddle horses also staked near the tents we were attempting to set up.

The storm struck with force, the wind, fiercely cold, almost lifting me from my feet as

I clung to the tent, nearly erected. It was instantly dark, and I could see only by the flares of lightning striking the prairie nearby and terrifying the horses, some of which were rearing, flinging themselves to the earth in their effort to escape. Tents began blowing away, heaving through the air like huge bats, further terrifying the animals. Abruptly with the wind came snow in fat, stinging flakes, fast, furiously whirling, driving at us on a level plane from the north and further reducing vision. Reason had by now oozed from my mind, leaving it blank. I had no idea of what to do, I a young man, the leader of my first trade expedition. Nothing like this had ever happened to me. Unable to think, I could merely cling to the tent, attempting to keep it and myself from leaving the ground. It was then that Arséne somehow struggled to me, seizing my arm and placing his mouth to my ear.

"What?" I yelled. "What?"

"The dun, my horse—he's gone. I can't find him. Please, Jean-Pierre, help me find him. Please, please."

"You've lost your horse?" I yelled, suddenly in a rage and completely irrational. "Well, go find him. Go on, go find him, little idiot."

"No, please help me, Jean-Pierre. I can't see anything. You have to help me. Otherwise he'll be lost," he cried, continuing to tug my arm.

"Va-t-en, petit morveux!" I screamed at him, hearing my voice rise to a screech like a woman's, telling him to 'Go away, little snot-nose.' "Go find your horse, and don't come back till you find him. You hear me? Don't come back without him!" With a great jerk, I freed my arm, sending him flying.

So much for reason. And my cursed temper. Goddamn my temper. You see, I had lost my reason. Clinging to the tent, I'd sent the child off into the storm. Am I proud of that? No, I am not. I had refrained from telling Hélène-Eulalie that part, only told her he had wandered off to look for his horse.

A little later Lefort slipped through the tent-flap covered with snow and resembling a bonhomme de neige. I was sitting upon a buffalo robe with my head in my palms. When he asked me excitedly whether I had seen Arsène, I remembered suddenly what I had said to the boy. I rushed out into the storm, shouting, "Arsène, Arsène!" I was a lunatic, crazy— or in Comanche, "poisá." But I didn't go far. At only a short distance from the tent I realized I was lost. I could see nothing but whirling white. In some manner I found the tent, groping until I bumped into its glow. Within that shelter by the light of a smoky fire Lefort and I stared at each other, realizing there was absolutely nothing we could do until the storm had subsided. Nothing we could do at that time to search for Colonel de St. Maurice's only living son.

Poor boy. While we were searching that vacant white shining prairie, Arsène was seated behind Toyamancare, or Big-Mountain, clinging to his waist, face pressed against the buckskin warshirt-back of this unknown Indian, seated upon his pony. And grateful to be there and alive. Later when the warparty reached the Comanche camp farther up that same river, and beyond the snow, Big-Mountain chose to test him at once, evidently wishing immediately to discover the mettle of his newest possession, the white boy whose life he had saved. Years later, after hearing Arsène's story, I tried to imagine my former pupil's introduction to that entirely unfamiliar, strange, and probably terrifying place, a Comanche encampment. I had to admire the boy he had been. Even as a child he had been game.

Big-Mountain's war party rode past the horseherd and its young guards and into camp well after the sun shone in a sky blown clear blue except for smudges of smoke from the lodges of the band. Immediately all life there, dogs and children, a few old men and many old women, warriors and their wives and in-laws, poured out of a grove of tepees to welcome their returning warriors and to stare at the strange white boy. The big warchief slid from his sweating pony, leaving the boy seated behind the pad saddle. Arsène told me that dressed as he was in buckskins among that crowd of sparely dressed, bare-skinned human beings of both sexes and all ages, he wished nothing more than to become invisible. He was especially aware and shocked that some boys not too much younger than he went entirely naked, their little penises dangling like worms before the girls and women, while the older boys wore only breechcloths. The older girls he noted were modestly clad in buckskin dresses, the little ones in breechcloths. The camp and its smoke even smelled different from anywhere he had ever been, mostly good, cooking meat, but with a sharp, exotic trace.

In spite of the staring eyes of that crowd of Indians, and all their chatter and clamor, his attention was fixed upon the freshly-painted warchief who had plucked him from the blizzard and in whose will he sensed that his fate lay. Big-Mountain abruptly broke off his conversation with several feathered important-looking men, with whom Arsène later realized he had been betting. The warchief strode to a group of boys about his age. Hesitating among them, then seizing one by the arm, he leaned and spoke to him for a moment, led him to the trampled earth around his pony, waving and evidently shouting that the crowd move back. People shuffled backward. Placing the Indian boy near the warhorse, he reached and seized Arsène, swinging him down from behind the saddle and placing him facing the other boy at a distance of three or four strides. Then, with a fierce expression—one to be taken seriously—and painfully gripping Arsène's arm, he mimed with his free hand that the white boy was to fight the other.

Arsène was too startled at first to think, but instinct told him not to delay. So while the other boy began cautiously advancing toward him, hands poised as if to seize him, Arsène, acting peremptorily, charged and pushed him so violently that the other, grasping for him and missing, nearly fell backward, staggering to recover. Arsène stood waiting, not sure what to do next. He had never fought before. The Comanche boy, angry now, rushed at him kicking in the air. He waited, backing, turning partway. He received a blow to his hip but swung round and caught the boy's foot. With all his strength, he heaved the foot upward and shoved forward. His adversary flipped backward onto the dirt, striking his head and slamming the air from his lungs, leaving him gasping, feebly trying to breathe and rise. The spectators cried out and pressed closer. In spite of his efforts the Comanche boy fell back and lay struggling to regain his breath. Again and again he tried to sit up but was unable to rise more than a hand's breadth. At last he flopped back into the dust, lying helplessly while still gasping.

"Bravo! Yo lo guardo!" came suddenly from behind Arsène, who had absorbed enough Spanish from soldiers at the post to know it meant, "I'll keep him!" He turned to see Big-Mountain, a stout, heavy, man with shining dark skin and a feather in his hair, stride to him with a ferocious smile, grip his arms, shake him gleefully, and toss him behind the pad saddle upon his warhorse. Evidently he had won his bet. Mounting the pinto, Arsène's new father pressed his pony through the noisy, staring crowd and trotted between tepees to a lodge with an old woman standing in front. The old woman took the rein of the pony as Toyamancare dismounted. In a peculiar way, Arsène-Christophe Alexandre de St. Maurice had come home—that is, to his new home.

Tossing twigs on the coals, which blazed and fluttered for a moment, I recalled the boy the colonel's son had been—as usual, almost with disbelief. When I had first met my pupil he had been a lively and affectionate lad of ten years, well-mannered, with an inquiring mind. Though headstrong and stubborn, he had been an industrious scholar. We became friends. After the first year our relationship more closely resembled that of older brother to younger, or even father to son, than of tutor to pupil. Colonel de St. Maurice was more than a half-century older than the boy, whose mother had died the year in which he was born, 1775, before my time. But I've been told she was a pretty child far younger than Monsieur de St. Maurice (the custom in La Louisiane being for girls to marry between the ages of fourteen and nineteen) and that he was inordinately fond of her. She, along with a daughter and another son she had borne the colonel, was torn away by a terrible pestilence that swept through the post one year. Since Arsène, the child, lacked living grandparents on either side, the loss of his mother, older sister and brother meant for him a solitary childhood without much affection.

As for the colonel, they say he never recovered from the loss, although he was a man of such fortitude and composure I could never detect a sign of his grief. Nevertheless I sensed it weighed upon his heart. Immediately after his wife's death he sent the infant Arsène downriver to his sister in Nouvelle-Orléans. This, his only sister, was a single lady and a notorious snob who raised the boy until he reached the age of ten, when he became my charge.

Arsène's aunt was a devout lady who had left much of his education to her favorite priest, a Father Crispin, evidently a dry and severe old man, while she occupied herself with her social life, as well as with his social upbringing, trailing him through the drawing rooms of her restricted circle, the most elevated in the Nouvelle-Orléans of that period, where he might be instructed by the example of other elderly ladies and a few old gentlemen with perfect manners. But I soon found that his true character combined imagination, invention and daring. While outwardly docile and respectful toward authority, the boy was, I discovered, inwardly in bitter rebellion against the doctrines and discipline of the Church—and, indeed, against all authority, including mine and that of his father. This attitude he successfully concealed most of the time, having in general the mien of a responsible little adult and usually accompanying it with the mild and courteous behavior appropriate to a grown man of gentle birth.

Of course I was younger then and something of an enthusiast. Monsieur de St. Maurice possessed a remarkable library, and I had been reading the philosophes, most particularly Messieurs Diderot, d'Alembert, Turgot, and Voltaire. Besides the fundamental subjects, such as arithmetic, Latin, history, grammar and rhetoric, selections from Virgil, Horace, and Cicero, I assigned and discussed with Arsène readings from the new authors. We even read and discussed passages from that old Jansénist, Blaise Pascal and, in contrast, from M. Jean Jacques Rousseau. Possibly it was unwise to introduce such novel ideas to an immature mind. Yet as I have said, I was an enthusiast and after completing the essential tasks and drills of the day we engaged in many impassioned discussions concerning what we took to be the flaws and virtues to be found within the works of the old and the new authors.

Arsène, though, would stand for little of Pascal. To the contrary he virtually shuddered at any writings reminiscent of piety. He had early and in secret become a rebel. No, it was to the ideas of Rousseau that he was powerfully attracted and to which he returned again and again, arguing for them vehemently. I remember that the concept of Rousseau which particularly seized my pupil's imagination was that of man living freely—I stress, freely—in Nature, as opposed to civilized man with his luxuries and effeminacy, "the garlands of flowers over the iron chains" of his slavery. Arsène admired what he understood to be the warlike virility and Spartan simplicity of the Prairie Indians, as described to him by a then younger and more voluble Canadian trader, a former illegal coureur de bois himself, Antoine Lefort. Especially the boy had admired the Indians' freedom, their life in the outdoors with their wants supplied by Nature, the open sky above them, far from the artifices and hypocrisy of Civilization.

While amused by my pupil's passionate interest, I was able to sympathize with his enthusiasm, since it recalled my own fascination as a sickly boy with the Indians and the frontier. Actually I'd been myself such an enthusiast for the Natural Life that I had committed to memory some declamatory lines encountered in a book belonging to my Bostonian Blue-Stocking mother, a drama by the English poet, Dryden, *The Conquest of Granada*. In the speech of its hero—whom I had of course imagined myself to be—he confronts a monarch who has condemned him to death. The child's interest had recalled it to me, and I had recited it to him in English, crudely translating my recitation into French. Although Arsène spoke very little English, he insisted upon memorizing this passage in its original language. He performed it for me again and again with dramatic gestures and atrocious accent:

"I am free as Nature first made Man,
Ere the Base Laws of Servitude began,
When wild in woods the Noble Savage ran."

Gazing at the stars, I pondered destiny. Le destin. I wondered then, and have many times since, whether it might be Arsène's destiny to become that curious creature, a Noble

Savage, whatever that might be. I observed him for years with almost the regard of an older brother. Eventually he provided my answer.

Seeing that the camp was secure, as Antoine Lefort had reported to me, and quieting, and that there was nothing I could do, I returned to my bedroll, shifted it so it lay almost touching that of my less-than-legal bride, slid my musket nearby, lay down in my buckskins. When Hélène-Eulalie sleepily reached out her hand, I pressed it to my cheek, then passionately to my lips, kissed and released it. After that, and a few murmurs between us, we drifted into the restful remainder of the night, with only a horse-snort or an occasional owl to disturb the silence.

On our return Colonel de St. Maurice, at the age of eighty, fell in love. This did not occur immediately after our arrival. Although he was delighted to welcome us home following a successful expedition and to hear news of Arsène, he was in the beginning puzzled and annoyed by the presence of Sehêbi and the little girl, especially when we asked him to allow them to live with us as members of the household. Yet the old officer and diplomat, veteran of both the French and Spanish armies, liked the Indian peoples and was respected by them.

I should explain, however, that the woman, like the child, was anything but prepossessing during those first days. The colonel remembered Sehêbi from her earlier visit during Arsène's first stay. But then she had been excited and pleased by the novelty of all she saw. She had been pretty and charming. This time she was subdued and morose, a somber presence uninterested in her surroundings. The child, too, for the first weeks remained sad, aloof, and fearful with downcast eyes, hugging her doll, silent around others in spite of Hélène-Eulalie's and Mlle. Bijou's efforts to draw her out. Monsieur de St. Maurice, who had originally worried that she would spoil the tranquility of his household and of his office in particular, began—after learning her history—to be troubled by her melancholy silence. Eventually he spoke to his niece of his growing concern, but there was nothing she or any of us could do except to reassure him, as Hélène-Eulalie did frequently, that the little girl would eventually grow accustomed to her new surroundings and to us and would then become happier.

She changed more quickly than we had expected. From the beginning she had been drawn to the old tomcat, especially perhaps because domestic cats were at that time unknown or a novelty to people of the prairie tribes. But Diablo had been suspicious of her attention and had rejected her advances by stalking away with lowered tail and ears drawn back. But after a week or two had passed and the child had ceased her efforts to stroke him, the cat appeared to have become increasingly intrigued by her, curling around the kitchen chair she often sat in and even rubbing against her bare legs, as long as she paid little attention to him. Then one day during the third week after her arrival, Diablo, without warning, sprang into her lap and began kneading her knees through her dress. We happened to be eating lunch at the time, and Mlle. Bijou immediately came beaming, with a tray of coffee, into the dining room to inform us that the little girl had smiled and was at that moment stroking the old, battle-scarred cat, who was purring loudly. This was an event of some significance, since it was the first time any of us had seen Ooa smile. The three of us, including the colonel, smiled at each other.

This little triumph, aside from the cat's part in it, belonged principally to Mademoiselle Bijou. From the first the Negro woman had devoted herself to the child, feeding her plentiful meals with tidbits offered in between in order to fatten her thin body, washing her face and hands, combing her hair, talking to her constantly in French, and—as soon as Ooa had come to trust her—taking her by the hand and leading her to the village, where she had had her fitted for two or three dresses. Several days later, following another trip, she had returned with the frocks, so that the child was afterward clad much like the other children, black or white, residing at the post.

Meanwhile her adoptive mother, Sehêbi, continued to grieve and to mope, according to her people's custom. She had become so immersed in her sorrow over Taoinan's, or The Flute's, death that she sometimes seemed oblivious of her adopted daughter, only clutching the child to her occasionally and comforting her in Comanche. At these moments it was as if she had momentarily awakened to her surroundings and the actual world. That world, which had seemed to fascinate her so before, she now rejected to the extent that she was able—the world, I mean to say, of the house, our river port, the fort, and the village. For the first week or so the weather had been clear with moonlight nights, and she had slept outdoors with the child in her buffalo robe by the vegetable garden. But then rain had begun gusting through the trees in a drenching south wind, and she had moved to the kitchen near its garden door. During the day, despite Mlle. Bijou's entreaties, she would not sit in a chair but insisted instead on sitting cross-legged upon the bare boards with her back pressing the wall while rain slapped the windows and drummed upon the roof.

During the early period after our return, Hélène-Eulalie and I had been so occupied at the trading house with the mass of details accumulated during our absence, as well as with attending to the hides, peltry, and horses acquired by the expedition, that we had lacked time for the new members of our household. But with the help of Antoine Lefort, and of his practical young wife, Simone, we were able to master the confusion and draw the affairs of the firm into a rudimentary order. Afterward its daily work might at least proceed unimpeded under the direction of Antoine and a new young agent comptable, or accountant. This burden lifted, she and I had more leisure to devote to Sehêbi and the child.

But even Hélène-Eulalie could not penetrate the web in which Sehêbi had wound herself at the start of her long and traditional stint of mourning. Having escaped immolation at his gravesite, she was, it seemed, nonetheless giving Taoinan his due. It became evident that nothing any of us said or did was going to deter her from expressing what seemed to be her genuine feelings. Even Hélène-Eulalie's piano, which had delighted her previously, failed to rouse her from her grief. The colonel's niece and I discussed her state and concluded at last, after futile attempts at cheering her, that it was kinder to leave her alone as she wished. With the child events evolved otherwise.

From the first the little girl had shown an interest in the colonel as well as his cat. One day during the first weeks when I had returned from work before our midday meal, Mlle. Bijou called me with a smile to a window with a view of the veranda. Monsieur de St. Maurice was clumping, with his two canes, back and forth upon the porch which stretched across the front and two sides of the house. It was his daily habit, as if pacing a schooner's deck, to exercise in this manner. I peered through the glass. Behind him at a short distance walked the child, keeping pace with him. It was a droll spectacle—she with a grave expression, the old man with a faint smile which revealed his amusement at her presence.

"How long has this been going on?"

"Just since today. Sometimes he tries to speak to her, but she doesn't understand."

"Does she understand you?"

"Usually I can reach her."

When the colonel arrived at the end of the walkway, he turned. The child, halting some ten paces behind him, backed against the railing and stood, with downcast eyes, until he had passed her, then fell in behind him again at the same distance and with the same sober expression, as if she were slowly marching behind a drummer.

I turned to Mademoiselle with what must have been a puzzled look.

She shook her head, made a humorous grimace and shrugged.

Later reflecting upon the child's behavior, I decided it meant for one thing that she was becoming accustomed to her new home and its inhabitants and was finding her situation less strange and forbidding than it had seemed at first. It also meant, I supposed, that she was beginning to be more bored than frightened and was probably wishing for playmates. It would be time soon to begin her schooling. Plainly she was now more nearly at ease in parts of the house that must have appeared odd and menacing to her at first, even the dining and drawing rooms. Sometimes she would wait, seated upon a chair in the shadowy parlor, for Hélène-Eulalie to come home and play the piano for her.

On another occasion one evening before dinner we heard a shriek from her that brought us all out into the central hallway. Even Monsieur de St. Maurice burst, stumbling, out of his office door and stood, leaning upon his canes. To our astonishment, Ooa was giggling. This was the first time any of us had heard her laugh. She was crouched, squatting, over the old cat, who was playing, using deft paw slaps and nimble jumps, with a pretty little snake ringed with red, yellow, and black—a serpent we all of us knew to be deadly. The two women, who were closer to the child than I, reacted. Hélène-Eulalie plunged the few paces to her, seized her beneath the arms and drew her backward, dragging her to a safe distance, while Mlle. Bijou, hissing at Diablo, swept up a small carpet, threw it over the injured snake and stamped upon it. For an instant Ooa watched, fascinated, then began to wail and sob. This was the first time any of us had heard her cry. For my part, as the colonel watched chuckling, I managed to wrap the mashed but still wriggling serpent (known as "Coral Snake" by the Americans) in the carpet, carried it outside and disposed of it. By the time I had returned the three adults had succeeded in explaining by French words and with their hands the danger from the snake to the child, and Ooa was looking abashed in the arms of Hélène-Eulalie, who was on her knees behind her. Even the colonel was bending over her, smiling.

I recall thinking it peculiar that the child should be drawn to the old officer and diplomat. Hélène-Eulalie suggested that perhaps there had been, in the massacred Osage village, some elder, perhaps a grandfather, of whom she had loving memories. In any event, as time went on she took to playing almost silently with her doll—or loitering—outside his office door when he was writing or reading inside. The colonel was aware and amused, possibly even touched, by her attention and responded with occasional kindly smiles and awkward pats on the head. These, from what we could judge by her appearance, seemed to please yet not entirely to satisfy the little girl, and she continued intermittently to haunt the hallway outside his office door and, though soon less frequently, to march at his back during his daily intervals of exercise.

By this time the child had mastered, owing to her daily talks with Mlle. Bijou and Hélène-Eulalie, a limited command of the French language, as well as of course the Comanche tongue in which Sehêbi spoke to her. Unfortunately while the colonel's hearing was adequate for conversation with adults speaking distinctly, it was unequal to the attempts at communication of a shy child with an uncertain accent and, after a few embarrassing failures, Ooa abandoned her effort to reach the old man orally despite encouragement from monsieur and from both women. Then one day the situation resolved itself.

None of us had been quite aware that the little girl wished to enter the colonel's office. It was his retreat and, as it were, a sacred enclosure in the household, containing as it did all of his books, memorabilia, and papers. Even Mlle. Bijou was not allowed to enter to clean or dust without permission. Hélène-Eulalie and I never passed the threshold without first knocking and being invited in. From the first it had been understood that the child would not be permitted within that sanctum. Of course if Monsieur de St. Maurice had been aware that she desired so intensely to inspect its snug, book-lined interior, he would surely have allowed her to inspect it under his indulgent gaze. As it was, one afternoon when Hélène-Eulalie and I were to meet with the colonel over some trifle concerning the new accountant, the child slipped in as we entered. The little girl stood looking about with an awed expression. I had closed the door before noticing her and was about to open it and gently usher her out when the colonel with a smile waved at me, signaling that she might remain.

"Tu peux rester, ma chéri," he said, still smiling. "Mais il ne te faut pas parler, n'est-ce pas?"

Gravely the child nodded. Still looking about, she seated herself on the floor near the door, while Hélène-Eulalie and I took the two available chairs. Our meeting was soon concluded. When we stood to depart, Ooa rose also. Slowly as if dawdling she went to the end of the room opposite the governor's escritoire. There between two books separated by bookends was the polished human skull which had adorned the office since my arrival. The child went to the skull and examined it carefully, running her hands over it gently. We watched as if suddenly frozen in position. Turning she looked at the colonel strangely, questioningly. Meeting her gaze with a smile, an encouraging expression, he shoved forward his escritoire and beckoned her to him. She went slowly to him, her eyes on his. When she reached him, raising her face, she began asking him softly about the skull, about whom it had belonged to and so forth. Probably he did not hear her words clearly, but he understood without hearing. With an extraordinary expression, clearly moved, he ran his hands over the child's hair, over her face, and quickly pulled her into his lap. His eyes glittered. At that she looked into his face for a long moment, then leaned her head into his chest. He drew her closer to him, and she remained still, looking down, her thin legs dangling.

Dramatic displays of emotion can be embarrassing. But there was a quality so powerful, one might even say sacred, about this moment and about the colonel's expression that I stood, along with Hélène-Eulalie, like one entranced. That was the moment, then, that old Monsieur de St. Maurice seemed to me to have recovered a love he had not felt, except for Arsène, since his second wife, that child bride, and her children, except for Arsène, had been torn from him by the pestilence. Quietly Hélène-Eulalie and I turned, opened the door and departed, leaving the two of them seated together in silence.

After that the office door was often ajar. The little girl frequently played with her doll, or the cat with a feather, upon its floor while the colonel read or wrote at his escritoire. Indeed they were often together. They seemed to speak little, but speech appeared to be unnecessary to their mutual understanding. In brief a harmony clearly existed between these two souls, and each it seemed derived something of perhaps ineffable value from the other's presence.

25

As Ooa became increasingly at ease, contented, and secure among us, Sehêbi appeared to sink more deeply into a melancholy solitude. During this period Hélène-Eulalie was exceedingly kind to her. Yet her sympathetic attention seemed of little avail. The Frenchwoman—who incidentally now considered herself to be in all respects but the legal one an American—did succeed after a series of rainstorms in persuading Sehêbi to move into Arsène's former room upstairs near mine. Ooa, however, was already sleeping on tanned bearskins provided by Lefort in Mlle. Bijou's tiny quarters off the kitchen. She did not wish to move, even to be with her "mother," of whom she was nonetheless clearly fond.

The child's reluctance to change bedrooms seemed further to dishearten Sehêbi, this to such a degree that Hélène-Eulalie began herself to be discouraged. This led to her repeating to me several days later what had seemed at the Pawnee-Piquée (or Wichitan) village an extraordinary proposal: namely that I assume the rights of a husband with the girl—in plain words that I copulate with her—in order to cheer her. Hélène-Eulalie now suspected that it might be my avoidance of this marital embrace that was responsible for Sehêbi's increasing melancholy.

I was once again surprised at the suggestion—or, rather, by its source. At first after our return I had regarded my situation with some complacency. The idea of a ménage à trois was not displeasing to me. Indeed it appeared to me a logical and pleasant solution to our predicament with Sehêbi. I had nearly recovered from my astonishment at Hélène-Eulalie's having originally proposed it. Consequently soon after our arrival I had been anticipating, with relish I must confess, taking upon myself the responsibilities of a Comanche chieftain, in this one respect at least. And with a clear conscience. Certainly it was what my good friend and "brother," Taoinan, had wished.

But the "solution" had not developed as I had anticipated. From the beginning there had been no hint of an invitation from either female. Sehêbi had been physically remote as well as despondent. Hélène-Eulalie had been distressed at and preoccupied by her young friend's melancholy. Neither had seemed particularly interested in me in any event. Truly at moments during the months following our return the unhealthy thought occurred to me that the three women might be conspiring against me. There were so many low-voiced conversations between Hélène-Eulalie and Mlle. Bijou which hushed when I approached, and so many sad and aloof glances from Sehêbi, that it seemed almost as if they had jointly found me guilty of some crime, perhaps merely of being male. But at my predominantly reasonable moments I realized the absurdity of my suspicions and rejected them entirely. Still my experiences during this period reduced any envy I might once have had concerning the polygyny of my male Comanche friends. It convinced me that one woman at a time would be all I would ever be able to manage—except perhaps briefly in instances of extreme temptation.

In truth there is not much to be said about our sad ménage à trois. It was from my standpoint a failure. Following Hélène-Eulalie's suggestion—or, rather, instruction—I went to Sehêbi's bedroom one night soon after she had moved into it. I found her not in her bed but in blankets upon the floor beside it. After expressing a momentary surprise, she received me as if she had been expecting me, throwing back the blanket. In the light from my candle, I saw she slept naked. Regarding me briefly and reading my intention, she rolled dutifully upon her belly and parted her legs, resting her head upon her arms.

I extinguished the candle. In an instant I had cast off my nightshirt. I had not been with a woman since the thunderstorm at the Pawnee-Piquée village and thus was primed for the encounter. Following a few preliminary caresses, my eagerness impelled me to enter her. I was quickly enjoying myself to a nearly intolerable extent. But during these fleeting moments of delight I became aware of a shuddering of her back in addition to the rhythmic motions of her hips and buttocks. I realized, with my ear now close to her face, that she was sobbing in a smothered fashion into the blanket. I was shocked. If I had not been so close to achieving my purpose, I might have lost my enthusiasm at this discovery. As it was, I was disconcerted yet not sufficiently so as to interrupt my pursuit of the momentary bliss that waited so near. A few more thrusts brought me my reward, so that after a second or two I was able to turn my attention to the girl gasping and weeping beneath me.

I remained for some time attempting to comfort her. At first I stroked her hair and her shoulder, speaking gently into her ear in both French and Comanche in my effort to discover the cause of this outburst, and especially to find whether it could be my doing. But my words seemed only to bring on louder and more convulsive sobbing. But then as I shriveled and withdrew, she suddenly wrenched over, revealing a startling strength, so that we lay face to face. But not for more than an instant. Throwing her arms around me, she pressed her wet cheek against mine, gripping me with such force I feared for the vertebrae in my neck, still weeping but less violently until finally she began to sob out "Jean-Pierre" once or twice and Taoinan's name over and again, with still more in Comanche that I could not understand. But by now, fond as I had been of Taoinan, her continued grief had come to seem to me excessive. Our embrace soon became an ordeal and I was quickly wishing to escape her grip, our sweat, her tears and saliva as soon as humanely possible. At last she did relax her arms and rest, seeming to doze. Gently I disengaged myself. Finding my nightshirt and candle in the dark, I located the door and silently slipped from the room, vowing not to repeat the experience until the girl had completed her mourning.

Back in my own bed I was unable to sleep. I thought of Taoinan with a pang, of indeed the only brother, mock or real, along with Arsène, whom I had ever had. Yet it did seem strange to me that after over three months Sehêbi still behaved as if he had died the previous day. Then I began recalling what he had once told me of his union with Sehêbi. It had been after his first series of successes as warrior and rising warchief. He had married and had collected a sufficient number of horses to be considered a wealthy man. But he was still dissatisfied. Something was missing, he said. He had made medicine and consulted with his guardian spirit. His animal spirit had directed him to travel north and see what he found. He had done so, riding alone. As he penetrated northward and westward, he encountered band after band of those Comanches called Yamparicas. All had been friendly, the leading men in each vying to feed and entertain him.

In the last band visited he had formed a friendship, after a longer stay than usual, with a warchief older than he. This man, whose name was Red Sparrow-Hawk, had a captive wife of the tribe known to the Spaniards as "Caihuas," or to the Americans as "Kioways." This wife, Beaver Woman, had a pretty little daughter, Sehêbi. Taoinan had found her entrancing. She in turn had immediately liked him, in spite of his deformed foot. Although only eleven years old, she had been of a daring and adventurous nature, already eager to leave her father's lodge and marry. The two men had talked and, despite Beaver Woman's tears, had reached an agreement. The Flute had returned to his own people and come back at the next round moon with his two wives, several of their male relatives as herders, and a small herd of ponies. A few weeks later, with the ponies presented, all promises having been fulfilled, Sehêbi, with her new Comanche name of "Willow," had proudly and gaily ridden off behind her husband. At eleven years she had become a grown-up favorite wife, honored by carrying his shield.

Out of curiosity I had been unable to resist asking my Comanche brother whether he had begun to sleep with her then. Not immediately, he had told me with a serious expression: he had taken time to "prepare" her. I asked no more. But when I had first met Sehêbi she had seemed joyful, a favorite wife who appeared still to be the favorite child she had been, spoiled by both her husband and his older wives, who spared her most of the drudgery of their lives and usually treated her more as a daughter or younger sister than as a rival. Consequently, I reflected lying there awake, Sehêbi had lost not only a kind husband but also the man who had, in effect, served for some years as substitute for her father. This double loss, I concluded, would have to suffice as explanation for her continued grief. After resolving this much for myself, I was able around dawn to fall asleep.

That morning at the dining table the old man was exceptionally cheerful. He had heard the previous evening from a visiting Caddoan Indian bearing a message that his son would be coming to visit him after the fall hunt, news that spread quickly throughout the house. As a result the conversation was more lively than usual for that time of day—that is to say, his exchanges with his niece were. I remained mostly silent. Hélène-Eulalie fell into his mood immediately, but I noticed that she regarded me strangely once or twice as we sipped our coffee. To what did she attribute my fatigue, I wondered? There was a chill conveyed by her gaze that contrasted with her blithe appearance and cheerful repartee with Monsieur. Not feeling my freshest after my nuit blanche, I soon became convinced that she was aware of my nocturnal call upon Sehêbi and would confront me with it during the day. Not that I felt guilty of anything. I had merely followed her instructions. Yet my abdomen tightened as if preparing to resist a blow.

At the trading house, where we were both occupied with recording an inventory of the stock, she ignored me—again a contrast to her usual companionable awareness. It was not until evening before dinner that she stopped me in the downstairs hallway.

"Poor Jean-Pierre, you look as if you didn't sleep last night." Her expression was pleasant, sympathetic, but her eyes were cold.

"Yes, I didn't sleep well."

"Any particular reason? Too much coffee?"

I had to smile, meeting that chilly gaze. "Why pretend? You know I visited Sehêbi, as you wished me to do. Remember?"

"Oh, how nice. And...was it good?" she taunted.

For a moment I reflected, while she watched me with a bitter smile. Annoyed, I almost replied that it was inappropriate for me to discuss it with her. But thinking better of that, I shook my head, shrugged. "No, actually not very."

"What? What do you mean?"

"She wept."

"She wept?" She leaned toward me with a puzzled frown. "Are you serious? She wept?"

"Yes. For Taoinan."

For a moment she continued to gaze into my eyes, frowning. "Poor Sehêbi." Turning, she walked away, her blonde head lowered, apparently reflecting.

That same day, as I recall, the mild monotony of our lives was broken by an incident at once trifling and revelatory. By revelatory I mean it illuminated a facet of Ooa's character of which we were all of us unaware. I as much as any. To me the shy and gentle child had seemed a person requiring constant protection from the cruelty and violence of the world. We all, from Mlle. Bijou to the colonel, felt that way I believe. We rejoiced inwardly at finding the little girl finally at ease, confident and seemingly happy among us. Hélène-Eulalie, in particular, took satisfaction in this. Yet I was seated reading on the veranda that same day when I learned that my protective feeling toward the child was exaggerated.

Ooa was on the road near the house, stooping, knees bent, drawing in the dirt with a stick. Not far from her was the old tabby, tail high, watching as two white boys a little older than she approached from down the road. Since this was a rare occurrence by the house, Ooa straightened and shyly watched them as they drew near. The cat, apparently curious, began advancing toward them for a short distance, then halted, turning a little sideways to look back at the girl. At that the smaller boy, perhaps to impress his companion, scooped up a small rock and flung it with decisive aim at the animal. The old cat, stung in the hindquarters, screeched and ran off. Ooa drew herself up and shouted. The boys began to laugh. Angry as well, I jumped from my chair to upbraid them. But the girl was quicker, sprinting toward the two as they waited, laughing at her reaction. They evidently failed to realize her serious intent until she was close. The taller boy, still laughing, reached out to seize her in order to shield the other. But Ooa dodged and swung her hooked fingers at his face in passing. Blood flowed immediately. The smaller boy, backing, still giggling, held out his hands protectively. She struck him with full momentum, flinging him backward onto the road, doubtless knocking away his breath.

Then she threw herself upon him. Frozen, I watched in astonishment as those seemingly frail elbows and knees pummeled the boy and fingers clawed at his face, which he tried vainly to protect. One of her knees evidently found his testes, I judged, since he had begun to scream as if being tortured. The older boy, pressing his bloody cheek with one palm, and blustering, was attempting with his free hand to seize one of the little girl's arms or legs, but she was moving too quickly for him to grasp either. By this time I was sprinting down the road, yelling, "Non, Ooa. Mais non, ma chéri. Non, non!" I feared for the boy's eyesight from the assault of those clawing fingers. As soon as I managed to drag Ooa from the boy, she relaxed in my hands, still weeping with rage. When the smaller urchin had recovered sufficiently to rise from the dirt dusty, bloody, and blubbering, I examined his clawed features and found his eyes unhurt. I scolded the two and sent them back to the village with a warning to avoid our vicinity in the future.

I found the entire household watching from the veranda. Mlle. Bijou was laughing uproariously, holding Sehêbi by one arm, evidently having done so to prevent her from running to assist the child, who plainly had required no help. As we returned, Ooa and I, my hand resting upon her thin shoulder, Madamoiselle emitted a victory whoop not entirely unlike those of Arsène, while a worried Sehêbi continued twisting to free herself. The colonel too was chuckling, leaning on his canes, having witnessed all from his office window. Hélène-Eulalie trotted quickly down the steps toward us, her expression one of puzzled concern. As Ooa and I neared her, I squeezed the child's thin arm, marveling at the force compacted within that body. No longer weeping, she turned up her tear-stained face to look at me quickly in embarrassment. I felt a pang in my chest. Yes, it was unnecessary to feel quite so protective toward her—within that delicate frame lurked a warrior parent, or rather some semblance to the big wolf, piaisa, crouched there prepared, when needed, to rouse and defend or attack. I realized then that, in spite of our lacking a blood bond, I had begun to love the child, and that she could not have been more truly my daughter.

Arsène too told me that he had not been a Comanche boy for long before he had begun to form an attachment to Toyamancare, or Big-Mountain, his Comanche father. Generally, while often gruff and abrupt, the warchief watched for his white son's safety and was generally kind to him, as if the tabebo boy were really his own by birth. His three wives and, in particular an old woman captive who lived with them, were also kind. Once when Arsène was first with the band, and before he had made friends and was feeling isolated and fearful, he had become aware of several old women standing together and peering at him with hatred as he passed. Uneasy, he had avoided their presence when he could. Soon afterward Toyamancare had called him into the lodge and had warned him, by signs and a little Spanish that these women had lost sons years before when Comanches and Spanish soldiers had been at war and had clashed in skirmishes or battles. Consequently they hated white people. Big-Mountain cautioned him to accept nothing to eat from any person other than his wives, for he had learned that the old ones wished to kill him. Later after Arsène had made friends and gained confidence in his new situation, he grew accustomed to the venomous looks that the old women gave him and dismissed them as a fact of his new life. The warchief's concern had made him feel more secure, more at ease and soon happier in the Indian camp. For this, and other care, he was grateful to the warchief and before long had begun trusting him and feeling toward him more and more as if he were indeed his father.

At Fort St. Jean Baptiste de Natchitoches our unhappy ménage à trois continued in much the same fashion. Odd as it seemed though, Sehêbi did appear to have become more cheerful by the evening following my visit. After the day's excitement and mirth, she played out by the vegetable garden with Ooa and her doll for some time. Previously she had seemed to take pleasure in nothing. Hélène-Eulalie, who was going about with a dour expression, gave no sign of noticing the change, although I was sure that she had. A few days later, when she had mostly recovered her good humor, she mentioned it to me, giving me a pained though insinuating look.

"No," I said.

"No, what?"

"No, I'm not going again."

"To Sehêbi? Nobody asked you to."

Yet she smiled a little pleased smile, while we talked of other things. Nevertheless I was confused in my mind about the woman and the girl. Whenever I thought about or looked at the colonel's niece, I knew—even when I was annoyed with her—that I loved her. But I was also strongly attracted to Sehêbi, although in a different way, perhaps for her youth and freshness—that is, when she was not in mourning. Strangely I seemed able to love them both. Still if I had learned anything from my night call upon Sehêbi, I had learned that it was necessary to choose. There was no doubt in my mind that the older woman was the one whom I believed I could not live without. Consequently even though I might have done so with an excuse and with relative impunity, I paid Sehêbi no more nocturnal visits. As for Hélène-Eulalie, while she had quickly become congenial once more, even affectionate, and though I courted her, there was not the slightest hint from her of an invitation to her bed. So although I'm an impatient man, I bided my time and reluctantly made do with abstinence.

I don't know what would have occurred if Arsène had not eventually arrived. We waited throughout most of October. Still he had not come, nor was there any word. Meanwhile we lived as we mostly had since our return. Even so Sehêbi had become more cheerful. Monsieur de St. Maurice, noticing at once, took advantage of her improved spirits to invite her into his office for an hour each morning. For the past several years he had been writing notes and making observations upon the native tribes he had encountered during his long military and diplomatic career at Natchitoches Post. These included, of course, the many Caddoan peoples who resided within and near the district, as well as the Norteños, or Nations of the North. These were the prairie peoples with whom we traded most rewardingly and included the Wichitan confederacy—Taovayeses, Kichais, Tawakonis—as well as non-Wichitans, the Tonkawas and the Comanches. He was eager to collect more information upon this last nation. Using the French language, a little Spanish, and hand signs, he questioned Sehêbi daily in this regard, while Ooa and sometimes the cat played upon the floor, or the child sat quietly upon a chair with the old tiger purring in her lap.

Then we heard for a second time from some Indians at the store that Arsène, or Ah-mah-bah-tay, "The One Without A Head," was on his way and would arrive soon. How they knew I do not know. But the news sent a tremor of excitement through our household.

Each of us, except perhaps for the child, who had become contented with her new life, looked forward to seeing him, surely the colonel most of all. We were having a stretch of unusually fine late autumn weather. I was seated upon the veranda reading—I remember well—a book I had discovered in the colonel's library, Nuits de Paris, by one Rétif de la Bretonne. I still recall his description of a scene at the Place de Grève during the later years of the Ancien Régime. It had compelled me to put down the book and reflect: at night the authorities were breaking two condemned criminals upon the wheel. The crowd was festive, talking and laughing throughout, while executioners broke the prisoners' limbs with iron bars. One young girl in particular incurred the author's indignation for her giggles and mockery of the men's struggles and screams. I was reflecting upon this incident with my eyes closed when a familiar voice roused me:

"Jean-Pierre, il faut que je te parle."

I started, opening my eyes. Sehêbi stood before me with an anxious expression. Clearly she was nervous.

"Oui?"

Her French had greatly improved. She began by saying she was sorry she had not come to my bed during the time since our return. But she pleaded that she had been "très, très malheureuse." A tear glided down her cheek as she continued to describe how unhappy she had been. Since there was but a single chair on the porch, I rose and stood facing her, leaning against the balustrade, taken by surprise, trying to look sympathetic. She went on to tell me that Taoinan had told her I had promised to marry her and, although she had believed she was going to die instead, she thanked me, along with Arsène and the others, for having saved her from death. She knew she should stay and be my wife, but she was sorry. She could not remain. There was no life for her at the post.

"But why?" I asked gently, placing my hand upon her shoulder. "Has someone been unkind to you?"

"Oh, no. Everyone has been kind. You've all been good to me."

"But why do you want to leave?"

"I miss my people," she cried. ("Ma peuple—elle me manque beaucoup!") "I miss First-Frost and She-Scolds-Her-Dogs," she wailed, beginning to sob. "I miss all the people and the prairie and the ponies and the buffalo meat and everything! I want to go back!"

I drew her to me. She sobbed on my chest, while I stroked her back. "You want to go back with Ah-mah-bah-tay, is that right?"

"Yes, yes, yes," she sobbed in a smothered voice. "Please let me go. I can't live here."

I thought for a moment and am ashamed to say I was suddenly feeling an enormous relief. "Of course you may go," I said gently, continuing to stroke her. "You'll take Ooa with you?"

"Oh, yes," she said, raising her head, trying to smile, sniffling, tearful eyes upon mine. "Yes, I must take Ooa."

"But...Monsieur de St. Maurice, he loves her, you know. You can't leave her for a while—until? He's a very old man. It would make him happy. She likes it here, and we'll be good to her. Hélène-Eulalie loves her too, and so does Mademoiselle."

"No. I can't leave her. She's my daughter. Taoinan gave her to me. No, I won't leave her."

I drew her to me, holding her tightly. A wave of affection swept through me, with a pang of regret. "Very well. I'll talk to Ah-mah-bah-tay when he comes."

She hugged me, pulled back, looked at me gratefully, the afternoon light shining off her wet cheeks. "Jean-Pierre, you are good. Tonight I'll come to your bed—yes, tonight and every night until I leave. We'll fuck and fuck. Yes? You do want me, don't you? It will be good again."

I backed to the balustrade in consternation, searching for the right words. I was much tempted, but I thought of Hélène-Eulalie and the likely consequences.

"You don't want me? That other night I was remembering Taoinan. I was so sad. This will be different."

"I know. But you see... It's Hélène-Eulalie—you see, she gets a little jealous. You know, jealous. You know what that means, no? Yes, we'd better not, since you're leaving anyway. We'd better not. You understand?"

She regarded me, frowning, puzzled. "Jealous? But we're both your wives? I didn't know that. Some wives do get jealous, though. I'm sorry, Jean-Pierre."

"Oh, well. It's because you're so young and pretty. Because you're so pretty."

She smiled, suddenly beaming at me. It was the first time I had seen her look happy since our arrival. It made me happy to see her look that way again after such long misery.

When she had left to find the child, I thought back at her recent more cheerful mood and smiled. I had been flattering myself that it had been my nuptial embrace which had raised her spirits. Now I saw it had been the news of Arsène's impending visit and the prospect of an escape from the Post. I shook my head at my own vanity.

26

Soon afterward the weather changed. From mild and dry, it became cloudy, cool, windy. There was a hint in the air of seasonal change, a first warning, as it were, of approaching winter. I kept glancing at the sky and thinking of Arsène. One day it blustered and rained. October was ending when he finally arrived on a late afternoon a little before sunset. I was in my room reading when I heard whinnying from the corral and then, listening carefully, distant replies. Suspecting it might be Arsène, I went quickly down the stairs and through the hall.

The front door was open. I found Mlle. Bijou, Sehêbi, and Ooa standing on the porch before it. The road stretched to its corner, empty, but the neighing from that direction had become louder. We were joined by Hélène-Eulalie and the colonel just as Arsène appeared around the corner of the road. He was coming at a lope, leading three horses, the first of which—a great sorrel with a blazed face—limped slightly and bore a pack saddle. I recognized César at once as he threw up his head and shrieked a whinny, to be shrilly answered by my mare. Beside me Monsieur de St. Maurice exclaimed and laughed at seeing his old horse. Arsène approached rapidly. I saw that although the weather was cool he was bare from his darkly tanned waist up and carried his lance and shield. He wore a single feather in his long black hair and even at a distance I could see his face was painted red, blue, and yellow. The women began to wave. Drawing near, Arsène whooped. At the same time Antoine came running up the path from the river.

They arrived at the porch steps at the same moment. Arsène slid off his buffalo horse, the insides of his buckskin leggings dark from the animal's sweat, and the two men embraced. Passing the rein and the leadrope, his shield and lance, to Lefort, Arsène ran up the steps to his father, seized the old man with a hug, nearly lifting him from the veranda. Both men laughed. He seized and kissed his cousin on either cheek, and she cried out at the force of his hug. He turned to me. We embraced, and he pressed his painted cheek against mine in the Comanche manner. He smelled of woodsmoke and horses. As we stood back, smiling, looking at each other, I noticed how he had filled out, how muscular, though still lean, he had become, noticed too the familiar scar and tattoo on his chest. He hugged a laughing Mlle. Bijou, but with Sehêbi and the child he was reserved, merely nodding at the woman and patting the child on her head. Yet when Sehêbi stared at him, instead of her old expression of distaste, and without even a smile, her eyes and her face glowed.

Sadly for his father, Arsène's visit was brief. He was worried about the lateness of the season and the possibility of encountering violent weather, particularly on the prairie through which the band would ride to their winter camp. During that evening's dinner I asked him who had become civil, or peace chief in the absence of the medicine man called "Red-Woman."

"It's still Red-Woman," he smiled. "They came back."

"What?" exclaimed Hélène-Eulalie. "Tell us."

He explained that having traveled far south, indeed two days' ride above the Spaniards' town and presidio of San Antonio de Béxar, the brothers had established a camp in a good location with plenty of water, grass and firewood, where they had planned to stay for a time. But a war party of Lipan Apaches, venturing into comanchería, had discovered and attacked Red-Woman's camp a little after dawn one morning. Fortunately all of the men had risen early, preparing to ride out to hunt. There had been a fight in which Tosapoy, or "White-Road," had fought with valor, like two men, even after a Lipan had shot an arrow into his side. He, along with Red-Woman, El Chamaco, and the other male relatives had at last succeeded in driving off the Apaches. But for a time the outcome had been doubtful. Several other Comanche warriors had been wounded, one of whom later died. Afterward Red-Woman had held a council in which the surviving men decided that they formed too small a group to continue safely as they were. The council had determined to return northward and attempt to rejoin their old band, now led by Big-Mountain.

This they had done. Red-Woman, humble and subdued, had visited, smoked with Toyamancare, and expressed his followers' wish. The latter chief had, in turn, convened a council, whose members had unanimously decided in favor of readmitting Red-Woman, White-Road, and their relatives and followers into the band. This had all been done, with rejoicing on both sides. Soon afterward the chastened Red-Woman had by tacit consent of all resumed his former position as Medicine Man (Puhahante) and also as civil chief, while White-Road, grim as before, had remained uncharacteristically inconspicuous, continuing to heal from the wound that had nearly killed him.

"So Red-Woman will select the site of your winter camp?" asked the colonel.

"How did you know?" said Arsène.

"I've been learning more about your people from Sehêbi. Her French has improved, thanks to your cousin."

"No," said Hélène-Eulalie. "It's Mademoiselle. I haven't had time."

"Well," smiled Arsène, to his father. "You may interrogate me. I'll tell you everything I know."

"No," the colonel said. "You'll make it sound so agreeable I'll want to move into your tepee with you. How would you like that?" He raised his wine glass with a smile. "But here's to you and your wives and my little grandsons, whom I hope I'll live long enough to meet someday."

With wine and continued good humor the dinner and the evening passed quickly and pleasantly away. Arsène, however, with his worry about the weather, remained for only a week. Much of the time he spent with his father, often in the office. Actually throughout that week both Arsène and Hélène-Eulalie spent many hours with Monsieur de St. Maurice shut in his office, to the evident annoyance of Ooa and the cat. Hélène-Eulalie confided to me that the long family discussions concerned Arsène's and her inheritances, a subject which I considered not my affair and which interested me not at all. I was still sufficiently young, you see, so that only the near future was of any concern to me. As a result I saw little of Arsène during his stay, what with my hours—and many of Hélène-Eulalie's too—required at the trading house.

Yet there were two evenings when he and I lounged by candle-light in the drawing room before the fire, after the others had gone to bed, and reminisced. I had always been interested in Arsène's stories of his early years as a white Comanche boy. I'd asked him if the other boys had tormented him at first. He had said, "No, very little." The other boys, it appeared, had been curious about him in the beginning, finding him, he thought, a kind of freak to be observed and studied. His prompt fight with the other boy, and his victory, had earned their respect, convincing them that he was brave enough to become their companion and playmate.

The difficulty at first had been communication. Besides his native French, Arsène knew a little Spanish and a few words of English. More helpful was the Prairie sign language which Antoine Lefort had begun teaching him even before the trading expedition on which he had become lost. He had found these haphazard lessons fascinating and had always begged for more, until he had become able in a desultory way to form and comprehend enough signs to make the gist of his meanings known and to understand much of what other boys wished to tell him. He was helped in his efforts by soon making a friend, one who became lifelong. This friend was the boy he had fought on his arrival, whose childhood name was, "Poná," or "snail," for no particular reason Arsène could discover.

He told me that during the first weeks he had been constantly nervous because of the unfamiliarity of almost everything around him and because of not knowing what to expect. He had done his best, he said, to hide his anxiety. He knew from the stories of Indians Antoine Lefort had told him that for his own safety he must be resolute and hardy. But he was not prepared for the conditions of his new life. For one thing, he was unaccustomed to going almost without clothes. A thin boy, he was often chilled. During the first weeks (and he had kept track of time in the beginning), particularly in the early mornings, he had sometimes shivered in spite of his efforts not to. The other boys, even little ones, found this amusing and laughed. He also became sunburned during those late spring days. His companions found his red and pealing skin comical as well. He learned they were comparing him to a snake, which sheds its skin. He was a curiosity to them, a source of surprise and amusement. They loved to hear him attempt Comanche words, especially long ones, such as "tosanebachcap," which meant merely "le givre"—or in English, "frost."

Then there were the ponies. At twelve years he rode well. Riding had been his principal sport and entertainment as a solitary boy at the post. But he was not prepared for the half-wild ponies of the band, some of which were scarcely broken. The little children and younger boys rode old gentle horses. But the more daring boys of Arsène's age joined older ones in attempting to ride wilder animals that more experienced and reckless youths rode in order to show off before the girls.

The wilder ponies were a challenge that separated the boys not only by age but by temperament and resolve. When Poná asked him to go with the older boys one afternoon to try riding some of the nearly grown colts, Arsène heard himself immediately say, "Jaa," or "yes," as if there were no doubt about his desire to do so, as if he had been eagerly looking forward to doing so, when actually he felt a chill beginning to prickle at his neck and slide down his back. But he was cheered when he noticed that his new friend, Poná, as they walked together toward the arroyo where older boys had led the ponies, appeared to be as nervous as he himself was.

An older boy was already riding when they arrived in the deep, sandy ditch. An experienced horseman, he was clinging with both hands to the horse's mane. Several large youths held a reata encircling the horse's neck, giving it sufficient slack to plunge and buck but preventing it from running off, while six or seven others watched. The pony reared and bucked, trampling the deep sand, which slowed its movements, making them difficult. Finally, as the animal seemed to tire, the boy released the mane and slid off from the side, springing away and taking care to avoid its kicks. The others laughed and exclaimed. Poná rode next.

The ponies were mostly a patchwork bunch. His was white with great brown spots, while others had black patches on white, even dribbles of spots of either color distributed at random on their coats. The older boys helped Poná mount, covering the eyes of his gelding until he was seated. When one of them removed the buckskin blind and jumped back, the pony sprang into the air, landed, and bucked again. On this jump Poná tore loose, taking to the air in a sitting position and coming down hard on his buttocks. All the boys laughed as he slowly struggled to his feet with a weak smile.

Older boys helped Arsène climb upon his backing, sidling pony. Though his heart was pounding, he tried to appear confident and nonchalant. Had they chosen a particularly difficult pony for him? He wondered, having noted the animal's wicked eye. But he had no time to speculate. Someone pulled away the buckskin from the horse's eyes, and Arsène tried to hang on throughout a succession of violent jolts which wrenched him in every direction. Then he was in the air, awkwardly twisting, falling with his arms out before him. He struck with his hands and chest and chin, and though it was sand, he slammed down with force. He had intended to rise at once and to walk away smiling casually. But he could not. There were spots before his eyes and he soon discovered his nose was dripping blood. Poná and other boys gathered around him and lifted him up. He tried to laugh. With gestures they showed him how to squeeze his nostrils together and dragged him over to an edge of the arroyo, leaning him against the bank, where he was able to stop the bleeding and gradually recover, while other boys tried to ride. He was disappointed in himself, but he quickly discovered that the others, even bigger boys, considered it no disgrace to be thrown. He found that they were treating him with increased respect, as one of them, one who had dared climb upon a half-wild pony and attempt to ride it. They were treating him as one of them. When he realized this he felt better, exhilarated, proud.

There remained marksmanship.

Almost from the day of his arrival at the Comanche camp, Arsène had been trying to learn to shoot arrows accurately from a bow Big-Mountain gave him. For a target he used a rabbit skin which he had tied stretched between the lower limbs of an elm. Beginning practice close to it, he propelled arrow after arrow either far beyond his target, missing it altogether, or into branches of the tree. He spent much of his time at first in hunting arrows. Gradually, though, he learned at least to strike his target.

Poná sometimes came and watched him practice at the edge of camp. The Comanche boy had no difficulty in striking the target time after time from a far longer distance. Seeing the ease and accuracy with which Poná shot arrows, placing them usually at the center of the rabbit skin, Arsène was inwardly furious with envy and frustration. But his new friend patiently showed him how best to sight along the arrow as well as teaching him the gentle release he himself practiced. After a time, overcoming his impatience, learning from his companion as well as from sustained practice, Arsène began puncturing the target until there were more holes than remaining intact hide. Still, when camp moved for the first time since his arrival he was once again discouraged on seeing little boys running here and there at the edges of the advancing line of travois hunting with miniature bows, shooting accurately in their play and sometimes even killing a bird, squirrel, or rabbit, feats he was far from yet achieving.

So he adapted to the life he had been thrust into. But I remember asking him whether he had not been homesick at first, whether he had not missed his father and our life at Natchitoches Post. At this question, asked when we were first reunited, he had appeared amused and embarrassed. Yes, he confessed, he had silently wept wrapped in a buffalo robe those first nights in a strange tepee. As it turned out, he had been homesick during the first several weeks. Everything had been so strange. He had missed his father, missed us all, as well as his secure existence at the post. The prospect of Rousseau's free life close to Nature, which he had yearned for, had begun to frighten him. Most of all, strangely it seemed, he had missed Mademoiselle Bijou, missed the black slave whose stern affection was the closest to mothering he had ever known. His aunt in Nouvelle Orléans had been so occupied with her social life that she had given him little warmth. She had, he once told me, a "un coeur sec." But Mlle. Bijou, unmarried and childless, had given him a mother's attention and affection, as well as a mother's guidance, and since Colonel de St. Maurice was often busy with his own affairs, she had in many respects compensated for the total absence of one parent and the partial absence of the remaining one. He had missed that in the Comanche camp.

He paused in the middle of a sentence, and sat for moment gazing at the floor.

"What's wrong?"

He shook his head. "Nothing." He looked at me. "You know, there was another... when I was first there. I almost forgot. Hmm."

"There was?"

"Yes. An old woman, slave for Big-Mountain's wives. She's still with us. She was a captive, a Charitica. We call them "the dog-eaters." But they're good horseman, good warriors."

"She was good to you?"

He nodded, an old whiteman's gesture I hadn't seen him make for a while. "Everybody calls her 'Cáco,' Grandmother. It was at first, when I was still in Big-Mountain's lodge. Some warriors had come in from a raid. Everybody was out at a dance, you know, celebrating. I was alone in my buffalo robe, sniveling. Suddenly there was a hand on my forehead. It was a cold night, and we'd had a fire. So I turned and could barely see her. An old woman. She had a wrinkled, kind face. She took my hand and held it between hers. As I remember I turned away and cried harder. But she kept singing a little song over and over and holding my hand and once in a while stroking my forehead. Well, I stopped crying, and she left. I think she came back a few times. Anyway, she was kind. I'd almost forgotten her."

"So you got through the hardest part."

"Yes. And then I forgot about her."

I remember asking him when and how he had become a leader among boys his age, for he was clearly that when we found him by the great bosque along Rio Pecos. With a little smile, he told me that whatever leadership he had possessed he owed to a foolish—indeed crazy—exploit during his fourteenth year. I asked him to tell me about it. He had been very lucky (avait de la chance), he told me.

The band had been hunting buffalo far north of its normal range, he said, close to la Rivière Rouge de Natchitoches. Scouts had discovered a large gathering of Caihuas, long before his people's treaty with them. This enemy was camped along the river. They had plenty of horses. At this news a group of older boys, haughty young warriors who had assisted in a few raids, declared they were going to steal that enemy's ponies. They made a commotion about their intention, with noisy recruiting, preparatory singing and drumming, night and day, parading on horseback before the girls, as well as arrogant responses to questions by their young admirers. As a result Arsène and some of the younger boys had become resentful and angry.

After talking with Poná, he had conceived a plan, a romantic and nearly impossible scheme. Yet his plan would work, he believed, if they were able to find, say, three more boys capable of maintaining complete silence. Poná selected three, all fourteen or fifteen years of age. Meanwhile Arsène spoke casually with one of the scouts who had sighted the enemy camp, flattering him by his attention. He learned that, since their own band was already camped on the Plains, they had only to strike directly north to reach La Rivière Rouge. They then had merely to follow that river eastward, taking care not to be seen by the enemy's scouts, to come upon the Caihua encampment, whose horseherd was grazing north of the river. This scout was so proud of his skills that—never suspecting young boys would attempt what experienced warriors viewed as a formidable challenge—he drew a map with a twig in the dust, showing features of the terrain, as well as the river and a bend with a ford where raiders might cross horses, in the event that there was high water. Enjoying the awed admiration of a boy, the older man provided detailed and valuable information about landscapes. In response to Arsène's questions he went on to boast of the strategy he himself would employ if, like the older, young warriors, he were going to attempt to steal that horseherd. Arsène committed it all to memory.

Each boy kept his secret, even from family and friends. Each sneaked from his tepee in the middle of the night, leaving on foot and joining the others at a large rock shaped like a lance-head a little beyond camp. They traveled rapidly during the two days it took to walk to the river. After that they followed its southern bank in the dark, sleeping—in a secure position—during the two more days of travel required to reach the enemy camp. The second night they forded the river, observing the enemy's many little fires and the motions of briefly illuminated, smoky figures near them, listening to the sound of drums and singing, as well as occasional whinnies and barking. At that moment, standing together dripping on the northern bank, and suddenly feeling all too young and inexperienced, they had had an awed realization of the enormity of the challenge they faced as well as the danger even where they stood at the brink of the camp with its commotion of people like their own, except that these people were enemies and would happily kill them. Arsène told me he was so scared he had to grit his teeth to prevent them from chattering. And the other boys, pale in the dim light, showed equal signs of fear.

Moving upstream, he took cover behind the bank in a sandy cove. There he held a final meeting, since the entire conception had been his. First he reminded the boys that they were not there to steal the entire horseherd. They would be succeeding if each could bring back even two good horses. They would have embarrassed the older youths who had been so haughty and insulting in their replies to questions and with their displays of bravado. His plan, he explained, was simple. They would first rub on the skunk scent he had brought to avoid alarming the dogs. Each would carry scraps of meat to throw to them if necessary. They would blacken their faces and bodies with charred wood. They would then circle the camp to where the horses grazed, possibly guarded by several older boys. They would creep near the herd, hide and wait until a little before dawn, when the entire camp slept.

At that time when the horse guards would be dozing, they would separate. Each would move silently into the camp and quickly cut loose every horse tethered by a warrior's lodge. He believed that could be done safely in the dark. Each boy would choose two ponies, lead them out and meet at their present location. When all were there, they would mount and race together into the herd screaming sounds they had laughingly practiced far from camp—growls and cries of bears and cougars. To confuse the enemy, they would not whoop or make any human noise. But they would stampede the herd, doing their best to disperse the ponies, sending them off in every direction. Later they would gather at the agreed-upon ford, after crossing the river. As soon as they had rejoined, they would gallop west and south, each riding a stolen horse while leading at least one other by a reata. In this manner all of them might change horses at intervals, so as always to be riding a fresh mount. Consequently they could return in half the time it had taken them to reach this place. If loose horses accompanied them to the ford, they would drive them along, ride them too. Meanwhile any enemy warrior who had managed to rope a horse would be in futile pursuit of the panicked and scattered herd.

Of course something always goes wrong with carefully conceived plans. For one thing there had been a moment of terror from an unexpected event. Arsène, crouched in the dark by a tepee, had been about to cut loose a fine black stallion when a dog somewhere howled. Immediately all of the dogs in the camp joined in a deafening chorus of howls which lasted less than a minute. He had expected the entire camp to wake and spill from the lodges. But silence ensued. No one appeared. Evidently this was a normal nightly occurrence. Beyond that his plan worked for the most part, except that the Caihua ponies, instead of dispersing, followed the mounted boys, followed their horses that is, crossing the river individually and in bunches, so that much of the herd arrived on the south side, milling together again, when the boys met. Alarmed by the clouds of dust marking their position, he and his companions fled south, followed by dust clouds formed in the sky by groups of the galloping stolen ponies, which would combine almost into a herd again whenever they halted.

On the morning of the second day the Comanche scout with whom Arsène had spoken trotted down from a hilltop and galloped toward them. Arsène and Poná, at the head of the herd, drew up their horses and met him, while the other boys driving fragments of the herd gradually caught up.

"You got plenty horses," the old warrior said. "Yours?"

"Now they are," said Arsène.

"You did like I said?" The old warrior was not a man who revealed surprise, although the wrinkles around his eyes stretched a little wider.

"Yes"

"Good. Your folks have been wondering where you were."

The following morning, early, Arsène saw what appeared to be horsemen emerge from a long shadow of a bluff on the prairie. Since the group was coming from the south, and they were well within comanchería, he was more curious than alarmed. As the others rode closer he recognized them as the young warriors who had been boasting of their intended horse-stealing adventure. The warparty apparently had recognized the younger boys simultaneously. Arsène drew up his horse and waited for his companions, now his triumphant and gleeful friends, to join him. At the same time the leading young warrior galloped up, staring at the ponies milling before him, and at the five smiling younger Comanches holding what had dwindled to about half of the original Caihua herd.

"Where did you find all these horses?" the young brave, Ecopisura, or Scraping Spoon, demanded, staring around in disbelief at the herd of loose ponies, not otherwise greeting the younger boys.

"We found them in the Caihua camp on El Rio Colorado," Arsène said proudly, his head held back.

"You're lying. That's not possible. You little boys couldn't steal from the Caihuas. They'd kill you. Tell me the truth. Where did you find them?"

"Ask my friends." Arsène ignored the insult.

"It's true," said Poná. "I swear it by the sun. He led us." He indicated Arsène with his chin. "We sneaked in at night and cut loose all the horses. They couldn't catch us in the dark, and we were riding their best ponies."

"No, no! That's not possible!" Ecopisura, eldest son of Tosapoy, was flabbergasted.

"We'll give each of you a pony, if you'll help us drive them back," Arsène offered. "But we'll choose which ones we give."

The older warriors conferred. Their leader, Ecopisura, in a fury, refused to accept a horse. Lashing his pony with his quirt, he rode back for the Comanche camp at a run. But the others, each unable to resist adding another pony with so little effort to his few, choked down their pride and joined the younger boys in surrounding the herd, adding a few loose bunches, as well as mares with colts, and stragglers. Following Arsène and Poná, they all set off together in the early morning sun.

That night the camp celebrated. All those Comanches, that is, except for the young warriors who had originally planned the raid and who had made such pompous preparations for it. They and their families sulked. Most pleased of all was Big-Mountain, who responded to the news at first by shocked disbelief, then by laughing uproariously and shaking his adopted son in delight, adding two horses from his own plentiful herd to Arsène's cluster. The men danced all night. The news of the boys' exploit spread eventually even to other bands and divisions, so that laughter, as if from a great joke, spread in waves throughout the tribe, and the white—or tabebo—boy who had planned the raid became known by reputation in all of comanchería. But as their exploit rapidly passed into legend, the individual boys were nearly disassociated from it and were, in effect, often overlooked. Still, within the band they continued to possess an elevated status, especially among younger boys and girls.

Also, although the band moved frequently, a party of horsethieves, probably Caihuas, succeeded in stealing back many of the horses, along with many Comanche ponies, within that year.

"Well, you were still a hero to the girls, right?" He laughed.

Arsène, nearly fifteen, had been taking a new interest in girls, and it pleased him from that point of view to be seen by them as the originator and leader of the famous raid and consequently as its principal hero. Furthermore Big-Mountain had already moved him out of the big tepee and provided him with a small lodge of his own, following the tribal practice for boys of a certain age who would soon begin, or had begun, dreaming voluptuously of girls. I recall that when he told me of his new status within Toyamancare's band, I asked him whether he had yet begun sleeping with girls. He told me with a smile that, No, the boys among his people were too shy, as he himself had been. It was the custom among his people for the girls, particularly the older girls, to make the advances. That had been, he said smiling, the real reward, apart from the horses, of his having been briefly a hero.

"Tell me about it."

Laughing, he said there had been an older girl, who, soon after his return, had crawled into his lodge one warm night and awakened him by laying a finger across his lips. For a moment he had been terrified. She took his hand and wrestled it down to her crotch, her pubic hair. He suddenly realized the figure kneeling over him was a girl and his fright changed to excitement. He began to speak or to whisper something, but again that finger pressed across his lips.

Telling me this, Arsène smiled, then laughed quietly for a while. She had slid off his blanket, he said, and run her hands over his thighs and belly. He had become as hard as flint, he said. Then she had kneeled over him and, holding his rigid penis, slowly sat down upon him in such a manner that it slipped into her deeply. She was wet inside. She had moved up and down several times and he had ejaculated. She then lay on him for a while, her cheek against his, face turned away. Every time he tried to speak, though, she laid a finger across his lips. Soon he was stiff again and again she mounted him, riding him up and down. After he had ejaculated a second time, she departed under the rolled-up edge of the tepee, leaving as silently as she had evidently entered. As she was leaving, he whispered to her to come back again. She said nothing but had returned a number of times. He would never know in advance," he said. And he never saw her face clearly, so he never knew who she was. But, he laughed, her visits got better and better, until he would look forward to them almost desperately, until finally she stopped coming. And he never knew who she was. That was his initiation to love-making, he said, and he wished he could do it all again.

"And if the girls get pregnant," I asked. "When they don't want to be? Do they care about their reputations?"

"Yes. You know those big smooth river rocks?"

"Yes."

"They get a couple of those and pound their bellies. That usually works."

27

With respect to my own sexual encounters, I did see a good deal of Sehêbi when I was at home. She had recovered her high spirits, her interest in the life around her. She not only spent many hours in the kitchen chatting in her constantly improving French with Mademoiselle, but she also played outside with her daughter and sometimes even wandered about the house, sitting alone, for instance, in the dim drawing room. She had become lively and attractive, fetching once more. Of course I was tempted, with Hélène-Eulalie so occupied with her uncle and cousin. The girl managed to let me know by her glances and expressions that she was still available, if I should want her. She had moved from Arsène's room and was sleeping on the veranda, where I might have been able to join her. But I had, for me, the unusual good sense to maintain my equilibrium.

Still, fond of her as I was, I felt a responsibility for her well-being, especially after she should rejoin her people. For that reason I detained Arsène late the evening before his departure, when the others had retired for the night. Dressed for his stay in shirt and trousers, he was quite amenable to sitting with a glass of Armagnac and engaging in a candid conversation. We spoke idly at first about the People, particularly his friends. He was worried about Sees-Fire, who had been acting strangely since Taoinan's death. He no longer could talk, communicating only by signs. He had, it seemed, lost his voice. After we both wondered aloud about this, I turned the conversation to Sehêbi, beginning by asking him who would provide for her and the child once she had returned.

"Taoinan's two other wives are with Big-Mountain. He has four others. But he's rich and she's pretty. I think he'd like to take her."

"Do you think she'd be happy?"

"With First-Frost and She-Scolds-Her-Dogs? Yes. When Taoinan was alive, the three of them were like sisters."

"Would you consider marrying her yourself? She is pretty, as you yourself just said. And charming, too."

"My wives wouldn't like it. Two of them are pregnant again. I think they'd be jealous. Mean to her."

"I see." I smiled. "You're afraid of your wives?"

He laughed. "No, I want peace in my lodge."

"You would take her if she were unhappy with Toyamancare, and nobody she liked would take her, wouldn't you?"

"I would—for you Jean-Pierre. I know you like her. My cousin knows too. She doesn't like it."

"Has she talked to you?" I asked in surprise.

"No. But I can tell."

I looked straight into his eyes. "Yes, I do like Sehêbi, as you said. But I love your cousin. We're going to marry, if she'll still have me."

"Good." His eyebrows arched.

"If she'll have me. Anyway, I'm glad you'll look out for Sehêbi. That eases my mind."

"I will."

I began to rise, setting down my empty glass.

"Wait." Arsène, still seated, looked at me intently.

I sat back down. "What is it?"

"I want to tell you a dream I had."

I waited while he thought. Raising his head at last, he looked at me gravely. "This happened a few nights ago. I don't remember it all. It seemed to go on for a long time. But I remember this part as if it really happened." He went on to tell me of riding on a trail in woods like those he had passed through on his way to the post. He came to a stream, an open space in sunlight. There was a boulder at the stream's edge. Seated upon it was Taoinan, The Flute. In the dream he was dressed as he frequently was in life, bare-chested, with breechcloth, horseman's leggings. Beside his normal foot dangled his deformed foot, both in moccasins. To Arsène's astonishment he had one male nipple and one swollen female breast. At this breast he was suckling a wolf pup which he cradled in his left arm. Arsène drew in his pony, stared and laughed in amazement. But Taoinan, unsurprised, returned his gaze calmly, as if he had been expecting him. Raising his free hand, he pointed upward. Arsène heard a rush of wings and saw a flock of crows ascend from nearby pines. As they rose rapidly into the sky, they became scalps. He watched until they disappeared into the blue, then turned quickly back to the boulder. Taoinan regarded him sympathetically, soberly, for what seemed in the dream a long time, as if he were trying to convey something with his eyes. But Arsène, baffled, could comprehend nothing. That's all he remembered.

"It seemed so real. What do you think it means?"

"I have no idea."

"You were his 'brother.' You knew him better than anybody."

"That's true." I saw that he still revered Taoinan. "But I have no understanding of dreams. What do you think it means?"

"I don't know. But I've thought about it ever since. I've thought maybe it could mean..."

"Go on."

"That our sons will be "wolves"—or like wolves, great warriors. They'll take many scalps. It could mean our enemies will be afraid of us and run away." He shrugged. "I don't know. It could mean something like that. What do you think?"

"Maybe. Who are your enemies now?"

"Oh, you know. The same—Apaches, Utes, Tonkawas, Huazas, Pawnees, Caihuas. They all want our country, our grass, our buffalo, our horses."

"Huazas?" Then I recalled that was the name the Spaniards of Béxar used for the people we call 'Osage.' "I see. You think the Huazas will run from your sons?"

He smiled. "I'm just guessing at the dream."

"Well. Are you sure you have enough enemies?"

He smiled. "Toyamancare says if we don't have plenty, we'll become women."

I smiled. "That's Toyamancare. Anyway, I think what you ought to do, when you get back, is talk to a Puhahante, medicine person. Somebody with big power."

"Of course, that's what I intend to do. I suppose I'll talk to Red-Woman. He doesn't have much power, but maybe... I just thought that perhaps, since you were his brother..."

"I'm sorry," I said. "I wish I could help. But I'm just a tabebo, remember? White man. I have absolutely no power. But on that subject," I blurted, because it had been haunting me. "Your shadow—it looks normal to me now." Call it intuition, but I had had throughout his stay a powerful sense that any reference to witchcraft would at present be a violation of our friendship.

His expression changed. Obviously he found even the reminder repugnant. "Oh that. Yes, that's stopped."

But from his tone and his stricken look, I suspected that it had not. I sensed that the subject was one he was determined to avoid discussing, even with me. I hadn't the heart to press him further.

He avoided my eyes as we rose. We embraced, and since he had announced that he, Sehêbi, and the child would be leaving early in the morning. I expected to see them off but said goodby anyway. After that we went, again smiling, still good friends, to our respective rooms.

Although I had gone to bed late and was tired, something woke me in the night—or rather early in the morning. Perhaps it had been the moon shining in my open window onto the floor. I thought I heard some noise outside and went to the window. To my surprise I found I had come to it just in time to watch Arsène and his female companions depart. The three of them rode out of the shadows by the corrals into the silver light of a half-moon directly overhead. Arsène, once more the Comanche warrior, was leading two pack horses. I noted that he had left old César behind. Following him first came Sehêbi, then Ooa, the child riding to the side and a little behind her mother. As the little group started down the white strip, Ooa slowed her pony, turned in her saddle and looked back for a moment. The moonlight full on her face made it pale, silver. I could not distinguish her features. Then she turned, kicking the animal into a trot, bouncing a little, in order to catch up. I watched the three of them until they turned the far corner and vanished, then crawled back into my bed. Before yielding to sleep again, I kept seeing a fragment of our farewells the previous evening when the child had suddenly embraced the colonel's crippled legs, pressing her face between them. Monsieur de St. Maurice, with the aid of a cane, had bent and gently raised her face to his, stroked her cheek and somehow managed to bend so far as to kiss her tenderly on the forehead. That was all. But the vignette kept reappearing in my mind until I once more lapsed into sleep.

Our breakfast in the morning was a quiet and solemn affair. The colonel ate and sipped silently, isolated in his thoughts. Hélène-Eulalie was also silent and pensive. She would not look at me. I suspected something was wrong between us but could not think what it might be this time. Plainly she was full of sympathy for her uncle at the departure not only of the son who was, in effect, lost to him, as well as the child of whom he had become fond.

"Please don't be sad," she said to him at last. "They'll be back. We'll make sure of that on our next trip, won't we, Jean-Pierre? You'll see them again. Ooa will be bigger, but she'll never forget you, so..." She looked at him sympathetically. "You mustn't think you won't see her again."

"I've no reason to be unhappy," said the colonel, raising his head, wiping his lips with his napkin. "Each of us has moments of happiness. In my lifetime I've had my share. More, really. Recently the child gave me something I thought I'd lost. No, I'm not unhappy, I'm grateful. I don't pity myself, so don't pity me." Looking from one to the other of us, dry-eyed, he began sipping his coffee.

For a time we ate in silence. Mlle. Bijou came and went in silence.

"I'll miss her too," Hélène-Eulalie said at last. "We'll all miss her."

I nodded. Yes, I felt a pain as if I were losing a daughter.

By the time we left the table, after Monsieur de St. Maurice's remarks and behavior, we were all in a more cheerful mood. With a smile and a nod he hobbled down the hall, went into his office—allowing the cat, tail up, to precede him—and shut the door. I was about to go to my room, prior to leaving for the trading house. But Hélène-Eulalie's stance and expression stopped me. She was standing stiffly erect, with her head a little to one side. Her chin was raised, along with her eyebrows. She wore a little imperious smile and her direct gaze was a challenge. If she had been a man I would have thought myself about to be offered a choice of weapons.

"What is wrong? What have I done now?"

"Tu a fait l'idiot," she said. "C'est tout."

"What?" She had never tu-toied me. The noblesse vous-voied each other. "Tell me. What have I done?"

Moving closer to me, she began to look more and more amused, perhaps at my expression. "Who could be jealous of such an imbécile?" she asked rhetorically.

"Jealous?" I asked, searching my mind. "Ah, Sehêbi..." I was now embarrassed, and she began to laugh. "Look, I had to tell her something. She wanted me to come to her bed. What could I say? I had to lie. You should be pleased with me."

"I know. She told me all about it. Told me not to be jealous. She was going away. Who could be jealous of a mufle like you, anyway? Tell me."

"Nobody," I said, feeling my face redden. Her calling me a boor annoyed me. I was becoming angry myself. "Of course, nobody could."

"Wait," she said, laughing, placing her hands on my shoulders. "Don't get angry." Moving her face close to mine, she now looked amused. "You were right. I was a little jealous. But you shouldn't have seen...and you shouldn't have dared tell her."

It was my turn to smile. I drew her to me, our faces close now. "But you'll forgive me?"

"What do you think, idiot?" she said, her expression changing to one of tenderness, looking at me with raised eyebrows, her great gray eyes.

I drew her close, holding her tightly, and brought my mouth down on hers. We clenched each other. Holding her, feeling her body pressed on mine, I could tell that with the departure, the anger and the laughter, her passion had returned.

So it came about that Hélène-Eulalie and I married again, legally this time and in her church. I had put aside my scruples, betrayed my Deist principles...for love of her. We had married quietly in the church on the hill one windy afternoon when no one else was stirring. The cherub-cheeked curé, half-aware I suppose of my Deistical leanings, had been as tolerant and brief as I had been well-rehearsed in my role by my bride-to-be. She and I had talked calmly and rationally of pros and cons for weeks previous to this occasion. Then one evening, when seated serenely on a sofa in the drawing room, we had each confessed that we needed the other person desperately and could not bear to continue living without that person. We began kissing, then breathing hard, until she panted, "No," broke away and ran upstairs alone to her bedroom.

After that we hurried to plan the ceremony, witnessed only by Monsieur de St. Maurice, who was borne to the church on a burro, and by Mademoiselle Bijou, and by Antoine and his wife, Simone. It was a cloudy, miserable, joyful day. We—including Monsieur le Curé—celebrated with two rare bottles of Champagne and a feast prepared by Mlle. Bijou at the colonel's house. At the close of our modest revelry the priest had acquired some difficulty in walking and was returned to his house by Antoine and the burro. The colonel, the bride and I, slumped in our chairs, chatted for a time in the drawing room before the fire. When we became drowsy, Monsieur de St. Maurice went tapping away with his canes to his room, while Hélène-Eulalie accompanied me up the stairs, hand in hand, and soon once again climbed, naked as she was born, into my bed—legally at last.

28

In the spring of 1800—barely May I think it was—I sent Antoine Lefort into the plains to trade for horses. There were a variety of rumors that year, the year that Spain retroceded Louisiana to France. One rumor had the United States going to war with France over the port of Nouvelle Orléans because of anticipated exorbitant duties upon the mass of American agricultural products transported down the Mississippi. This was not a preposterous idea. People were angry, greatly aroused. We had also learned that Americans farther east were beginning to migrate westward, even though many would be unwelcome in territories under the French or Spanish flags. But they came anyway.

There was a sense among us that we were on the brink of great events, great changes. Colonel de St. Maurice told us he expected, within a few years, a migration of Americans from the southern states to the Mississippi River, and even beyond. It would be impossible to contain that growing and increasingly restive population, he contended. People— whole families he believed—would come, whether legally or not. For the southern states immigrants would require horses. Horses, then, would increasingly be the staple of our sales to the migrant American public, who would travel westward in waves seeking new lands offering new opportunities. They would spread along our frontier, some spilling over. It was time to begin preparing for that or risk missing the possible bounty to follow.

Antoine and two fellow Canadians crossed the prairie, following La Rivière Rouge to the great canyon near its source. The Spaniards call this canyon "Palo Verde." Big-Mountain's band, Those-Who-Go-Far-Alone, frequently established their winter camps within it, where there was wood and water, grass, and protection from the blizzards of winter. Lefort had no doubt learned of this favorite location during our trading visits.

Toyamancare and his people greeted the traders warmly but were reluctant to part with their ponies, even though they owned more than a thousand head. For one thing many of the horses were in poor condition, having been fed at winter's end mostly upon bark stripped from young trees. There was some doubt they would be able to survive spring snowstorms in crossing the prairie to La Grande Forêt and beyond. In the end though, Antoine and his friends contrived to accumulate some thirty head of average ponies in fair condition. Somehow they succeeded in driving them back to the post without losing any. We sold all but three which we needed ourselves, so that the expedition was more or less successful, but one that we decided we would never repeat during that time of year.

For me, outside of the moderate profit the trading company made, the interest of the expedition lay in what Antoine told me of Arsène. He had found him agitated. Now I should note that Arsène was in some respects closer to the Canadian than he was to me.

Antoine had thought that the man he had known as a boy was behaving oddly, appearing anxious, distracted. Antoine was at first curious, then concerned. Finally one morning, brilliant with sunlight, when the two of them were alone and he noticed the younger man shrink suddenly back into the shade of a small tree, he asked him directly whether anything were wrong, told him he didn't seem himself. Arsène started and stared at him for a moment.

"That's right. I might as well tell you, Antoine. El Chamaco's been witching me."

"El Chamaco? Because of Tosapoy?" Antoine remembered that it was partly owing to jealousy of Arsène that Tosapoy, or White-Road, had cut the throat of his independent and disobedient wife, Tabo-ui.

"Yes. I think White-Road is behind it."

"Witching? How?"

Arsène frowned, became thoughtful, stared at him. "Watch." He stepped into the sunlight. At first nothing seemed unusual.

"Alors...quoi?"

Then Lefort noticed that as his friend moved, his shadow followed independently, having become distorted, moving jerkily, swollen here and shrunken there, but never quite corresponding to the precise shape or motion of Arsène's trunk or limbs. Abruptly, while Antoine watched, the image washed inward upon itself, becoming Arsène's ordinary shadow.

"Did you see that?"

Antoine, staring, said he had and found it, "drôlement bizarre—un type debout dans des flots, n'est-ce pas?"

"Mais non. Voyez-vous. Ce sont des flammes."

"Ah, mon dieu, je voie. Tu as raison. C'est du feu." Shocked by the image of a man standing, not in waves, as he had first thought, but in fire, Antoine reflected: "You need to talk to someone with big medicine. Big Puha. Not Red-Woman, of course."

"No, not Red-Woman. That's the trouble. They're half-brothers. Tosapoy, too. There's nobody else with power."

"No? You sure? Have you tried talking to El Chamaco himself?"

"No, why would I do that?" He had become extremely pale.

"Let me think about it," Antoine said. What he kept thinking about was the threat implicit in his young friend's shadow, a threat conveyed obscurely and no less seriously because of bumbling El Chamaco's role. About that, he had to do something. But what?

He told me he had pondered for several days while trading. (One cannot hurry bargaining with the People.) He was baffled until he thought of the blind arrowmaker, the one who led the little children in games. He recalled that on our return journey from the great divisional meeting on Rio Pecos, the old man had said he had "seen" the giant ogre owl, Piamupitz. Taoinan had told him that the blind man could frequently "see" what ordinary sighted men could not. This showed that he had "Puha" or power that ordinary men lacked.

So Antoine went to see the blind man at his lodge one morning, bringing as a gift, slung over his shoulder, a buck he had shot. The arrowmaker, seated in the doorway of his small lodge, invited him to enter. The two sat and smoked, passing the pipe for a time. After the Canadian had explained Arsène's troubles, the old man reflected with his eyes half-closed.

"Has Ah-mah-bah-tay talked with El Chamaco?" the arrowmaker asked.

"No. I asked him that."

A long silence followed. Prepared for a lengthy visit, Antoine waited patiently.

"I can 'see' El Chamaco," the blind man said at last, his eyes still closed. "I've 'seen' him often. He's the same, not happy." He lapsed into silence, evidently reflecting.

"Why is that?"

"He believes nobody respects him. Everyone admires his half-brothers. Tosapoy is a great warrior with many wives and ponies. Red-Woman is a Puhahante, with big power, big medicine."

"And El Chamaco's camp crier."

"Yes. He thinks 'only camp crier.' He rides badly. He's a poor warrior. Has only one wife. Only three ponies."

"So he wants more wives and ponies. He wants everybody to look up to him. What about the witching?"

"He learned that from his brother, Red-Woman. He's doing it for Tosapoy. But he likes doing it."

"Of course. So what is Ah-mah-bah-tay to do?"

The arrowmaker sat silently for a long while. "You know, I can't 'see' him. Maybe because he's a tabebo, whiteman, like you. I think he has to talk to El Chamaco. But tell him to come to my lodge tomorrow morning. Maybe then I'll be able to 'see' him and help."

Arsène, doubting the old man's Puha, had delayed in visiting him. Antoine had been compelled to return with the new ponies to the post; he had departed feeling baffled.

Meanwhile on his return Antoine learned from the gossip of French Canadian friends of the furor caused by the shameful act of another trader and former coureur de bois named Gustave Barré. Most trappers and traders, like Lefort, knew him, or at least knew of him. This man, who already had an ugly reputation on the frontier, was presently the topic of indignation wherever voyageurs gathered.

It appeared that on a brief visit to St. Louis for supplies he had married a young white girl from a destitute family, taken her with him on a trading expedition to the Pawnees. Tiring of her, he had sold her to a chief who had offered a number of ponies for her, sold the child that is without her knowledge and deserted her, taking the ponies and leaving her with the tribe. Evidently he had boasted of it. Antoine, along with his friends, was outraged and could talk of nothing for some time but of what a vaurien vicieux the trader was, a disgrace to all of them. Barré, they agreed, though a shrewd and brave trader, was a man lacking any principles and the slightest degree of honor. Although Antoine finally ceased talking about the scandal, he never got over his indignation, which ultimately made his debt to the man more painful.

Until I saw The One Without A Head I waited and wondered.

That summer during our annual expedition to the Comanches Arsène told me about his meeting with the arrowmaker. It had shaken him. He said he had finally entered the old man's lodge after having been again invited to do so. But he was skeptical of the other's power. The two men had smoked. He had believed the arrowmaker would show some deference toward him since he was a warchief. But the old man was completely self-assured, even self-important, blind and frail as he was.

"You were a 'wolf,' weren't you?"

"Yes."

"Why did you leave them?"

"I got tired of living that way."

"Did you kill many people?"

"What? No."

"I see in your heart there's one you're sorry you killed. A woman. Isn't that so?"

Arsène started.

"You know, this is a very bad spell. Very bad. Does your heart hurt?"

Arsène remained silent.

"When you came to us... When you came with Big-Mountain, a boy, you were sad. You cried...sometimes. At night. I can 'see' that. Isn't that true?"

"Yes. At first. For a while. I got over it." He was embarrassed. Comanche boys of twelve were not supposed to weep. Yet he was surprised, impressed that the old man knew.

"How did you get over it?"

"How? I don't know. Just time, I guess. New friends."

The old man was silent for a time, smoking the pipe. He passed it to Arsène. "Here. You smoke."

Arsène smoked, feeling increasingly uneasy. He thought back for a time. Suddenly he started. "Well, yes. There was someone who helped me. I forgot. She didn't come often, or very long. But she helped me during my worst nights."

"Who was that?"

"That old woman, the Charitica slave. Everyone calls her Cáco, Grandmother. I guess maybe I should go see her. I never thanked her. Do something for her. She makes me think of an old Painted Arrows woman I had to kill. Yes, you see, we were crawling toward their camp and..."

"Maybe it's the same woman."

"What?"

"I just said 'maybe.'" Who knows? Anyway, if you have a clear heart you'll be harder to witch. I think so. But you must see El Chamaco. Be nice to him, make him feel good. I 'see' there's something of yours he wants very much. I don't know what it is or what it's for. Some tabebo thing. He's afraid to ask you, thinks you're mad at him."

"He does? What kind of whiteman's thing?"

"I know it's black, like a bundle of feathers, that's all. But if you want to stop the witching, you'll have to give it to him. Otherwise you'll probably die."

"What? Probably die?"

"Yes, I think so."

29   *Summer 1800, By the Washita*

I remember that our summer 1800 expedition left Natchitoches Post weeks later than its customary time of departure. Metal arrowheads, blankets of stroud cloth, dark blue or red, failed to arrive until mid-June that year. Perhaps a ship was late in reaching Nouvelle-Orléans. Who knows? I have forgotten the cause. But these items were in such demand among the Indians that it was impossible to depart without them. When we finally rode past Fort St. Jean Baptist leading a string of packhorses, it was already the end of the third week in June. Progressing in those first days through pine forest, we frequently crouched under downpours which drenched us and our horses while not, however, penetrating the tarpaulin-covered goods in the packsaddles, the responsibility of Antoine Lefort. Nevertheless he and Hélène-Eulalie, riding beside me at the head of the caravan, carried on much of the time a cheerful conversation, elated, in spite of dripping branches—as I was too—to be bound again for the sunny winds of the prairie.

By the time some three weeks later that we arrived at our familiar Red River crossing, the weather had turned agreeable. While two engagés, under the direction of Henri Tournier, erected the tent for Madame and me, they and the remainder of the party chose to profit by the beauty of the evening and spread their blankets or robes under the Milky Way, the Comanches' 'Wolf's Road,' beside the final flickerings of their fires.

On reaching the Pawnee-Piquée (Wichitan) Red River villages we found we had missed our Comanche guide. The head chief informed us that the young man had, after some weeks, tired of waiting and had ridden away to rejoin his people. He had left a message informing us that the band would be moving slowly up the middle waters of the Washita River, which we might intersect in two or three days by riding directly north from the village.

Yes, the Washita. Scouts had reported buffalo along the Washita that summer. After striking the river, the chief continued, we should follow the stream toward its source to the northwest. By so doing we would after a few days encounter Comanche lodges, which remained at each site for some days before advancing farther upstream.

The directions proved to be accurate. In less than a week Lefort, riding in advance, returned to tell me he had seen tepees and the Comanche horseherd far ahead of us along the river. Since it was by then late afternoon, I directed the men to halt at the next suitable campsite. While they were engaged in removing packsaddles, picketing horses and building fires, I dispatched Antoine forward once more to the Comanche camp in order to announce to the headmen our planned arrival the following morning, so that they might observe their ceremonial welcomes. In addition, I asked him to find Arsène and to invite him to dine with us that evening.

It was dusk before the two men rode up, tossed their reins to an engagé and joined us at the cookfire before our tent. Antoine took me aside at once and told me of crossing tracks of unknown horsemen along the Washita, said he had shown them to Arsène. I reflected, then shrugged, told him we would discuss that later. After we had greeted and embraced each other, we sat around the fire and ate the venison and squash which Tournier had prepared. Arsène did not look well. His walk was stiff, off balance. Once he tottered or staggered. I was shocked to see him moving in the spasmodic manner in which his shadow had moved the last time I had seen him. He had not painted his face, which was haggard and sallow. His hair hung in a long braid on either side of his head, with a red line drawn along its part and an eagle feather drooping in his scalplock. Firelight flickered upon and reddened his features, giving him a feverish look, while he ate slowly with his fingers, talking as he did so. Seated cross-legged opposite him in buckskins, Hélène-Eulalie, her face nearly as tanned as his, leaned forward eagerly listening, while Antoine and I sat energetically chewing to her right.

"So it seems we came too late," she said, turning to me. "We won't be able to see Toyamancare or his sons, or any of the others, will we?"

"It's too bad," said Arsène. "They wanted to trade, but his medicine was strong. They left about ten days ago. He didn't want to wait any longer."

"You don't know when they'll be back?" I asked.

"No. The Panismahas live above the Pawnees. On the river they call the 'Loup.' The South Loup. A long way."

"Was it a big warparty?"

"Twenty-seven men. Many of our best."

"When are you meeting them? And where?"

"Next big moon—down the river where we started. Whoever gets there first will wait."

"And Sehêbi..." exclaimed Hélène-Eulalie. "Did she go with Toyamancare? You said he'd probably marry her. And Ooa—what about Ooa?"

Arsène looked up from his tin plate with an embarrassed smile. "No. I was going to tell you. She's with me. The child too."

"They are?" asked Hélène-Eulalie, clearly astonished. "I thought you disliked each other."

"We found out we didn't."

"When?" I asked. "On the way back?"

"Yes."

"I wondered about that." I laughed. "So you married her? And took the child too?"

"I did."

"But...you told me..." said Hélène-Eulalie. "Your wives...aren't they mean to her?"

Arsène's haughty look appeared. "They wouldn't dare. She's my favorite now. I've talked to them. They're good to her, and the girl too. My little boys like Ooa. The women are pleased at that."

"So you married her. That's good. And she's your favorite wife," I said. "What made you change your opinion?"

He looked at me a moment, offended, then slowly smiled. "You haven't changed, Jean-Pierre. Well, I'll tell you. She's pretty. But that isn't all. I found on the way back from the post I could talk to her. That we could talk. She's clever. She's seen life at the post and life with the People. She understands things others don't. Of course there are other smart women in the band, but she's...different."

"Good."

Hélène-Eulalie smiled at her cousin across the fire. "You were smart to have married her. I think she's just right for you."

As soon as my own wife had left us to go to her bedroll, I asked Arsène quietly whether he had talked to El Chamaco and whether the sorcery had stopped.

"Yes, I did see him." He looked around behind him into the dark beyond the firelight. "The witching is better now. It hasn't stopped, though the boils have. It seems that El Chamaco can't control it any more. Neither can Red-Woman."

"What do you mean?"

"Well, it is better. You haven't noticed anything, have you?"

"You still look sick. In fact, sicker. So it hasn't stopped?"

"Not entirely."

"You say El Chamaco can't control it now? You got him to try?"

"Yes. What do you think he wanted of mine? Begged for."

"I don't know. Something black. I remember that."

"At first he tried arrogance, like Tosapoy. That didn't work. It's not in his nature. So when he finally asked me for what he wanted, he was very humble, like a little boy."

So what was it?"

Arsène appeared amused. "Have you ever seen my Spanish umbrella? It's black. I bought it from a soldado at the post. But I hardly ever used it. He begged for it. I gave it to him to get him to stop the witching."

"And he can't stop it?"

"He thought he could. He's embarrassed. He went to see his brother. But Red-Woman can't stop it either."

"You were going to see the old one they call Cáco."

"I saw her," he sighed. "She wasn't getting enough to eat. Big-Mountain's wives and boys get first choice of the food. They get the best meat. She gets last choice. But she's lost her teeth, or most of them. She can't chew much. They don't care."

"Well. So you're going to hunt for her?"

"She told me she was always hungry. Yes, I am. I should have thought of that sooner. I thanked her for being good to me when I was first here and sad. I told her I'd hunt for her and bring her food and she could cook it for herself and me the way she liked it, and she could eat it. I told her I'd take care of her, and she wouldn't be hungry any more."

"She was pleased, of course?"

"She cried."

I nodded. "And by the way, Antoine told me you passed some tracks of horsemen on the way here."

"Yes." Arsène frowned. "I'd like to know who they were. With Big-Mountain and the others away... If we had to fight... But up here it's unlikely."

It was late. The engagé who had been guarding the ponies was relieved by another man. He released his horse to the herd and came to stand by our little fire. We three chatted for a moment. Arsène, after giving me a significant look, said, "Alors, bonne nuit," and went off to his bedroll. I soon went to mine, leaving the former guard squatting alone warming his hands by a few dusty coals and fitful flames.

We arrived early next morning within sight of the Comanche camp by the river after first passing the grazing horseherd. Arsène led us into a meadow brilliant with dew and traversed by a tributary creek, where we might camp. It was located some thirty rods below the nearest tepees and about ten from the Washita, which sparkled and splashed white over rocks, running shallow for some distance. While the men unsaddled and picketed the horses, Arsène, Hélène-Eulalie, and I rode into the smoky, noisy encampment.

Everyone seemed occupied, either working or playing, the women cooking or attending to children, the men smoking, talking in small groups, often holding their horses by a lead rope, young boys kicking at each other, shouting, and racing among the tepees, dogs trotting beside us, the few little mongrels barking, the big wolfish ones howling. Everyone looked up as we passed, the women especially, pleased and excited by the presence of traders, the men reserved but genial, a few of them raising a hand. There was a relaxed, good feeling about the camp on this morning, as if everyone was contented in the fresh sunlight and enjoying the day. Arsène and I dismounted at the big lodge of Red-Woman, once again civil chief, while Hélène-Eulalie, still seated upon her one-eared pony, held our horses.

We rejoined her sooner that I had expected, stepping out into the sunlight a short time later. Formerly tall and thin, Red-Woman had gained weight and seemed to have shrunk nearly to the size of his brother, El Chamaco, who lighted the ceremonial pipe, which we smoked in turn. The civil chief was changed otherwise too, humbler, no longer so impressed with his own importance. I had expected a long speech of welcome. But after we had all smoked and I had presented him with a gift of tobacco, he said only a few words, to which I replied and the ceremony was over.

Arsène then introduced the serious topic of this occasion. He informed Red-Woman of Antoine's report, imparted to him when Lefort had first located him in camp, that he had crossed hoofprints of what might have been a scouting party descending from the north. These he had seen, himself. Antoine had first observed its marks along the riverbank where the stream curved westward. The prints of several horsemen had followed the Comanche tracks for a way, then abandoned them to point northwest, like the Washita itself, but higher. With many of the band's leading warriors absent, Arsène was concerned about the identity of these riders, whoever they might be. It worried him, he confided, because any engagement at present with an enemy would find the band weakened. And it was his responsibility to defend the People. At any rate he felt it necessary to share our discovery with the civil chief.

"You have sent out scouts?" asked Red-Woman.

"Yesterday."

"Then we must wait. Maybe they are friends."

"Probably not friends if they come from the north. They could be Pawnees. But they hardly ever come this far south and east. Or Osage, but they don't come this far west. I don't know who they could be."

"Let's see what the scouts tell us."

I spoke to Arsène of the difference in Red-Woman when we were again mounted and moving toward his lodge.

"Yes, he has changed since he came back. He's more sensible. But you know, Toyamancare is really head chief now, head war chief and peace chief too. Red-Woman is thought to have little Puha, little power. He's peace chief, really, mostly in name."

"And you?" I asked.

He smiled. "When my father's away, I'm head warchief—and, really, civil chief too. Big-Mountain doesn't trust Red-Woman."

"Bravo!" said Hélène-Eulalie. "I'm surprised you didn't go with the war party. But glad you didn't."

Arsène rode along with a thoughtful expression for a moment. "I was up there once when I was a 'wolf.' It's a long, long way. Besides we visited Sehêbi's people last month, almost to the mountains of Nuevo Mexico."

"Did she see her mother?"

"Yes. All her relatives."

"It was kind of you to take her."

Arsène did not respond to his cousin, riding the remainder of the way beside the river with the same thoughtful expression, as if he had not heard. I knew it was not good among the People for a warrior to reveal affection for a wife. It suggested he was weak.

Beside Arsène's big lodge was the smaller one of his women. Presumably Sehêbi slept in his. No one was visible. Before Arsène could call out, Hélène-Eulalie had swung down off of her pony and was running toward the lodge, crying out, "Sehêbi!" From the big tepee came a little shriek. Sehêbi rushed from the doorway, and the two women embraced, both talking at once, leaning back to look at each other, embracing again, laughing. Sehêbi was weeping as well as laughing. From what I could see, she looked well, as well as I had ever seen her appear. Arsène and I dismounted. At that, Sehêbi disengaged herself and ran to take the reins of the three horses, pausing an instant to smile at me, tears still slipping down her painted cheeks.

"Jean-Pierre, ça va bien?"

Without waiting for a reply, she rushed off with the horses.

"Come see my new lodge," said Arsène, looking back as he stooped into the doorway of the tepee. The morning was already turning warm. The sides, raised for ventilation, allowed air to circulate as well as sunlight to enter. "My wives made it." The shelter was roomy and clean, with robes and blankets upon its floor and the two buffalo robe beds at the edge. Opposite the doorway, the owner's bowcase and arrows, as well as a buffalo-horned headdress, hung from a pole. I nodded at the headdress.

"That means you're a warchief?"

"Not a big one."

"Like Big-Mountain?"

"Yes, he's head warchief."

"But he just wears an eagle feather."

"Yes, he doesn't care. All he really wants are more horses." He smiled. "He never has enough."

Hélène-Eulalie turned as Sehêbi entered. "And how is Ooa? I want to see Ooa."

"She's playing. Don't you hear them?"

For some time we had been hearing the shouts, laughter, and screams of children.

"Can we go watch?"

This time we walked, with Arsène shooing away the dogs. Moving upstream, we passed several tepees, one before which a woman was sewing moccasins with an awl, and another by which a dark, well-proportioned young man was brushing his long hair with the help of a trade mirror. He called a greeting as we passed, and Arsène replied. He looked familiar.

"Who was that?"

"Deer's-Ears."

"Oh yes, I remember." Ears-of-a-Sorrel-Deer had been called, Poná, or "Snail" as a boy. Arsène's best friend, or "brother," he was about the same age. He was handsome and appeared to be light-hearted and good-natured.

We arrived at the group of children just as they appeared about to start a new game. Two boys of about eight or nine years, naked like all the boys that age and younger, were still scampering about near an old man but, as we approached, they flung themselves down at the end of a row of girls and other boys, apparently ranging in age from about four years to nine or ten. It was difficult to tell because they were all seated upon the grass with their backs to us, their legs extended before them, except for one little girl who held the old man's hand. That child and the old man appeared to be the only ones aware of our presence. In the instance of the man, this was odd because his milky eyes proclaimed him to be blind.

He was, I realized, the arrowmaker, Basin-Paunch, who had seen the ghost bird, or Piamupitz and who had counseled Arsène. He appeared quickly to take note of us and looked away. The little girl who, like the old man and the other girls, wore only breechcloth and moccasins, led the arrowmaker to the middle of the row of children, released his hand and ran to sit at the far end of the row by the two boys. The children were beginning to giggle. Stooping, the old man began to move up and down the row, fingering the bare feet and legs of the children, some of whom began to laugh or shriek with excitement. Finally he selected one, a little girl, whom, with surprising strength, he raised by her feet, slinging her upon his back, so that she hung face down, hair dangling. He packed the child back and forth before the row, while the children screamed questions at her:

"Do you have a pony?"

"Yes," cried the girl.

"Do you have a bridle?"

"Yes."

"Do you have a tepee?"

"Yes."

"Do you have buffalo meat?"

After more questions and responses, always "Yes," the row of children jumped to their feet, rushed to the arrowmaker and pulled the red-faced child from his back, threatening that they were going to eat him. He tried to fend them off, but like a swarm of bees they came at him from all sides, tickling until to our astonishment the old man began to giggle and snort and whoop and laugh in a strange jig, leaping up and down and throwing his arms in the air and all around him, driving the children to further efforts and greater hilarity. One little boy, unable to control his laughter, rolled upon the grass.

The spectacle was so strange that we too were laughing, even Arsène. Beside me, Hélène-Eulalie was laughing so hard that tears shone on her cheeks. I had been unsuccessfully seeking to spy out Ooa, when suddenly from among the mob tickling the arrowmaker she turned and saw us. Her cry was lost in the uproar. But she ran to us, to Hélène-Eulalie that is, and flung her arms around her, looking up into her face with delight. The woman went down to her knees on the grass in her buckskins and embraced the child. They remained in that posture for several heartbeats, cheek pressed to cheek, while the other children, all at once noticing, paused in their game and stared, and the nearly toothless old man stood, still smiling, gazing blindly in our direction.

Walking back by the river, we wandered to Arsène's lodge, Ooa between the two women and holding a hand of each. Later Hélène-Eulalie and I were standing chatting with Arsène prior to returning to our camp when a big black, dusty animal indistinguishable from a wolf, parted the branches between bushes at a little distance and warily emerged. I supposed it was not a wolf or it would not have stood staring at us as it was doing. Hélène-Eulalie, while conversing with Arsène, suddenly noticed the animal.

"Look. Is that yours?"

Arsène turned. "No. She's been hanging around lately. I don't know who she belongs to. I think she has pups. Her teats are swollen."

"She's probably hungry, la pauvre."

After examining us carefully, the animal approached cautiously, halting about twenty feet away, staring at Arsène with her yellow eyes, her plumelike tail slowly waving.

Arsène crouched, holding out a hand, and called her to him. The wolfdog approached him warily. When she was within several feet, he reached an open hand slowly out toward her. The animal backed and growled. At her growl, Arsène whirled and kicked a moccasined foot sideways toward her. Dexterously the dog leapt away, avoiding the kick, then stood at a little distance, grinning at him, her bushy tail waving faster.

"Look, she likes you," laughed Hélène-Eulalie. "She's flirting."

Arsène moved slowly to a rack where strips of buffalo meat were drying in the sun.

Removing a large strip, he drew his knife, and cut it into several pieces. Again he called the animal to him, squatting, holding out a morsel. This time she advanced cautiously to barely within reach of his fingers. Motionless while we watched, Arsène continued to hold out his hand. Finally the dog snatched the gobbet from his fingers, leaping backward. But Arsène continued talking softly to her, saying, "pia'isa," over and over. By the last cut of bison meat, he was rubbing behind her ears with one hand while she chewed meat from the other, simultaneously growling and whining. Finishing, she leapt away and trotted off, turning before reentering the brush, fixing us with her yellow eyes, to grin once more, her teeth gleaming white in her black face.

"Is she a wolf or a dog?" Hélène-Eulalie asked.

"I don't know. Both, I think."

"She has pups somewhere," observed Hélène-Eulalie. "What's her name?"

"She doesn't have a name. I just call her, wolf, 'piaisa.'"

"But doesn't 'pia' mean 'mother?'" I asked.

"'Mother' or 'big.' In this case, 'big.' It might as well mean the other. My people admire the wolf. It's our brother or sister."

"I wonder where she's hid her pups," murmured Ooa, who had been standing, clinging to Sehêbi, watching intently this transaction between man and canid.

That evening as I sat smoking at twilight before our tent a visitor arrived. It was Toyamancare's brother-in-law, Tuchubarua, or Bearbird, who rode his burro out of the dusk. I had never exchanged a word with the man, but he dismounted and approached my tiny flame and held out his hand as if we had been old friends. In Comanche I offered him food, hoping he had eaten, since Hélène-Eulalie was visiting Sehêbi. But no, he declined. Pausing he glanced down at my saddle on the ground, reached and absently drew a horse pistol from its holster and, holding it with both hands, examined it minutely. Since the weapon was primed, I was immediately alarmed, wondering even if he had come to kill me. But no, he replaced the pistol and seated himself opposite me at ease. Baffled as to his intentions, I offered him a cigarillo, which he accepted. We smoked together for a time in silence. Disconcerted, I waited for him to speak, but he remained mute, looking around at our camp, or at the emerging stars, his clown's broad features good-humored. I attempted politely to learn what he wished from me, tried in broken Comanche. He allowed me to do so then, after a pause, replied, to my astonishment, in fluent Castilian. Again I was disconcerted. His command of that tongue was far superior to my own. If he found my surprise comical, he refrained from revealing it. In any event since it seemed to me he was simply being sociable, we had a topic for conversation.

It evolved that many years before, when he had been a boy, and Comanches and Spaniards had been at war, he had participated in a raid upon una villa nueva mexicana at the age of about fourteen. He had been captured, sold at a Taos trade fair as a family servant—that is as a slave—and had lived with and served a prominent Santa Fe family for four years. He had managed finally to steal three horses and escape at night. In the interim he had mastered the Spanish language, which he seemed to enjoy speaking, as he had clearly relished my surprise. A moment later, tossing the butt of his cigarillo into the fire, he surprised me again:

"Sabes? Somos casi parientes, tu y yo."

Como? Nearly relatives? What did that mean?

He smiled at my astonishment, explaining that he knew I regarded Arsène as a younger brother. Arsène was his son-in-law, having married three of his daughters. Por eso we were almost related. Stammering, I tried to demonstrate pleasure at this news, dumfounded as I was by the situation. But still at ease, he asked me for another cigarillo, lighted it, blew smoke toward the stars, and began speaking—at random it appeared at first—of Arsène. Of Tosapoy—White-Road, that is. Of how his son-in-law had discomfited that redoubtable warchief and overcome his Puha. This it seemed was what he had really come to tell me.

Arsène had been among the rearguard during the return from an attempted raid against the Osages the previous fall. The would-be raiders had suddenly encountered, drawn up facing them across a river, a sizable warparty of Osages, who mocked them with obscene gestures. Realizing he had lost the vital advantage of surprise, and even though his party had outnumbered the enemy, Big-Mountain had turned back, acting against the protests of his rival, White-Road. After that both warchiefs had ridden with Arsène in the rearguard, anticipating trouble, accompanied by seven other warriors. On the third day of their return journey, a small pursuing party of Osage warriors had overtaken and ambushed them in a dense strip of woods. These warriors had apparently intended to separate the Comanche rearguard, kill its members, and flee with their scalps and horses.

Arsène later told me that on the third day he and his companions were traveling as usual behind the main body. The enemy, about thirteen in all, had evidently galloped in a wide circle, to the north, had left their ponies with a boy, preferring to fight on foot against Comanche horsemen. Termed 'los ligeros,' 'the fleet ones' by the Spaniards and reputed to cover seven English miles in an hour at a rapid wolftrot, the Osage warriors had hurried to surprise the rearguard from the north side. A bit of luck had saved the Comanches, he said. Aware before their riders of the hidden enemies, Toyamancare's pinto and several other ponies had suddenly balked, snorted, and pricked their ears toward the right flank of the party. Toyamancare, in the forefront, instantly sensed the group's peril, though the 'fleet ones' remained invisible.

"Adelante!" he shouted, whooping, lashing his horse, falling forward onto its neck. In a body Arsène and the others, also ducking and heeding his cry, followed, their ponies springing into gallops. Startled as well, the enemy warriors concealed in the forest shot their arrows above the horsemen, missing in their confusion. They burst from the trees and hesitated, knowing that Big-Mountain's warwhoop would attract the main force.

At a distance of five or six rods, Toyamancare drew up and turned his pony to look back, as did Arsène and the others.

"Everybody not afraid, follow me!" cried White-Road, challenging Toyamancare. "Unless you're scared without your big horse," he taunted Arsène, swinging his quirt against his own pony's rump, and charging back toward the enemy.

"No," bellowed Big-Mountain. "Don't be fools! Tontos! Wait for the others!"

But Arsène was already urging his horse behind that of White-Road. The Osages, taller, bigger men than Comanches, raced to meet them, their shields and lances raised. After an instant's hesitation, Toyamancare and the remainder of the rearguard rallied and lashed their ponies to follow. The antagonists clashed in dust and confusion. But enemy warriors quickly surrounded White-Road, who had failed to slow rapidly enough. Arriving an instant later, Big-Mountain and others engaged the principal attackers with their lances. White-Road, aware of his predicament, whirled his pony and attempted to fight his way back to his companions. It was then that an Osage warrior thrust a lance through the heart of his eldest son, Ecopisura, or Scraping Spoon, who was attempting to rescue his father. In response, finding himself in an opportune position, Arsène plunged his lance into the chest of the killer, feeling it strike bone, slip by and go deep, jerking it out as quickly. That warrior dropped his weapon and staggered, falling. Another of the giants seized the tail of White-Road's horse just as three of that pony's hoofs were rising, wrenching it to the side. The warchief, clinging to his shield and lance, leapt from the falling animal. Under cover of Toyamancare's lance, he rebounded. Simultaneously Arsène kicked his pony forward. Shifting his own lance to his left hand, he leaned to White-Road, grasping him from beneath the right shoulder. The warchief sprang upward, struggling, clutching his rescuer as he pulled himself up behind him. Arsène kicked and urged his mount forward, until he broke from the mêlée and galloped between oncoming, whooping Comanche riders of the main force. He drew up after they had passed and, still panting, flung his free arm and elbow backward, striking White-Road and sending him tumbling to the earth. In the dirt the man, stunned and shaken, gazed up in furious, shocked astonishment. Arsène, full of accumulated anger, was suddenly enraged, as he told me later, remembering how the warchief had murdered Rabbit-Knife, his friend, remembering the man's bloody hands, bloody knife, her severed, gaping throat spouting blood. And how wife-murder went unpunished among the People. He stared down with hatred at his old foe.

"You just killed your son!" he cried.

White-Road gazed up in disbelief. Arsène continued to glare at him. He confided to me that he had gone crazy for a moment and had almost lanced the warchief with the shining, bloody blade that had just slain an Osage. Only the prudent thought of the living sons' duty to avenge such a death—as well as the memory of his own impulsive dashes—had restrained him. His intention, he said, must have been visible on his face, because for an instant he had observed a flicker of fear cross the fallen man's countenance. Finally the warchief whose life he had saved turned his face to the ground, beginning a struggle to rise. As Arsène rode off a glance behind revealed the older warrior still attempting to struggle upward, a crippled beetle in the dirt, while Osage braves slipped away in every direction between the trees, leaving one dead, one a captive.

Bearbird laughed quietly recounting this part, repeating himself several times, as if taking huge pleasure in the recital. The lofty warchief, Tosapoy, or White-Road, surly to other men and considered "mean" by the camp women, had been humbled at last. And his own son-in-law, my little brother, had done it.

Later when I praised his rescue to Arsène, he observed thoughtfully, "A warchief must not be rash. You lose men that way."

"Be like Toyamancare?"

"Like both my fathers."

Bearbird, soon after his account, bade me goodnight and still occasionally chuckling rode away on his burro, calling back to me out of the dark, "Adios, primo!"

Next morning we ate hastily while an engagé led in and unhobbled the packhorses. Even before Hélène-Eulalie, Antoine, and I had finished our breakfast of coffee and pemmican, the men had struck the tents and saddled the riding horses. In another half-hour they had loaded each packhorse with its bales of goods, and we were ready to depart. Indeed we were so timely that our packtrain was winding upriver before the Comanche caravan got under way. But in riding through the People's camp we passed the pole frames of tepees, while the women of each family wrestled with the hide covers, folding them into sufficiently small bundles so that they would fit upon the frames of the travois, many of which were already fastened to standing horses. Old women shrieked at each other and at darting children, while the mistresses of the lodges occupied themselves with rawhide wardrobe cases, parfleches for meat, pots, kettles, buffalo paunches filled with water, and other goods gathered together before loading. Dogs wove in and out of this confusion, seeking any morsel that might drop during the seemingly chaotic preparations. Older warriors sat by the embers of their fires, some of them smoking a pipe or a cigarillo, and holding the rein of their favorite pony. As we passed, Arsène's wives smiled shyly, with several horses standing nearby already hitched to travois, while Sehêbi waited seated upon her pinto, her face newly painted, wearing her white buckskin dress, and proudly holding Arsène's shield. She greeted us with a faint smile as we passed. Last of all among that household, a wrinkled old woman bent over a little naked boy, clutching his hand and apparently talking urgently to him. That, I thought, must be Cáco, looking like a true grandmother absorbed by her duties and as if she had always been a part of that family.

We struck out along the river, following its course beside a straight interval of that twisting stream. Looking back, after perhaps a quarter of an hour, I spied horses and riders in the distance behind us. To our left was a wide field. I told Antoine to have the men pull aside from the riverbank and to hold the packtrain there until after the band had passed in its entirety. Directly before us projected a rocky knob descending to the river on its north side. The caravan, I could see, would want to circumvent it to the left and rejoin the stream upon completing the detour. Hélène-Eulalie was also studying the little obstruction.

"Why not ride up there while we're waiting? We can watch as they go by."

I had no objection to this plan. A little later, after a scramble, we reached the summit, where we had a fine view in every direction. I was able even to make out one of the Comanche scouts, far ahead, riding across a clearing in the woods on the opposite side of the river.

"I think that's Arsène leading," said Hélène-Eulalie, gazing back.

"Yes."

Quite close now, and advancing steadily, crept the scattered caravan, its own packhorses loaded with baggage as well as, often, a child or two clinging to their backs, and its travois scraping over an occasional rock, and usually led by an old woman, either mounted or afoot. On either side rode the older warriors, their lance blades, fashioned from Spanish swords, gleamed in the morning sun, with sometimes favorite wives riding their ponies behind, carrying their husbands' sacred shields. Young unmarried women, cheeks painted with round spots of vermilion, rode self-consciously within the cavalcade, while the younger warriors, painted and feathered, raced their ponies back and forth along either side, showing off. Apparently oblivious of risk, small naked boys and a few girls ran the same paths, while farther to either side older boys with diminutive bows and arrows hunted for birds, snakes, and squirrels. Threading among the entire procession were the dogs, the few little mongrels and the big wolfish ones, scarcely keeping from under the horses' hoofs.

Arsène passed nearly below us, riding his bay gelding, relaxed in the saddle, but holding his lance erect. Alert, he had noticed us from a distance, and nodded as he passed. Behind him rode Sehêbi on her pinto, proud and dignified, looking neither to right nor left, bearing his shield. Next came the three sisters, brightly painted, each riding her own pony, calling back and forth to each other and laughing. The first girl led a packhorse. The second two horses were dragging travois. The old woman, Cáco, led the last pony, trudging energetically, looking back and forth, her nearly toothless mouth open.

"Look, there's Ooa," said Hélène-Eulalie. "Oh, look—in the travois."

In the frame of the first travois, in a kind of basket, rode one of Arsène's little naked sons. Circled by his hands were three black necks and heads, faces constantly turning to look around them.

"Her pups," cried Hélène-Eulalie. "And look, there she is."

On the far side of the travois and quite near trotted the black wolfdog we had seen the previous day. She turned her head frequently toward her pups, as if concerned, but still seemed content to pace along beside them. On our side, striding rapidly and carrying a big switch, was Ooa, wearing only a breechcloth, concentrating mostly on the little boy, who looked at her anxiously from time to time, and those three miniature black dog-faces, peering here and there.

"Look how serious she is," laughed Hélène-Eulalie. "And severe."

As we watched, a big hairy wolfish dog approached the travois to sniff toward its basket. Ooa shouted at it and swung her switch. The big dog leapt to the side and quickly trotted away, giving a quick look back. Ooa, the little Screech Owl, continued to stride with the cavalcade, occasionally waving her switch, appearing important and serious about her responsibility.

30

For a fortnight we traveled by the river, wending northwestward in a leisurely fashion. The weather was agreeable, with hot days and pleasant nights, the heat frequently moderated by breezes or a thunder shower. We would spend a day or two at each campsite, then move upstream. We had so far encountered no bison, but there was an abundance of deer, as well as herds of wapiti in the woodlands, while the band's horses were thriving on grass by the river. The agreeable days and nights, the relaxed and nearly festive mood which persisted within the band, were marred however by two incidents. The first lasted for less than a few heartbeats. Yet this occurrence seared a memory into each of us, especially Hélène-Eulalie, that was never forgotten.

We knew there was a prisoner in camp, an Osage captured during the skirmish in which White-Road's oldest son, Ecopisura, had been killed. We scarcely saw the man, whom White-Road was said to have delivered bound to his relatives in order for them to inflict appropriate vengeance. At each encampment a tepee was set apart from the others. A thread of smoke curled from it, day and night. Perhaps by accident, perhaps by our hidden desire, we saw the captive only from a distance while moving camp, imagining however one of the tall and insolent warriors whom Antoine had described to us. But Lefort, who saw the body later thrown out for the dogs and wild animals, said that the man was not what he, or we, had imagined.

The incident itself was merely a scream. Yes, a scream. A gargling sort of scream. Yet that scream vibrated with such agony, communicated such horror, that all of the camp seemed to hesitate for an instant. It was a sound that penetrated, followed by silence. It froze my spine. I looked at Hélène-Eulalie, whose appalled features reflected its sound. And at Arsène, who had blanched.

"Ils l'ont cassé. Pauvre type," remarked Antoine. "Je crois qu'on lui a coupé la langue."

"Cut out his tongue?" gasped Hélène-Eulalie. "No, they wouldn't do that?"

Antoine shrugged. "Ces sauvages...vous savez, Madame."

I glanced at Arsène. He said nothing.

In the end we found that it was worse—worse to us, with our prejudices, at any rate—than we had imagined. Lefort informed us later that the fellow, poor fool, had not been Osage at all. He had been one of the simple Canadian tramps who reside with the Osage, marry or live with one of their whores, who strut before strangers and impersonate their leading warriors. The chiefs, who tolerate them with amused scorn, call these men,

"Bohèmes," Walkers-Over-The-Earth. Lefort called them vagabonds, poor simpletons who in contrast to the bold coureurs de bois, the voyageurs, who occasionally live among the Osage people, serve as butts of cruel humor, as pitiful clowns. This man, we later learned, had accompanied the war party to remain with the horses. Instead a boy and an injured warrior had remained, and the Bohème had run along with the others. The poor fellow had endured days of torture, had proven himself, we came to believe, braver than he had known and perhaps worthy of his pretense. Antoine told us that if the man were lucky they had held him down and he had drowned in his blood. The incident projected a shadow across the remaining days of the expedition and prepared us for misfortune to come. The second incident was ambiguous, not necessarily ominous: one scout sent ahead and northward had not returned. He was two days late. So far Arsène told us he believed the young warrior had merely been delayed. But he was going to be concerned if the scout did not arrive soon.

Still in the camp, all around us, the gala mood persisted. The scouts dispatched back to investigate the tracks heading northwest from the Washita returned puzzled, though not alarmed. They as well as Arsène and even Lefort agreed that they were most likely the hoofprints of a small party of Caihuas. They were possibly even following us to seek an opportunity for acquiring ponies. Consequently Arsène increased the number of boys guarding the horseherd. At the end of this mostly tranquil period we reached a crook in the stream where we were to spend some days hunting and curing meat prior to returning down the Washita.

The campsite was almost an island, with a narrow entrance to the west from the meadow where numerous boys and a few older girls took turns in overseeing the horseherd between forest and river. We set up our tents at the farthest end of the stream-encircled strip, opposite the opening to the meadow. Before us spread the Indian camp, its tepees raised mostly along the riverbanks, leaving a clear space in the center reaching from our tents and bales to the field with its multitude of grazing horses, crows underfoot resembling flyspecks, and its distant mounted figures.

In the evenings we lay about at our ease. The men shared a large tent backed to the river, while Lefort, Tournier and I slept in another pitched before it. At a little distance south of ours, and situated for privacy, a third tent belonged to the women, in this instance to Hélène-Eulalie and her two guests, Sehêbi because elle avait ses regles (was menstruating, that is) and could not, the People believed, share her husband's lodge without destroying his Power (Puha), and Ooa because she wished to be with the two women. Each evening we built a fire in the space between our tent and the bales piled as a breastwork some two rods before it.

Arsène joined us for our evening meals, often providing them. Except for Sehêbi, who remained isolated according to tribal custom, we regaled ourselves with venison and wapiti, with stories and attempted humor. The entire Indian camp appeared still to be in a festive mood those moonlit summer nights and drums announcing dances or gambling games thumped after each sunset. Sometimes Arsène brought Deer's-Ears with him and after our meal the two young men would lie by the fire joking back and forth in rapid Comanche and laughing together, until Hélène-Eulalie would demand that her cousin stop and share his stories with the rest of us.

At times I believe their stories were scarcely repeatable. But I recall one occasion when Toyamancare's name was mentioned, and I asked them why they were laughing.

"Oh, it's about his favorite horse," explained Arsène. "You remember his racehorse, Jackrabbit (Piarabo)? Well, he dotes on that horse."

"He's taught it tricks," laughed Deer's-Ears. "He acts like it's a person."

"He hunts on it?" asked Antoine. "I would. One could run down an antelope."

"No, he hunts on his buffalo horse."

"That's what's so funny," Deer's Ears said. "He only races it. He's taught it to bow. I've never seen a horse do that before."

"Well, he's made it a pet," said Hélène-Eulalie. "My horse is a little like that. He comes when I call. What's funny about that?"

"It wouldn't be funny for a woman or a boy," Arsène explained. "But for a great warrior, a chief like Big-Mountain, to have a horse trained to act like a dog, that follows him around—that's unusual. That's funny."

I had never seen Arsène in such high spirits, so light-hearted. For most of our visit the grim warrior was absent, replaced by a stern-featured but amiable young man. He was clearly enjoying his family and his life, especially the sociable intermingling on the trail and in camp, the dancing, gambling games, feasting, and the relaxed pace he had set on our progress northwestward. It was also apparent to me that he enjoyed the prestige he had gained in the chase and in war as well as his present importance as paraibo, or chief, in the absence of Toyamancare and—presumably—any rival warriors who had accompanied that indisputable headman of the band.

Each evening at the end of our quiet conviviality, Arsène would mount his horse and ride in the moonlight the short distance to his lodge where his three plump wives, Cáco, and his sleeping sons awaited his return. Hélène-Eulalie and Ooa would retire to the women's tent while Antoine and I would quickly review the names of those of us whose turn it was to stand guard, as well as the required hours of each. In the present instance, although we were apparently quite safe upon our quasi-island, it was fortunate that we followed our usual practice. That very night, I believe it was, when Arsène and Deer's-Ears had joked over Big-Mountain's attachment to his racing pony, Antoine came into our tent several hours before daybreak, with a scrap of moon still reflected on the grass outside the doorway, and woke me even though it was not my turn at watch.

"What is it?"

"The horses are nervous. Maybe there's a bear or a cougar somewhere. Maybe not."

"I'll be right out."

We had turned the pack animals in with the herd but had picketed our own mounts to our camp's rear, back of the men's tent in the grass by the river's edge. I rose, pulled on my moccasins, seized my musket, its powder horn and lead balls and a loaded horse pistol, and went quickly into what seemed a peaceful silvery morning with no hint as yet of dawn. Lefort, quite visible by moonlight, was standing by our breastwork smoking his pipe.

"Anything else?" I asked. For many men I would not have risen. But I trusted Antoine's instincts. Clutching my musket, I laid the big pistol on the turf to the right of my feet.

"There have been owls. From several directions."

"And you're not sure they're owls."

"They may be. But maybe not."

"Go back and wake Tournier and then the others. I'll stay here."

"I could be wrong."

"Yes, you could be right. If you're wrong, all we lose is a little sleep."

As I waited, I recall becoming increasingly skeptical. I even regretted having asked Lefort to wake the engagés. The morning was so serene, with its dim moonlight and the constant rush and splash of the river around us, and otherwise the silence, without a camp dog barking or howling, that the very thought of an attack seemed improbable to the point of absurdity. Furthermore upon reflection it seemed to me extremely unlikely that any of the People's enemies would seek them in this location within comanchería, far from the band's habitual region. Yet I determined, if only to show respect for Antoine, to persist in vigilance until sunrise, when the entire camp would awaken.

Antoine soon reappeared bringing with him Tournier, our cook as well as next in command after Lefort. Bearing his musket casually, muzzle down, Tournier paced sleepily back and forth behind our barricade of bales, pausing intermittently to peer into the silvery encampment before us. Antoine and I remained at the middle of the barricade, leaning upon it and exchanging inconsequential remarks from time to time. From my perspective, however, it was ironic that we did so. Normally I am not an indecisive man. I am inclined to pity such individuals. Yet for the past few days I had myself become indecisive, uncertain of the immediate course to follow. The person with whom I had been wishing to discuss this matter was standing, smoking his pipe, at my elbow. Yet for some time I had been unable to broach the subject troubling my mind—partly, I suppose, because I hated to reveal irresolution, a weakness so unlike my normal behavior. Finally though, as the faintest tint of the dawn glow began diluting the moonlight, I managed to tell the Canadian that I sought his opinion on an important matter.

"Bon, dis-moi, donc," he grunted, turning to face me, removing the pipe from his teeth.

"You remember some time ago Arsène asking how long we could wait to meet the others?"

"Yes."

"I said, since we had come this far, I supposed we should wait."

"I remember."

"Now I'm beginning to wonder. Are we wasting our time? I'm getting impatient. What do you think? All this lying around is pleasant, but we're not here for that. Who knows how long it will take Big-Mountain to reach the rendezvous?"

"Maybe he will never arrive."

"What do you mean?"

"They're in dangerous country, among enemies."

"You think they'll be killed?"

"It has happened." He puffed on his pipe. "But no. I don't think they will be killed.

It's possible, but Toyamancare's a good leader. He has good men. But they may be late."

"Do you think we would do better to leave this band? Head west and try to find some Yamparicas?"

Lefort reflected. "Those Yamparica Comanches, they trade with the New Mexicans. We might have trouble finding a band with many horses. These people are friendly and have horses and hides."

"They know us, too. We know them. So what do you think? Stay with Arsène and the others?"

"Yes. I think so—écoute!"

Dawn had arrived. For the last few minutes I had been idly watching a figure which had emerged from its lodge. This man—for it was certainly a man—had looked about, stretched. Carrying what appeared to be a reata and bridle, he had set off for the pasture where the horseherd had spent the night. I had watched him pass through the opening that formed the exit of the camp to the meadow beyond. His figure was scarcely out of sight when there came from that direction an abbreviated shriek—a shriek, that is, begun full-throatedly and arrested, followed by silence.

"What?" I looked at Antoine. He was peering into the distant field, his rifle raised, where all we could make out was agitation, a circular flow among the distant, still silvery horses. "The Caihuas? For horses?"

Immediately the camp awoke, with a variety of voices, cries, from its lodges, women's and men's. All of the dogs began to bark or howl, and several of its children to join them in bellowing. Warriors began appearing from their lodges, quickly seizing their shields and lances, gliding to their horses, picketed nearby. But the first to rush from his tepee and to spring, armed, upon his pony, was Arsène, whose shape I recognized. Without waiting, he leaned forward and rode, bearing lance and shield, at a gallop out of sight. Now a confusion of men and horses surged forward into the space in the middle of camp, so that we were no longer able to see the gap before the meadow. More men were mounting their ponies riding away. From the field came a Comanche warwhoop and then warwhoops which were possibly not Comanche, followed by more whoops and scattered musket shots, with an ever greater turmoil in the space between the rows of tepees, as an armed struggle appeared to be developing between the scarcely prepared defenders and a body of invaders.

"Mon Dieu, what's happening?" Hélène-Eulalie stood a little behind us, disheveled in her buckskins.

"Osage, I believe," said Antoine, without turning, sighting along his rifle.

"How could they have found us here?" I murmured. "Not Osages. Not possible."

Behind Hélène-Eulalie, at a little distance, were Sehêbi and Ooa, the woman appearing alarmed, the child frightened. It was almost gray daylight now, though well before sunrise, rendering everything within view more or less visible. Gripping and resting my musket upon the bales before me, I concentrated upon distinguishing friend from enemy in the haphazard engagement developing before us. The Osage men—for they were Osages—now identifiable by their gleaming bald heads topped by roached hair, were attacking mostly on foot, swinging warclubs behind shields or thrusting lances, while those Comanche men who had been able to mount their ponies, battled principally with shield and lance from horseback. While some raiders pressed the defenders, others ran at random into tepees from whence came screams of women and children. Two Osage warriors in the near distance, in contrast to their companions, rode what I knew to be good horses from the herd. Both warriors were tall. Indeed one was a giant who loomed larger than the pony he rode, his feet near the ground. With raised shield he swung a great hatchet, or tomahawk, against his smaller adversary, whom I recognized as Deer's-Ears, causing the Comanche to shield himself and back his horse in order to avoid the ferocious hacking of the larger man.

"Shoot," I urged.

I had been wondering when Antoine would fire. I glanced at him just as he drew his trigger. Flinching at the deafening report in my right ear, I watched the massive bulk of the enemy warrior topple from his horse. He rose to his hands and knees on the grass, still holding his axe, and resembling an enormous near-naked infant, until an arm collapsed and he rolled to the side and lay feebly struggling to rise. Did I imagine hearing a groan from the enemy warriors? Perhaps. In any event the second tall horseman, bearing shield and lance, now raced toward our breastwork, drew up, stared hard for hardly an instant, ducked and whirled his horse and rode away.

I had a clear look at him. He was big-boned and darker than the rest. From his head down this warrior was dressed as the other raiders, in breechclout and moccasins, but he wore a headdress and mask formed from the head of a buffalo, with horns and eye-holes, shaggy beard. Lefort, head bowed over his rifle, was ramming a charge down its barrel. The Buffalo—as I came to think of this person—paused before us for the briefest instant, staring from three rods away—a bold act. Tournier and I were so startled we failed to fire. By the time we had recovered, he had whirled his pony and was gone, weaving among the combatants, leaving our end of camp.

But it was perhaps The Buffalo, who appeared to have authority among the raiders, who dispatched young men to succor the bleeding giant, evidently a chief. The wounded warrior still intermittently flopped his arms, a tortoise struggling to roll from its back. We soon became aware that, while two of the raiders were assisting their presumed leader to rise, shielding and supporting him, another two were darting between tepees, approaching us from the front, on either side.

"Attends, wait," said Antoine. "Until they're close. I'll take the one on the right. You, Henri, the one on the left. Jean-Pierre, wait, in case one of us should miss."

"What can I do?" asked Hélène-Eulalie calmly.

I turned. She was kneeling between Lefort and me, a little to our rear. Behind her crouched Sehêbi, as if about to spring, steady-eyed as a lynx, a knife in her hand, with the frightened child.

"You could load for Antoine," I said. "There's a trade musket in our tent."

"I'll get it."

A succession of events next developed so rapidly I cannot as yet vouch for their sequence. As Hélène-Eulalie rose, bent over, to go to our tent, warwhoops sounded, very close, from behind it, with musket shots and shouts from the engagés on guard there. At the same moment whoops sounded from before us. I turned to see two warriors running from the closest tepees on either side. Antoine fired and the man on the right seized his middle and fell forward. But following the rifle's report, I turned at a little shriek from behind. A young Osage, standing for an instant like a dripping bronze statue, was poised before our tent. As his eyes met mine, he sprang forward, his warclub raised. But Ooa was directly in his path, having backed from her place by Sehêbi at the charge of the two warriors toward our breastwork. Nearly tripping over the child, the youth seized her arm, swinging back his warclub. Ooa screamed something, apparently in the Osage tongue, and the raider arrested his club in midair. The child's tugging to free herself from his grip, had turned the youth partially, so that his back was directed toward Sehêbi. As he released the girl, Sehêbi was upon his back, wielding her knife. She evidently struck bone in her fury or she would have disabled or killed the man. Without a sound, he reached a hand behind him, caught her arm and hurled her from him to the earth, at the same time swinging his warclub at her head. But as the young woman slammed the grass, she rolled. He missed her head, striking a shielding arm, sending the knife flying. While appraising the three of us at the rampart, he lifted his club again, grasping her hair.

"Jean-Pierre!" cried Antoine, while loading his rifle. "Attention!"

I swung around and fired, my muzzle no more than a rod from a warrior charging with shield and lance. Wounded by Tournier, he had been playing dead, it appeared. My ball struck his femur, knocking him down. An instant afterward, Tournier, who had reloaded, shot him once more as he attempted to rise, this time killing him. Lefort, too, was firing and loading, powder horn and ball, firing and loading, his rifle now creating havoc among those raiders intermingled with the Comanche defenders struggling before us.

Twisting back, fumbling in the grass for my pistol, I found Sehêbi still trying to fight free, clawing with her hands and kicking, while the youth gripped her hair, his club lifted but his eyes now fixed upon Hélène-Eulalie who, kneeling to my left, was leveling my pistol with both hands at his chest. There was an explosion and smoke as she drew the trigger. The raider dropped Sehêbi, staggered for an instant and toppled backward. At this moment three of the engagés, who had been successfully battling Osage swimmers behind the tents, came running to assist us. One of them, Jean Hugue, reached the dying youth, placed his musket at the young man's forehead and, with his moccasin on his neck, drew the trigger. A whoom and smoke, more gunpowder smell. Beside me, still kneeling, her head bowed, trembling, Hélène-Eulalie sobbed convulsively. Sehêbi, clutching her injured arm, clambered to her feet, slipped quickly to the child, embraced and gripped her tightly with her good arm. But Ooa, as if unconscious of her Comanche mother's presence, continued to stare, with a look of fascinated horror, at the dead warrior, the remains of his bloody, shattered skull.

Thus ended our part in the battle, the planned massacre which had failed owing principally to Antoine Lefort and the accuracy of his rifle. The battle itself terminated soon afterward, the warparty fleeing with most of their dead and all of their wounded as suddenly as they had come. They drove the Comanche horseherd before them. Except for those horses which had been tethered within the encampment, none remained. All of those which had been grazing in the field, including our own pack animals, were presently on their way to a distant Osage village.

But a loss of horses was not what troubled me at the enemy's departure. I had done my best to comfort my wife, upset as she was at having slain a fellow human being, even one intent on killing and scalping us all. I had examined Sehêbi's arm and found it wounded. I had quickly consulted with the men, who had shot two of the swimmers, of whom one had escaped in the stream. I had then left Antoine in charge of our camp, had vaulted our breastwork and had raced to the cluster of Comanche men, all talking and gesturing at once, gathered near the entrance to their camp. For what increasingly troubled me was not knowing the whereabouts of Arsène. I had seen him ride out early, before the other warriors. I assumed he had returned and had led the others in battle. Yet I had felt throughout the raid a nagging anxiety concerning his return. That anxiety was not reduced when I reached those warriors who on foot or mounted were talking of the wounded, of the dead, and of the disappearance of their warchief, Ah-mah-bah-tay. Finally pressing through the throng, I found Deer's-Ears still mounted. Looking down at me from his pony, he knew what I wished to know without my asking. His expression was somber.

"Ah-mah-bah-tay is gone. I've ridden all over the field. There are the bodies of three boys and Ugly-Game, who went out before anybody to get his horse. They killed and scalped them all."

"No, no. Ah-mah-bah-tay's horse?"

"It's gone too."

"So you think they've captured him?"

"Yes. What else can I think?"

"That's too terrible," I said. "No, that can't be true. He must be here somewhere."

"No, he's not here. We've looked everywhere. Even in his lodge. They killed his wives and old Cáco. He wasn't there. They've taken him, and we have no horses, not enough to chase them."

"His little boys?"

"Two of them got away, under the edge of the lodge. They killed the other, with the women. The old one was holding him. They scalped the women."

"I'm going to go after them," I heard myself saying. "Come to my camp if you want to go. Soon. You and anyone else who'll go."

He leaned from his horse, looking into my eyes sympathetically. "You'll go alone? What can you do if you catch them? You, alone?"

"I don't know. But I'm going. I'll leave soon. Come along if you wish." I left him, staring in disbelief. I, myself, scarcely believed what I had been saying. It was not reasonable. It was stupid. But I had to go, futile and possibly fatal as pursuit seemed. I wanted to break down and weep like Hélène-Eulalie. It was crazy, poisá, I knew that. But, walking quickly back to our camp, with my head down, I knew I would go.

31

There are always preparations for a journey. But Antoine and I, rushing, omitted all but the essentials—water, dried meat and mesquite meal, buffalo robes, powder and shot. We saddled our horses quickly. To my satisfaction, all of the engagés, even the man wounded by an Osage swimmer, Totin, volunteered to come. The wounded man I ordered to remain, along with Tournier, to afford some protection for the women and child. I kissed Hélène-Eulalie goodby, and then stood looking into her eyes for a moment. She blinked tears. Her features convulsed and recovered to their normal disciplined calm. I shut my eyes. We kissed again, embracing violently, and I turned away and mounted my mare. I waved at Sehêbi and the child, who stared at me, dazed, expressionless.

Tournier tugged two bales aside and we rode off at a trot, eight of us. The Comanche camp was in tumult, stunned by the raid, its deaths, the loss of its horses. As we rode through, women were wailing and howling, already in leather rags, with slashed, bloody arms and legs. We glimpsed several through tepee doorways preparing the bodies of the five dead women for burial, while men in other lodges, I supposed, had begun preparing the bodies of the four warriors killed. Others, both men and women, were caring for the wounded and throwing the possessions of the dead into the Washita. They hardly glanced up at us as we rode out of their camp. At the north end of the pasture, we located the trail of the enemy and horseherd. With Antoine and me leading, side by side, weapons in our hands, we began—saving our horses to the extent possible—following the tracks through the trees.

During those first hours I conferred with Antoine. He knew the country and the Osage people. I did not. He advised that we should track the raiders at a rapid, steady pace. But we should not draw too close behind them upon the prairie, where horsemen may be perceived at a great distance. The enemy would be hurrying, with scouts both before and behind them. Since we constituted but a small party, our chance of rescuing Arsène, and of surviving the rescue, would depend upon our surprising the enemy, for instance at night or at dawn, and perhaps stampeding the horseherd and carrying Arsène away with us during the confusion. After the warparty had entered La Grande Forêt, the Osages would feel secure in their own country, being within about a week of their village, and would draw in their scouts and relax their vigilance. In any event with the advantage of the wooded terrain we would be able to approach them closely while remaining concealed.

"What's the matter?" I asked. "You look troubled."

"Nothing. I recognized some of those I shot. They were from the Black Bear clan."

"Friends?"

"Well, no. I just recognized them."

We reached the Grande Forêt in three days, traveling northeast mostly by daylight, resting the horses at night and at intervals throughout the day. Fortunately rain had fallen recently, and the grass was green in many areas. Usually on such a trip one would lead at least an extra horse, as all Comanche war parties did, each man saving his favorite for battle. But possessing only the horses we rode, we took care not to injure or exhaust them. Still we made good time, each of us being well-mounted and the raiders' tracks mostly clear and easy to follow. The days, as we rode through wood and prairie, over cuestas and hills and across valleys, were mostly sunny and hot, with clouds forming in the afternoons, often followed by wind and a thunderstorm, and we progressed hour after hour at a steady walk or at a dogtrot, grateful whenever a shower would drench our faces and cool the steaming horses.

We owed our two delays to the rivers we forded before reaching the Cimarron, which we followed eastward to La Grande Forêt. They were the Río Canadian and its northern fork, Río Nutrio. Indeed it was only at the first of these that we were compelled to pause more than briefly. We reached our ford in late afternoon the first day. At the river's bank, I recall drawing up my horse and regarding the stream with dismay. There was no doubt that it was the ford to cross. The tracks of the enemy and the horseherd were clearly marked upon the earth near the bank. Disturbed soil could be seen on the far side where they had lunged up the low incline. But the river was high, a reddish color, with froth like the bubbles of soap, here and there, rushing wildly with little waves and a splashing, hissing sound. Previously during the afternoon we had heard distant thunder and seen flashes in a dark sky to the northwest while hot sun still bore down upon us. Now we saw the evidence of heavy rains upstream.

"What do you think?" I asked.

Antoine shook his head. "We'll have to wait."

We watered the horses, loosened cinches, removed bridles, and allowed the animals to graze, while we ourselves drank and ate a little, sitting and lying on the grass. Lying with the lead-rope in my hand, I must have dozed. There was a shout and the men's loud voices. I sat up.

"What is it?"

"A party behind us," someone said. "Look, coming out of the woods."

"They're Comanches," Antoine said, after a moment. "Look, there's Deer's-Ears in the lead."

"Seven of them," I said. As the horsemen filed toward us, I recognized Deer's-Ears followed by four men about his age. Two boys of sixteen or seventeen years, already warriors with bows and shields, brought up the rear. I had thought it curious that not one Comanche had joined us, even while taking into account the band's present crisis and its shortage of horses. Undoubtedly most warriors, occupied with their own losses and griefs, had considered our effort futile, our mission doomed. But Deer's-Ears had come to assist us, against all odds, in achieving the unlikely rescue of his friend. I greeted the little group warmly, gratefully, as they drew up and dismounted, shaking the hands of all, even the boys, who deserved the respect usually reserved for men by risking their lives in joining us.

"The river's high," Deer's-Ears remarked, his eyes on the reddened, frothing stream. "You going to try to cross, or wait?"

"I think we'd better try to cross." I continued to watch the stream, with a growing, uneasy sensation. It had subsided a little since our arrival upon its bank, but it retained its swift and ominous aspect. Yet if we waited until morning, as I would ordinarily have done, we would lose the remaining daylight hours at a time when minutes were precious. It was necessary neither to draw too close to those we pursued nor to fall too far behind them. "Shall we try it?" I asked Antoine. "I'll go first."

Lefort nodded, evidently a little surprised.

Deer's-Ears continued to stand, holding his pony, gazing at me. "Red-Woman was making medicine for you, Bluejay. For Ah-mah-bah-tay and us."

"Good. I think we're going to need it." I exchanged a look with Antoine.

Deer's-Ears continued to regard me with a grave expression.

"You and your friends danced, of course?"

"No time." He looked worried. "It's bad medicine to leave in daylight, but we had to, to catch you."

"We'll be all right," I said. "We'll get The-Headless-One and bring him back."

My words seemed to satisfy him, and he turned back to his companions and began conversing with them, while Antoine and the engagés began tugging at cinches and bridling their horses. Moments later I sat on my mare at the river's edge and stared at the roiling, turbid water before me, with Antoine and Deer's-Ears on either side, the others waiting behind. I had no conception of that water's depth. Now looking back after all the years, I must confess its look intimidated me. I swim but not well. If the mare and I were swept downstream, if I were swept off of her. If...If... I thought, hesitating.

"You want me to go first?" asked Antoine, after a moment.

"No. I'm going. Wait till I'm on the other bank." Taking a deep breath, I urged the mare forward into the rushing water, which surged and foamed around her knees. It was a wide crossing, some eighteen rods with, as I discovered, several temporarily invisible sandbars and a partially submerged islet, with two green saplings growing from it. For much of the distance the ruddy water frothed around the mare's knees or lower around her fetlocks as we crossed first one sandbar, then after a deeper interval, the other. Near the far shore we easily mounted and crossed the islet, descending into the main channel which flowed between that speck of land and the far bank. There the mare had to swim a short distance, which she did vigorously, though the current bore us somewhat downstream. Her hoofs touched bottom and, achieving traction, she propelled us powerfully up the low embankment to level ground, where she startled me by shaking like a dog. I turned her sideways and beckoned to Antoine and the others, traders and Indians, waiting on the other shore. I sat there watching them ford with a feeling of elation as they advanced toward me single file.

When all had gathered on the bank, with dripping horses and legs, we proceeded on a northeasterly route toward the Río Nutrio, continuing to ride up and down bare hills with—occasionally—fertile valleys in between. After riding a short distance, Deer's-Ears trotted from the rear of the procession to take a place beside me. For a time we rode in silence, I watching the sky, where thunderclouds appeared to be forming. The air was cooler and pleasanter now that the sun shone level rays from the hills at our backs.

"Did you see the dead chief?" he asked.

"What?"

Even Antoine straightened in his saddle and stared.

"You didn't see him? I wondered about that. It was too soon for him to stink. They'd hidden him with branches and leaves, not far from the trail."

"Osage?" I asked.

"The chief Kills-Far hit."

"How did you find him?" Antoine asked. He continued to show surprise and to look piqued. He prided himself on his ability as a tracker and usually missed nothing.

"Crow found him. He flew up when we got close, and we went to look. There were blood spots on the path, not many but a few."

"I saw them," said Lefort. "There are still some, more now."

"Yes. I think they're scared now their medicine's bad."

"The Osage are brave men," Antoine replied, somewhat testily.

"Yes, they're brave enough," Deer's-Ears said. "But you killed their chief. He was the one we found—the big man. Maybe too big to take back. You shot mostly older warriors. The best ones. The others are young. They don't know what to do—that is, they do, but I think they're scared their power has left them. So many hit, some maybe dying. It's a bad way to go back. It would be a good time to fight them now."

"That one with the buffalo mask. He's a leader," I said. "He's still with them."

"That's true," conceded Deer's-Ears. "The buffalo chief is still with them. Maybe he made them leave the big dead chief behind."

"Who knows?" I said, with a weary shrug, remembering Arsène again, a captive. "Who knows?"

As we rode in silence, I reflected upon the dead chief and the others Lefort had shot with his rifle. Weapons change but man doesn't, or only little and gradually. I bore no grudge against the Osage people, even though they were our enemies and would surely have killed us and seized our goods had they been successful in their attack. Antoine had prevented a massacre. I was very glad of that, since we would have been among the victims. Hélène-Eulalie and Sehêbi and possibly the child too. These Comanches were our friends. But I could see that by our presence, by our goods and our superior weapons, we were interfering in the lives and customs of the tribes. In the end I feared that by our interference and by taking upon ourselves the role of Fortune we would destroy them. And still while suspecting this, I knew I would continue to be a Comanche trader.

While I had been ruminating, Deer's-Ears had returned to speaking about the civil chief, of how in council after smoking, Red-Woman had sworn on the sun he would employ his most powerful medicine, taught him by his grandfather, Long Wolf. It was one he used rarely, because it was so dangerous. Unless used right, it could kill those it was intended to help. But he would use it right to safely restore the three groups, Toyamancare's,

Bluejay's, and Deer's-Ears' to the People, and would pray to bring back Ah-mah-bah-tay too. He vowed to begin fasting at once and to climb a nearby bluff where he would remain without food and pray constantly until his medicine was answered. Deer's-Ears was greatly impressed, indeed convinced, and to close the subject I had to feign also to be convinced.

We reached a creek a little before darkness replaced the last gray light. Dismounting, we unsaddled and hobbled the horses. We camped in a wood, ate cold meals with no fire, established a guard, spread out our robes, and slept, most of us, throughout the night. As for me, I dreamt before dawn of a blonde woman in a pale blue dress standing on the windy prairie, shading her eyes with one hand, gazing at the empty horizon. I woke and lay yearning for that woman, either in blue dress or in buckskins, speculating upon whether I would see her again...during this life.

At first light I woke the camp. We ate, saddled, and rode off at dawn. By sunrise we had nearly reached the Río Nutrio. But as we approached that river, already dazzling at some distance in the glare of the early sun, Antoine, riding beside me, suddenly exclaimed and began pointing around him at tracks upon the earth. The hoofprints we had been following had become confused, overrun, reversed, the majority of them pointed back in the direction from which we had come. Others went off north and south, up and down the river.

"What happened here, I wonder?"

Our little caravan had halted. Engagés and Comanches both were leaning from their horses, riding back and forth, examining tracks. Antoine, who had loped directly to the river, was investigating there a clump of willows by the bank. He dismounted, squatted, and peered at the dirt. Mounting his horse, he rode back at a fast trot.

"Bear tracks," he said, signaling the words with his hands to Deer's-Ears, who had ridden to us. "There was a big bear, and two little ones."

Deer's-Ears smiled. "The horses started back to the Washita. They like it there."

We spent a short time following tracks. They told a story. The horses had taken fright at the appearance, presumably out of the willows, of a large mother bear and her cubs. They had panicked and run in various directions, though mostly through the wood and prairie behind us. Their Osage herders had evidently had a difficult task in reassembling them and then driving them across the river. These indications gave me hope. As Lefort pointed out, the already troubled warparty had evidently lost a significant amount of time and possibly horses too at this place. Perhaps we were not so far behind them as I had at first feared. Conversely we had still to take care not to approach them too closely. Here I sent two of the young men ahead to watch for their scouts.

The following day was for the greater part windy and uneventful. The Rio Nutrio was a wide and shallow stream, with little risk of quicksand, since the tracks of the other party were visible across the water. Cheered by the discovery of our enemy's difficulties, I led across a prairie toward our third and final river, the Cimarron. I recall that during our noon halt two of our already small group deserted. I sat up from dozing to see two mounted figures diminishing in the distance from which we had come. One of them, I quickly learned from Deer's-Ears, was Canaguaipe, whose name translates to "The-Feeble-Effeminate-

One." He was a sullen and truculent young man who had appeared to resent every order I gave. The other was the younger of the boys. Apparently, according to Deer's-Ears, The-Feeble-Effeminate-One doubted my power, believing the Osages would kill us all. I was not altogether displeased at his departure. The-Feeble-Effeminate-One, I surmised, was probably one of those men who distrusted me because I rode a mare. No Comanche warrior would ride one. Mine was gentle and quick and smart. I liked her and I was not going to change horses because a few warriors believed my choice made me less of a man.

"I think your power's strong," said Deer's-Ears in response to my question. "So do the others. Besides, Red-Woman is making medicine for us."

"Good." I swung up into my saddle. "All right, amigos. Adelante!"

We paused after fording the Cimarron late that afternoon. Consulting together, Antoine, Deer's-Ears and I decided that as we were all tiring, both horses and men, it would be sensible to camp early, providing an opportunity for rest, nourishment, and hunting. We had eaten no fresh meat since our departure, and a multitude of tracks by the river, deer and wapiti, along with those of smaller animals, seemed to promise a plenty of game nearby. Following that decision, we dismounted in a grove of oaks, where we soon discovered that our enemies had recently paused and eaten, possibly early that very day. We found gnawed bones of deer, hot coals in the ashes of two fires, as well as large spots of blood where wounded men appeared to have stretched out in the leaves.

"Bien," said Antoine. "We approach them."

"And Ah-mah-bah-tay," Deer's-Ears added.

"The-Headless-One," I repeated. "You'll see. We'll catch them tomorrow in La Grande Forêt."

32

After a short night, we departed at dawn, following tracks of the enemy eastward along the Cimarron. After the sun had risen a distance above the prairie, and we were continuing northeastward along the river, Deer's-Ears abruptly halted his pony and slipped to the earth, where he stooped and swept up a strip of hide, examining it and holding it for Antoine to identify. Lefort turned the length of buckskin in his hands, inspecting it carefully.

"What is it?"

"Those people call this a 'captive strap.' Each warrior carries one in what they call his 'heart sack.'"

"Important to them?" In my mind, I saw Arsène, bound.

"Yes. Normally no man would drop such a thing."

Further encouraged, we continued along the river bank into the sun's rays at increased speed, alternating between a fast walk and a trot, sometimes even breaking into a lope, yet keeping the two young men well-advanced, and periodically drawing up to peer into the distance. For our midday meal we halted briefly under great cotton trees where a creek from the south joined the river. We proceeded once more immediately afterward. Several hours later Antoine drew up his horse and pointed north across a predominantly level prairie:

"See that trail?"

"What trail?" I noticed, after a moment, a dim breach in the landscape before me. It created a mostly straight line rising and falling with the grassy terrain into the distance, wavering a little like a badly made part in unruly hair. "That's a trail?"

"Osage war trail."

"To the Pawnees?"

"Yes, the Pawnees use it too."

"They raid each other?"

"Yes. They use it when the rivers to the east are flooding."

As we pressed on, I looked back. "Do you suppose Toyamancare took it?"

"No. I don't think the Comanches use it. It's shorter, but not as good a road as following the Cimarron." He looked at me speculatively. "Only war parties use it. But you know, because it's between two enemies, there's little hunting there. Too dangerous. So there are many buffalo. If one is willing to take the risk."

"You have?"

"Once, a long time ago. When I was younger and more foolish," he said, smiling with his eyes, and falling silent.

A little before the sun slipped again behind the horizon, we reached La Grande Forêt, that strip of post oak and blackjack extending vast distances north and south at the eastern limit of the Great Prairie. This boundary of Nature's designing, which we Americans now designate the "Cross Timber," consists of at least double rows of woods, comparatively narrow in some regions, as for instance by our usual route to and from the Wichitan villages, and as much as fifteen leagues, or two days travel, wide at others. According to Antoine, this latter was the width of the first strip at our present location, where the Cimarron passed into the forest's westernmost verge on its way to join the Rivière des Ark in the region where that northern stream descends into the country of the Osage. Reaching this barrier, we had achieved our first goal. We might now approach the raiders closely enough to strike them and—if my grandparents' Providence, or Antoine's chance, were with us—to save Arsène.

At the edge of this low and not easily penetrable forest we first noticed a deep, double buffalo trace running north and south, along with their droppings, and disappearing in the distant prairie in either direction. But more disquieting were the tracks of a large group of horses which joined those of the enemy and the stolen horseherd immediately where a well-trampled, irregular trail entered the woods. Deer's-Ears discovered these and pointed them out to Lefort and me. In doing so the Comanche suddenly looked disheartened.

Antoine sadly shook his head. "Here they were joined by more."

I was compelled to agree. Regrettably, if this conjecture were true, and if the new group was composed also of Osage warriors, our chances of a surprise attack and of rescuing Arsène were greatly reduced. There were probably now too many of the enemy for us to contend with. What to do? The men, both engagés and Comanches, who had quickly grasped the situation, were sitting their horses looking at me. It was too late to turn back, foolish to go ahead. And yet.... For a moment I reflected, then without a word, without permitting myself to think, turned my horse's head into the woods. We rode for a time in silence. Although I heard twigs snapping and scraping behind me, I did not look back. At length we reached a little clearing, where I allowed myself to pivot in the saddle while still riding forward. Behind me, advancing in single-file and led by Antoine with Deer's-Ears immediately following, came what appeared to be our entire group, with the boy at the end. I had a moment of pride at their having chosen to follow me, then the suspicion that we would probably never return on this path, that I was leading them, all of us, to our deaths.

The evening was clear, luminous, with a star or two, and a tinge of pink in the sky behind us. But twilight would soon be turning to dusk and, close as we were behind the objects of our pursuit, I knew we must camp presently or risk losing the trail and blundering in the dark forest. Fortunately we came soon to a little creek, tributary doubtless flowing to the Cimarron, now a short distance south of us. Beside it was a rude path, probably an animal track. I halted and sent Lefort up a way to explore for a suitable campsite. As we waited silently for his return in the twilight, I began hearing noises, the sounds of tearing twigs and parting branches, and possibly hoofs crushing leaves. These sounds seemed to me to come not from the north, Antoine's direction, but from the east, directly before us. The others heard also. We believed ourselves to be a half-day to a day behind our enemies now. But these riders were approaching us. Deer's-Ears moved up beside me, listening. Moments later we heard what could only be an occasional murmur of human voices.

"More Osage," whispered the Comanche, gazing at me in alarm.

It was still sufficiently light so that I could distinguish the dismay in his face, as well as those of the others behind us. Quickly dismounting, I placed a warning hand over my mouth, signaling that they should also dismount and follow me. Leading the mare, I made my way, quietly as I could up the creek, hoping that the crackling and snapping of branches and the murmured conversation of the advancing party would cover the sounds of our withdrawal, or that the unknown individuals, whoever they were, would attribute them to the retreat of wild animals at their approach. Already on the lower path some deers and a bear had hastily departed from our vicinity, so that such an assumption would be reasonable.

A few hundred paces up the stream we met Antoine descending. By this time the noise of the approaching group was carrying, though faintly, to our new location. The Canadian seemed to grasp the situation instantly, dismounting and leading his horse to confer with Deer's-Ears and me. After a hurried, whispered consultation, I sent the others upstream to a tiny meadow Lefort had located. Their instructions were to wait there for us, keeping the horses quiet, either until we returned, or the boy, whom I had posted partway, should call them, or until they heard Deer's-Ears whoop, in which case they were to come at once prepared to fight.

33

I had noticed a giant boulder on our way up the dim path. At some time in the distant past it had either split in two or, perhaps after rolling, had come to rest against another mossy giant, leaving a V-shaped fissure between them. Passing our reins to the others, weapons in hand, we ran silently down the track and concealed ourselves behind these great rocks, positioning our bodies so that each of us was able to peer through the gap while remaining invisible to any person traveling upon the nearby trace, a condition improved by the screening branches of several small oaks. Our breathing had barely slowed when we saw, in patches as it were, the lead horseman approaching from the east upon the trail, which widened near the stream. This horseman, mounted upon a pinto, was clearly an Indian warrior carrying a lance. Strangely as he paused at the creek to allow his pony to drink, he looked to me—impossible as it seemed—like a Comanche...indeed, looked familiar. The horse, too, a splendid black-and white creature, was familiar.

"Diable!" exclaimed Antoine in a whisper. "It's Toyamancare."

"No, no, that's not possible," I whispered.

"Yes, yes," whispered Deer's-Ears, greatly excited. "And there're Bearbird and Sees-Fire."

A second and a third horseman drew up beside the first. Looking around them, they also allowed their ponies to drink. Seeing the three men, recognizing them in the deepening twilight, I had a dizzy feeling, as if I had been a child whirling in circles and were about to tumble. But my two companions surely were not dreaming. I called out: "Hóla, los amigos Comanches! Hóla, Toyamancare!"

There was an instant of silence, when the three men, each seizing an arrow from the bowcase on his back and fitting it to his bow, pointing it around in our direction, gazed excitedly, almost comically about, trying to locate the source of my call.

"Whose spirit are you talking to me?" Toyamancare finally demanded, throwing out his chest, drawing himself straight upon his horse, facing in our direction.

"No spirit," I called. "It's me, Bluejay. And Kills-Far, and Deer's-Ears. Here, behind the big rocks."

"When did you die? Tell us who killed you," Big-Mountain insisted.

"Are you really there, Deer's-Ears?" called Bearbird, now pointing his bow directly at the crack between the boulders.

"Yes," said Deer's-Ears. "And you? We thought you were up fighting the Panismahas."

"We went to the Rio Arkansas," said Bearbird. "But Piaisa warned us there not to go farther, so we came back."

"Red-Woman's medicine," Deer's-Ears murmured.

"I think they're men," quietly declared Bearbird, regarding his companions, lowering his bow. "That's Bluejay—my primo. No Comanche talks like that. And it's Deer's-Ears' voice."

In reply Sees-Fire gave a strangled grunt, eyes huge, lowering his bow, signaling frantically with a hand, "No—spirits!"

Toyamancare looked doubtfully from one man to the other. "Deer's-Ears," he bellowed at last, evidently forgetting we were in Osage country. "Come out so we can see you."

"Wait," I demanded. "We'll all come out. Put away your bows. We are not spirits, Toyamancare. We're your friends. Don't shoot us."

There was no reply, but the two men lowered their bows. Meanwhile other warriors had begun crowding their ponies behind the warchief, bows in hand, craning to see what was happening. Deer's-Ears strode boldly down the path, while Antoine and I followed more slowly and cautiously, our eyes on the drawn bows. Deer's-Ears strode to Toyamancare and held out his hand like a Frenchman or Spaniard. After a moment's hesitation, Toyamancare grasped it, appearing satisfied at once of the other man's corporeality. But the warchief was more reluctant to shake the hands that Antoine and I proffered, as if he feared that tabebos were more likely to be tricky, deceptive spirits than Comanches were, and he seemed not to see them, so that after a moment we let our arms fall. Deer's-Ears continued explaining the cause for our being in La Grande Forêt. Sees-Fire, wide-eyed and frozen upon his horse, continued to stare at us in alarm.

"The horseherd, the entire horseherd," Toyamancare lamented in the thickening dusk. "That's what we were beginning to wonder about."

"And Ah-mah-bah-tay, added Deer's-Ears. "They captured The-Headless-One and took him too."

"All my ponies and mi hijo!" moaned the warchief, looking around in the gloaming. "There's a good campsite a little way behind us. We'll go there and talk about what we're going to do. Where are your horses?"

Lefort ran a little distance up along the stream and called to the boy. Shortly the others, engagés and Comanches, appeared on the trace, leading our horses. After cries of reunion and embraces among the Nuhmuhnuh, we proceeded eastward by the trail, which widened and shrank unpredictably, at times becoming almost a thicket in the near-dark, where we were compelled to duck and fend off branches and still, at that, accumulate scratches. Finally we arrived at what appeared to be a grassy expanse containing at a little distance a grove of lofty trees with a small pond fed by a spring. Here we halted and began unsaddling, watering, and picketing the horses, while at the same time the Comanches of the two parties conversed rapidly, with immediate wails and demonstrations of anguish by those men of the warparty who had lost wives, children, or other kin.

By the time Toyamancare had called the Comanches to a council—under the stars, as a fire would be too dangerous—and by the time I had stretched out on my buffalo robe under a tree, Antoine and I had managed to splice together an account of the warparty's wanderings since they had separated from the band nearly a month before in the mountain canyons of the lower Washita. In brief it went as follows: after riding directly north to the Cimarron, reaching the river near where it enters La Grande Forêt, they had followed that stream in its northwesterly ascent almost to the Rivière des Ark, or Arkansas. But on entering a wood a little before the river's dip southward, they had encountered, sitting on its haunches in a path directly before them and blocking their progress, a large male wolf, who whined and howled as they drew near and, as they halted before it, proceeded to stand up and bark at them, not budging from its spot.

At this intervention by an animal the People regard as a brother, Toyamancare had turned his horse and ridden back the way he and his warriors had come. The party had halted, smoked, and discussed in council what they should do. Unanimously the warchief and his men had decided that Piaisa's behavior had been too clear a warning to ignore, that some mortal danger must lurk ahead, and that he was telling them they must abandon their plan to fight the Panismahas and, without proceeding any farther, return to their families. They had then retraced their route down the Cimarron until they had reached the westernmost strip of oaks indicating La Grande Forêt, where they had discovered recent spoor of buffalo moving directly northward by an old trail. Excited by the opportunity to hunt and gain fresh meat, and still ahead of time for their rendezvous with the band, they had followed the trail until it intersected another river, where in a small prairie, they had found a little gang of cows. They had succeeded in the chase and had slain a number of cows and calves. They had then, feeling no urgency to depart, passed many days in curing meat, in additional hunting and feasting, and in lying about, smoking, joking and enjoying themselves.

On their return to the Cimarron they had discovered the fresh trail of the Osage war party, the same trail we were then following a little west of them. They had correctly believed it to be that of Osage warriors with a big horseherd, although they had thought the horses to have been stolen from the Pawnees, the Osages' neighbors to the north. Toyamancare's lust for horses was immediately aroused. The other warriors, too, were enthusiastic about the prospect of stalking the Osage party, attacking at an opportune moment. They chuckled at the thought of stealing the horseherd, even though they were aware of the danger involved in penetrating a country frequented by the Osage people, and sometimes even by Pawnees, those enemies of both Comanches and Osages. But the tracks of so many horses were an irresistible lure, and they had decided to attempt acquiring some Osage scalps while collecting an extraordinary quantity of horses.

After a half-day's travel, their scouts had come within sight of the Osage rearguard and had been compelled to slow their progress, since the enemy was frequently delayed, owing to the difficulty of driving the horseherd through the rows of thick forest without losing large numbers of them. Later the raiders had halted by a creek and had unaccountably remained in that location for so long that Toyamancare and his men had become impatient and had almost decided to attack then, instead of waiting until the following dawn. Finally the Osage party had continued upon its way, moving slowly. The Comanches had examined the grove where their enemies had stopped and had found, with little searching, the body of a warrior barely hidden in a depression by the creek. The man had been shot in the chest. The ball had been removed. Yet he had died. Searching in the leaves near the corpse, Sees-Fire had found the ball itself. He had regarded it casually at first, believing it to be a musket ball, but then had noticed ridges raised and grooves indented upon it, marking the lead as having been fired from a rifle.

He showed it to Toyamancare, and the two of them had studied it, pondering, rifles at that time being rare upon the southern prairies and not even found among most traders. They had passed it around. They and other members of the war party looked at each other and wondered aloud. The only rifle in their experience belonged to Kills-Far, whom they knew had been due to arrive with the trade caravan not long after their departure for la Rivière Platte and the Panismahas. Could it be that the Osage warriors riding before them had discovered the location of the band high up the Washita, so far from their usual camps? If so, there had been a fight, as evidenced by the dead warrior. But if their people's camp had been struck by surprise, what about their wives, children, relatives and friends? What had happened to them? And the big herd of horses the Osage warparty was driving before it, could it possibly be that those ponies were not Pawnee horses? For the Pawnees did not have great numbers of horses like the Comanches. Could it possibly be that those horses ahead of them were actually Comanche horses? Were, in fact, their own ponies, which they had been planning to steal? Yes, the ponies, but their wives and families—this sudden doubt had seized all of the Comanche men at once. What about their wives and families? What had happened to them?

They had progressed a little farther but more slowly and tormented now by anxiety when their suspicions had been confirmed. A horse had neighed from the forest ahead. Their ponies had responded, ears pricked forward, excited. Toyamancare had drawn up, alarmed, signaling his men to be prepared to fight. But out of the woods to the north had crashed a single mare followed by a colt. It was a sorrel-and-white pony the entire party recognized, a mare belonging to the deceased Tichinalla, or Ugly-Game. She had evidently escaped among the trees from her Osage captors with her bony, tired colt. Big-Mountain and the others knew then that their first surmise had been correct and, after briefly conferring, they had reversed directions to travel to their own people, taking along the mare and colt. They had of course required another half-day to return to the creek where we had encountered them.

On reaching the campsite Toyamancare selected members of his warparty to stand guard, permitting my volunteers and me some hours of uninterrupted sleep. Lying on my robe between the bulging roots of a cotton tree, I was giving way to my fatigue, drifting off, when Deer's-Ears appeared with a report of the council. Although all of Toyamancare's party were anxious to rejoin their families as quickly as possible, he said, the council had determined to pursue the enemy at first light, believing them to be about a day ahead and probably tired, moving slowly, unsuspecting, and in disarray. The plan on reaching the raiders was to attack at the first opportunity, surprising them, striking first to rescue Ah-mah-bah-tay, then to recover the horseherd, and last to avenge those Nuhmuhnuh wounded and killed during the raid. I drowsily concurred and soon lapsed into sleep, broken at times during the night by distant thunder and the occasional illumination of the eastern sky. But

I slept well until a little before dawn, when I woke with an effort from a very bad dream, or cauchemar.

This dream was confused, but its ending, out of which I struggled awake, stayed with me—indeed remains with me today. I had of course been thinking frequently of Arsène and his captors during our pursuit. In the dream I remember still there had been a suffocating odor of carrion. This odor had seemed to awaken me, while still dreaming, to discover a figure bending above me, clearly visible by a chip of moon shining directly overhead. It was The Buffalo, bending closer and closer to scrutinize me through the circular white eyes of his mask. What struck me most was not only the nauseating odor of his breath but the strange blackness of his body and a peculiar humming. As his face drew close to mine, I saw not only the bloody nostrils but noticed that the darkness of his chest and body was owing to the thousands of flies sitting upon him, humming, with little fluttering wings, completely covering his exposed skin. At only a hand's length from my face the great buffalo head paused, and I could see within the peep-holes of the white circles the true eyes of a man examining my features, as if to memorize them. These real eyes were the most frightening part of the dream. I tried to cry out for help and could not but somehow raised my head and jerked awake with a sense of horror.

I could not shake off the feeling, like a cramp in my spine, until after sunrise. But earlier, while we ate hurriedly, I kept reflecting upon the dream.

"You know," I said finally to Antoine, "The Buffalo was a tabebo. I just realized it."

"What? Why do you think that?"

"I wondered why he was so dark. Burned by the sun, of course. But darker than that. I just had a quick look when he came close. But now I'm sure. He must have been hairy. Many tabebos are hairy, Indians are not."

"If he was white, he must have been a Frenchman."

"Why do you say that?"

"Some traders up north go on warparties."

"Why?"

"For adventure, plunder, to ingratiate themselves, or maybe because they married Indian women."

"So The Buffalo may be a Frenchman. Maybe he would help Arsène."

Antoine grunted with a shrug. "Some are worse than the natives."

Later it was good to ride rapidly behind or beside Toyamancare and to progress along the trail in the gray light of early morning. With this partial return of daylight he had evidently become convinced that Lefort and I were truly ourselves, men and not spirits and had, with a little embarrassment it seemed, embraced and invited us to ride at the head of the column with Bearbird, Sees-Fire and him. As for the latter warchief, who had continued to be mute, he rode at a prudent distance from us and occasionally eyed us suspiciously as we sped through the varied countryside.

I write here, "varied countryside," by the way, because it must not be imagined that in this region La Grande Forêt is one vast thicket. No, wide as it is, it is made up of undulating hills, often covered by post and blackjack oak, as well as by valleys in between, and interrupted by arroyos, little creeks, and even stretches of prairie. We now hurried through this dawn landscape, climbing and descending, according to hill or valley, and following the vague trail through bands of oak, in order to overtake our enemy as swiftly as possible. But strangely it now appeared that he too had begun to hurry, just when we had finally combined to a force sufficient to meet him on equal or superior terms. Each morning for the next three days Toyamancare believed we would catch him, and each day we were disappointed. We followed the clear trail of hoofprints, a multitude of them, through prairies into woods and out again, and even encountered and collected five stray ponies from the herd along the way, indicating that the Osage warparty was now speeding toward the Arkansas River and its village beyond on the Verdigris. As I say, for three days we chased them, finding their campsites colder and colder, less and less recent and giving every sign of increasingly brief occupancy. I was of course anxious. We were all worried I believe. I recall asking Deer's-Ears on that third day—yes, it was the third day—why he thought Toyamancare, in particular, was beginning to look more and more troubled and grim.

"Some of the men want to turn back. They're all thinking of their families."

"Will they just leave?"

"Maybe."

"But they must want their horses back?"

"Yes. They do. But they know there's not much chance. When we get to the edge of La Grande Forêt, Toyamancare has promised them to turn around. He says we must turn around there anyway."

"What? When will that be?" Shocked, I tried not to feel anything.

"Maybe today. Maybe tomorrow."

"Even if we don't catch them? Why?"

"Osage country. Too close. And they're going too fast now. They've got the herd to choose from. We have only the ponies we brought, and they're tired, even the spares."

"Why do you think they're going so fast?" Antoine and I had discussed this and failed to reach a conclusion.

"Maybe too many good warriors dying. They want to get back to their Puhahantes, to try to cure the wounded. Maybe they think their medicine's left them. The hawk, their emblem, has flown away. Trouble with the horseherd. Too many bad things happening. Those young men are confused and scared, I think."

I slept badly that night. It was a short night anyway. Toyamancare started us off in the dark the following morning. Antoine had told me we would surely leave La Grande Forêt by the end of this day, and I was filled with foreboding, a sense of dread, nearly convinced we would have to abandon our rescue attempt. Which meant abandoning Arsène. I felt something close to despair, to weeping. To forsake a friend in danger of torture and death is a terrible, terrible deed.

I remember we were emerging from a patch of forest onto a segment of prairie during an unusually colorful sunrise, when to my surprise Toyamancare drew up his pony to study for a moment, as I thought, the extraordinary view before us. Curious as to what he saw, I stared too.

The low sun, between clouds, was red. Except for open patches of blue and high streaks of rose and white, the clouds were an intense red. The sun, in fact, shone a red light upon the grassy plain before us, coloring everything it touched crimson, up to the opposite line of woods. Toyamancare, sitting his pony with lance in hand, had dropped his rein and was shielding his eyes with the other, squinting into the red landscape before us. As the warchief was not given to esthetic contemplation, I too squinted toward the distant treeline, trying to see whatever it was he saw. I made out nothing but a scattering of reddish shapes. Drawing forth my spyglass and focusing it upon one of these, I found it to be a horse, a red-tinted horse. But some motion caused me to shift the glass and bring it to bear upon an even stranger object. Nearer to us but in the direct, level path of the sun's glare, a mounted figure was approaching before an uneven line of grazing horses. Its pony was red, the figure carmine, wrapped in a red blanket, hunched forward so that its face was invisible. The sight, reminiscent as it was, gave me a shock. It resembled the swaddled corpse of Taoinan supported by two women as they led his pony to his place of burial. I passed the glass to Antoine, who put it to his eye. He started visibly, turning to me: "Nom de dieu!"

"No, no. It's impossible."

He placed the glass again to his eye. At that moment the figure, now at a slight angle from the sun's direct path, raised its head. With my unaided vision I could discern a face, although its features were a reddish blur.

Lefort gasped. "C'est lui!"

"What? Who? Not Taoinan. Impossible."

"No, c'est lui. C'est Arsène-Christophe!"

I plunged my heels into the mare's flanks, giving her her head. She bounded forward and we dashed at a run across the prairie, far ahead of all but Antoine, who had followed me. The Comanches and engagés trotted cautiously behind us, anticipating a trap, since Osage warriors might easily have concealed themselves within the wood we were recklessly approaching, or might even have been hanging from the far sides of the loose horses. As I drew close I saw that the blanketed figure had once again lowered its head, as its pony began trotting toward the mare. I drew up sharply beside the red horseman, whose pony had halted and, reaching, gently shook his shoulder, saying, "Arsène, mon vieux. Regarde moi."

Was it really he? The figure raised its head and stared at me with a confused, dazed expression, pale, blear-eyed, with stubble-beard, dried line of blood at his throat, dried blood on his face. He looked as if he had been exhumed. But it was indeed Arsène. He passed a hand over his eyes. "Jean-Pierre," he murmured. "What are you doing here?"

"We've come for you." He stank, I noticed, of death, of carrion.

The grazing ponies, too, had raised their heads, watching the horses of the men, who advanced with muskets or bows or lances and shields at the ready. Several among the horses began to whinny and tentatively to advance toward the others, which neighed in reply. From the oncoming Comanches came a whoop, a joyous cry from Toyamancare. Many warriors passed us and rode on to collect the loose horses. But the warchief rode to Arsène, threw a crushing arm around him, and pressed his cheek to the stubble beard of his dazed adopted son. This rough movement caused the blanket to drop from that young man's blood-stained body, showing him dressed as usual in moccasins, breech-clout, leggings and exposing on the left side of his head, partly under his loose hair, a gash whose red-rimmed depth revealed the white gleam of his skull, as well as three ugly scarlet marks on his chest and abdomen. As the leading warchief flung himself from his horse, Arsène gazed at him and at the others surrounding us with a baffled expression.

"It's your people," I explained. "Your friends, come to bring you back."

"Yes," he said, his eyes fully open, blinking, "Of course." He continued to look around him as if he had just awakened and were trying to determine where he was and why he was there.

"Piarabo!" cried Toyamancare joyfully. "My little jackrabbit." The warchief had slipped a heavy arm around the neck of the pony, was hugging it with a grin and was regarding us all triumphantly while tears slid off his jaw. As for the horse, it masticated a mouthful of grass, whose blades dangled from its lips, dripping green slobber.

34

We rode back to the woods from which we had come, two men and the boy herding the loose horses. There we dismounted within the margin of the forest in a glade of scattered sunlight and shadow, tethered our horses, and relaxed upon the oak leaves in order to await the return of the five young warriors that Toyamancare had dispatched to capture or kill the Osages pursuing Arsène. When the warchief had demanded of Arsène whether he was being followed, his adopted son had seemed by an effort to focus his thoughts and to ponder the question before replying that, yes, he had once glimpsed three men in the distance behind him. He added that the men were impeded, however, by their apparent duty of collecting and herding loose ponies that had earlier escaped or were also upon his and Piarabo's trail. He was yawning as he spoke and appeared, even as he sat his horse, to drift in and out of a state of confusion. Riding beside us westward to the strip of woods, he sat once again wrapped in the red blanket, with bowed head, leaving guidance to the pony, which proceeded beside ours. But within the edge of the woods when we were about to dismount, he raised his face, and stared again at Toyamancare, his faculties plainly once more focused.

"Ahpi," he said, addressing the warchief as father, "if there are prisoners, will you let me dispose of them?"

Toyamancare appeared surprised. "Yes, netua, my son," he said, with equal formality, after reflecting a moment. "You may do whatever you wish with any captives." Then he asked the question we had all been longing to ask. "Tell me, tua, how did you get away?"

"How did I escape?" Arsène said slowly, as if puzzled by the question. He held up his hands, wrists together, as if they were bound. "Barré. Barré freed me."

I looked at Antoine. He was not a man who revealed his emotions. Yet now he appeared dumfounded, incredulous.

"Did you say, Barré' the trapper? The trader? Not that Barré."

"Yes, the same, I think."

"Did he put you on Piarabo?" asked Toyamancare.

Arsène lightly touched his forehead, yawned. "Later, Ahpi. I can't talk. I've got to sleep. Jean-Pierre, help me down. My head aches."

As I helped Arsène off of his horse, I glanced again up at Lefort. He still wore an astonished expression. Had the matter not been so grave, I would have laughed. The merciless Barré, the satanic Barré, whom Antoine had mentioned more than once as a man without conscience, a disgrace to French Canadian traders—that very Barré had apparently saved Arsène from an agonizing death.

"Wake me when they come back," asked Arsène a moment later, as he lay down wrapped in his stinking blanket beneath a tree. "Don't forget."

The young warriors did not return for three or four hours. Meanwhile we drank water from our buffalo paunches, ate jerked meat, and lay in the shade, talking or dozing, the Comanches grouped together as well as the engagés, although the two groups were on cordial terms. As I sat with my back braced against an oak, drowsing, I became aware that Bearbird was standing by my mare regarding a horse-pistol in its saddle holster. I recognized him from the rear by his unique headdress, a black three-cornered hat festooned with scarlet plumes.

"Hóla, Bearbird," I called.

He turned, his features grave. "Hóla, primo. You hear about my daughters and grandson?"

"Yes. I'm sorry."

"I have two left. Two boys. And my grown sons."

"Take it out and look at it," I continued in Castilian.

He withdrew the pistol and examined it carefully, holding it up to his face and peering. I remembered having earlier primed the weapon and at first watched nervously. But he was careful, keeping the muzzle aimed toward the ground. Reassured, I began wondering where he had obtained the hat, of which he was evidently proud. Probably from a Spanish official. No other warrior in the band wore anything like it. But then he possessed a reputation for being different from any other Comanche. Deer's-Ears had told me about my "cousin" during our trip. Evidently his eyes were weak, and since a notorious incident many years before, afterward related throughout comanchería, his comrades always, as we Americans say, "kept an eye on him" during battle.

The incident had made him famous, although not entirely in a favorable sense. As I had heard it, he had during one windy, dusty skirmish with Utes near the Sangre de Cristo range of Nuevo Mexico, somehow in a cloud of dust become entangled within the wrong warparty and begun releasing arrows at his friends, while urging the confused Utes to follow him and fight harder. Both groups had been so stunned and the entire incident had occurred so rapidly that the Ute warriors had not touched him. One of his companions, recognizing him among the enemy had called him back. He had galloped the short distance to rejoin his friends, who afterward always made certain of his whereabouts during a battle.

Bearbird replaced the pistol in its holster and sauntered back to his group, while I continued to drowse.

There was noise and excitement well before the returning warriors reached our woods. A lookout saw them as they emerged from the distant trees, driving before them four ponies. Upon another, led by one of the Comanche men, was mounted what appeared to be a prisoner. The news spread at once, with everyone running to the edge of our forest to look, except for several of the younger warriors who leapt upon their horses and raced out across the prairie to meet them. There was even greater excitement when the news spread that the returning young men had brought with them, fastened to a lance, an Osage scalp. This meant, as it turned out, nothing less than our freedom to depart upon our return journey immediately. The need for vengeance for the sake of the People's dead in the raid had now been satisfied by a single enemy scalp, as well as by a prisoner, and we did not need to pursue the raiders farther.

Arsène looked up at me as if stupefied when I woke him, staring as if he could not comprehend why I had done so.

"You asked me to wake you. They've come back with a captive."

"With a captive?" He regarded me, dazed. "Who?"

"Your Comanche friends. They fought the Osage men who were tracking you. They brought back a prisoner."

For another moment he looked puzzled, then appeared suddenly to comprehend. "Ah, a prisoner. I see." He began to struggle to rise and fell back. "Help me up, will you, Jean-Pierre. I don't know why I'm so weak."

"You're weak because you have a cracked head."

Deer's-Ears and I, each holding an elbow, helped him stagger to where Toyamancare and several older warriors stood awaiting the triumphant return of the young men, who just then rode into the forest from the bright light of the intervening prairie. The recovered ponies came first, whinnying to ours, which were tethered or picketed among the trees, and which nickered in reply. Four of the young men, painted and armed with bows and lances, drove the animals before them and passed us. The fifth led the horse bearing the prisoner who was, like the Comanches, bare-chested, his bald, roached head gleaming in a patch of sunlight, his wrists bound behind him. He appeared to be eighteen or nineteen years of age. His captor drew up before the head warchief amid whoops and triumphant cries of the surrounding warriors, while the prisoner looked about him with disdainful dignity. The captor, Encantime, or Beetle, after greeting the warchief, urged his horse forward and handed the lead rope of the other horse to Big-Mountain.

"How did you take him?" asked the warchief. "Will you give him to Amabate?"

Encantime proudly held up his lariat and signaled his assent. Passing his shield and his lance, from which dangled a bloody scalp, to a nearby warrior, he dismounted and yanked the captive roughly from his horse. This individual, recovering his balance, stood looking boldly around him. There was, I saw, something wrong with his left ear, an ugly wound attracting flies. A lance or arrow has apparently grazed his face, no doubt at the Washita, leaving a red gash and tearing the ear in two, an upper flap and the lobe. Evidently they had festered.

"Ah-mah-bah-tay," called Toyamancare. "Here's your prisoner. Tell us what you wish to do with him." He turned, called behind him, "Dead Hide! The fire—ready?"

"Jaa!" a shout echoed from the wood.

Allowing the blanket to fall from his shoulders, Arsène walked unsteadily to the captive, halting no more than two paces before him and leaning forward to stare into his face.

"Ah, Munnepuske, c'est toi," he uttered in surprise. "This man was my jailer," he explained, turning to Toyamancare and the rest of us. Turning back, he sniffed, made a face.

The young Osage gazed back with hatred and defiance. For several moments, Arsène, standing with the younger man in a ragged oval of sunlight, his red-and-white head-wound gaping, he looked searchingly into his enemy's features, while the youth glared back, now appearing puzzled and a little shaken. "Was he brave?" (teconiuap) he asked the captor, who stood nearby. "Very brave?"

Beetle looked surprised. "Yes," he replied slowly, with reluctance.

"Cut him loose," said Arsène.

Beetle stared at Toyamancare, then at Arsène. He drew his knife, went behind the captive and sawed apart the rawhide bonds that held the man's wrists, swung round and held the point of the blade at his throat. The prisoner's hands dropped to his sides. He stood drawn up straight, features frozen, still defiant, prepared it seemed for a fatal thrust.

There was silence, as if the group of men gathered around, traders and Comanches alike, had ceased to breathe. Somewhere in the woods a horse snorted.

"Munnepuske, go," said Arsène, with a wave of his hand.

The Osage stared, uncomprehending.

"Go, va-t-en!" Arsène yelled, with a wave of his hand that caused him to stagger.

This time the warrior understood, looking wildly about him for an instant, fanning flies from his torn ear, before turning and sprinting between the trees into the prairie. Beetle and the watching men appeared stunned, paralyzed with disbelief as they saw the Osage, captive a moment before, race out into the field. Instants later, when the fugitive was halfway across, I turned at rapid footsteps behind me. Bearbird had run up panting and to my alarm holding one of my horse pistols. Before I could protest, he raised it in the air and fired, a loud report. Throwing back his head, he gave a long, loud and chilling Comanche warwhoop. In the prairie, the running man glanced over his shoulder and began sprinting even faster, ducking and dodging over the grass with extraordinary speed.

"Look," cried Bearbird, pointing. With lips and tongue he made an explosive sound, a giant horse-fart. "Piarabo!" he shouted, his jester's features for a moment comic once more.

The man's zigzag flight was indeed like that of a jackrabbit—was, when seen in a certain light, droll in the extreme. Men, even Big-Mountain, began to chuckle, then to laugh, until all of us were laughing. At the far edge of the prairie, a tiny figure, bald head gleaming, paused and peered back before plunging into the trees. Even at that distance he could not have failed to hear our laughter.

35

We returned for the night to our previous campsite where there was sufficient water for men, water and grass for horses. We made our camp in the grove at a short distance from the Comanche encampment, on the opposite side of the pond. I saw that Arsène was comfortably placed under a great cotton tree upon my buffalo robe. Antoine had previously lacked time to hunt, although he had now ridden away to do so. Consequently the best I could provide for the colonel's son was pemmican and cold spring water, the former of which he ate, chewing slowly, while drinking thirstily. I made sure that all of our horses had been watered, that they were safely hobbled or picketed with access to grass, and that we had placed ourselves in as advantageous a defensive position as possible, forming a crude circle among the trees. I went then to confer with Big-Mountain in order to learn the plans for the next day's march. He was seated smoking with several of his leading warriors, apparently in consultation, so that I returned to our camp.

I was astonished to find Arsène sitting braced against his tree, head raised, with eyes shut, a melancholy expression, wet cheeks: in my absence he had sawed off locks of his hair, which had been hanging loose, from the left side of his head. This had the incidental effect of completely exposing his wound. But I knew it could mean only one thing, that he was mourning his slain son and wives. Who had told him? I had asked Deer's-Ears not to mention the dead until his friend was stronger. Someone had. It didn't matter who. I sat down in the shadows of a nearby elm, drank water from my buffalo paunch, and began chewing pemmican. It was early afternoon, warm, and the camp was silent. Nearly everyone seemed to be prone, dozing or asleep. I was about to stretch out myself when I noticed Arsène watching me. He did not appear to be confused.

"That was magnanimous, what you did," I said, hoping to cheer him. "Monsieur Arouet would have been proud."

His expression did not alter.

"How's your headache?"

"Not bad, now. You saw Sehêbi before you left?"

"Yes. The girl too."

He closed his eyes again.

I was about to lie down when Toyamancare appeared. He went directly to the man he called "son," squatted, and examined the wound, which I had earlier examined, finding it clean. Arsène opened his eyes, watching. Toyamancare drew his knife, peering closely. There was a loose flap of scalp dangling at the bottom edge of the wound. I had decided to leave it undisturbed. But the warchief, without a word, began severing it. His patient stiffened, still watching, inflating his chest, arching his back, gritting his teeth, not flinching. After removing the flap and tossing it away, Toyamancare drew herbs from a pouch he wore, shoved them into his mouth and chewed vigorously. This was, I realized, the pouip I had heard of. He then spat the herb, with abundant saliva, into his hand and pressed it into the wound. At this, Arsène did flinch. I thought he was going to faint, but his eyes cleared and his color returned.

"Why did you let that Osage go?" the warchief demanded. "You shouldn't have done that."

"They let me go."

"The Frenchman let you go."

"He's an Osage, I think. Like I'm a Comanche. I think he's married to an Osage woman. Anyway, that youth was a brave man. I could tell."

"We should have roasted him."

"They didn't roast me. Just a few red coals."

"Did you know they'd killed your son and your wives?"

"No. I didn't then."

"Would you have freed him if you'd known?"

"Maybe not. Maybe I'd have killed him. But maybe not."

"They've made you poisá, loco. That's what it is—that tap on the head. You're crazy now, but you'll be all right, and then you'll be sorry for what you did." Rising, Toyamancare turned and strode away without a word to me and without a further word to his son.

"Furieux," I said. "He'll get over it."

"So you think," said Arsène, "Voltaire would have approved?"

"I know he would have. It was a magnanimous act. Jean Jacques too."

Again he smiled faintly, inscrutably. Was he pleased or ironic and amused?

"You never change, Jean-Pierre," he said mildly, closing his eyes again, smiling. "I like that."

With the help of a round moon, we departed early the following morning. Antoine had killed a deer the previous afternoon. Seated by our tiny cookfire, we ate heartily that evening and again in the morning before saddling the horses. I had difficulty in waking Arsène. He was confused about where he was and what we were all doing there, but he drank a great deal of water and ate some venison. As we were riding out in the silvery light, at times in the open and at times ducking and leaning between branches, following the trail through the pale oak thickets, I recalled my thoughts riding the same route eastward, my premonition that we would not return. That premonition had proven false, like so many. As Lefort had said, on a eu de la veine—we'd been lucky. But luckiest of all he considered Arsène. Although some might ascribe his escape and recovery to Providence, I was inclined to agree with Antoine. According to the Canadian, Ah-mah-bah-tay had inherited la chance of the old man, his father, who had advanced in rank and survived under two different governments, in two different armies, that of France and that of Spain, for so many years on the frontier, having lived even beyond the epidemics that had killed his first wife and their other children and had decimated Natchitoches and the Mississippi riverine communities at least twice during his lifetime.

Toyamancare and his warriors led our cavalcade, while we followed and the engagés served in effect as rear guard, with the recovered horses and their herders before them. I rode near Arsène, who was still by his Comanche father's sufferance mounted upon Piarabo throughout our return journey. Sometimes Antoine joined us. We rode westward until the margin of La Grande Forêt, then south across the Cimarron, the North Canadian, the Canadian, following them southward when possible, to the Washita, and along that stream until the canyons and waterfalls of the mountains on the lower river where the People were encamped and praying for the return of both our parties.

There were times when Arsène's eyes had a bewildered look and others when he was himself, times when he suffered what were apparently extreme headaches, when he rode with his head down, his face fixed in an impassive expression, hardly guiding his horse, times when he silently grieved, and times when he would engage in lucid conversations with us, and we would listen carefully. Out of these favorable hours, as we went along, I constructed a story, grafting twig to twig to fashion a tree. This was an account of what had happened to him and how he had resisted what had seemed to be his doom from the time he had raced from his lodge on the morning of the Osage raid to the hour we had encountered him resembling a bound cadaver riding upon Piarabo through that scarlet sunrise.

To start with, he remembered being rushed upon and surrounded by mounted men out of the half-light, as well as others on foot, all of them reaching for him or striking at him with warclubs. A horseman seized his lance near the blade. As he tugged and struggled to free the weapon, another man grabbed his leg from the ground and began dragging him from his horse. Dropping the lance, he drew his knife and was slashing at this person when he glimpsed an object swinging toward him. Instinctively he raised his shield, diverting some of the force of the blow, but it caught him nonetheless on the side of his head, and he remembered the impact and nothing more for a time. There followed a blur of days and nights and days, it seemed, of riding, his wrists bound before him, ankles tied beneath the horse, head aching severely. There had been halts of varied duration and on several occasions he had been given water, which he had drunk thirstily. And sometimes even meat, which he fed himself with his bound hands. But then again perhaps he was wrong. Perhaps they had stopped at night and left him tied. That seemed possible too. He remembered that several men had appeared to be badly wounded, with the others concerned about them. There was even a moment when one of these had apparently died, and there was a commotion about leaving the body concealed under branches and leaves. Some of the younger warriors had evidently wished to take immediate revenge upon him.

One of these was the young man who had been assigned to guard him. He became nearly certain on glimpsing that youth, waiting on his pony behind him, place a finger in his mouth and point it, wet, directly at him.

"What does that mean, anyway?"

"'You must die,'" said Lefort, who was riding near us at the time.

"That's what I thought."

But older men had prevented them from doing him harm. This incident, he told us, had fully awakened him to his situation, a prisoner of an Osage war party, and to his extreme danger. He had decided that the safest course was, temporarily at least, to pretend to be constantly as addled as he felt most of the time.

Another thing. It must have been during the first hours, sometime shortly after he had regained his senses, a man wearing a buffalo mask had loped along beside him and peered intently into his face, apparently having noticed his stubble beard.

"Bon Dieu! Tu es blanc. Dis moi, fumier. Tu es Français?"

Arsène gazed at him a moment, dimly comprehending that the Buffalo had noticed he was white and was asking if he were French. "Non, je suis Comanche."

"Ah, mon pauvre. T'es foutu, Comanche. T'es devenu un Peau Rouge. Tu vas payer. Tant pis. Tu vas mourir dans le supplice. Moi, Je m'en fous. Adieu, guerrier." The Buffalo, after taunting him, promising death by torture, swung his quirt against his pony's flank and loped away toward the front of the party.

He recalled that the man had returned several times during the days that followed, without his mask but with the same intense dark eyes and bold stare, tall and stooped, head held forward like a bull's, graying black shaggy hair, deeply lined face, and still the blue-painted beard that had made part of the effect of the buffalo mask. He had posed other questions in the French tongue, and Arsène had responded to them hoping to gain an advantage.

"Who was the tireur d'élite with the rifle?" The Buffalo asked.

"Antoine."

"Antoine who?"

"Lefort."

"Not Antoine Lefort! Down here? Not possible!"

On another occasion, during a long halt to rest and water the horses, The Buffalo, immediately recognizable by his bold carriage, strolled to where he was seated upon the earth by his horse, having been pulled off by an older warrior.

"What's your French name?"

"Arsène."

"Arsène what?"

"Arsène-Christophe Alexandre de St. Maurice."

"The governor's son?"

"My father's no longer lieutenant governor."

"And you're a Comanche. What a fool! And I suppose you belong to a warrior society, n'est-ce pas?"

"I did."

"The 'wolves'?"

"Yes."

"I knew it. What a fool! Whiteboy who wants to play Indian! Poor fool!"

On yet another occasion, when the warparty had halted for the night after entering La Grande Forêt and the warriors were occupied in eating and in tending to the wounded, The Buffalo approached him where he sat, bound, leaning against a tree.

"Lefort is with that trading party?" he asked, standing, a big-boned tall man, gazing down.

"Yes."

"Your father's firm?"

"Yes."

"He's your friend?"

"Since I was a boy." He looked up at the tall, scowling coureur de bois. "You won't help me, will you?"

The Buffalo almost smiled. "I wondered when you'd ask me. If you were French I might. But I despise Comanches. Why should I help you? You're nothing to me. Even if your father would pay ransom, I wouldn't help. Yet," he mused. "You know, nevertheless, I might cut your throat someday. You'll beg me for it."

Arsène confessed that it hurt his pride to ask. But he did ask, that much. Only that. Because he was afraid. He was ashamed to tell us, he admitted, but he had been very afraid. No, not of death. Not so much even of the torture, although he wouldn't lie, he was afraid of that. No, what he feared most was disgracing himself—himself and his people. "If I show pain," he had said, "they'll laugh and despise me and the Nuhmuhnuh." As a result he determined to increase his efforts to discover a means of escape. Failing that, he would kill himself, if he were able to.

But he knew he had little time. Once at the Osage village, he believed he would be guarded constantly. He would have no chance for either. Presently his captors were agitated because of the dead and wounded, mostly older men. The young warriors were preoccupied with the remaining wounded and even with the Comanche horseherd, whose many ponies continued to turn back in the direction from which they had come, evidently missing their accustomed range. The animals' persistent attempts to flee caused frequent delays, slowing the progress of the warparty's return and further flustering the young men, so that they had become careless. For instance Arsène noticed, during his periods of clarity, that the buckskin strap surrounding his wrists had stretched a little and that his captors, increasingly fatigued, no longer troubled to secure his ankles at campsites during the day. Exhausted from earlier riding both day and night, they now paid little heed to him, providing enough water and food to keep him alive, otherwise mostly ignoring him. They were of course saving him, he suspected, for later festivities.

Meanwhile during his periods of lucidity, which were lengthening, he kept looking for opportunities, while at the same time feigning to be dazed and somnolent. He soon made two important observations. The first occurred as the warparty prepared to camp for the night in a stand of trees by the Cimarron at a spot near the eastern edge of La Grande Forêt and only a few days ride from that river's confluence with the Río Napeste, or la Rivière des Ark. The young men responsible for the horseherd caught up and drove the animals near the site and held them in the luxuriant meadow by the trees beside the river. Once the horses had begun to graze, a single man could keep them there, unless there was a thunderstorm with lightning. As they passed, Arsène still mounted and waiting for his guard to take him down, noticed among the horseherd Toyamancare's Piarabo with a group of other ponies trailing him. Looking around him, he realized that the Osage men had chosen the handsomest horses to ride and had passed over his Comanche father's favorite, unaware of its swiftness. The sight aroused a flicker of hope. If he could in some manner extricate himself, catch and mount that pony, he might have a chance, he reasoned. The thought quickened his heartbeat.

He made the second observation during dusk while seated back from one of the cookfires, his ankles bound once again, his guard sleeping nearby. One of the wounded men, evidently shot in the shoulder, with a red hole in his back, staggered to the fire, flopped onto the ground, drank for a long while from a buffalo paunch, then attempted to cut meat from a bone he held. Seemingly too weak to accomplish this, he angrily tossed down his knife and chewed at the bone. Apparently unable to swallow what he had chewed, he spat it into the fire, and—as his alarmed companions called him—weakly, awkwardly rose and staggered away.

Arsène, his eyes first on the knife, then upon his young guard, managed quietly to crawl to the fire, kick the thing into the ashes, and kick dirt over those. He remained by the little fire, since his guard still slept, while his other captors seemed to be conferring at another, slightly larger fire, one of several. After a time the young Osage awoke. He came down to the fire, where he looked sharply at his prisoner, then sat down, appearing sleepy and bored. He too was wounded, dried blood, much of one ear gone. The youth seemed to disregard the pain. Though hampered by his bound wrists, Arsène, speaking slowly in French, asked the young warrior his name. The guard looked surprised, doubtful, and for a moment suspicious. Arsène knew the youth wished to kill him.

"Munnepuske."

"Qu'est-ce que ça veut dire?" asked Arsène, inquiring for the meaning of the name, hoping to engage this enemy in conversation and by so doing to render him less suspicious, less vigilant.

Munnepuske looked for a moment as if he would not respond. "Celui qui n'a pas peur," he declared proudly at last. Throwing a baleful look at the captive, he lay back, placed an arm over his eyes and, after a short while, indicated by his breathing that he slept once more, while flies circled or settled upon what remained of his ear.

Later several young men came and woke He-Who-Is-Not-Afraid. Arsène knew that they too wished to kill him. They stared at him and said, "pi-she."

"Means 'bad,'" said Antoine.

Arsène believed that their leaders would not permit his murder at present. But he suspected that the young men had decided to play with him. Yes, the fire. They would test him to see whether he was worth bothering with further. For a moment they talked. One youth held part of a dry branch in the fire. When it burned, he waved the flames around Arsène's head, his face, singeing his hair, which he could smell. After some moments, as the flames dwindled, the youth tossed it into the fire. Munnepuske then, using two twigs, withdrew a red, flaring coal from the fire, stood over him, dropped it upon his chest. His body jerked. The young warriors bent over him, scrutinizing his face. The pain had been intense, he said, as the coal burned through skin and settled deeper. He had grunted, knowing he must not cry out. His life, he believed, depended upon his enduring the pain. Next one, then the other, of the youths dropped a coal, first upon his chest, then upon his abdomen, while watching him carefully. He arched his back, panted, held his breath, panted and held his breath, holding back cries. Finally after a time the coals burned less intensely, though the pain remained. Soon Munnepuske approached again with a length of burning resinous branch which he had removed from the flames. He held it with an impassive expression above his victim's abdomen, lowering and raising it nonchalantly. He was watching his prisoner closely when a peremptory call came from a man with a deep voice. Munnepuske moved quickly away, throwing the firebrand back on the coals. It struck with an explosion of sparks.

"Tomorrow we will kill you," he called back with a satisfied look. The three young men departed rapidly, leaving Arsène alone with his pain and fear.

The council continued and continued. Night came on, the full moon dim behind clouds. At last he lay back exhausted, deciding he would pretend to sleep and hoping that when his captors believed him to be sleeping, they might let him lie where he was.

He woke later, at first confused, the pain still intense, not knowing where he was or how far he had dozed into the night. Munnepuske was gone with his fellows to a nearby fire where, from what Arsène could see, everyone slept. But there was a disturbance at a little distance. One of the wounded men had, it would seem, become delirious and was groaning and crying out at intervals, while his comrades, exhausted as they were, slept on. In addition, not far away wolves howled dolefully, evidently having smelled the odors of meat cooking in the camp. Overhead the moon was a pallid blur. A few flames flickered from the embers of the fire.

Arsène quickly dug out the knife. He first attempted to sever the strap around his wrists. He found it impossible, no matter what he did, to cut the leather while gripping the knife. Trying to cut while clamping the knife between his teeth also proved futile. Dropping the knife, he blew upon the coals of the fire and forced his wrists down upon them, raising them and placing them back time after time. But the effort proved excruciating, with the strap too tough to more than darken. Meanwhile the sounds of the wounded, possibly dying, warrior had become increasingly distressing to him. As his own frustration increased and verged upon despair the sounds of another man's agony seemed to prefigure the cries he might himself soon be making. Strangely he felt pity at such extreme suffering, even by an enemy, but tried to ignore both the sound and the emotion, which weakened him.

Beginning to be desperate, he rolled upon his side and, drawing up his legs, managed to sever the rawhide strips binding his ankles. He sat up and tried to secure the knife between his feet and cut with it, but the blade pulled loose at each attempt. He told us that then, weak as he was, he felt near to crying like a child. Fumbling with the knife, he dropped it into the final flickering of the fire and burned his fingers retrieving it. His chest, abdomen, and wrists hurt greatly, his head ached. He did not believe he was sufficiently strong to go into the meadow, avoid the horseguard, catch and mount Piarabo, and ride away. There was an alternative remaining though. He thought of plunging the blade between his ribs into his heart. At that moment he felt so certain of approaching death that he began quietly singing his death song, a murmuring absorbed by the noise of the delirious warrior and the nearby howling of wolves.

After a time though, suddenly furious at himself for giving in, he began struggling to his feet, intending to try, with a final effort, to catch the horse. Abruptly a hand seized him from behind and raised him to his feet by his scalplock. He dropped the knife as his head was yanked backward and he felt another blade keen at his throat.

"He held me like that for a long time," explained Arsène, as we rode along, side by side, Antoine riding and listening intently on his other side. "I believe he was trying to decide whether to kill me or not. The blade would press, then draw back, again and again. Blood ran down my neck. If I'd flinched or begged, I think he would have cut my throat. But I didn't move, except my eyes." No one was stirring in the campground, which lay quiet finally in the light of a moon which suddenly gleamed through a crack between clouds, he said. Involuntarily, at last, he gave a faint cry, gasping in pain from the pull on his hair and the cramped position of his neck.

As he told the remainder, he kept clearing his throat, speaking with harsh emotion:

"Ferme ta gueule!" The Buffalo whispered, commanding "silence," while simultaneously starting violently, with a grunt, and as he did so slackening the scalplock.

Arsène straightened and saw that a part of his shadow was assuming a series of running shapes. Unlike anything he had seen before, it had taken the successive forms of wolves, black shapes which, in effect, poured out of the dark and ran away, a small pack. When they ran across grass they were supple black silhouettes, but when they chased through the shadows of trees their shapes became silver, the color of the moon. Yet the last wolf silhouette pivoted from under a great tree and circled, silver to black, leaving the others, as if this splinter of the soul, or whatever it was, had changed its wish, racing back to Arsène's actual shadow and submerging—or as it were—dissolving, within it.

"Sacré..." exclaimed The Buffalo. His eyes opened fully. "Nom de Dieu! Tu as du pouvoir. Où as-tu appris ça?" He crossed himself. "Non, je'n te tuerai pas. Viens." Now evidently convinced that the man he held had supernatural power, he vowed not to kill him. Gripping both of Arsène's wrists, he sawed the buckskin apart, then kicked the strap and recovered knife into the ashes. The Buffalo propelled him by the arm from the guttering fire into the near dark. There in the strip of woods, Arsène tripped upon a prone figure wrapped in a blanket. He started violently and pulled back.

"Celui-là est mort," muttered The Buffalo, tugging him rapidly between trees to the edge of the meadow where the horses grazed. Still gripping Arsène's arm, he gestured at the distant silhouette of a horseman, slumped, with his head hanging, whispering as he gestured that the horseguard slept.

"Alors, mon sorcier, pas de maléfice, n'est-ce pas? Ne jettes pas un sort sur moi. Je t'ai sauvé la vie, n'est-ce pas? De plus—écoute, ceci est important—si tu vis, dis à Antoine Lefort qui t'a sauvé."

"Et qui êtes vous?" he asked, nodding in agreement to inform Antoine and not to lay a curse upon his interlocutor, who appeared now to regard him with awe.

"Dis lui que Gustave Barré t'a sauvé."

"Merci!" whispered Arsène to the dark into which the notorious trader had vanished. So it was Barré who had saved him! He shook his head. Still weak but feeling, with hope, renewed strength, he reflected momentarily, recalling that he wore only his moccasins and breechcloth. He crept back into the strip of trees, where he quickly located the corpse of the Osage. Already it stank of death. After an instant's hesitation, he unwrapped and rolled the body out of its sheath, threw the blanket over his shoulders, seized the dead man's knife, bowcase, and a length of horsehair rope. He made his way again into the dark meadow.

From his position at the edge of the woods, he gazed once more at the horseguard's drooping silhouette, then bending forward, glided as silently he could into the field, staggering a little, slipping between the ponies, which shifted as he drew near while continuing to graze. He moved carefully, humming and murmuring to them as he went, especially when passing their rumps. Venturing among them afoot was very dangerous. When alarmed, these half-wild animals might not only kick but bite and strike to the side with a front hoof. He lost time in seeking Toyamancare's pet but finally recognized the animal and called to it softly. Piarabo came to him, sniffing, nuzzling his hand. Clinging to its mane, or hanging an arm around its neck, he managed to knot the rope around its jaw, tossing the loose end over its back. Seizing the mane near the withers, he succeeded by a supreme effort in drawing himself upon the horse's back and in swinging his legs to either side. He reined the pony around, pressed its ribs, heading it westward. Hardly believing he was awake, he started it at a walk, lying forward upon its neck, under the clouded moon, between the shapes of grazing horses, back in the direction from which they had come, heading once more toward La Grande Forêt. The pony required no urging.

36

We traveled fast for the sizable party we were. Even the loose ponies walked or trotted briskly along, under the direction of their Comanche herders, as if they too were aware we were moving toward their home range. Except for Arsène's account I remember little of our return trip, riding at first through La Grande Forêt, its undulating hills marked by intermittent bands of dark, green-leafed oak, interspersed by occasional grassy valleys and scalloped by wooded arroyos and ravines, some containing temporary creeks, others mere rivulets, or—more often—dry runnels. We turned our horse's heads south at its western verge and continued, crossing with ease or difficulties the Cimarron, the Río Nutrio, the Canadian, until we reached the Washita and followed its banks along its southward course.

The single incident that clings in my memory, strangely, is a hunt by actual wolves. Up to that time I had of course seen many wolves and many deer. I had watched wolves seize a crippled buffalo calf which could not run with its gang of grown bison. But I had never witnessed a successful deer hunt by those remarkable, clever canids. We were upon an expanse of rolling prairie, with its short grass and lack of brush and trees affording clear views, when we all at once perceived, from our hill at a little distance, seven white wolves in pursuit of a magnificent buck, all running at great speed. They evidently did not see us. The buck was plainly tiring, while the pack continued to gain upon it. At last, when the wolves were leaping, snapping to sever its hamstrings, the animal dove down the bank of an arroyo. There as we could see, the buck was overpowered, briefly thrashing its antlers and front hoofs, and attempting at once to fight and leap free, with wolves at its neck and flanks. Almost instantly though, it was torn down, quickly vanishing, still struggling, beneath the bodies of the wolves ripping it apart, devouring it alive. For some curious reason this hunt, entirely as intended by Nature, or even by Providence, as many would have it, made an impression upon me which I have not forgotten. Why, I cannot tell you. But I recall that at the time I remarked upon it to Arsène, riding beside me.

"That's what I thought I was," he said, reflecting, "a wolf."

"But no longer?"

"No, I admire wolves. They're like us, our relatives. But no longer."

"And the witching? Your shadow? Still bothering you?"

"No. I haven't had it since that night. It's stopped."

I smiled. "You'll have to tell El Chamaco when we get back. Tell him he can keep his umbrella."

"Yes." He paused. We rode in silence for a time. "But I did have a bad—a strange—dream a few nights ago."

"Oh?"

"You know, dreams are important to us. Nothing to do really with the witching. But it was strange."

"Well?"

"I told you about Cáco, the old woman. They killed her when they killed..." He swallowed. "She looked horrible, like a corpse. But with tears running... She was talking to me. But I couldn't understand... Couldn't hear anything she said." He paused, swallowing again. "You know she'd been holding one of my boys, when..."

"Yes. Go on."

He cleared his throat. "But here's the strange part. She wasn't speaking with her mouth."

"No? What do you mean?"

"No. There was no blood. But her throat under her jaw was open. Her neck. A black hole. She was talking through that gap, two flaps of skin, above and below, like lips, and all the time crying. It was horrible, and I was weeping myself. Then I grabbed her and pressed her to me and said, "Stop, stop, you can be my grandmother. Stop, please stop." His face flushed, he cleared his throat and laughed roughly: "Infantile, no? Doesn't make any sense. Isn't that a strange dream, Jean-Pierre?"

I had to agree that it was. I turned my head so as not to see the tears in his eyes.

On another of his good days, when his headaches relented, Arsène told us of reining in near the summit of a hill on the morning of his flight, among a clump of trees, and looking back. He was sure he was being followed, since he had from time to time heard hoofbeats behind him during the night, when he had ridden swiftly under a veiled moon, slowing periodically so as to rest his horse. To his surprise he made out in a brown meadow far back the little group of loose horses which had kept upon his and Piarabo's trail. He was relieved at this knowledge. But farther, far behind the meadow, and several tracts of trees, he saw three horsemen, whom he knew to be Osage. He was surprised to see that they were pursuing two horses, apparently attempting to add them to the little herd they had already retrieved. He started off again, weak, hot, and thirsty, dozing intermittently, giving the pony its head.

The day went by, he told us, with the pony choosing its own gait, sometimes walking or trotting, sometimes moving at an easy lope. His head aching badly, Arsène rode by instinct, clinging to the mane, merely staying on, his eyes sometimes shut. Later in the day he became aware that Piarabo had stopped and was grazing. They were in a dell with a creek, green by its edge. He said he was so weak he feared that if he should dismount he would be unable to climb again upon his horse. Yet his thirst and the sight of the clear stream drove him to do so. Half-falling from the pony, he crawled to the creek and let his face slip into the water. He drank his fill, prostrate in the grass for what seemed a long time, falling asleep and waking and sleeping again.

The sky was tinged pink when he woke. He sat up, quietly sang two of his medicine songs, prayed to his guardian spirit. Afterward he was stronger, he said, and managed to stand, stagger to the pony and, after leaning upon it a moment, to clamber upon its back. He rode off into the woods, still giving the animal its head between the trees upon a sometimes vague trail. The sky had grown dark and a big moon had risen when he realized he had left the dead man's bowcase, with its bow and arrows, behind at the creek. He should have despaired then, he told us. He dared not risk going back. He was hundreds of leagues from his people without food and, now, with no means of hunting or even of defending himself except for the dead man's knife. This, he said, he intended to use against himself if necessary. But he insisted he was tranquil, almost confident and unconcerned, simply riding along without thinking about what would happen. He would not die by Osage fire. He did not fear death. He believed he would live. He was thinking a long time of Taoinan, he told us, and of his two fathers, when a big owl hooted, "hoo, hoo-oo, hoo, hoo," a deep-voiced black shape in a tree above him when he passed. It flew after him from tree to tree for a time. After that, he said, he felt almost happy, so much more hopeful he was sure he would be saved.

After a time, going at a walk through the endless silvery woods, he fell asleep again. When he woke, he told us, he was riding out of a forest in a red sunrise. Some of the horses that had been following Piarabo had caught up with him and were grazing beside him on the prairie. He thought he saw horsemen with lances far ahead in the red light from the sky. The horsemen looked like Comanches, and he said to us, "Je croyais que vous étiez tous irréel, une vision donc," and he shut his eyes to see whether we were still there in his head. We were not, but it was restful in the dark, and the red light so painful, like his headache, that he dozed again, thinking that a vision of the People was a good sign. Then, he said, something was shaking his shoulder, and he heard my voice and thought it was still good medicine he was dreaming. Reluctantly he opened his eyes and was astonished to feel and see me rocking his shoulder.

"What are you doing here, Jean-Pierre?" he quoted, laughing at himself. He could laugh about it now. Even to me it was amusing. We had left La Grande Forêt far behind, crossed the Río Nutrio, and were riding for a time southward along the Canadian side by side. There was the flow of splashing, sparkling ripples. The two horses liked each other, Piarabo and my mare, and walked along contentedly. Our cavalcade was placid. Antoine was ahead, riding beside Deer's-Ears. On our long journey the two men had become friends, although they rarely spoke. And Arsène looked well. He was feeling well at that moment, without a headache, his mind clear. We rode along quietly. But I had to ask two questions:

"Since the witching stopped, have you had any more trouble with pain...stiffness, your joints?"

"No. Since that night, nothing at all."

"Good," I said. "Another thing. I'm curious. Why do you think Barré decided not to kill you? Freed you instead?"

He frowned, considering. "I don't know. I think at first, it was the witching, my shadow, the wolves. He thought I had the power to put a curse on him. But also it had to do with Antoine. That's why he did it. Not for me."

"I've never seen Antoine so troubled by anything. He loathes the man. He's happy for you, of course, but he can't understand it."

The days were hot in mid-August, with smoke in the sky to the north. There had been thundershowers over scattered parts of the prairie. Other portions had remained parched. Possibly the fires had been ignited by lightning. Or, although the season was early, possibly by Indian hunters. Antoine thought by Pawnees. In any event the smoke, brought to us by a west wind, blurred slightly the wavering outlines of hills and occasional clumps of trees, and we could sniff it in the air. Travel was hot and monotonous. Anything that broke the tedium was welcome.

I recall one afternoon all of us laughing—Comanches and traders alike—at a commonplace event that, as it happened, evolved into what many among the People came to believe an instance of <u>Puha</u>. We laughed because at the head of the column, riding beside Toyamancare, Sees-Fire, his mouth open, had gagged and choked on swallowing a fly. One of the big ones that annoy the horses, it seemed. The news passed instantly down the line, until all of us were laughing at this trifling incident. But as we learned a moment later, as soon as he had recovered his breath, Sees-Fire had begun angrily to chide his friends for their mirth—when abruptly he had stopped, on noticing their surprised expressions. He too then realized, even as he digested the fly, that he had been speaking. Speaking! All of us in the cavalcade hailed the recovery of his voice, an event accepted by his friends as akin, in their view of things, to a little miracle, while others of us considered it at the least a fortunate accident.

The monotony broken, and the question of the miraculous raised, I ventured to ask Arsène a question which had lain restive in my mind since his capture. He was riding beside me, still smiling at Sees-Fire's mishap, as well as from pleasure at his friend's recovery of his voice—the voice he had lost after Taoinan's death.

"Tell me. I'm curious. I've been wanting to ask you."

"Yes."

"When you were a captive, did you pray?"

He appeared surprised at the question. "Of course."

"To...the Supreme One?"

"No, he's too far away. Behind the sun."

"To whom, then?"

"My Animal Spirit. I made medicine to my Animal Spirit."

I was silent for a while. "Would you mind telling me...who is your animal spirit?"

He considered for a moment, his head down. He looked around us. No other horseman was near. "It's a secret. I don't want to lose Puha. But you won't tell, will you?"

"Of course not."

"You're like my brother, so I think it's all right

Riding side by side within the long cavalcade under a blazing sun in a pale blue sky across the prairie, he told me about his sacred Animal Spirit, his Medicine:

It was immediately after he had led the horse-stealing foray that his Comanche father, Big-Mountain, decided he was now a warrior and must, for his protection, seek his Animal Spirit. He was first instructed by the band Puhahante, or medicine man. Soon afterward he went out one windy morning, he said, carrying his buffalo robe over his shoulder and his pipe and flints in his hand. By this time he was accustomed to most weather and was comfortable in breechclout and moccasins. Since much of the nearby prairie was flat, he had decided on the single hill within sight of the camp, climbing to its summit from the east side. Four times he paused to light his pipe, as told to do, smoke and pray to the spirits for Puha, power. At the top he lay down his robe and seated himself where he could not see the camp with its tepees, tiny horses and people. That night, doubtful and worried he might be an exception to born Comanche seekers, he lay loosely bundled in the buffalo robe, keeping his head covered as directed. That requirement, to him the most difficult of his instructions, gave him little trouble the first night, although the fluttering of part of his robe in the wind and the hiss of the wind in the grass and in the rattle of leaves from a nearby shrub made him start several times.

The second night was worse, the third worse than that, the fourth worst of all. At the beginning he had been tired from his preparations and his apprehension, so weary that after a wakeful beginning he had slept gratefully and peacefully. But the third and fourth nights he seemed not to sleep at all. Hunger, mild at the beginning, had begun to torment him. Then, more difficult, were the little sounds he began hearing about him, as if some animal, or animals, were creeping close by. He seemed to feel something very near gazing at him, perhaps sniffing him. He thought once he felt a warm breath that stank like carrion. He had found it hard not to raise his head from its hairy tent, sit up, and stare into the near dark to see if it were not a cougar (toyarohco) or bear (guasápe) standing over him. Yet he had forced himself to keep his head down, believing he must prove worthy of power, surmising that perhaps the spirits to whom he prayed were testing him and that, as the Puhahante had warned him, all his preparations and prayers would be lost if he should sit up or raise his head from its buffalo robe cover before his guardian spirit came.

The fourth and final night, though, it was not large beasts or reptiles he feared. Half-starved and exhausted, he seemed to sense the intangible presence of spirits gathered over and about his buffalo robe. But eventually dozing, he restlessly shifted a little, and started, certain that something had moved near his face, in fact under his head covering. Now frozen, he felt something softly brush his cheek, soft as...feathers. Stiff with terror, he felt the pressure of something hard as bone—or perhaps a beak?—against his temple by that ear.

"Buenas noches, blanco," whispered a husky voice. "Were you a Spaniard before you came to the People? Please tell me."

"Non, non," he managed to squeeze out of his chest. "J'étais Français auparavant."

"Ah, pardon. Très bien. Speak up," the voice went on in French. "Please look at me. I will be your guardian spirit."

Terrified as he was, Arsène moved his cramped neck. The robe slipped completely from his head. He stared. Standing on its talons and little legs, leaning its round, neckless head, with its two erect tufts, close to his nose, was a big horned-owl. Its yellow eyes, round, unblinking and enormous, gazed steadily into his. "But...but?" he stammered. "Piamupitz... is he? No, no, of course not. Pardon. Excuse me. I mean..."

"Ecoute, young man. Everything has its opposite. We all have relatives we're ashamed of. He's a freak, a monster. We don't acknowledge him. He's not one of us."

Arsène was shivering uncontrollably. "You're not here to tell me...that I'm?"

"Yes. I know, I know," the voice floated out. "No. Not at all. Don't be afraid. The People believe we big owls are messengers of death. Partly true. To them sometimes we are. But you're a whiteman, tabebo. A quite different culture. We're symbols of wisdom to you. Voltaire a dit ça? Non, je ne crois pas." The bird chuckled, a sound like the rustle of dry leaves. "But flattering, don't you think? I heard your prayer. I listen to all of them, you know. I like your attitude. Something different. So I decided to be your friend, your Animal Spirit. A new experience for me. Call when you need me. Donc, au revoir, jeune homme." With a huge spreading and silent fanning and lifting of wings the owl slowly rose and vanished into black night.

Though mystified, Arsène almost collapsed with relief. He'd really feared no spirit would come. So that's how it was! He now had an animal spirit. He wondered if all of them were as odd as his. To his surprise he found himself exhausted and so sleepy he could not hold his head up nor keep his eyes open. He wondered if he'd been dozing. With a single glance around, and seeing nothing but the shapes of trees and shrubs vaguely swaying in the breeze, he rolled back into his robe, covered his head, and lapsed into a dreamless sleep.

"And that's how I got my medicine. And this time when I prayed, it saved me."

I thought about this, impressed by his conviction, riding along afterward in silence, struck by his unusual vision. For that must have been what it was, a dream or a vision. No? So his medicine supposedly came from the great horned owl. Maybe so. Why not? I did not think of his belief as superstition, you understand. One man's belief is another's superstition, and vice versa. Since history's beginning, men have believed everything. Been willing to die for their convictions, no matter how strange. And more than anything been eager to kill for them.

A few days later the weather cooled. It was a fine fresh morning. We were now able to make out the distant pale mountains into one of whose canyons we were to descend and rejoin the People. We were riding along in silence, when my self-styled primo, and Arsène's father-in-law, Bearbird, fell back and rode on Arsène's far side. After greeting us, he too rode quietly for a time, the plumes of his hat bobbing to the horse's walk. Once more I studied the hat that was fixed firmly over his loose black hair on the right side. He had cut off the left side in mourning. Three-cornered, with red plumes, it was undoubtedly one of the gifts presented from time to time, sometimes with full uniforms, by Spanish officials to important chiefs and warriors. His expression was melancholy, more thoughtful than usual. He was of course grieving for his daughters and a grandson, although he had two grown sons, respected warriors, who had survived.

"You freed that Osage," he said at last to Arsène, not as an accusation but as a statement.

"Yes, I did."

"They don't like that. But if he was valiant, I think it was all right. Yes, it was all right."

I was surprised to hear him distinguish between the others and himself. Usually it was "we."

"Good."

"Do you want to be peace chief?"

Arsène looked startled. "Not now. Maybe when I'm old. Why?"

"I think you'll be civil chief someday. And my grandsons, your sons, will be great warriors. You can honor them, make them part of your bodyguard."

"Well, if it should happen, that would be good."

Shortly, saying nothing more, Bearbird trotted away, joining the warriors at the foremost of our caravan.

Arsène regarded me at first with a puzzled, humorous look, then relapsed into silence. Grieving again? I thought so. No doubt the words of his father-in-law brought to mind again his murdered wives and son. He maintained this mood for the remainder of the afternoon, remaining wrapped in silence until the end of that day's march.

In the morning two days later we arrived, still following the river, at the canyon where the band was camped. From the ridge where we had halted we could look down upon the tepees, the tiny figures of people and a few horses, all in a great meadow near the Washita. Toyamancare sent the boy down to the camp with the news of our arrival, while we dismounted and prepared for our triumphal return. Arsène, embarrassed by his black stubble of a tabebo, also spoke to the boy, ordering that he send Sehêbi immediately to him with his soap and razor. Although the People would still be mourning their dead, the fact of vengeance accomplished, even if signified by a single scalp, would be a cause for triumphant celebration—as was of course our unexpected rescue of Ah-mah-bah-tay.

Meanwhile we all bathed in the river's shallows. The engagés and I put on whatever clean clothing we had thought to bring, most of us little or nothing, while the Comanches, some using trade mirrors, applied paint and dressed in their best leggings, with a few in fringed warshirts. Arsène, like the other warriors, was rubbing his horse with grass to make him shine. But Piarabo was, even in summer, a shaggy, unkempt beast and not much could be done with his appearance. His virtues were all under the hide. Gazing down at the encampment, I could see small figures running about, horses being caught. The feelings of excitement there were doubtless equal to those that all of us were concealing, I suspected, watching several horsemen from the camp begin to gallop up the hill toward us. I turned away to assist Arsène in fastening an eagle feather, offered him by Big-Mountain, into his hair. This act was complicated by his half-bare head and his healing, but still wide, wound. I had succeeded in tying the big feather in his scalplock when three horsemen dashed up onto the ridge among us, their horses blowing, the riders shouting with joy. One of them rode to us, and slipped from her one-eared pony. It was Hélène-Eulalie, regarding first Arsène, then me, with tears in her eyes, his razor in her hand. I jumped forward and embraced her fiercely.

I am one of those who expect things to end badly. Indeed such attempted rescues against all odds usually do. But sometimes on extremely rare occasions—or so it seems to me—they do not. There are such occasions. In my heart, I really did not believe it before.

This was one of them. Nobody had expected us to return with Ah-mah-bah-tay. Indeed we had not, in our own hearts, expected to do so. But somehow, by an unusual concatenation of events, we had been able to restore him to his people. The camp below was already wild with joy, according to Hélène-Eulalie. There would be a scalp dance tonight, and perhaps for several nights more.

People had feared that both our parties were dead. Now already they were crediting Red-Woman for saving us all, owing to his great newfound Puha. For it was he, they believed, who had sent the wolf, Piaisa, to turn back Toyamancare and his warparty. They even thought he had sent the big fly to bring back Sees-Fire's voice. Red-Woman soon became known among the People as a great Puhahante, medicine man.

Perhaps they were right. Who knows? I do not, in general, believe in miracles. My private opinion was that a male wolf with a den and mate with pups nearby was attempting to turn Toyamancare and his warriors away from them. Then again, if the Comanche warparty had proceeded they might indeed have all been killed, either by the Pawnees on the Platte or farther north by the Panismahas on the Loup, or Wolf, River. Perhaps Piaisa did save them from death. Who knows? At any rate, I said nothing. Why should I have? There is a time for jubilation and no matter what was the cause of Arsène's and our survival, I rejoiced with the rest.

Women of the band paraded out from the camp to meet us, singing and led by She-Scolds-Her-Dogs carrying a lance. We wound down the hillside in a stately procession, with Beetle foremost, proudly gripping his scalp-bearing lance. He was followed by Big-Mountain, Sees-Fire, and Ah-mah-bah-tay, riding side by side. Arsène, shaved and painted, still wore the death-stinking red blanket stripped from the Osage corpse. The eagle feather dangled from his scalplock on his hairless side next to his red-and-yellow cheek. Behind them rode Bearbird and the other Comanche fighting men, then Lefort and I, followed by the trader-volunteers, and finally three Comanche herders with the recovered ponies. The women, then men, boys and girls, some few on horses, some afoot leaping and running, a few drumming, greeted us in a near-delirium of joy, all singing or crying out, even though some of the women, ashes on their heads, wearing leather rags, slashes and scabs on their legs and arms, were still mourning their dead. Among other individuals I observed the camp crier, El Chamaco, attempting to control his cavorting pinto pony while holding above his head with his free hand the opened black umbrella, and behind him I noticed the blind arrowmaker, Basin-Paunch, prancing and capering among the crowd, hand in hand with a little girl, surely his granddaughter. To add to the frenzy, the band's wolfdogs were racing among them, howling. I had never witnessed such a jubilant welcome, such exultation, such exuberance, nor heard such a deafening tumult.

37

It was a relief to reach our own camp. Our familiar tent was pitched among cotton trees at the meadow's edge by the river. The engagés proceeded to their own tents and wearily dismounted, prior to picketing their horses. Hélène-Eulalie, who had returned before us, stood with a smile before our tent. Ooa was standing beside her regarding us gravely with big eyes. The woman scarcely appeared pregnant. Even in dirty buckskins, hair disheveled, face and hands tanned by the sun, a few lines on her face, gray eyes alight with pleasure, she looked beautiful and desirable to me. Old Tournier, smiling gap-toothed, greeting Antoine, as Lefort continued on to their shared tent, then grasped the reins of my horse, as I too dismounted and went quickly to buss the child and to embrace Hélène-Eulalie once again.

Within the tent, tossing my hat on the ground, I could hear the little girl talking to a puppy outside. "What's she doing here?" I asked quietly. "Why isn't she with Sehêbi?"

"It's embarrassing. She's been living with me. She wants to go back with us—live with us."

"Live with us? Why?"

"She's frightened. Ever since the raid she's been having nightmares. She doesn't want to be with Sehêbi. She clings to me."

"She sleeps here?"

"Yes. She's very afraid."

We exchanged a long look.

"I'm sorry."

"So am I."

Again we embraced, a long kiss and embrace.

"I'll speak to Arsène," I said at last. "He'll have to work it out with Sehêbi. If it's even possible."

That evening the encampment vibrated with an excitement accentuated by boys racing their horses at the edge of camp and the pounding drums at the dancing ground. Tired from our journey, I had slept much of the afternoon. But Ooa, who had ventured to the dance circle with another child, informed me that men and boys had cut down and stripped a small tree and sunk it in the earth with the scalp attached at the center of the circle. She seemed unconcerned that the scalp was Osage. Men had also laid a large fire nearby. It had now been lighted. When the sky grew completely dark, with the moon in its last quarter over the eastern mountains and already rippling upon the Washita, reverberations of the drums swelled, suddenly combined with singing. We knew the dance had begun. The three of us went, threading between tepees, hurriedly dodging children and dogs, and stepping carefully with other late individuals, to the great fire illuminating the scalp-pole, the drummers and singers seated next to it, and the dancers themselves, shuffling in the firelight.

We stood watching for some time. The dancers were those men, and the boy too, who had constituted the war and rescue parties. Painted and wearing their finest garb, they stamped and shuffled the earth with moccasined feet, erect or bent, gesturing with bows, warclubs, or lances, from time to time raising their faces to emit warwhoops, as they circled the pole, while the singers sang with the drumming, and spectators occasionally joined the chorus.

"Look, there's Arsène," said Hélène-Eulalie, who stood with her fingers entwined with those of Ooa.

"Ohhh, look at his head," cried the child.

Bare-chested and wearing leggings and moccasins, Arsène was dressed like other dancers with, however, a striking warbonnet—feathers vertically arranged within and around a red headband, downy tufts at the tip of each. He wore it high and cocked to the side, above his wound. It was similar to the headdress which had been presented to Taoinan and discarded with the warchief's other belongings after his death. Arsène gripped, in his right hand, a bow and some arrows which he occasionally shook at the stars. We watched him circle innumerable times, dancing with effort and a somber expression, near Sees-Fire and Big-Mountain. But after a while when he passed the great fire, I began noticing that his wound was draining past his ear down his neck. Or was it sweat?

Twice more he danced by us until, abruptly, he began to stagger. Apparently losing his balance, he reeled and dropped to his knees. He remained, panting it seemed, on hands and knees, with lowered head. Instantly, while the drumming and singing continued uninterrupted, a figure broke from the spectators, rushed to him, seized him under the arms in an attempt to raise him and, evidently, to tug him from the dancing ground. It was Sehêbi. Her expression was alarmed, frantic. I was reminded of the time she had flung herself as desperately upon Taoinan's corpse. But Toyamancare and Sees-Fire, dancing nearby, quickly dragged her away and thrust her from the circle, next seizing Arsène, who seemed to be protesting, and helping him, while themselves still half-dancing, to the group of drummers and singers, seating him there near the fire in an honored position and rejoining the dancers. Apparently dizzy, Arsène shook his head again and again. He did not attempt to rise or to move back within the dance circle. I observed Sehêbi watching him. Her expression as she stood in the front row of spectators was one of mingled anxiety and great pride.

When we left the scalp dance in the middle of the night, the camp was still celebrating. The dancing would continue until dawn. Arsène would continue to sit with the drummers and singers until the end. There would be feasting. But I was weary, and we departed. In the tent, undressing in the dark and preparing to enter our buffalo robes, it turned out there was another inconvenience involved with the child. Ooa had a puppy, one of those of the black wolf or wolfdog, who had disappeared at the time of the Osage raid. Arsène's remaining two boys had taken the others. The puppy slept with the child. The little girl slept with Hélène-Eulalie. But Hélène-Eulalie would not permit the dog under the robe with the two of them, which was where the puppy was determined to be. So there was a scuffle, with the woman remonstrating, the child chiding the dog, and even a giggle, as the dog continued to try digging and burrowing within the robe until finally it gave up and slept, and Ooa quickly fell asleep.

Tired as I was, I could not sleep. After a while, I thought I sensed a restlessness in the other bed. "Are you awake?" I asked quietly.

"Yes. I can't sleep. You too?"

We lay there and had a long quiet discussion, as married people who have been separated for a time will do. She informed me, to my surprise and satisfaction, that during our absence, and even while traveling downriver, she and Tournier had carried on a modest trade for buffalo robes and peltry. Of course barter for horses had been impossible. I told her the details of our trip and of Arsène's captivity, escape, and rescue, omitting those of witchcraft which I had never told her, so as not to alarm her. I hardly believed them myself, although I had actually seen his shadow contort.

"It still astonishes me," she murmured. "After all Antoine told us about Barré— evidently an evil person—that he found it possible to free Arsène. Don't you think it's extraordinary?"

"Arsène thinks it's because...he wanted Antoine to owe him."

"Hmmm. That's part of it."

"Of course, it was a gamble, une affaire de chance. Because it must have seemed doubtful Arsène could actually escape. He must have concluded it was possible."

"Yes. That's right."

"Well, what do you think?"

"I think..." she said, and was silent. "I think it was Barré's pride. He reflected. If he'd murdered him, Antoine would never have known. But giving Arsène a chance to escape meant Antoine might know and would be obligated to Barré, and Barré could then feel superior to Antoine. Yes, that's it. Barré's pride saved Arsène."

I considered that an astute observation, an explanation though partial, by an astute woman who didn't know the entire story, and I was soon able to sleep. I slept comme une souche until dawn when I was having a pleasurable dream in which I was sharing my bed with Hélène-Eulalie. I was stroking, caressing the top of her head with increasing excitement when it occurred to me she had cut her hair, that it was now short. I was so surprised that I woke to discover I had been stroking the pup, which had moved upon my robe. There was also a disagreeable smell. Staring in the half-light, I saw that it had committed a misdemeanor, not, happily, upon my bed but upon the earth at a short distance. The animal slept soundly curled near my face. I left it there. I should have risen and removed its crotte, but I was still sleepy and, instead, rolled away from the dog. Shortly I drifted back to sleep, still breathing the stink and reflecting that if this were what marriage with children meant, I had perhaps been a fool to abandon the liberty of my former life for it.

By now I calculated the month to be early September. We were eager to leave. But there was, it seemed at first, a serious obstacle to our departure. Of the eight packhorses with which we had arrived, there remained but one. My wife and Tournier had borrowed two ponies from the People and had packed and led their own, walking down the river along with most of the women and older children, including Sehêbi and Ooa. I realized I would have to bargain for several ponies in order to transport our belongings and goods back to the post. But Toyamancare, Sees-Fire, Red-Woman and, indeed, Arsène himself, were too occupied for several days to be approached concerning this delicate subject. So we waited and traded with the Comanche men who had returned with us. Unfortunately trading for horses, the most valuable commodity for the firm, was impossible with the present scarcity of those animals among this band of the Numuhnuh.

But that morning we witnessed by chance a curious spectacle. A group of the People, no more than a dozen, passed us at a little distance, some mounted, many walking, with a few horses dragging heavily loaded travoises, with children and dogs beside or behind them. They made for the river and continued to descend along its bank. Antoine rose abruptly from his seat by the coals of our cookfire, hurried to my saddle, with its gear, and returned with my spyglass, which he trained upon the forlorn cavalcade.

"Who is it? Can you tell?"

"Tosapoy, or Chemin-Blanc. I thought it was."

"No. Really?"

"Please. Let me see," asked Hélène-Eulalie, rising, taking the small telescope that Antoine offered. "Yes, it is. With his new wife and sons and some of his relatives, but not all. His brothers are not with him."

"Not with him? May I look?" I could see, from the side, as they trailed down the Washita, a young girl riding directly behind the warchief. She was holding what appeared to be his shield and lance. The three older wives and others of the party rode behind her. Neither Red-Woman nor El Chamaco was present. Also absent were many of his relatives and many of those who had formerly constituted his faction. "I didn't know he'd married again. In fact, I haven't seen him since we got back."

"Yes, while you were all away. Sehêbi says the girl's meek. She'll never quarrel with him. She's proud to be married to a great warrior. It appears that her family is too."

I shrugged. "Chacun à son gout."

"He did save his wives and small children during the raid," observed Hélène-Eulalie. She did not mention Arsène.

It turned out that White-Road, after the death of his son, Ecopisura, had mourned for longer than was customary. Even after that he had continued to avoid other warriors, especially Arsène and Toyamancare. People suspected that he had remained with the band to see whether those two chiefs would return. Now since they had, he was departing with the individuals who chose to follow him to a different band of the Kotsoteka Comanches.

The scalp dance and feasting continued for three nights. Meanwhile Toyamancare, Red-Woman, and the lesser chiefs held councils determining honors for those who had merited them during the raid and our two expeditions. The first of these I learned was for Arsène, and not because of the false rumor, believed to have originated with Basin-Paunch and Sees-Fire, that Amabate's captor, wrongly called, 'Buffalo,' had actually been Piamupitz, the great cannibal man-owl, who had spared his prisoner because Ah-mah-bah-tay's Puha was so strong. No, the reason was that the People regard with respect and awe a warrior who, in effect, returns from the dead—that is, for example, a wounded man who is left apparently dying by his comrades and who recovers and eventually struggles back to the tribe. Although this was not precisely the case with Arsène, the chiefs considered that any warrior who was wounded and captured by an enemy, without having surrendered, and who managed to return alive merited equal respect. As a result he had been presented, for one thing, with the headdress similar to Taoinan's that I had seen at the scalp dance. In addition the leaders had given him a new name. He was no longer to be called, "Ah-mah-bah-tay," or "The-Headless-One," but "Tosaporua," or "White-Bear," meaning more accurately, I believe, the silver bear or the one we Americans name the "grizzly." Arsène, when I was able to speak with him privately within his tepee, was pleased but smiled at his new name, since he gave the entire credit for his survival to El Chamaco's witchcraft, Barré's decision, our efforts, and to his Animal Spirit.

On the fourth day I went to Arsène's lodge in early afternoon. Sehêbi was seated, cross-legged before a pot on a smoldering cookfire. At first she did not see me. One of the little naked boys was embracing her, arms around her neck, his back to me, while the other was scampering about, chasing, alternately, each of the two puppies. Her expression I can only describe as beatific, as she chuckled and stroked his hair and talked into his ear, until her eyes met mine, when it turned suspicious, cold. The other boy ceased his play and looked at me, a tabebo, shyly and with distrust, fingers in his mouth. Sehêbi appeared older and a little heavier, a mature woman. Her look had become sorrowful, reproachful, as she welcomed me, as formerly, in French. I surmised that she knew of Ooa's wishes and had probably informed Arsène.

"Is he awake?"

"Yes. Go in. I'll bring food."

Arsène greeted me gravely. He had been smoking, perhaps praying. Had I interrupted his mourning? Perhaps. He looked tired but well. His headwound, I noted, was closing and appeared to be healing. He passed me the pipe.

"So you're now White-Bear."

"Yes. But the same man. No better." He smiled. "I suppose you've come to ask about horses."

"How did you know?"

"Because you'll need them to get back." He continued to smile faintly. "I can't tell you now, but don't worry. You'll have horses."

"Because we must leave as soon as we can. As you know, we're already late. Your father will have been worrying."

"I know. Tomorrow you'll see."

"Good," I said, faltering a little. I could hear Sehêbi outside talking quietly, gently to the little boys. "I have another thing to ask you."

"Yes?"

"It's about the child—Ooa. She's been having bad dreams. She's very frightened. She doesn't want to stay here. She wants to go back with your cousin. She wants to live with us."

"Yes. Sehêbi told me."

"I'm sorry about that—for her."

"What does Hélène-Eulalie think?"

"She loves Ooa. She wants to raise her."

He bowed his head, pondering for a long time. Outside it had become entirely silent. "You too, Jean-Pierre? You want to take her? You'll have your own, you know."

"Yes, I want to take her."

Again he thought for a long moment, then raised his head. "Very well. You may take her. I have already talked to Sehêbi. She understands. She has our boys."

Shortly afterward, while Arsène and I were speaking once more of his rescue, Sehêbi entered the lodge with a pot of meat. She was pale and looked at me with a face of stone, as if I had pried a knife between her ribs into her back. But she placed the pot between us, saying nothing, and left.

"She heard us."

"She'll argue and weep again," he said, reaching into the pot with his knife for a gobbet. "But she'll have to accept it."

I ate quickly, thanked him, made an excuse, and departed. No sooner had I proceeded a short distance than I heard Sehêbi's raised voice coming from within the tepee, Arsène's calm reply. I hurried off guiltily, guiltily, feeling bad, as fast as I could walk.

That evening fat El Chamaco, camp crier, who now always called me "brother," came to our camp to inform us that in the morning, when we heard drumming, we were to come to the dancing ground—Kills-Far and me especially. There was to be a ceremony honoring us. With Arsène's remarks about horses in mind, I assured him we would be there. Meanwhile, we prepared our pack saddles and remaining trade goods, as well as the bales of robes and peltry, made them ready for departure. By a little after sunrise the following day, we had struck and packed the tents and were impatient to leave, lacking only the necessary horses. Then we sat by our subsiding cookfires, smoking and talking sporadically, waiting.

As soon as drumming began late that morning, most of us hurried to the dancing ground, with Tournier, my wife, and the child remaining to watch the camp and its array of baggage. As we arrived, both men and women were dancing. A gusty breeze had risen, and puffs of dust from their feet blew sometimes onto the spectators. The scalp pole still flew its black pennant, flapping like a crow's wing. Men and women had formed into two lines, confronting each other and dancing forward and backward in unison. Finally they made a circle and moved, dancing to the drums and singers, around the pole until, abruptly, with several thuds of the drums, it all stopped. The dance had ended.

Red-Woman, dressed in buckskin leggings and warshirt, made a speech. His appearance had altered greatly. Whereas before he had been tall and bony, he was now visibly shorter, with loose gray locks, a paunch, and wrinkled. As if physically diminished. His expression was dignified but mild. Very strange. I did not listen much. All I was able to think of were horses. I continued to look around, and none were in sight. Toyamancare, Arsène, and the other council members, dressed in their finery, stood by the drummers. Red-Woman went on commending the Comanche members of the warparty against the Panismahas, as well as Deer's-Ears and his volunteers who had accompanied us, naming and citing them individually and, it seemed, endlessly. But then he began to speak of us, the tabebos, the traders, and to praise us, especially Kills-Far, for having driven off the enemies with his rifle, and having shot plenty of them. He even praised me for having led the rescue party to deliver Ah-mah-bah-tay—now White-Bear—from his captors. For that, he proclaimed, they wished to honor us. We needed horses in order to return to our own country. They could see that. At these words I began listening carefully. They would now give us horses. There was a great pounding of the drums. Then, silence, and another pounding sound, that of hoofs.

Boys, riding at a lope, entered the dance circle between parted spectators and drew up before the drummers, singers and council members. Dismounting, they passed the reins first to Toyamancare, then to Arsène and the several other warchiefs and elders. In all there were seven healthy appearing ponies of all colors, including one, a beautiful pinto gelding, which I recognized as Toyamancare's own—the one, indeed, he had ridden while leading his war party. I regarded it in disbelief. Arsène, or White-Bear, led a fine blue roan to me and gave me the rein. I gazed at him and the other officials, stammering thanks. But no one was listening to me. Slowly Toyamancare came forward leading his pinto warhorse. While I watched in awe, he moved in a slow, stately manner to Antoine Lefort and, with a few words of praise and appreciation, handed him the rein. Antoine, who rarely showed emotion, appeared overcome. He struggled to say something but was plainly so moved he was unable to speak. Realizing that, standing drawn up, chest thrown out, Big-Mountain extended his hand. Lefort seized, gripped it, looking into the warchief's eyes, and shook it vigorously. It was a rare moment, and I seem to recall having tears in my own eyes as I looked from Toyamancare to Arsène, who stood before me, painted and dignified, yet amused at Lefort's and my consternation, eyes revealing his delight.

I made a brief speech, thanking the council and the People for their generosity, when they had lost so many ponies, in giving us not only the means to return to the post, but magnificent gifts to Kills-Far and me. There was a last, celebratory dance, again performed by both men and women, with the usual drumming and singing, which was to be followed by more feasting, to which we were invited. But I pleaded our need to saddle and pack the horses and prepare to depart. We were, in effect, excused and immediately proceeded to lead the two saddle horses and the others back to our camp, where the men quickly saddled and loaded those to serve as pack animals. Within a short time, we were ready, impatient to start off.

I then discovered that Hélène-Eulalie and the little girl were not with us, had disappeared. My wife's one-eared gelding was saddled, ready to go, as was my mare, a calm and gentle animal, which I had saddled for the child. The packhorses, in a line, occasionally pawing impatiently, restlessly switching their tails, stood with their packsaddles, ready to go. Old Tournier, who had taken a liking to the little girl, had sewn a bag for her puppy, a hide sack now attached to our one remaining original pack animal. Antoine and Tournier, along with the engagés, stood by, or near, their horses. I was becoming increasingly annoyed. My temper smoldering.

"Go," I said finally to Antoine. "You might as well go, and we'll catch up."

"Attend, les voilà."

Running toward us came Hélène-Eulalie and the child. Ooa carried a switch, and the puppy scampered before them, sometimes glancing back at her.

"Sorry," the woman gasped, as she mounted her horse. "We said goodby to Sehêbi."

I was too angry to respond.

Tournier scooped up the dog, placed it, yelping and struggling, in the sack, arranging it so that only its head protruded, while the little girl came to me for assistance in mounting.

"Elles pleuraient, toutes les deux," she said in a confidential tone, with a severe expression.

"But you didn't cry?"

"No, I don't cry."

I could picture the two women weeping in each others' arms. Sehêbi would, of course, I thought sourly, blame me for the loss of the child.

Moments later I mounted the handsome blue roan, which pranced and bucked once as I turned it but, after pressure on the reins and a lash with my quirt, quickly settled into a comfortable dogtrot. We had not reached the river, when Arsène joined us, riding a nondescript bay gelding. He, Hélène-Eulalie, and I rode side-by-side downstream, in and out of shadows, along the line of big trees for a time, mostly in silence. We were all feeling too emotional, I believe, at this parting to say much. Finally we embraced, and he started upstream.

"Come visit us," I called, when he had gone a little distance.

"I will," he called back.

"Soon! Your father wants to see you. Before...you know."

"Yes. I know. I will."

Turned in the saddle, I watched his back for a moment. He was still wearing the warbonnet.

I loped back to the head of the column beside Hélène-Eulalie. I looked at her, but her face was turned away. I was no longer angry. As I reached toward her to stroke her back, she leaned away from me. Again I twisted in the saddle, gazing at the cavalcade behind us. Antoine, seated straight on his new pinto, brought up the rear. Next came the engagés riding haphazardly by the packhorses, which walked along in a row, led by Henri Tournier. Foremost among the pack animals was our old sorrel. Beside him, and behind Tournier, was the child on the mare, riding gravely, regarding the pup, whose head, bobbing with the horse's gait, was facing her. After a long look back, I turned, watching sunlight on the splashing Washita and on the trail ahead, with the tracks and traces of White-Road's party, proceeding downstream. Shortly I reined the roan against the one-eared pony, reached, hung my hand on Hélène-Eulalie's far shoulder. She glanced at me and sighed. This time she leaned into me. We rode along like that for a while.

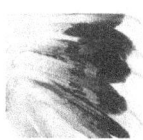

All I have written here happened long ago, when I was young. We are now Americans in reality, whereas formerly we might have been thought to be Spaniards or Frenchmen. This continent has changed. In 1800 we discovered that thanks to the might of Napoleon Bonaparte, Spain had returned La Louisiane to France. In 1803 that monarch sold it and us, as it were, to the United States of America. We began to live, without moving a pace, in the Territory of Orleans. Nine years later, still without budging, we became residents of the State of Louisiana, having joined the great union of American States, for whose liberty I fought briefly so long ago.

There are of course many of French and Spanish heritage among us, settlers or their progeny particularly, who are displeased by this arbitrary transformation of allegiance. But when they have had sufficient time, I believe they will be reconciled to a superior and more just form of government. As for my wife Hélène-Eulalie, and for me, we see our citizenship in the new nation as an honor and boon freeing us, momentarily at least, from the weight of history. There is still hope in this young country.

During this period, anno Domini 1821, the Great History has evolved, punctuated by Grand Events. Our petty history, too, has driven its path into that unknown we name the future. Looking back upon the past thirty-three years, I note how certain of the affairs of Europe have affected us even here, in a place so remote from its Grand Events. For instance our change from subjects of a monarchy to citizens of a republic. Others have scarcely mattered to us. For an approximate half of those years Napoleon Bonaparte, with his battles, conquests, aggrandizements and ultimate defeat was all the news—until his banishment to the island of St. Helena. Colonel de St. Maurice before his death followed the little emperor's career and campaigns with constant interest whenever the news arrived. For the rest of us, even Hélène-Eulalie, occupied as she was with children and household affairs, with Ooa and the two boys, these historic tides flowed too distantly to signify much. With a few exceptions, such as our local French patriots who puffed up at Napoleon's victories, the officers and men at the post as well as the populace were mostly as indifferent as we were to the foreign drama.

Occasionally the international turmoil all but touched us. We caught a whiff of gunpowder from the coast in General Jackson's victory over British troops in the battle of Nouvelle-Orléans in 1815, even though our war with England, begun in 1812, had officially concluded. As would be expected, we were quite aware of the treaty four years later between our nation and Spain fixing our western boundary with la Provincia de Tejas at the Sabine River. We were far more interested, however, in events on or beyond this frontier—viz., the earlier explorations of Captain Lewis and Lieutenant Clark to the Pacific. This bold venture much discomfited Spanish officials, as was demonstrated in 1806 by their dispatching Captain Francisco Viana with a large body of troops to La Rivière Rouge to turn back a second expedition dispatched by Mr. Jefferson, and departing from this very port, to explore the course of the stream deep into northern New Spain. With his superior force Captain Viana succeeded in turning that party back. Of course in our own Territory of Orleans about the same time General Wilkinson, Army of the United States, charged former Vice-President Burr—the killer of Mr. Hamilton—with a conspiracy to sever us from those states. Although the press made much of the trial, Burr was acquitted of treason.

The same year saw the repatriation of another American officer here at Fort Claiborne (formerly our Natchitoches Post) after a period of captivity by the Spaniards. The man was Lieutenant Z. M. Pike, about whom a fuss was deservedly made upon his safe return. I chuckled to learn that while the lieutenant had explored the great distances to the source of the Rio des Ark in the Stony Mountains, he had failed to accomplish one of his missions, namely to find and establish relations with the Comanche peoples, having traveled at first too far north, then as a prisoner too far south, of comanchería. Colonel de St. Maurice would have enjoyed conversing, assisted by an interpreter of course, with the young lieutenant. Unfortunately the old man had died...let me see, yes, three years before, in 1804, at the astonishing ripe age of 85. Appropriately perhaps, that was also the year that Clark and Lewis departed up the Missouri River, possibly signaling the start of the end of our entire frontier.

It was the same year that Arsène-Christophe made his last visit to his father. He certainly visited in 1804, some days after the colonel's death and seventeen years before his own. It was four autumns after our return from the Comanche camp in the mountains of the lower Washita. I am bound to mention though, in passing, that during our return journey when we had all but attained the post, a trifling incident occurred which just failed of making me a cripple. I had already discovered that my gift horse possessed a sense of humor. (I have found, by the way, that certain geldings like to jouer des farces, or to play what we Americans call, "practical jokes.") Why did Arsène give me such a beast? Because of course the Comanches castrate most of their stallions and ride geldings to the chase and to war, unlike some other tribes. Aside from his sense of humor the blue roan was a fine horse, provided that his rider was constantly alert. I mount him still for short distances. I first learned of his whimsical disposition through his habit of removing my hat when I was saddling him, or fumbling with his lips at the fringes of my buckskin hunting jacket, only to rip away a strand or two. Often when I first sat him in the morning, especially if the weather was chill, he would buck playfully until I slapped him with my quirt. Several times when I was relaxed in the saddle and turned to look back, for example, he would buck, on one occasion enough to loosen me. I should have been forewarned, but mostly he behaved well and I was careless.

We were only about a league from the post and fording a shallow but rocky creek. I had dropped a little behind to inspect a packhorse's cinch. In midstream I reached down to test that girth. Sensing me off-balance, he bucked, sending me flying. I landed on my back with a great splash—fortunately not on my head. As it was I struck rocks and for some moments was stunned with pain and unable to rise. It would have been comical but for that. As it was, presumably only the horse was amused. Hélène-Eulalie and Antoine reached me quickly and drew me to my feet. I tried to laugh and to conceal my pain. Even so, that pain quickly became so intense it compelled me to take to my bed for several days upon our return, and I have since that trifling incident suffered such grief with my back that to this day I can't endure to be in a saddle for more than two or three hours. My nights are sometimes troubled by similar pain. The worst of this is that our expedition to the Washita and the trip beyond became of necessity and much to my chagrin and sorrow the last expedition I was able to lead to the Comanches. Indeed it became my last journey to the prairie. I was exiled forevermore from that bracing place with its dangers and joys, as well as from the People's pastoral world of dominant horseman warriors, of the imagination, of hardship and delight, pleasure, pain and beauty.

I further recall at the time of that return twisting once—my quirt poised above my horse's flank—to watch Ooa riding beside Hélène-Eulalie as we passed Fort St. Jean Baptiste advancing toward the colonel's house. Ears back, the roan proceeded in a decorous manner. Perhaps because of my pain, I had a premonition at that moment that the old man had died during our prolonged absence. His heart. I could almost see Mlle. Bijou, clothed in black, appearing upon the front veranda as we approached to inform us of his death. And I foresaw the disappointment and sorrow in the eyes of the child at the news. And yet, as we drew near the building, as we actually approached the house, there upon the veranda before the open front door stood Monsieur de St. Maurice, leaning upon one cane while holding the other and simultaneously shielding his eyes from the sunlight, peering down the road at us. What he saw was our string of packhorses laden with bales and the bearded, shaggy engagés, bare-skinned under their hats and darker than Indians, riding here and there at one side or the other.

I was leading on the roan. Behind me rode Hélène-Eulalie and the child side by side with, behind them, the packhorse bearing the dog. Last were Lefort beside Henri Tournier. When quite near the house I observed that Monsieur was searching persistently with his eyes among us, apparently without finding the person whom he most wished to see. I realized as we turned away from the packtrain, waved, called out and rode to greet him that the missing person he had hoped to see was his son.

His consolation was the child. Ooa had climbed the steps behind us and approached him shyly with her arm and hand extended. Turning from Hélène-Eulalie and me, he smiled, bent down, supported by a single cane, grasped her hand and, leaning farther, kissed one cheek, then the other. After that they were often together as before, quietly, without much speech between them. Frequently she played almost silently with her dolls in his office, where I had noticed on first entering some days after my release from the worst pain that the skull formerly wedged between volumes on a shelf of his library had disappeared, its space occupied by books. Otherwise all was the same, from the colonel's escritoire to a cushioned chair where the cat had habitually curled. We learned, however, that the old cat slept there no more: he had sallied one night to hunt, as was his habit, and had never returned. The colonel had never found him, despite an energetic search by Mlle. Bijou.

Monsieur de St. Maurice's end came, as I have written, just four years after our return from the Washita. His death was sudden, although perhaps he had anticipated it. I suspect this because during the weeks before his fall he had spoken and speculated frequently about Arsène-Christophe. He was especially proud of that warchief's behavior, from our report, as a captive of and fugitive from the Osage warparty. Hélène-Eulalie and I realized that he longed to see his son, possibly for a last time, although he gave no hint of illness. Unfortunately we could provide no rational hope, aware as we were that Arsène might ride up any day that autumn of 1804 or fail to appear for another year or two. Still the old man hobbled daily around the veranda, taking care not to trip over the dog, which was a nuisance, as young animals can be. The colonel would halt on each turn around the porch and gaze down the road, as if looking for a painted rider bearing a lance and loping, with flying hair, toward the house on a pied pony. For him that rider never arrived.

It was on a Sunday morning, I believe, when we heard the sound of Monsieur de St. Maurice's collapse on the veranda. Mademoiselle Bijou had taken ten-year-old Ooa to church with her. My wife was playing the piano, profiting by the absence of our four-year-old first born, Roger-Philippe, who had also accompanied Mlle. Hélène-Eulalie was in the middle of a quiet passage, as I remember, when we heard the crash. The piano ceased. It seemed we knew simultaneously what had occurred. I was upstairs in my bedroom. I ran down the stairs and the hallway out the front door. But she had reached the colonel before me and was on her knees bending over his face. His eyes were closed. He was breathing irregularly. She was squeezing his wrist, feeling for his pulse.

"We must take him to his room," she said, turning to me. Her face was white, her eyes large. "Can we do it?"

"I think so."

She was strong. I took him under the arms, she beneath the legs. We managed without difficulty. His bones bore little flesh. He was light. We laid him in his bed, stripped him to his undergarments, and slipped a pillow under his head. He was scarcely breathing and unconscious, very pale.

"What shall we do?"

"Nothing," I said. "I'll go to the church and fetch the curé as soon as the service is over."

"Yes. That's good. I think he had a seizure." She drew a blanket up to his shoulders, turning to me again with a look of anguish. Tears were forming in her eyes. "Hurry back, will you, as soon as you can?"

I took her in my arms and pressed her to me, then quickly left the room and the house.

Monsieur de St. Maurice lingered for three days, watched continually by either Mademoiselle Bijou or my wife. It must not be thought, though, that I shirked my part in this melancholy duty. After the birth of Roger-Philippe, Hélène-Eulalie, occupied as she was with the child as well as with Ooa and household matters, had found little time to assist me with the affairs of the firm. As a result I spent much of each day working in my office in the town, mostly in ordering goods, or in related correspondence, and in overseeing such details of the business that our manager was too busy to consider. Beyond these duties I did my utmost for the stricken man.

An American infantry company had replaced our former militia at the post that summer. One of the older lieutenants, a drunkard with a face the color and texture of rare roastbeef, professed medical knowledge. Something of a buffoon, he nevertheless gave an impression that an intelligent though melancholy spirit lay beneath his tiresome impersonations and jocosity. I had sought out this officer that Sunday and fetched him to the colonel's bedside after the curé had departed. After examining the old man, the lieutenant told the three of us, Hélène-Eulalie, Mlle. Bijou, and me in his physician's pompous manner, that Monsieur was dying and that no treatment on earth would be of avail. This time there could be no doubt. We accepted that judgment, already apparent to us, and resigned ourselves to waiting.

Colonel de St. Maurice died on the third night after his fall. What French people call, "l'agonie," was brief my wife informed me. That came just before dawn, the mucous in the throat, convulsive gasps, a great heaving of the chest, then silence. She told me she went to the window, waiting for first light, and wept there a little. But in those hours of waiting, over the preceding nights and days, she had long since said goodbye and had already shed tears until her eyes were pink. We buried him that day in the churchyard after a service. He had not wished to have an elaborate, official funeral. We all wept, except for small Roger-Philippe, unable to understand what had happened. Ooa, also with red-rimmed eyes, silent and sad-faced, was annoyed by her dog and would not play with him all day. Hélène-Eulalie had adored her uncle. For me his death was like losing my father again. Mademoiselle Bijou, too, continued to grieve. In short, Monsieur de St. Maurice's absence left a vacuum in the house. There was a sense of its spirit missing.

Arsène arrived three days later. We were eating breakfast on a fine October morning, all of us except for Roger Philippe, who had eaten in the kitchen. We ate mostly in silence, each of us refraining from glancing at the empty chair at the table's head. We looked at each other, however, when we heard Ooa's dog howling, with brief barks, outside the front of the house.

"Is there somebody outside, I wonder?" said Hélène-Eulalie.

"He doesn't usually do that, unless it's a stranger," said Ooa—or Louise Marguérite de Saint-Aubin Fouquet—as my wife had named her, though we all persisted in calling her by her Comanche name, the little owl.

"I'm not expecting anyone," I said, setting down my napkin.

We heard the front door open abruptly, rapid footsteps coming down the hall. At that we stared at each other, startled, and at the doorway. I was halfway out of my chair when Arsène appeared, pausing within it. He wore his feathered headdress, making a striking figure as he stood, hesitant, an elktooth necklace dangling over the tatooed scar and burn traces on his chest. But he had not, for once, painted his face. He appeared travel-worn, as if he had not slept, and far older than his twenty-nine years.

"My father?" His eyes were fixed upon the empty chair.

We looked at him in consternation, momentarily speechless, searching for the proper words.

"I'm too late." He had read the truth in our faces. A look of extraordinary pain passed like a shadow across his features. "I already knew. He waited for me, didn't he? Too long."

Hélène-Eulalie sprang to her feet and went to him in three strides. Seizing his shoulders, she gazed into his eyes. She embraced him, drawing his head onto her shoulder, holding him. I was on my feet now. Ooa, her chair pushed back, was staring, big-eyed, open-mouthed. The kitchen door flung open. Roger Philippe trotted in, followed by Mlle. Bijou, who halted, her hands reaching for the child. My son drew back and gaped at his mother and the dark, feathered figure she was gripping to her. Arsène's back, his entire body, was shuddering. I realized he was weeping. My wife turned her head, signaling me to clear the room. Hurriedly, I ushered Mlle. and the children into the kitchen, following behind them. I halted by the shut kitchen door, stunned by the rapidity of these events. We then heard what could only be sobbing, a man's passionate grief. Mademoiselle Bijou and I looked at each other, astonished, appalled.

I took each child by the hand and led them out the back door. Together we walked down the path to the river, I ignoring my son's questions until we reached a grassy bank above the port. I seated myself and took the boy upon my lap, rubbing his back. Ooa's black dog joined us, wagging its tail, trying to climb upon the girl, who pushed it away. It lay down, pressing its jaw on her knee, staring up into her face. We sat together watching the loading and unloading of barges and pirogues and the sluggish, serpentine rhythm of the water, el Rio Colorado de Natchitoches, la Rivière Rouge, The Red River, easing down toward the city of Nouvelle-Orléans, to the gulf and open sea.

Despite the long journey he had made to reach us, Arsène remained only a few days. On the third day I was in the kitchen on some errand when Mademoiselle Bijou, who had been bent over the stove, straightened and turned to me with a hesitant expression, as if not sure whether to speak.

"What is it?"

"Oh, nothing important." Her features were wrinkled into an indecisive expression.

"Tell me, please."

"Well, it's Monsieur Arsène. It's very strange, that's all." She shook her head.

"Yes?"

"I went to church early yesterday morning…to light a candle and pray for…Monsieur." She hesitated and continued. "I rested there for a time upon my knees. Finally I got up and went to the door. I was about to go out when I saw Monsieur Arsène standing at his father's grave. His head was down, as if he were thinking. I didn't wish to disturb him, so I backed farther into the church and waited. I didn't think he'd be long." Again, she hesitated.

"Yes?"

"He wasn't. He looked around him as if to see if anybody was watching. He didn't see me. Suddenly he crossed himself. Yes, crossed himself."

I stared at her.

"He got down on his bare knees in the dirt there, Monsieur, lowered his head and joined his hands. He was praying, Monsieur. He was praying. I'm certain of that. Isn't that strange? I thought you would like to know, you who were so close to him when he was a boy."

"It is very strange. Thank you for telling me. Very odd. Yes, thank you."

During this brief visit Arsène did not, as he had before, change into European clothing. The weather was mild. He dressed as usual in little, all of the time, indoors or out. After his outburst of sorrow, however, he was genial to all of us. Warm and polite with Mlle. Bijou, gallant with his cousin, fraternal with me, cordial with the children. It was as if, for this visit he was behaving like his father—or better, perhaps as he believed his father would have wished him to behave, even while dressed, or undressed, as he was, like a courtly French gentleman or officer, even a member of the noblesse—but not altogether different, truth to tell, from his manner as a boy.

In particular during that visit, he haunted his father's office. Sometimes he sat in the colonel's chair for long periods, apparently thinking intently, gazing out the window. Sometimes he paced around that little library, occasionally withdrawing a book from a shelf, looking hard at its title, opening it and peering randomly at a page, then shutting and replacing it. At other times he would sit in the tomcat's cushioned seat, holding one of the old man's leather-bound books, with its gold-printed title, unopened in his hand, his back to the open door, staring out the window, sitting like this at times for hours. None of us disturbed him. In fact, Ooa, or Louise-Marguérite, who loved that office, would not enter when he was there. She recoiled from and avoided Arsène, as if he reminded her of all she wished to forget.

One night when I was up later than usual, reading by candlelight in the parlor, I passed by the office on my way to bolt the door. The room was lighted by a single candle. I saw Arsène's silhouette from the back. He was facing the window as usual. On my way returning down the hall I paused and entered, placing my own candle upon the colonel's escritoire.

"What are you reading?" I took the book from his hand. It was *Réflections ou Sentences et Maximes Morales* by La Rochefoucauld. I passed it back. "Can you still read?"

"Of course. It's difficult. I've lost the facility. But these are brief. I can make out most of them."

"What do you think of them?"

"They're diverting."

"Will you join me in a glass of your father's Armagnac?"

"I suppose so." He looked simultaneously annoyed and pleased, his thoughts interrupted. "Why not?"

From a cabinet in the corner, I poured a little of the brown-gold brandy into two small glasses and handed him one. "To your father's memory."

"Yes, to him."

I settled into the chair before the escritoire. "Tell me, I've been wondering. You said, when you first arrived, that you already knew he'd died—although you didn't quite. What did you mean?" It was a personal question, but we had usually been frank with each other.

He regarded me for a few moments, sipped from the glass. "Yes, I've been wanting to tell you, Jean-Pierre. It's hard to talk about. I had a dream." He lapsed into silence, looking down.

"You don't have to tell me. We can talk about something else. For instance, when you return, will you go back to the Pecos?"

He looked at me for a time with a faint smile. "You're always so delicate, Jean-Pierre. I appreciate that. No, I want to tell you. It was a very strange dream. I do have strange dreams, don't I? I wonder why. I was riding through a dark forest, no moon or stars. It was cold. I was shivering. I didn't know where I was going, but the horse seemed to know."

I leaned forward, looking at him encouragingly.

"Piarabo?"

"No. Just a horse." He paused, annoyed. "I saw a light before us. The horse was taking me toward it. I saw it was a fire. As we drew close, a big wind came up, shaking the branches around us. When we reached the fire, I saw it was blowing sparks into the air. I dismounted, wondering why all those sparks didn't set the woods on fire. But they didn't. I went to the fire, holding my hands out, rubbing them together to warm myself. Then I saw two eyes watching me from the dark. They were like green flints in the light of the fire. I shivered. 'Who are you watching me?' I asked.

"Tzena, the coyote, came a little way into the light, on the other side of the fire, where the sparks were blowing around him. He was a big male, as big as Piaisa. He just sat there and stared at me. 'What do you have to tell me, Tzena?'"

"Were you afraid?"

"Of course. *Your father is dead*, he said, in Taoinan's voice. He didn't open his mouth, but I heard him in my head. *He waited for you a long time. But you never came.*

"'That's true,' I cried out. I could suddenly feel the tears on my face, even in the dream. That's what I'd been afraid of. 'What should I do? What should I do?'

"Tzena's eyes never left mine. *You must go to where he is buried. You must pray there in the tabebo manner. Then you must decide again whether you will live as a tabebo, as he wished you to do, or as one of the People.*

"'Ne tzaré Nuhmuhnuh!' I cried out. 'You know I'm Comanche!' Then the wind blew so hard it snuffed the fire, sending sparks flying. It was very cold and they came down as flakes, snowing thickly. It was a black-and-white-dark, and I was staggering in the snow, like that time I was lost as a boy, bumping into trees. I don't remember any more." He took a sip from his glass. "That's how I knew. Wasn't it a strange dream, Jean-Pierre? What do you think?"

"Have you decided whether you'll come back to us? Everything is here for you. As you know, your father left you and Hélène-Eulalie almost everything."

"You know I'm a Comanche."

I finished my glass, setting it on the escritoire. "I know. That is a very strange dream, especially Taoinan's voice. Well, I must get to bed. The dream is simple. You've made your decision."

"Yes, I suppose that's all it is. It's true, I have. Why then, the dream?"

I stopped in the doorway and looked at him.

"But, you know," he said. "There were times I've envied my father's life."

"Why?" I asked.

He was silent, brooding, the candle guttering, the volume still in his hand, no longer

The-Headless-One but White-Bear, the Comanche chieftain. I left, carrying my candle down the hall, casting, as I climbed the stairs with it, a little nimbus of uncertain light.

While we were concluding breakfast in the morning, taking our last sips of coffee, Arsène told us he would depart the following day. Hélène-Eulalie immediately became pensive, fell silent for a time.

"Dear Arsène," she said at last. "I truly wish you would stay with us. We've talked of this over and over. But you insist you will not, and since you will not. You know your life is dangerous. Frankly, you could be killed at any time, and this house wouldn't even belong to us."

"To you," I quickly said.

"Don't be silly. No, Arsène, I don't mean to sound crass. But, you know, legally...our situation would be épouvantable. When we die, for example, Roger-Philippe would have no inheritance."

I was surprised. I remember her saying, "épouvantable." We had talked of this. Clearly it pained her to speak of it. But the woman was not sentimental. Though infinitely sympathetic, my wife has the mind of a realist.

Arsène smiled, amused at our distress. "You know I want none of this. What would I do with it? The house, the furniture, money? I know you would give me money any time, if you had any to give. I know you would take me in, if I should ever come back. But I never will, I promise you. Except to visit."

"I hope you'll visit us more often," she said, her voice breaking. "You do see, my dear cousin, don't you?"

"Of course I do," laughed Arsène. "You're making too much of this." His expression became grave. "But as for visiting more often, I don't know. It's terribly far. A hard trip. They've made me civil chief, peace chief. Red-Woman wants only to be Puhahante. So I have responsibilities. It's difficult to leave. You see?"

"I'd love to go out on the next trip with Antoine," I said, "and so would you, wouldn't you?"

Hélène-Eulalie shrugged helplessly.

"But with my back and the work and the children..." We gazed at each other, acknowledging the sad truth that our lives had greatly altered and that, in fact, if worst should come to the worst, we might never see him and he might never see us again. Meeting Arsène's eyes, I felt a chill in my chest. There was, for an instant, pain in his gaze.

"So," he said cheerfully. "There's a notaire in the village, isn't there? Get the papers, and I'll sign them. I'll go to the trading house with you, Jean-Pierre. I'll take some presents back." He looked from one to the other of us and laughed. "Don't look so solemn. I'll be back. Not right away. But I'll come back. I promise. And don't worry about me. I have, as Antoine says, la chance, no? I have Puha. So don't worry. We'll see each other again." He stood up from his chair. "Come, Jean-Pierre I'll ride to the village with you. How soon will you be ready?"

He departed at first light the following morning before we rose. I did not wish to see him go. We had embraced and said our farewells the previous evening. He departed doubtless leading his spare pony, which was packed with gifts and the belongings he cared to take. Those belongings consisted principally of two more pistols, with powder and shot, and his father's sword. In addition he took with him an English grammar and a French-English dictionary he had found in the colonel's bookcase. I had asked him,"Why?" Because, he told me, there were more and more Americans moving from the east to the frontier. He foresaw even then that he would have to speak and deal with them. He would be responsible for that. And he was correct. He was right, too, about another thing: we were to see each other again. Rarely, yes, but as it turned out, four more times.

39

Our commerce became increasingly uncertain after 1805, when the U.S. Government established a manufactory of Indian goods at Natchitoches. At first the tribes were loyal, but as the years passed and rival traders undersold us, it became more difficult to maintain a profitable business. The new competition, in any event, made my task more laborious, increasing the number of hours I was obliged to work. More responsibility shifted to Antoine Lefort, who continued to lead the annual expedition and to deal with the Indians, who respected and trusted him. The Pawnee-Piquées and other tribes of the Wichitan confederacy, in particular, as well as certain of the Comanche bands—including, of course, that of Arsène—preferred to deal with him rather than with our rivals. Indeed so did those Indians we Americans call, "Kioway," a smaller tribe which had concluded a treaty with the People in 1806 and become their allies about that time.

In 1808 our second son, Paul-Maurice, was born. It was the year Napoleon chose to occupy Spain, creating patriotic turmoil in New Spain. Antoine reported on his return from the prairie that the Pawnee-Piquées and Comanches had gathered a force to attack the Osages. He did not know the result of this campaign. He learned it, however, the following summer when he arrived at the Red River villages and was startled to find them burned and abandoned, the latter act apparently perpetrated by the Wichitan's Osage enemies. When Lefort located Toyamancare's and Arsène's band farther south on the Rio de los Brazos de Dios, he learned that the campaign had been successful in nearly destroying an Osage village, taking scalps and carrying off several women. But warriors of that people, craving retaliation and not finding it easy to locate roaming Comanche bands, had focused their vengeance upon the Pawnee-Piquées, some of whom had fled south to take refuge among their fellow Wichitans, the Tawakonis, while others had joined the Nuhmuhnuh. Never again would a trader find welcome or barter at the charred villages by the Rio Colorado de Natchitoches, la Rivière Rouge.

Arsène visited us again the following year, I believe it was. Yes, I remember it being the start of what is now called the Mexican War for Independence in 1810 between native-born patriots and royalist forces, or Criollos and Gachupines. Roger-Philippe must have been ten years old and Paul-Maurice two. I recall that the boys were at first frightened of, then fascinated by, their Comanche relative, whose rare visits they increasingly looked forward to.

Arsène did not come again for five years, reappearing, this time with Antoine, his traders, and a herd of horses in 1815, five months after the Battle of Nouvelle-Orléans. Hélène-Eulalie had just departed downriver with Ooa and the two boys. From Nouvelle-Orléans they were to board a vessel for Le Havre, France, the way being clear owing to the end of our war with England, as well as the restoration of Louis XVIII to the French throne. Although my wife had sworn never to return, the changed circumstances persuaded her to do so, her principal desire being to find an appropriate husband for Ooa, then at the advanced age, for a Louisiana demoiselle, of twenty-one years. Hélène-Eulalie was also determined to place Roger-Philippe, then fifteen, and Paul-Maurice, then seven, in an American school on the return trip, after introducing them to their French relatives in Paris. With this intent in mind, I had written my Uncle Elliott some months before, requesting that he find a good boarding school for them. In time I had received his reply, not only naming such an academy in Boston but promising to oversee and entertain the boys during the time they would be in New England. It was indeed a generous offer from my favorite uncle, as well as of course from his wife, my Aunt Priscilla. We accepted immediately, and I began in my reply, and in the ensuing correspondence, to resolve the details.

There was, nevertheless, the matter of money. Living upon the frontier as a célibataire, or unmarried man, and with my needs met by the generosity of Colonel de St. Maurice, I had rarely thought of money. Indeed I had entertained a certain contempt for it. But after my marriage and, especially, after children, I found myself thinking of little else. My wife, it is true, had arrived with a small inheritance from her father. She had inherited more with the colonel's death. Even I had inherited an interest in the firm of de St. Maurice et de St. Aubin. My resources along with my salary would have supported me amply had I not married. I had never regretted my marriage, however, the exchange of my narrow life for a fuller one with my beloved Hélène-Eulalie. But as Natchitoches itself changed, becoming more civilized, I came to believe that Civilization, like the new vessels propelled by steam, operated principally through the propulsive force of wealth. Travel for my three, boarding school for my sons, even a husband for Ooa all proved costly, keeping me at my desk for hours straining my wits to conceive of means to make the firm more profitable and ourselves more prosperous. Hélène-Eulalie, herself, paid for the travel and once in Paris, so she wrote me, even for Ooa's fashionable gowns. Out of pride, I vowed to repay her. Eventually I did.

But happily, acquiring a husband for Louise Marguérite proved an effortless task. From a bony figure of a little girl with an anxious, peaked face, she had grown into a slender, brown-skinned, quiet young woman with dark eyes and fine features. She had become, in short, a beauty, the belle of little Natchitoches. But this belle contrived, it seemed, to discourage rather than to attract suitors, whether American officers from the fort or the sons of planters along the river. She appeared actually to distrust the young men of this frontier, perhaps young men in general. For that reason Hélène-Eulalie, who, it must be said doted upon our adopted daughter, now a bright, sensitive young woman, determined to remove her from this place and bring her to one where she would encounter men of a more cultivated variety.

My wife succeeded brilliantly, as I had anticipated she would. Most gentlemen introduced to the girl in Paris were, as it happened, stunned by the exotic features and demeanor of this New World beauty, charmed by her lack of coquetry and by her frank, though reserved behavior. She married, as it turned out, a cultured widower, a relative of Hélène-Eulalie's, one according to my wife, able to provide for her and to appreciate her as far more than un beau objet.

But to return to Arsène's 1815 visit as well as the firm's and my need for money: after consulting with Antoine Lefort, we sat with Arsène in the colonel's office and discussed possibilities. Antoine suggested a plan which sounded practicable and appealed to all of us. In the end we adopted it. To begin with, Arsène would establish each year a rendezvous site where we would meet him for trade. He would invite other bands to attend. This alone would give us an advantage over our chief rivals, the American traders from the Natchitoches Indian manufactory, who had always to search out roaming bands each spring. Next, Arsène suggested a means of augmenting our trade of horses, the most profitable branch of our business. Our firm would equip several local mesteñeros, or mustang-catchers, while he provided young men to show them where they might find quantities of wild horses. These young Comanches would assist in capturing and breaking the ponies. A certain percentage of these horses would go to Big-Mountain and his people. The remainder would belong to de St. Maurice et de St. Aubin to be sold to buyers in the interior. We agreed upon the plan and, the following spring, put it into practice. A little to our surprise it proved to be an outstanding success. Big-Mountain and the Comanches were pleased. We and our buyers were delighted. Gratefully I looked forward to a succession of profitable years and an end to my worries about the firm's—and my own—fortunes. But fate, la malchance, intervened and our plan had to be abandoned the following year.

We learned in the winter and spring of 1816 that smallpox (la tásia) had struck the People and was said to have spread, or to be spreading, throughout comanchería. We worried, of course, about Toyamancare's and Arsène's band—and, especially, about Arsène himself. But earlier that winter we had learned from visiting Pawnee-Piquées that Toyamancare's band had vanished. There had been no word of them, and nobody knew where they were. Mademoiselle Bijou prayed for them in church. I worried and hoped. By 1817, the year that, to my great joy, my dear Hélène-Eulalie returned from France and New England, the news from the prairie was that—although entire bands had perished—the disease had subsided and that survivors of cette peste affreuse were recovering and beginning to return to their normal lives. But about Toyamancare's and Arsène band, Those-Who-Go-Far-Alone, we heard nothing. My wife, joyous and triumphant upon her return, having left Ooa well married and the boys in a good school, joined me now in wondering and worrying.

We heard nothing for two more years. Our anxiety had turned nearly to sad resignation. Antoine, on his trading trips, learned nothing from other Comanche bands. None of them had heard anything about Toyamancare's band since before the start of the epidemic. Perhaps, as some Comanches had suggested, his band had been one of those in which everybody had died. We had almost ceased to hope, occupied as we were with the struggling trading house and with our daily lives, when in the fall of 1819 we learned that Arsène lived.

Strangely I received the information indirectly from the American lieutenant with the whiskey sunburn. The man was something of a nuisance. He came frequently to the trading house and would lounge there until I appeared from my office. He was not only a drinker. He was a performer, a humorist, a mimic. Since I spoke English, when he was bored he sought me out, boring me in turn, exhaling his drunkard's breath at me, and wasting my time. But not on this occasion. I was behind the counter, standing by the clerk, and looking over an inventory list. The officer was telling me a drawn-out tale of Americans who had settled west of the frontier, illegally of course, in the vicinity of nearby Nacogdoches. Several of them, he said, were riding along the Camino Real one day, close to the town, seeking two of their horses suspected to have been stolen by the Wichitan Tawakonis. One of these squatters, for that is what the illegal settlers are called, was an itinerant preacher named McConnell. The lieutenant knew McConnell who, he had once told me, believed in a complicated theory that the Comanche people were really Jews, descendents of a lost tribe of Israel.

Well, drawled the officer, mimicking the squatters, these Americans trotted round a corner in the road and just about slammed into a party of Comanches, all painted up and armed with spears and bows and arrows and muskets. Well, they didn't look like they was on the warpath, and it was too late to run anyhow, so they just rode up to the leaders and asked if anybody spoke English. One of the lead Indians rode out, and McConnell held out his hand. This chief, all paint and feathers, shook it, then the hands of the others. The preacher asked if he spoke English.

"Poqito," the Indian said. "Little."

"Have you seen any Tawakonis? They stole our horses."

"No, no have seen no Tawakonis. No horses."

"Seen any other Indians?"

"No. No Indians."

"Well, I guess we'll just have to keep on looking, then. Thanks, chief. My name's McConnell. What's yours?"

"Como? What you say?"

"Your name? Who are you?"

"Me? I am the noble savage."

"What? What did you say?" McConnell couldn't believe he'd heard what he'd heard. "What did you say?"

With that this Indian puts one hand on his chest, with his lance and shield in the other, and declaims a poem, you know, in English—declaims:

"I am as free as Nature first made man,
Ere the base laws of servitude began,
When wild in woods the noble savage ran."

Can you beat that? McConnell nearly fell out of his saddle. The other men just stared, open-mouthed.

The lieutenant leaned back and laughed, his cheeks and purple nose redder than ever.

"Would you mind saying that again...chief?" McConnell asked. "I'm not sure I heard right. Yes, please, say it again."

◇◇◇◇◇◇◇◇◇◇◇◇◇◇◇◇◇◇◇◇◇◇◇◇

So the Indian puts his hand on his chest again, and declaims it again. This time the preacher listens carefully, and he memorizes it. Just like that. Memorizes it. I got it from him. Meanwhile, the other squatters are still staring, with their eyes bulging out of their heads, and with open mouths.

"Adieu, Messieurs," the Indian says, in French, without so much as a wink or a smirk, and something like, "Bun journy." And he rides off, with the others following. But—are you all right, Mr. Fouquet?"

The lieutenant ceased giggling and chuckling. He stared. It must have been my throat seizing spasmodically, choking me as I laughed and laughed. But that is how we learned Arsène was alive.

40

Arsène's stay was, as usual, brief. He had ridden in on a black gelding the week following his encounter with the Nacogdoches preacher. He came alone, leaving his party camped and trading near the settlement. We laughed, with Hélène-Eulalie, about his recitation to McConnell. But as we quickly discovered, he disliked the American squatters, saw them as a threat to his people. Meanwhile he told us how he and Toyamancare's band had survived the epidemic.

At first news of the disease he, as peace chief, had moved the band out of the region, riding toward Rio Pecos but stopping short of it at the great western wall broken by canyons. They had traveled as inconspicuously as possible, avoiding all the favorite camping spots where other Comanches might be found and successfully shunning other bands of the People. They had turned south at the wall and followed it until they reached a canyon with a stream running within it and with pasturage and firewood and more grass on the nearby prairie. They took refuge there, concealed themselves, sometimes moving to a new canyon when the firewood and grass gave out, but remaining in the vicinity, eating deer and wapiti and even ponies when there were no buffalo, lived among themselves isolated and hidden for three years. In the end they had emerged without having lost a single warrior, woman, or child to the tásia.

That autumn was mild. The pleasantest moments during Arsène's stay occurred during the evenings after we had eaten and Mlle. Bijou, bent and crippled with rheumatism, yet more determined than ever to rule the household, had cleared the table. Hélène-Eulalie, Arsène and I would move out upon the veranda, where we had placed chairs. We would chat quietly, with long silences, the black dog at her or my feet. On clear nights we would lean back and gaze at the stars.

"Anybody care for Armagnac?" I would sometimes ask.

Some evenings we did, some we did not. The light from the lamp in the hallway would glow at the open door, while that in the colonel's office would gleam out the window, enabling us to see each other's faces when we cared to make the effort. There were, of course, insects, always insects buzzing and whining, especially mosquitoes. But when the bugs became too insistent and we began slapping our hands and faces, Arsène would stuff and light his pipe—not a ceremonial pipe, but a pipe for enjoyment. He would puff for a time and pass it to me, and I would puff and pass it back.

Our conversations would begin idly with gossip of the post and town, sometimes turning to talk of those close to us, like Mademoiselle or Antoine. I recall Arsène remarking that Antoine seemed a happier man on this visit than he had appeared to be for a long time.

"You know why, don't you?" asked Hélène-Eulalie.

"Well, I heard Barré died."

"Killed by the Pawnees," I said. "That's part of it. Tell him."

"Did I ever mention Simone coming to me? Oh, some time back. Maybe before your last visit?"

"I don't think so."

"She was worried about him. He was so bothered by his debt to Barré. He could think of no way to repay him. She said it preyed on his mind. She was tired of hearing him talk about it. It was getting on her nerves. He was even talking about traveling to St. Louis and trying to find the man. Leaving her and the children in order to do so. What did I think she should do?"

"I'm sorry," murmured Arsène. "I never realized..."

"He wouldn't want you to know. It was between Barré and him. So I thought and thought. Finally I suggested that Antoine send up some very, very nice gift by, you understand, one of his Canadian friends going up the river. They all know each other, it seems. Someone among them could locate Barré and eventually get the present to him. And that would end the matter. Fini, and he could forget it."

"Did he?"

"Yes," I said. "But Barré died first."

"That really didn't matter. Antoine had made the gesture. Maybe Barré even heard about it before he died. You know how news travels. At any rate, it freed Antoine."

"What was the present?"

"We heard about an American gunsmith in New Orleans," I said. "Antoine went down. A few months later up the river came the most beautiful rifle you've ever seen. The man made it. Like Antoine's, only beautiful. Beautiful wood, ornate stock, fine steel. He sent it up with old Tournier. And I'm sure it'll come back down someday, either with Tournier or some other trader."

"And now Antoine's happy?" asked Arsène.

"Now Antoine's happy," said Hélène-Eulalie. "And so is Simone."

As the hour grew late, the topic would invariably turn to Arsène's annoyance at the American squatters in buckskins, those backwoodsmen who, with their families, were slyly invading la Provincia de Tejas, building their squalid cabins in the woods beyond the Sabine River and advancing slowly but persistently toward La Grande Forêt, La Grande Prairie, and comanchería, toward the People's buffalo range. Arsène compared them to grasshoppers, aahtaquine.

"They've already stolen the eastern part of this province."

"Why do you care?" Hélène-Eulalie said with a smile. "You're not a Spaniard. You might have been a Spanish officer, of course, but you didn't want to be."

"The Spanish officials in Béxar make no attempt to stop this invasion. What's the matter with them? They're going to lose the province. Can't they see that?"

"They can't get their own people to settle it," I reminded him.

"But why do you care?" Hélène-Eulalie insisted. "Surely you have enough space."

"I can see what's happening. Even Big-Mountain or Red-Woman can't see that. These people aren't like Spaniards or Frenchmen. They're lawless. They have no laws. Borders mean nothing to them. Did you ever consider, Jean-Pierre, that all those horses we sold you, and you sold to them—someday they'll ride them across our land? Maybe across our backs? We were fools."

"No. I never thought of that."

"Someday we'll be fighting them on the prairie, on our own land. Here, smoke."

"I wouldn't worry," laughed Hélène-Eulalie. "We Americans are convinced your country's only a big desert."

Arsène believed in the truth of his prediction. I could not see the future as clearly as he, nor was his cousin able to. But of course we now know that his premonition was well-founded. Of that last visit, however, what I remember most is his departure. He left before sunrise. Hélène-Eulalie had embraced him and said her farewell the previous evening. Still, she had intended to come down but failed to wake, an omission she always regretted. I, having an uneasy feeling, dressed in the dawn light, descended the stairway and went out the front door. He was holding his black horse about to mount but, seeing me, he turned and came toward me with a smile. In the wan light he looked far older than his.

"I've enjoyed this visit. You've made me feel like a civilized man."

It was an extremely strange thing for him to say. "You know you don't have to go. Or you can go and come back."

"To what, Jean-Pierre? To be a clerk in your store?"

"You know it's your store, if you want it."

"I don't want to leave the band. They're my people. I'm their Paraibo, their chief. I need them, they need me. I'm a Comanche, Jean-Pierre."

"What about Big-Mountain?"

"He's an old man. He leaves decisions to me now. Don't misunderstand me. It's a good life, mostly. I wouldn't want any other. It's that I worry about the future. I can see it coming. Nobody else can."

"You had a dream? A vision?"

"Perhaps." He smiled faintly, saying, "aahtaquine." Clearly he wished to quit the subject. I was surprised. But his expression had suddenly become jovial, mischievous. He had caught me gazing absentmindedly at the elktooth necklace, tatoo, and scars on his chest and abdomen. "So. you still think I'm a savage, don't you, Jean-Pierre?"

We were saying goodbye, standing facing each other, he holding the rein of his pony, both of us suddenly a little self-conscious, striving to be light-hearted, to keep our emotions in check.

Of course he knew I didn't. "Yes," I laughed. "But not ignoble."

"But you, Jean-Pierre," he said, still smiling, greatly amused, risk becoming..."

"What?"

He gave a wicked chuckle, his eyes laughing also. "You're so...comfortable. My cousin too."

"Tell me. What?"

"A domestic animal."

"Is that all?" I laughed. "Well, yes. I'd thought of that. Like an old horse, or an old dog with fleas. You're probably right. I'm enjoying domesticity. Maybe it's not as good as life for a noble savage—in summer. But it's good."

We both laughed, laughter tinged with melancholy. I remember sensing that he suspected, as I did, while we embraced, that this time it was possibly not au revoir but adieu.

 41

Hélène-Eulalie had compelled her cousin to promise to return within a year, this time bringing Sehêbi and his boys. But two years later, in 1821, with all the news about the independence of Mexico from Spain, and the opening of a trade route from Missouri to Santa Fé, he had still not appeared. We began once more to wonder. While he had always been reluctant to entangle himself in promises, he took seriously those to which he did commit. We told ourselves that his tribal responsibilities had delayed him. But by the month of October, although we no longer discussed the delay, we were each living in a state of mild anxiety.

As I recall, it was the time of a full moon. When I descended the stairs one morning and went onto the veranda to observe the weather, which was fair, blue sky and sunlight, a promising day, I saw a tepee nearly concealed among trees upriver, somewhat removed from the port. Immediately I knew there must be a connection with Arsène, although I believed he would have come to the house, even at a late hour. Hurrying to the kitchen, I told Hélène-Eulalie and Mademoiselle what I had seen. We three returned to the veranda in time to see an Indian woman, with a man behind her, trudging up the path from the river. As the pair drew closer, we recognized Sehêbi, older and heavier but still a handsome woman. The man behind her looked familiar, but I could not quite recognize him. We called and waved, leaving the house to meet them. In response, Sehêbi raised a hand in the greeting sign, let it fall. There was no enthusiasm in their demeanors, no joy in their steps.

"They bring bad news," I said, speaking my thoughts, then wishing I had not.

"Don't," Hélène-Eulalie began. "Maybe it's nothing to do with Arsène."

Reaching them a little way down the path, I recognized the man as Deer's-Ears, who had been Arsène's closest friend since boyhood, indeed his "brother." We embraced, all of us, Mademoiselle too. They avoided our eyes.

"Arsène, he's all right?" Hélène-Eulalie cried in French to Sehêbi.

Her face, Deer's Ear's evident distress, answered the question.

"Not...dead?" I asked hesitantly.

Again, their expressions answered.

Hélène-Eulalie gasped, looked at me in anguish, tears already in her eyes.

"Come," I said in Comanche. "We have coffee and food."

We sat at the kitchen table, the tears flowing down my wife's face. Mlle. Bijou, choking from time to time, violently clearing her throat, served us coffee, adjusted the damper on the stove, and angrily stirred a pan of eggs.

"Tell us what happened," I said. The void in my chest was glacial.

Sehêbi told us in her broken French, sometimes turning to question Deer's-Ears, who had evidently been present. We quickly learned the principal fact: one of the squatters, whose motives Arsène had so distrusted, had shot him fatally. But in the period of a few days, by talking with Deer's-Ears in Comanche and by hand signals, I was able to fashion a complete account of what had occurred, from beginning to end. Not that it made us less unhappy to know the full truth, but we had to know, and in the end knowing made it easier to accept his death.

Meanwhile, as I have written, I required some days of smoking and talking with Deer's-Ears, of questioning him, before I was able truly to visualize the details of that fatal event. Arsène's friend had apparently chopped the hair from the left side of his head in mourning. The hair had partially grown back, but he was clearly still mourning the loss of his "brother," and I was obliged to question him gradually, over a number of hours, with tact and patience. As for Sehêbi, she had finished with all the excesses (in my tabebo opinion) of Comanche women's mourning, but she bore her grief, like her new scars, still in her expression, in her eyes. They only gleamed with pleasure and pride when I questioned her about Arsène's boys, Bearbird's grandsons, raised by her and already young men, whom she referred to as "our sons." Each had apparently distinguished himself as hunter and warrior. Each already had no difficulty in raising a war party to follow him on a raid or to steal horses. In response, almost as an afterthought, it seemed, she asked about Ooa. But when I had told her the girl was married and happy, far away, she murmured something and never asked again.

Near the end of our friends' stay, Hélène-Eulalie was in the kitchen one morning training a new girl, whom Mademoiselle had chosen from the small free black community in town, since she herself had received her freedom and a sum of money upon the colonel's death and was finally preparing to yield her nearly lifelong responsibilities. Sehêbi approached me and asked me to conduct her, The Willow, to the church, which she wished to see once more, with its silver and gold and its pictures with gilded frames and its little lights. She told me she wished to make one of the little fires for White-Bear, as she had seen my wife do. I willingly obliged her. Later, when she had lighted her candle and we were leaving, she turned and looked back from the doorway at the altar and banks of burning candles, her eyes resting especially upon the gruesome image of the crucified Jesus.

"What will you do now?" I asked as we descended the path toward the house.

"I'll go to Deer's Ear's lodge. He has asked me. I like him."

"He's a good man, isn't he?"

"Yes. He's kind to me." She stopped in the path, turned and faced me. "I'll never come back here." She gazed into my eyes, her face sad and strange, a big woman now, her lined face still comely. "I loved The Flute, and I loved White-Bear. They're both dead. I'm sorry I was no good at fucking when I was married to you."

"That's all right—all that's a long time ago."

"I'll never see you again after this time. I never loved you like the others, Jean-Pierre. But I liked you."

Touched, I patted her shoulder, leaning, looking into her eyes. Suddenly, surprised at myself, I embraced her vigorously and kissed her on the mouth, a long final kiss. For an instant she looked back at me archly when I pulled away, with a little pleased smile and, for an instant, something of the old coy look. Then she turned and started again down the path, and I followed.

At the house, on the veranda, I questioned Deer's-Ears a last time.

Arsène, it seems, had devised a plan to warn those settlers who had approached most closely, even though still in the piney woods, to the prairie and to comanchería. With a small party of warriors, including his "brother," he had ridden many leagues from south to north, pausing at each of the foremost clearings and cabins. There he had admonished the occupants, often discovered working in their corn patches, not to advance farther but rather to stop or withdraw, or their property and lives would be in danger from his and other Comanche raiders.

Of course this was partly a bluff, as Deer's-Ears admitted. The Comanches did not raid east of La Grande Forêt. But the bluff had had a visibly powerful effect. Indeed, Arsène had considered it too powerful. The families they had approached, isolated as they were in the woods, had been terrified upon seeing his party of painted and armed horsemen ride out of the forest. Arsène had feared that their terror was depriving them of their senses to such an extent that some, especially woman and children left alone, while their man hunted, were failing to understand what he was telling them in his limited English. Consequently he had decided it would be preferable for his party to conceal themselves while he spoke with the squatters. Deer's-Ears and others had warned him against appearing alone, saying it would place him in danger, that it was good for the tabebos to be afraid. But Arsène would not be dissuaded.

At first the plan had succeeded. That was perhaps a bad thing, Deer's-Ears opined, for it may have made White-Bear too confident and thrown his warriors off their guard. Because one day Arsène had left them at a little distance and ridden to a solitary cabin, where they could hear someone chopping wood. While the others had lounged on their ponies, Deer's-Ears, worried, had followed, remaining hidden behind trees but close enough to watch, alert, sitting his horse, bow in his hand with an arrow fitted to it.

In the little clearing before the cabin a tall grizzled man in dirty buckskins was chopping wood. A gaunt, pale woman stood in the doorway of the shack. She was holding an infant, while a little before her and behind the woodsman two ragged boys of eleven or twelve years wrestled. A third, younger boy watched, jumping up and down, occasionally shouting, encouraging one of them. An eviscerated buck hung from a branch, while antlers and bones were scattered before the dwelling. When Arsène appeared out of the trees, Deer's-Ears said, the woman quickly drew back toward the dark interior, hugging the baby to her, while the boys ceased their struggle, froze, and stared. The man, however, dropped the axe and seized his rifle, which was leaning against a nearby sapling. He stood with the butt of the weapon on the ground, barrel in his hand. Scowling and spitting, he appeared more venomous and enraged than afraid.

Immediately Arsène's calm voice was speaking to him in his halting English. The squatter listened, glaring, slouched over his long rifle. His jaw, with its shaggy beard, was raised defiantly, his expression contemptuous. When Arsène had finished talking, the backwoodsman spat and crazily roared out words, shaking his fist at Arsène, as if commanding him to leave. White Bear, said Deer's-Ears, replied quietly but, after a moment of abuse, turned his horse, so that his back was toward the man. He raised his head, beginning to call out or whoop. At the same time the woodsman, still spewing words, swung up his rifle and fired. Arsène, his cry cut short and knocked from his horse, lay convulsed by its legs. Deer's-Ears, stunned, raised his bow, whooped, aimed through the drifting powder smoke, released his arrow, all in an instant. At first, he told me, he thought he had missed, seeing neither feathers nor shaft protruding from the buckskin shirt. But when the woodsman dropped his rifle, struck his chest, threw his head up, reeled and fell, rolling on the ground, his legs kicking, Deer's-Ears realized that his arrow had passed entirely through the man. The woman shrieked, vanishing in the cabin, with the boys after her. Responding whoops and breaking branches sounded from the woods behind him.

He rode, weaving between trees, to where White Bear's black horse stood above its master. Hurling himself from his pony, he knelt over Arsène. A large bleeding hole below the scarred, tattooed chest showed where the ball had exited. Deer's-Ears knew his friend had been killed. No one could survive that wound. Yet the eyes in those ashen features contorted by pain watched him. The lips trembled. He leaned closer. But with the woman's and infant's screams, and his companions' whoops and one of them slamming the axe against the door, he could hear nothing. Leaning farther, he placed his ear nearly against the lips and heard a faint whisper, as if from very far away:

"Make...boys...Nuhmuhnuh." The eyes shut in a sudden agonized expression. Arsène cried out in a vomit of blood.

Deer's-Ears sprang up, jumped over the scalped woodsman, sprinted to the cabin. The infant lay already dead, thrown in a corner. The woman lay sprawled, newly dead, bleeding, scalped, her mouth and eyes open. The smallest boy writhed in speechless terror, held by Dead-Hide, who gripped him by the hair, holding a bloody knife. The two older boys cowered in another corner, the bigger one holding a butcher knife toward the two warriors advancing upon them.

"Niatz!" he bellowed. "Stop!"

The warriors turned, freezing in place.

"Hear me. The crazy tabebo killed White-Bear. Dying, your chief told me, 'Make boys Nuhmuhnuh.' We lost warriors from the tásia. Many. We'll need many to fight these people when they come into our country. We'll fight them with their own people when we can. Take these boys and tie them on horses. And burn this place."

The men, Dead-Hide, Beetle, Hoarse-Bark, and The-Feeble-Effeminate-One regarded him with fury in their painted faces, yet hesitantly.

"I'm your warchief now. White-Bear wished it. Do as I say. We've got to ride out of here." He said he walked, not looking at the others, to the boy with the knife. Gesturing, holding out his hand, he ordered the boy to give him the weapon. The oldest boy, who was visibly trembling, tears streaming down his cheeks, gazed at the warriors, at his dead mother and the baby, back at the warriors, and at Deer's-Ears. He stared at Deer's-Ears. Slowly he turned the big knife in his hands. Holding it by the blade, his eyes upon Deer's-Ears, he proffered the shaking handle. Deer's-Ears grasped the knife, then pointed to the boy and to himself, indicating that the boy would be his. Seizing him by the arm, he propelled him roughly from the shanty.

Soon afterward White-Bear's body was tied upon his horse, the three boys were mounted, tied on other ponies. The cabin, its dead inside, smoked, flared up, and blazed as the painted horsemen departed, riding at a trot through pine forest, westward, toward La Grande Prairie and its buffalo.

When Deer's-Ears concluded telling his story, through Sehêbi the first time, he collapsed upon the kitchen table, sobbing, his face in his arms. Sehêbi maintained a stoic expression, except for the tears gliding down her cheeks. She had already grieved. An ache in my throat, I had to leave the room, glancing back as I exited to see Hélène-Eulalie, weeping, embracing and comforting Sehêbi, while Mademoiselle wept into her raised apron, and the black wolfdog trotted from one person to another, looking toward each face with an anxious expression.

I must report that I did, however, have a final glimpse of Arsène, when he came to me, or rather I went to him, in a dream. Of course I must surely have dreamt of him at other times, but this is the fragment I remember. It was after our Indian friends' departure. I was melancholy, suffering backaches, troubled nights, with bizarre dreams, most of which I could not recollect. But a single shard of one, a fleeting picture, as it were, returned to me at breakfast one morning, and I did recall that fragment vividly. And still do. I was riding up a prairie knoll mounted upon César—who had of course died years earlier. As I gained the top of the hillock, I saw what appeared to be a green Indian dancing. Drawing close, I recognized him as Arsène. But no, he was not dancing but stamping the buffalo grass.

"Jean-Pierre, you're riding César!"

"Arsène, what are you doing?"

He regarded me with an embarrassed smile, continuing to stamp, but still as if he were dancing. He was painted entirely green, except for yellow stripes upon his cheeks. Even his headdress was green, its feathers resembling long leaves. The grass underfoot, I now saw, was swarming with grasshoppers—aahtaquine—to the Comanches. They were crawling over him, climbing his leggings, buzzing and flying, landing on his face, even his nose, as he brushed them off, slapping them down. But they continued to stick to him nearly faster than he could shed them.

Listening to him panting, I stared in amazement.

He continued to gaze at me with that constrained, embarrassed smile: "Ahhtaquine. You see, Jean-Pierre? Ahhtaquine!"

Indeed, I saw, and see yet more clearly today.

About a year later, the following autumn, I recall that on a night of the full moon, it being a beautiful evening, I went for a walk with the dog. It was an unusually warm evening for the season. Despite insects, we had left windows open. Hélène-Eulalie was playing the piano, familiar compositions. I could still hear the music as the dog and I proceeded down the white, moonlit road, I sauntering, content after a good meal, he adapted and fat, trotting, pausing here and there to sniff, occasionally to paw where he sniffed, and to urinate, then rejoining me. I was about to turn back approaching a great, shaggy tree illuminated by moonlight when there came from the dark between branches the sound of a large owl, a hoo, hoo-oo, hoo, hoo. Oddly, this sound in conjunction with the melody played by the distant pianist, raised a chill up my spine, though not from fear. I was moved, somehow, to respond, mimicking its voice, even to the rhythm of its notes. Abruptly, out of the upper shadows, a great dark wingèd shape, partly silvered by the moon, descended, gliding, hardly flapping, swooping closely, silently, above my head. The dog and I watched it vanish into the woods. Did it think I was teasing it?

This, of course, could happen to anyone. It is a part of Nature, after all. I am not a superstitious man. I do remember, however, a sensation of warmth, of elation even, suffusing my body. Oh, memory, may I never lose you! I strolled with the wolfdog, that mix of tame and wild, back to the house a strangely happy man, feeling blessed by fortune, feeling even that "inconvenient emotion" that La Rochfoucauld wrote of two centuries before, as the sound of the piano augmented, carrying out the lamplit window into the moonlight.

That wise duke also penned this maxim, "L'espérance, toute trompeuse qu'elle est, sert au moins à nous mener à la fin de la vie par un chemin agréable." Ah yes, Hope, deceptive as she is, leads us to the end of life by a pleasant road. N'est-ce pas? Hélène-Eulalie possesses her Faith. I have my Doubt...and Hope. For what? For what I do not know. Perhaps for an explanation of this riddle we live in after I, too, turn to carrion.

But meanwhile I am an American man with extraordinary memories and am able to feel that inconvenient emotion for a few of the living and a few of the dead. We have sufficient money to live upon, having sold the trading house this year. I—we—have, along with our gray days of ennui, melancholy, and the times of bitter words, moments of laughter, of happiness. A sufficient amount to eat and drink, good Bordeaux included, which we purchase by the pipa, or cask. An excellent library. Good fireplaces, with plenty of firewood. Even at rare moments, joy. What more does a life have to offer? For what more could one wish?